Jonathan the Visionary

Jonathan the Visionary

by
X. B. Saintine

Translated, annotated and introduced by
Brian Stableford

A Black Coat Press Book

ISBN 978-1-61227-751-6. First Printing. May 2018. Published by Black Coat Press, an imprint of Hollywood Comics.com, LLC, P.O. Box 17270, Encino, CA 91416.

TABLE OF CONTENTS

Introduction

"L'Histoire de Jonathan le visionnaire" (here tr. as "The Story of Jonathan the Visionary") by X. B. Saintine was initially published in 1823 in volume 2 of *Le Mercure du dix-neuvième siècle*, where it served as an introduction to a series of stories allegedly told by the eponymous character, three of which—"Séthos et Cléophas" ("Sethos and Cleophas") "Le Jeune boyard" ("The Young Boyar") and "La Mésalliance" ("The Misalliance")—appeared in the same volume. The remainder of the series, amounting to seventeen stories, one of them containing three subsidiary stories and divided into four parts in its periodical publication, appeared in subsequent volumes of the *Mercure*, culminating with the last of the subsections of "La Vengeance" ("Vengeance"), "Le Chérif de Maroc" ("The Cherif of Maroc"), in volume 9 in 1825. They were the only items of prose fiction contained in the periodical during those years (it was suspended later that year, although a new *Mercure* soon reappeared under a slightly different title from a different publisher, with a broader editorial policy).

The short-lived *Mercure du dix-neuvième siècle* was an important early showcase for the French Romantic Movement; it was advertised as being published by "the members of a Society of Men of Letters," whose prime mover, the periodical's most frequent contributor and the signatory of the editorial in the first issue, appears to have been Pierre-François Tissot (1768-1864), a radical Republican journalist and pioneer of the Romantic Movement. Tissot had previously worked on the newspapers *Le Constitutionnel* and *La Minerve*, both of which had been suppressed by Louis XVIII's censors because of their political activism, and the *Mercure* had to maintain a careful diplomacy in order not to suffer the same fate. Other members of the Society included Adolphe Thiers, Félix Bodin and, of course, "X. B. Saintine." Among the poets whose work the periodical published during that phase of its existence were Victor Hugo, Alphonse de Lamartine and Madame Desbordes-Valmore and it routinely featured satirical fables in verse; its reviews typically contained fervent propaganda for "*romanticisme*," not only in French literature but German and English literature as well.

Saintine's was one of the lesser-known names on the list of the periodical's founders, and remarkably little seems to have been recorded subsequently regarding his biography. The author of the article on Saintine in Pierre Larousse's *Grand Dictionnaire* (1866-76) was apparently unable to find any information about his life, apart from a birth-date in 1798 and death-date in 1865; that dearth of information was inherited by numerous subsequent reference books, extending all the way to Wikipedia. Other sources, however, record that the author's baptismal name was Joseph-Xavier Boniface, that he was born in Normandy, not far from Cambrai, and that his brother, who retained his patronymic, became an educationalist and the author of several elementary school text-books.

Xavier Boniface was apparently conscripted into the National Guard in 1814—at the age of sixteen, if the dates given in the different sources are correct—and was embroiled peripherally in the conflicts of the Hundred Days in 1815. While in garrison, he met his fellow conscript Eugène Scribe, already a successful playwright, and the two wrote a vaudeville together under the name of "Xavier." Although Boniface returned thereafter to his studies in medicine, his fate had been decided, and his commitment to a career in letters determined. He soon selected "Saintine" as his preferred pseudonym—the X. B., of course, standing for his real name. He won a poetry prize awarded by the Académie Française in 1817, and continued writing vaudevilles in profusion; the Larousse article credits him with two hundred, but in a brief obituary note added to a review of *La Seconde Vie* (1864; tr. as *The Second Life*) in *Bibliographie Catholique* in 1865, Alphonse Berthet quotes the convincingly exact figure of 157—approximately one every three months throughout his long career. He was

8

sufficiently successful in his writing for the stage eventually to buy a house in Marly, to which he retired with his wife and children, while retaining his many friendships in Parisian society. His health was apparently frail, however, and his death long anticipated.

The short stories that Saintine published in the *Mercure* were a second string to his literary bow, but one that was far less successful financially than his work for the stage; their publication in the periodical was presumably due, at last in part, to his sponsorship of it, and he might well have financed its first printing in volume form himself. He continued to write prose fiction in various lengths throughout his career, however, eventually becoming very successful in that endeavor too.

Saintine's first story series was reprinted in two volumes as *Jonathan le visionnaire, contes philosophiques et moraux*, advertized as "publié par X. B. Saintine,"—which presumably refers to the author's pose as the "editor" of stores recounted by the immortal Jonathan—and issued in Paris and Brussels by Baudouin frères, the printers of the *Mercure*, in 1825. In addition to the stories already cited, volume one contained: "Les Bienfaiteurs" ("The Benefactors"); L'Enfant du sorcier" ("The Sorcerer's Child"); "Le Poète de l'Hellénie" ("The Poet of Hellas"); "Les Arinzes" ("The Arinzes"); "Heur et Malheur" ("Good and Ill Fortune"); "Tam-Garaï, le bon Baian" (Tam Garai"); and volume two "Les Deux écus" ("The Two Coins"); Bébut l'Ambitieux" ("Ambitious Bebut"); "Le Pecheur d'Ormus" ("The Fisherman of Ormus"), "Le Métaphysicien" ("The Metaphysician"); "L'Ermite de Lac Majeur" ("The Hermit of Lake Maggiore"); "Le Jumeaux" ("The Twins"); "Les Contradictions" ("Contradictions") and the remaining two stories included in the text of "La Vengeance": "Le Hottentot-Boshi" ("The Hottentot-Boshi") and "L'Almamy de Bondou" (The Almamy of Bondou"). A second edition followed from A. Dupont et Roret in 1826, as *Contes philosophiques et moraux de Jonathan le visionnaire*.

In 1932 a further item connected with the series appeared in two parts in volume 40 of the *Revue de Paris* as "Histoire d'une civilisation antédiluvienne" (here tr. as "The Story of an Antediluvian Civilization") which bore "the signature Jonathan-le-visionnaire (X. B. Saintine)." As the title indicates, the story provides a synoptic account of complete history of a civilization in Ethiopia, only a few distant echoes of which survive in the societies known to history. The first section, which deals with the origin of the society, is an unusual venture in the subgenre of prehistorical fantasy, written before the first discovery of human fossil remains began to provide clues regarding the early social evolution of the human species. The final section, which deals with the "decrepitude" and collapse of the civilization, providing a quasi-prophetic indication of the manner in which the present civilization might develop and degenerate, begins with a farcical digression but then settles into a scathing account of how our the future of western civilization might be transformed and destroyed by dramatic scientific and technological advancement.

In 1937, by which time Saintine's reputation as a novelist had been solidly established by the success of the classic *Picciola* (1836; tr. as *Picciola; or, The Prison Flower*), one of the core prose works of French Romanticism, the author was quick to produce a new version of the 1825 portmanteau, repackaged as *Les Soirées de Jonathan* [Jonathan's Soirées], which omitted six stories from the first version and added four new ones, preceded by a revised and vastly expanded version of "L'Histoire de Jonathan le visionnaire." The six stories that were dropped were: "La Mésalliance," "Séphos et Cléophas,", "Le Poète de Hellénie," "Les Arinzes," "L'Ermite de Lac Majeur," and "Les Jumeaux". Three of those retained were retitled: "Tam-Garaï, le bon Banian" as "Gloire et vertu" [Glory and Virtue], "Bébut l'ambitieux" as "Les Deux ambitieux" [The Two Ambitious Men] and "Le Métaphysicien" as "Un Coup de Soleil" [Sunstroke]. The four that were added were: "La Prophétie de Jean de Milan" (here tr. as "The Prophecy of Jean de Milan"); "L'Ile du cocotier" (The Island of the Coconut Palm"); "Le Cheveu blanc" ("The White Hair"); and "L'Histoire de l'académie de Berchtolsgarden" ("The History of the Academy of Berchtolsgarden"). Although the introduction claimed that the reprinted stories had been revised, most of the changes made to the texts were trivial.

"Histoire d'une civilisation antédiluvienne", to which a passing reference is made in the prologue to *Les Soirées de Jonathan* was not reprinted therein, nor in the 1853 reprint of that text, nor anywhere else during Saintine's lifetime. It seems probable that *Les Soirées de Jonathan* was put together in a hurry, in order to cash in on the success of *Picciola*, and appearances suggest that the text included as its introduction might well have been originally planned as the opening chapters of an abandoned novel, or at least as part of a more elaborate frame narrative. It is noticeable that the prologue as printed undergoes a drastic change of tone and direction in its flippant final pages. If it was, in fact, an aborted novel, it would have been interesting to see a complete version giving a fuller account of Jonathan's extraordinarily extended history and the nature of his immortality. I have appended the new material from the second collection to the translations of the first version and the translation of "Histoire d'une civilisation antédiluvienne" in the present volume.

"Histoire d'une civilisation antédiluvienne" was reprinted, however, in a further version of *Jonathan le visionnaire* published posthumously in 1866. That version is again revised, although the changes made to the stories that it includes are mostly minor; they are "Heur et Malheur"; "LÎle du cocotier"; "Le Jeune boyard"; "Bébut l'honnête home" (a second retitling of "Bébut l'ambitieux"); "Le Pecheur d'Ormus"; "Guy d'Albrot et la chatelaine d'Oudales" ("Le Cheveu blanc"); "Un Coup de soleil"; "Les Arintzes" ("Les Arinzes"); "La Vengeance Africaine" ("La Vengeance"; the three included stories of which are retitled "Tamus le Saab," "Messiael l'Almamy" and "Abdallah le chérif"); "La Prophétie de Jean de Milan"; "Séthos et Cléophas"; "Tam-Garaï" ("Tam-Garaï, le bon Banian"); and "L'Enfant du sorcier". In this version the stories are irregularly distributed within a frame story, which recapitulates the earlier account of the narrator's encounter with Jonathan in its first section, and also recapitulates the end of the prologue to *Les Soirées de Jonathan*, in slightly abridged form, in its final section. The bulk of the frame narrative, however, consists of a more elaborate account of the narrator's dealings with Jonathan after their meeting in Paris, including an earlier expedition to Normandy than the one detailed in the climax. If the prologue to *Les Soirées de Jonathan* was, in fact, adapted from chapters of an abandoned novel, the new episodes introduced into the 1866 text might well be based on other chapters from the same abandoned work; if not, they are almost certainly based on sections of text that were intended to be inserted into the 1937 text but removed when its format was recast.

The addition of the third version of the collection to the previous two produces a highly unusual bibliographical complexity. Again, I have added the new material relating to Jonathan's biography as a further appendix to the present volume, noting therein a few of the changes made to the stories, although I have also added notes on some of the more substantial changes made to them in the footnotes to the translations of the stories themselves. The end result is admittedly complicated, but hopefully provides a satisfactory account of the evolution of the project.

All eight of the stories from the two earlier versions of the portmanteau that were omitted from the 1866 edition of *Jonathan le visionnaire* were separately reprinted in another Saintine collection from the final phase of his career, *Contes de toutes les couleurs* [Tales in All Colors] (1861), two of them under variant titles. It seems highly probable that the two collections were compiled at the same time and that the new edition of *Jonathan le visionnaire* was intended at that time to make up a set with *Contes de toutes les couleurs* and reprints by Hachette of some of his earlier collections, including an 1859 reprint of *Les Métamorphoses de la Femme* [The Metamorphoses of Woman] (originally 1845) and reprints in 1860 and 1861 of two previously-published omnibuses, one headed by *Un Rossignol pris au trébuchet* [A Nightingale Caught in a

12

Siege-Engine] and the other *Antoine*, which had accumulated other items with those originally published in *Récits de la tourelle* [Tales of the Tower] (1844). There might be several reasons why publication of the revised version of *Jonathan le visionnaire* was delayed until after the author's death, but the most likely one was anxiety regarding possible political repercussions.

The three versions of the portmanteau were published under different regimes in markedly different circumstances, the first during the reign of Charles X, the second after the July Revolution of 1830, during the reign of Louis-Philippe, and the third during the Second Empire. Although Saintine was not as radical a Republican as some of his collaborators on the *Mercure*, equally moderate Republicans had run into dire trouble following the *coup d'état* of 1851, when several of the leading Republican pillars of the Romantic Movement were exiled, including Victor Hugo, Alexandre Dumas and Edgar Quinet. Saintine escaped that penalty, but he had to live nevertheless with the rigorous censorship introduced by Napoléon III, and must have been keenly aware of the fact that, given his history, the censors would look very attentively at everything he published. Although there is little in the stories narrated by Jonathan that was likely to cause offense, "Histoire d'une civilisation antédiluvienne" is a different matter, and there is a distinct possibility that its fierce political satire would have raised hackles in 1861 that it had not raised on its initial publication in 1832, when the political climate was far milder.

The possibility of political suppression was, however not the only factor that might well have inhibited Saintine's adventures in satire and speculation at various points in his career. If the introduction to *Les Soirées de Jonathan* really was an aborted novel, that might well be a symptom of the difficulty that authors have always had in marketing fantastic fiction, in the teeth of editorial and critical opposition. Although a few of Saintine's shorter stories are flamboyantly fantastic, all of his published novels and the greater number of his novellas are naturalistic—mostly set in distant historical periods, historical fiction being far more likely to escape political censorship or suppression than contemporary fiction—as are the vast majority of the dramatic productions that represented the main strand of his production.

Although Saintine indulged his liking for fantasy in collections of tales for children, including an exercise in the popularization of science similar to those undertaken by S. Henry Berthoud, *La Mère Gigogne et ses trois filles* [Mother Gigogne—a character featured in popular puppet shows—and Her Three Daughters] (1864; reprinted several times as *Science enfantine* [Children's Science]) he might well have been one of several members of the Romantic Movement who would have liked to give their imagination freer rein in their serious endeavors, but were obliged to operate under the burden of an editorial yoke in that respect for much of their careers.

In his last book, however, *La Seconde Vie*, Saintine cast caution to the winds and indulged his eccentricities wholeheartedly, in a collection of tales of visions and visionaries, many of which pretend to be autobiographical and at least some of which really were based on actual dreams and accurately reflect his meditations on the subject. One story describes a consultation between the narrator and a physician, in which contemporary theses regarding the nature of dreams are discussed, but the most interesting items, in their relation to the hypothetical exploits of Jonathan is "La Chine à Paris" (tr. as "China in Paris"), which features a vision of the future in which Europe has been conquered by China, and "Prométhée" (Prometheus"), which recapitulates the author's arguments regarding the role played by scientific advancement in cultural decadence, but offers a more hopeful view of the prospects of Western civilization than the one implied by "Histoire d'une civilisation antédiluvienne."

Although the stories contained in *Jonathan le visionnaire* stand up very well in their own right, if read in isolation, the portmanteau is definitely more than the sum of its parts. Although the mysterious Jonathan only features as an active narrator in a few of them, the pretence that that the other stories are also items of his reportage places them within a context that is extremely broad both temporally and geographically, sustaining the contention that the questions addressed by the underlying moralism of the tales really are eternal and universal. That bold reach fits in very well with the ambitions of the Romantic Movement, of which Saintine's short stories are early prose productions, following rapidly on the heels of Charles Nodier's pioneering endeavors and ahead of the Movement's heyday in the 1930s, when Honoré de Balzac, S. Henry Berthoud, Jules Janin, Théophile Gautier, Joseph Méry and others began to publish short stories prolifically in a number of new publications that were very hospitable to such material. Saintine's work was, therefore, genuinely pioneering, and it is probable that his 1825 collection influenced several of the writers who followed in his footsteps—certainly in the cases of Berthoud (a fellow native of the Cambrésis) and Méry.

The fact that Saintine employed Oriental settings in some of his stories was not unusual, as Oriental fantasies had a long history in French fiction going back to Antoine Galland's publication of *Les Mille-et-une nuits*, but "Bébut l'ambitieux" is unusual in its use of a real historical setting and its determined use of data accumulated from the accounts of Persia given by French voyagers. A similar determination to utilize extensive background research is also shown in the subsidiary portmanteau employing African settings, which was far more unusual as an endeavor. It is arguable that Saintine is a trifle excessive in the employment of exotic terminology and his addition of supplementary footnotes (many of which were deleted from the later versions of the stories), but his determination to incorporate real details of natural history and anthropology into his stories deserves credit for intelligence as well as originality, and he ought to be recognized as the real founder of the school of "travelogue fiction" subsequently developed prolifically by Méry and others.

The most striking originality on display in the 1823 collection, is, however, to be found in its fantastic material, especially in "Les Arinzes"—which might be regarded as a sketch for "Histoire d'une civilisation antédiluvienne" in its brief description of a prehistoric civilization that has vanished from human memory in spite of providing the seeds for several of the world's great religions—and "L'Enfant du sorcier." The latter story is seems to be surprisingly rapid spinoff from Mary Shelley's *Frankenstein* (1818)—a probability further increased by the suspicion that "Les Arinzes" might have been inspired by Percy Shelley's "Ozymandias"—and if so, the influence must have been direct; the appearance of "L'Enfant du sorcier" in the *Mercure* in 1824 was more than a year in advance of the melodramatic adaptation of *Frankenstein* titled *Le Monstre et le magicien* [The Monster and the Magician] staged at the Porte-Saint-Martin theater.[1] Unlike many tales prompted by Mary Shelley's novel, Saintine's story takes up the theme of the novel's subtitle, "The Modern Prometheus," in a robust fashion, featuring a bold experimenter who not only wants to recreate a human being from primal clay but wants to improve on the divine plan and create an improved human, thus making the story a very early example of a speculative account of engineered superhumanity.

Although Saintine was a somewhat eccentric contributor to the development of *roman scientifique*—Jonathan proudly asserts that the only sciences he is able to take seriously are alchemy and astrology—there is a Voltairean skepticism in his work that has much in common with other contributions made by the Romantic Movement to the evolution of that genre, and "Histoire d'une civilisation antédiluvienne" is a truly remarkable work seen in that context; it antedates the three major contributions to futuristic fiction made by other leading members of the movement, Charles Nodier, in "Hurlubleu" and

---

[1] Available in *Frankenstein and the Hunchback of Notre-Dame*, Black Coat Press, ISBN 978-1-932983-38-8.

"Léviathan le Long" (both 1933; tr. as "Perfectibility"),[2] Félix Bodin's *Le Roman de l'avenir* (1834; tr. as *The Novel of the Future*)[3] and Louis-Napoléon Geoffroy's *Napoléon et la conquête du monde* (1836, tr. as *The Apocryphal Napoleon*),[4] and it is worth noting that Saintine was personally acquainted with all three of those authors, and that all of them would surely have been regular readers of the *Revue de Paris*. His influence on Nodier is very obvious, and on the other two at least probable.

Seen from the viewpoint of today, the most unusual aspect of the vision of a technologically advanced and highly automated society depicted in the final section of "Histoire d'une civilisation antédiluvienne" is not its content, whose elements were soon to become stereotyped, but the fact that scientific and technological advancement is represented not as an aspect of progress but as crucial symptom of social decrepitude, a kind of terminal social disease. In that regard Saintine was more radical than any of the other contemporary philosophers who were skeptical about modern science, and who argued against what they saw as technological excess or mismanagement. At the same time, however, he obviously had a strong interest in some of the scientific controversies of the day, the ongoing argument about the generic status of the orangutan being satirically reflected in both "Histoire d'une civilisation antédiluvienne" and "The History of the Academy of Berchtolsgarden."

The latter comedy, as well the most extravagant of the fantasies in *Les Soirées de Jonathan*, "Le Cheveu blanc," and the climax of the prologue to latter volume, suggest that Saintine found difficulty in taking fantastic notions seriously once the initial phase of his career was over, but the movement of his satire in the direction of blatant farce in those

---

[2] In *The Germans on Venus*, Black Coat Press, ISBN 978-1-934543-56-6.
[3] Black Coat Press, ISBN 978-1-934543-44-3.
[4] Black Coat Press, ISBN 978-1-61227-579-6.

items also broke new literary ground, and has an engaging blitheness. His vaudevilles extrapolate the same farcical wit, but they contrast markedly with his novels, most of which are earnest, not to say a trifle grim. His later short stories are various, but his quirky sense of humor is very noticeable in *Les Métamorphoses de la Femme*, the more recent items in *Contes de toutes les couleurs*, and most especially in *La Seconde Vie*, in which some of the more flamboyant comedies are striking early exercises in proto-surrealism.

Saintine's literary reputation, such as it is today, rests almost entirely on *Picciola*, an intense account of psychological survival in which a deeply disenchanted political prisoner is relieved from his descent into madness by his preoccupation with a flower growing between the stones of his exercise yard. The author attempted to recapitulate the theme in *Seul!* (1857; tr. as *The Solitary of Juan Fernandez*), which purports to tell the true story of Alexander Selkirk, the castaway on whose experiences Daniel Defoe supposedly based the core element of story of Robinson Crusoe. As several stories in the present collection demonstrate, the ideas of disenchantment, isolation and psychological survival had always been a source of fascination for Saintine, and "L'Île du cocotier" might be regarded as a precursor of *Picciola* and *Seul*—as, for that matter, might his first novel *Le Mutilé* [The Mutilated Man] (1932).

Although *Picciola* certainly deserves its reputation as a key text of the Romantic Movement's heyday, however, it is by no means the case that Saintine's contribution to the movement stopped there, or that it was completely stifled by the Second Empire's censors. His short fiction covers a remarkably wide spectrum, both thematically and tonally, while always retaining a firm moral anchorage, and remains one of the finest and most ambitious nineteenth-century extensions of the tradition founded by Voltaire's *contes philosophiques*.

Several stories from *Jonathan le visionnaire* were translated into English not long after their initial publication, all presumably pirated and all of them published without any credit being given to Saintine. They include:

"Heur et malheur," as "Luck and Ill Luck" in *The Atheneum, The Monthly and European Magazine* and *The Museum of Foreign Literature and Science* in 1827, *The Mirror of Literature, Amusement and Instruction* in 1828 and *The American Masonic Record and Saturday Magazine* in 1829;

"Bébut l'ambitieux" as "Bebut the Ambitious" in *The Oriental Register* and *The Museum of Foreign Literature* in 1828;

"Le Pecheur d'Ormus" as "The Fisherman of Ormus" in *The Oriental Herald* in 1828, *The Extractor* in 1829, *The Magazine of the Beau Monde* in 1835 and *Johnston's Penny Fireside* Journal in 1842;

"Tam Garaï the bon banian" as "Tam Garai, the Good Banyan" [*sic*] in *The Monthly Magazine* in 1829, *The Story-Teller* in 1843 and *The People's Journal* in 1847;

and "Le Jeune boyard" as "The Young Bayard" [*sic*] in *The Ladies' Cabinet of Fashion, Music and Romance* in 1841.

The following translation of *Jonathan le visionnaire* was made from the version of the 1825 edition reproduced on Google Books. The translation of "Histoire d'une civilisation antédiluvienne" was made from the relevant volume of the *Revue de Paris*, also reproduced on Google Books, and the translation of material from the 1866 edition from the same website. The translations of the new material from *Les Soirées de Jonathan* were made from the version of the 1837 edition reproduced on the Bibliothèque Nationale's *gallica* website.

Brian Stableford

The Story of Jonathan the Visionary

What should one think about magic and spells? The theory is obscure, the principles vague and uncertain, and which approach the visionary; but there are embarrassing facts, affirmed by serious men who have seen them; to admit them all or to deny them all appears equally inappropriate, and I dare say that therein, as in all extraordinary things that emerge from the common rules, there is a division to be found between credulous souls and strong minds.

(La Bruyère, *De quelques usages*.)[5]

Several years ago, while traveling in Italy, I found myself in the company of a rather large number of Frenchmen and foreigners, men of intelligence and taste. We were going to Cosenza, the capital of nearer Calabria, and, after having passed Rossano, forced to abandon our carriages in order to cross the mountains, we were walking together in a small caravan, glad to be thus rendering one another mutual aid against the tedium of the journey or against the malefactors with which the region is filled, especially since the famous earthquake of 1783, which completely destroyed the town of Cosenza and plunged so many families into poverty.

From time to time we called a halt, and then, after a light meal, all grouped on some hillock, with our weapons at the ready, we loved to discuss the mores and modern costumes of the land through which we were traveling, the antiquities of

---

[5] The philosopher and moralist Jean de La Bruyère (1645-1696) published *Les Caractères*, of which "De quelques usages" is chapter XIV, in 1688. It was a highly controversial book, to which many of the contemporaries described therein took great exception.

Italy, and all the successive changes that the inhabitants and soil of that beautiful country had experienced. Several of us had traveled a great deal, and piquant comparisons drawn from the customs and habits of all the peoples of the world gave an infinite charm to our conversations.

We were in the middle of one of those interesting narrations when we suddenly perceived that a man clad in a woolen cloak, his hair retained in a net, surmounted by a large hat, was standing nearby and listening to us. At the movement we made in putting our hands to our weapons he smiled and reassured us with a gesture.

"I beg your pardon, Messieurs; like you I am a traveler; I am going to Cosenza, and, knowing from experience the danger of traveling alone in these mountains, I have come to beg you to receive me in your little troop. When I approached, a very interesting and, especially, very true story seemed to be claiming your entire attention; I feared distracting you, and abandoned myself, without thinking about it, to the pleasure of listening."

The man had a mild and honest air; his exterior, although eccentric, was decent, and we accepted him as a companion.

On the road, interrogated by us about the region, which he seemed to know perfectly and the common goal of our journey, he replied: "I can only give you a few details about Cosenza, although I have lived in the town in three different epochs. The last time I left it, the earthquakes had still respected it, and I confess that I am only going there today in order to observe the effects of those cruel games of nature, the contrast between a populous and flourishing town and its debris dispersed in the solitude."

"Monsieur," I said to him, "how is it that, while you are still young"—for in spite of the deep wrinkles that traversed his forehead and gave him an air of austerity, he seemed to be aged forty at the most—"a town that ceased to exist in 1783 has left you memories of its splendor?"

He said nothing.

One of our companions observed that the stranger had also claimed to have lived in Cosenza in three different epochs; he still remained silent.

We all looked at one another, darting incredulous glances, and stopped interrogating him.

Another halt, another conversation. This time, the stranger seemed at first only to take very scant notice of what was said, but from time to time, an ironic smile or a movement of impatience betrayed his thinking. Our discussion concerned the large number of religions that divide humans and impose on their minds different morals and duties, just as varied climates impose other forms and needs on their bodies.

Sir B***, an English colonel, recently returned from India, was entertaining us with curious observations that he had made of the religions of the Brahmins, and all the mysteries of science deposited in the Vedas and Sanskrit books. When Sir B***, with the arrogant confidence that one shows when, proud of a new discovery, one believes that one will only find disciples, and not judges, in one's audience, developing the ancient precepts of the Valouvrians and the Gymnosophists, after having caused all the artillery of his erudition to thunder in telling us about the six sciences of Nyayam, Vedantan, Sankiam, etc., the heresies of Agama Shastra and Buddhism, was detailing with the greatest fervor the mysterious rites that only he, among Europeans, had been able to know, he suddenly heard our new companion say, in an approving tone: "That's true!"—taking as his point of departure Sir B***'s observations on the religion and science of Hindu priests, revealing entirely to our eyes the ocean and wisdom of superstition of which he had only been able to glimpse the shores.

Dr. K***, so well-known in Germany for his voyages in North America, gave us in his turn some geographical and philosophical details regarding Florida and Louisiana. The stranger listened at first with attention, but soon corrected a few errors of locality with which the doctor agreed, astonished nevertheless that anyone could know more than him about places that he had traveled for thirty years of his life.

"You cannot judge from the beauty of those regions to-day," his antagonist said. "It would be necessary, like me, to have seen them when the Natchez, still faithful to their picturesque customs and usages in harmony with that primitive and sublime land, transplanted their huts from the banks of the Ohio to those of the Iberville."

"But you're putting me in a terrible embarrassment," replied the doctor, holding back a burst of laughter, "for the Natchez vanished from the region after 1730, and I am forced, either not to add faith to your discourse, or to believe that you are more than a hundred years old."

At this point the doctor's laughter was communicated to the entire caravan. The stranger stood up, and we continued on our way.

Each of the individuals making up our troop had his turn with the hundred-year-old man; to one he let slip that he had been at the battle of Marignano,[6] which seemed to date his birth to the beginning of the sixteenth century. To another, a knowledgeable antiquary, he gave formal denials regarding the antiquity of certain monuments, with no other evidence than the words: "I know! I'm sure of it!" We expected in incessantly to hear him cry: "I saw them constructed!" but he doubtless restrained himself, for he seemed more annoyed than satisfied by the calculations that we might have made of his pretended age.

Finally, when we come to talk about the energetic speeches and sublime words that historians place in the mouths of dying heroes, and the last words of Epaminondas having been cited by one of us as model of the genre, he interrupted the narrator and said, in an emotional voice: "The death of Epaminondas was devoid of ostentation, like his life. "He had ceased to live when he was carried to his tent, and Plutarch and Diodorus lied about it! Oh, the most virtuous of

---

[6] The Battle of Marignano was fought in September 1515.

24

men! After so many years...! Oh, my..." And tears seemed to flow from his eyes, as at a memory of amity.[7]

Immediately, we were unanimous in declaring him mad. "He's the elder brother of the Wandering Jew," said Dr. K***.

"Addled brain, but great learning," replied Sir B***.

Already we were no more than a few leagues from Cosenza when we heard a strange noise around us, and our little troop was suddenly surrounded by a large number of bandits. We were preparing for a vigorous defense when one of them advanced ahead of the others and approached us, shouting: "Ransom your lives!"

That honest negotiator was nearly sixty years old; he waited for our response for some time, but then, perceiving in our ranks the intimate of Brahmins, the contemporary of François I and the friend of Epaminondas, he fell to his knees, seized by terror.

"Jonathan!" he cried. "God save me! Yes, it's him...! I was very young when I saw you, but your features remain engraved here, and have not changed at all. Mercy! Mercy! You've come back again! Wasn't it enough that your presence in this place has already caused the earthquake that that has ruined us all? My father told me that he had it from his grandfather that your arrival in Cosenza had caused a similar disaster a century before! Mercy, Jonathan!"

And at that terrible name, the entire band surrounding us fled, crying: "It's Jonathan the sorcerer!"

As for the latter, he covered his face with his hands, saying: "Superstitious beings! Haven't I enough to lament? They attribute to me a misfortune whose cruel consequences I tried to prevent; I warned them about the disaster, and they believe me to be the cause of it!"

This time, we no longer knew what to think of our singular traveling companion. There are things so simple that reason alone cannot explain them, and it is also necessary for reason to accept extraordinary things that it cannot compre-

[7] The Theban statesman Epaminondas died circa 362 B.C.

hend. Doubt overtook us with regard to Jonathan, and doubt, in this case, was to take a step in favor of the bizarre man that we had initially take for a madman, and at whom we might have laughed unjustly.

We all drew nearer to him, with the exception of a Neapolitan who, until then, had shown himself to be a man of intelligence and common sense, but who, from that moment on, kept himself apart and continually made the sign of the cross throughout the remainder of the journey. Jonathan appeared to be plunged in profound meditation, and did not reply to our multiple questions.

Finally, we arrived within sight of Cosenza in the evening and arranged to stay the night in a small inn situated at the foot of the mountain. It was there, weary once again of our importunities, that he adopted a singular means to avoid them. When Dr. K*** spoke to him he replied in English; Sir B*** immediately presented himself as interpreter, but only received replies in Spanish. We had a Castilian among us, who entered the lists in his turn, only to beat an immediate retreat on hearing the Muscovite dialect assault his ears. Jonathan hoped to rid himself thus of our curious solicitations. But, perceiving that by clubbing together we could comprehend the various languages of Europe, he took refuge in those of Asia, in which Dr. K*** and Sir B*** followed him for a while but finally lost him in Malay and Siamese jargon.

The next day, when we awoke, we learned that Jonathan had disappeared, and I heard no more mention of him during my sojourn in Italy. A few months later, I returned to the capital of France.

"Paris has always been the rendezvous of those stupid fops, those effeminate men, veritable brutes of civilization who, in the midst of the prodigies of the human mind, live without seeing and without thinking, and who, endowed with the same faculties of which the development in the soul of the likes of Columbus, Newton, Voltaire and Lavoisier, produced the discovery of a world, enlightened humankind, explained and analyzed the universe, spend their life inspecting their wardrobe, attentive to the cut of their garments, picking their fingernails and showing themselves in public promenades in order to amuse children with their ridiculousness."

"What would you say, then," replied Madame ***, to whom I expressed myself thus in a moment of jest, "About a man who, already at a mature age and possessing great learning, is nevertheless infatuated to the ultimate degree with the fault that you have just identified?"

"I would think of him that his learning is only an effect of memory, and that reasoning plays no part therein."

"You might be mistaken. Monsieur Gernonval, of whom I'm speaking, thinks and reasons; his reason sometimes goes astray, but that is more the voice of his overabundant imagination than his judgment."

"I don't understand what you mean."

"But here he comes now; listen to him and you'll understand."

And I did, indeed, see entering Madame ***'s home a man dressed in the most ridiculous and extravagant fashion. Everything that the art of attire has of refinement, and everything that fashion adopts in the way of luxurious baubles, served as his adornment.

Jonathan! I was about to exclaim—for it was him again—but his name expired on my lips, so stupefied was I to see the sorcerer of Calabria in a costume so different from the one he had been wearing on the day of his first appearance. Since then, I had formulated the project of penetrating what that inconceivable being was; that something supernatural presided over his destiny I had no doubt.

I affected not to recognize him, in the fear of inconveniencing him. I even listened to everything he recounted of the bizarre and the marvelous with an air of credulity that was not simulated. The man was beginning to take possession of my imagination powerfully. He perceived that, and seemed from then on, as he spoke, to be addressing himself more particularly to me than to the others; for several people had come into Madame ***'s home since his arrival.

When he withdrew, everyone interpreted what he had heard in his own way; only I remained silent.

"Well, what do you say about our visionary?" Madame *** said to me, finally.

"He confounds my mind," I replied, "And it appears to me to be easier to believe him than refute him."

"Are you going to think that he's as old as the world," added a newcomer, "or that the soul, after a thousand transmigrations, has rallied all the memories of his previous existences, as he would perhaps like to persuade us? For he seemed to me to have a great liking for Pythagoras, Cagliostro and all the illuminati of ancient and modern times."

"I don't know what to reply," I said, "but I'd prefer to believe in a single miracle, a single deviation in the eternal laws of nature, than to think that all hazards have collaborated to sustain his impostures; that a thousand miracles have been made in order to prevent one; for it isn't the first time that I've found myself in his presence, and what I have seen speaks as loudly in his favor as what I've heard."

"His air of frankness seduces you," replied my antagonist, "And it's doubtless not from that side that he's attackable; the name of visionary that we've given him suits him completely, for I'm convinced that he adds complete faith himself to what he advances. *Fortis imaginato generat casum*.[8] His dreams and reveries soon become as many verities for him; he's a lunatic, an inspired individual, a dreamer—in sum, a visionary—but he isn't an impostor."

Jonathan—for I shall conserve for him the name under which I saw him for the first time—knew that I had taken his defense ardently, and that my confidence in him was complete; that seemed to put me in favor in his mind, and I took

---

[8] "A strong imagination begets the event": a scholastic dictum quoted and discussed in one of Montaigne's essays.

advantage of it so fully that that after a while I became his disciple, his confidant and his friend.

"I noticed your surprise," he said to me one day, "When you recognized me in a modern and bizarre costume; but, apart from the fact that I have long adopted the attire in usage in the country in which I am living, the numerous emotions experienced during my long existence have created within me, so to speak, a need for eccentricity and extravagance that I sometimes satisfy with a pleasure that you are fortunate enough not to be able to understand. Oh, how sagely the Eternal has marked the ordinary measure of human life! I have seen everything, felt everything, and my sensations today are no longer anything by themselves but reminiscences of my first century.

"A citizen of all lands, a contemporary of many ages, it seems that God has forgotten me on earth in order to leave an irremovable spectator there of all the changes that have occurred. I have seen Rome in its cradle; I have seen anthropophagous peoples devour their enemies in the same place where the queen of the Arts, Athens, once stood; I have witnessed the noisy feasts of the Sicambres, the bloody games of the Bructeres. After having seen the torch of knowledge extinguished and reignited, I have followed step by step the new progress of the human mind, and I have repeated with Solomon: 'All is vanity!'"

"What!" I said to him. "Do you not at least render justice to the scientists of our era, who, stripped of all the arguments of the schools, are marching with a firm and free step along the road traced by reason and experience?"

"All is vanity!" he repeated. "They can only see with the eyes of the body; their reason has killed their instinct; none of them is able to divine, and it is only by means of the imagination that one can grasp the ensemble of the creator's works. But no, each of them wants to engender his own universe. Buffon considers the earth as a fragment detached from the sun; Burnet sees it as a ball of water; Palissy as a mollusk. The

29

atoms of Epicurus and Gassendi were succeeded by the subtle matter of Descartes or the material substance of Spinoza, over which the gravity of Newton has finally triumphed.

"Believe me, there is nothing but contradiction among the scientists; I have seen systems succeeded by other systems too often! In one of my ancient voyages in France, I was nearly imprisoned for having invoked the sentiment of Aristotle in a discussion with a professor at the University; thirty years later, I was threatened with being burned alive in the same country for having spoken irreverently about the same philosopher to the same professor. Innate ideas and the materiality or immateriality of the soul have caused me to run more risks to my life than the hundred battles that I have witnessed.

"Today, I no longer take sides either with scientists or with kings, and in this very century, which you call that of reason, I prefer to be known in France for the way I tie my cravat than for my fashion of thinking about the actions of the government. I have endured all forms of power, and I don't prefer any of them; I have studied and delved into all the sciences, and I only believe in astrology and alchemy."

"Is that possible?" I exclaimed. "It seems to me that of all the sciences, they are the most vain and the most false."

"Always basing thought on that of others, only seeing by means of the feeble eyes of those who surround us," he said, in a bitter tone, "do you only add faith to the things you understand? You do not believe in yourself, then, for the causes of your existence are a mystery to you, in spite of the reveries of the philosophy of Montbard.[9] Is it possible to think, then, that for so many centuries, public credulity would not have been enlightened if those sciences had not presented some foundation? Would so many brave men have died on pyres, martyrs to intolerance, if they had not been convinced of verities, objects of their research?

---

[9] The reference is to Buffon, born in the commune of Montbard, who eventually acquired its château.

"The hermetic sciences disappeared, as well as the others, in the revolutions of the globe, but was not their power authentically proven in antiquity, even by those who had an interest in denying them? Did Moses not recognize, before Pharaoh, how far the power of the disciples of Zoroaster could extend? Did Saint Peter refuse to believe in the marvels of the art of Simon, the so-called Magus? Have not your historians, including the sage Rollin, proven the authenticity of the oracles of Rome and Greece? Whether that is white magic or black magic, aided or unaided by the demon, is not the point. But that sacred fire, conserved by a few initiates in India, still shines there in all its brilliance.

"Beware of deceiving yourself; Europe, discouraged too soon by fruitless trials, and which allows imposture to sit upon the tablets of Ptolemy, will soon recover from its errors; the discovery of the magnetic fluid will explain in due course the mysteries of the second life, of somnambulism and dreams, in which unknown objects present themselves in their real form, and will aid in revealing entirely in those countries the temple of Zoroaster and the emerald tablet of Hermes."

I did not understand him sufficiently to oppose him, and the movement of inspiration that seemed to have gripped him in pronouncing those last words imposed on his adversary the necessity of employing with him other weapons than reason.

After a moment's silence, I said: "Jonathan, is it to that marvelous art that you owe the prolongation of your existence?"

"I can reveal nothing! Perhaps I've ready said too much. But no," he said, softening his voice, "I won't repent of my confidence."

He affected to change the subject, and we returned to his voyages.

"In less than a century," he said to me, "France has changed its face considerably. When Louis XV was on the throne I lived in Paris under the name of Monsieur de Saint-Germain and frequented the society of philosophers."

"Has not Grimm mentioned you in his correspond-ence?"[10]

"That's possible."

"What do you think of that time, compared with ours?"

"You have exchanged pleasure against reason. Then, however, I saw philosophy, a new religion, still on the defen-sive, conserving a proud and imposing attitude. Today, strong-er than ever, I see it, after the victory, ready to renounce all its advantages."

"With how many anecdotes and piquant facts your memory must be furnished!"

"Yes," he replied. "In the dread of forgetting them, I have related a few of them, which I want to leave you as a pledge of memory. At first I had the intention of publishing them for the instruction of men; you will be my editor if you judge it necessary." He went to fetch a little box, which he handed to me. "Here they are. I have been a witness to, some-times even an actor in, all the stories that you will find here. Several, doubtless, will seem to you bizarre and incredible; come to find me, and I shall give you a clear and frank expla-nation."

As soon as I had quit him, I had nothing more urgent than opening my box. I found it full of little scrolls of every form, color and material: paper, silk, birch-bark, papyrus, parchment, etc., etc. A large number of the stories were writ-ten in languages that I could not understand; I made every possible effort to have them translated; the best professors of the Collège de France assembled several times in my home in order to clarify the difficulties that vulgar translators could not vanquish. In the end, I read and devoured everything. Some of the narratives seemed to me very simple, respiring the tone of

---

[10] Author's reference: "Vol. VII, p. 193." The reference is to the journalist and diplomat Friedrich Melchior, Baron von Grimm (1723-1807); the first volume of his *Correspondance littéraire, philosophique et critique* was published in 1753, and later ones covered the entire period up to the Revolution.

frankness and verity; a few others appeared to me to merit a title other than that of histories, and I immediately ran to Jonathan's house in order to ask him for the "clear and frank explanation." He had moved, and no one has heard mention of him since.

Not being able to wait for an interval of a century for him to condescend to come back to France in order to give me his explanation, I have made the decision to submit to the public the anecdotes collected by Jonathan. A few timorous individuals have seemed to doubt the entire veracity of these accounts. That is an insult to my friend. However, to free myself of all responsibility in that regard, I have consented, after many altercations, to entitle them "tales," and to add to the name of Jonathan the title of "visionary," in order not to alarm persons sufficiently superstitious not to believe in astrology and alchemy. Furthermore, by way of conclusion, I shall say with Montaigne: "The stories that I have borrowed I refer to the conscience of those from whom I have taken them."

X. B. Saintine.

(In the course of this work, the notes of Jonathan's editor are signed X.)

The Young Boyar

(Wallachia)

We hardly think at present; and if we do think, it is only to obtain enlightenment in order to dispose the future. The present is never our objective. The past and the present are our means; only the future is our object. Thus, we never live, but we hope to live.

(Pascal, *Pensées*, "Human Vanity")

The sun was beginning to gild the summits of the elevated monuments of Bucharest, the capital of Wallachia, when a young man, who was recognizable by his short cloak and his richly-plumed astrakhan bonnet as the illustrious scion of a family of boyars, emerged from his residence, situated on the bank of the Dumbrowitz, and plunged into the mountains. On seeing the rifled carbine encrusted with silver and nacre that was slung over his shoulder and the large toothed dagger that he had in his belt, one might have believed that the hope surprising a chamois or a wild deer, or even triumphing over a bear, the terror of the land, was the sole occupation of his thoughts. One would have been mistaken. He was twenty-five years old; he was in love; and his age perhaps preoccupied him more than his amour.

"Twenty-five years!" he murmured, in a low voice. "A quarter of a century! Doubtless the better half of my existence! And what have I done thus far that can legitimate the employment of so many years?

"I have a thousand projects of happiness, but how can I carry them out? I would be so happy, if I have the time, but the desired moment always retreats before me. My marriage to Anna has been put off for another year, by the order of the voivode, her father. How long that year of waiting will be! To marry at twenty-six! I shall scarcely have tried the roles of father and husband; I shall barely have raised my family...and old age! Oh, how short life is! Is it not a revolting contradiction to give a man, the king of creation, a reign of such short duration, when there are twenty species of animals that live for centuries? They are not endowed with reason, however; they have not been the particular objects of the Omnipotent's attention."

While mechanically loading his carbine, he added: "That deer grazing on the tip of that rock is perhaps six times my age already, and perhaps might live another six times as long as I shall live."

"Yes, if you are maladroit," replied a voice that seemed to emerge from under the ground.

The young Wallachian recoiled in surprise. Then, suddenly perceiving at his feet a wretchedly-clad man lying on the sand of a dry ravine, he cried: "Who are you?" while directing his instrument of death toward him.

"Alas, clement Lord, "When you have killed me, you will not live for any longer, and the deer will not live for any less."

"Who are you, in sum?"

"A man who, in order to save his life, has come to confide it to the fury of the tchimbers[11] and the voracity of the bears."

"Who, then, is threatening your life?"

"Your relatives."

---

[11] Author's note: "A species of wild bull." That meaning of the word, which refers elsewhere to a kind of garment, appears to be idiosyncratic to Saintine. He used it again, in the novel *Chrisna* (1855 in *Revue contemporaine*; book 1859; tr. as *Chrisna, the Queen of the Danube*), where it features in the title of the first chapter; in the dedication to the book—to his son, a diplomat—Saintine claims to have visited Hungary and encountered Zingari there.

"What crime have you committed, then?"

"That of having one sense more than other men."

"What is your name?"

"To tell you is to risk a great deal, for you're carrying a very fine rifle and you have the right of life and death over me and my race."

"How?"

"Clement Lord, I am a Zingari, the chief of all the Zingaris proscribed and condemned by your people."

At those words, the young hunter recoiled involuntarily with a gesture of scorn, for the Zingaris or Tziganes—the word means vagabond—were a nomadic people descended from Copts and Nubians, who, having obtained from their ancestors a few secrets of necromancy, the dispersed heritage of ancient Egypt, had peddled them throughout Europe. As civilization, the mother of incredulity, had been established in that part of the world they had been driven back to the regions most propitious to the development of their art.

For many years, they had been living in Hungary, Moldavia and Wallachia, where a few of their bands still live, but in that era, whether because a part of their secrets had been lost or because, as because doubtless ill-intentioned historians have suggested, they profited from the confidence that they inspired and the free access that was granted them to the riches houses of the land to exercise occult talents other than the art of divination, which demanded less knowledge and more skill, they had fallen into complete discredit.

They often seemed to haunt the open roads more willingly than the interior of cities. A decree of proscription having not been sufficient to drive them away, the voivode of Wallachia had authorized his subjects to hunt them legitimately. It was that measure of public safety that constrained the unfortunate Kaboul, of whom we are speaking, to take refuge in the heart of the mountains, even though he was a stranger to the excesses of his brethren and spent his life honestly, composing philters and contemplating the stars.

As we have said, at the fatal name of Zingari, Assan Corati, our young hunter, recoiled in amazement. Educated at the University of Padua, however, like all the opulent youth of his nation, he had liberated himself from some of the prejudices of his native land, in order to adopt others in a foreign land. Thus, his Wallachian horror for the sons of Egypt yielded to his Italian confidence for every species of the marvelous. Furthermore, even among his persecutors, Kaboul enjoyed a high reputation as a savant and honest vagabond.

Assan reassured him regarding his fear, even assuring him of his protection, and soon returned to his original idea. "You overheard," he said, "the plaints that I was uttering regarding the strange distribution of instants between humans and certain animals?"

"Your carbine is lying peacefully in the grass, and you're provoking a discussion," Kaboul replied. "I'll take advantage of that to satisfy my natural need to talk and to prove to you, which I am glad to do, that a miserable Zingari is sometimes the equal of a boyar for reasoning. You were lamenting the brevity of human existence? But does not man have thought, with which he can divide his moments infinitely, and make centuries of his hours?"

"Sixty minutes, employed however you please, is nevertheless only an hour of life."

"Elapsed in dreamless sleep or in idleness, they only form a long series of monotonous instants, which, once passed, only leave an imperceptible point, soon confounded, compacted and forgotten with a thousand similar points that compose the void of our existence; but occupy each of those instants in projects and actions, weigh upon each moment, see nothing with indifference, and you are happy in the present, the past leaves you memories and the future opens before you full of hopes. You have lived."

"Yes, for an hour. In your magical secrets, savant Kaboul, is there not one that prolongs life?"

"I possess it," the latter replied, smiling. "Would you like to make use of it?"

"What, sage Kaboul! You possess it, and you deign to dispose it in my favor?"

"Very gladly; I will give you, if you wish, two hundred years of existence."

"Oh, my friend!"

"More than that, and don't lose sight of this prerogative attached to your new life: the future will be at your disposal, and you will be able to grow old as rapidly as you desire."

"I shall make scant use of it."

Kaboul suddenly drew away from Assan, and the latter saw him climb rocks, descend into the depths of precipices and hang over the edge of torrents, murmuring strange songs in an unknown language. Finally, he came back, carrying in his hand a large quantity of herbs of every sort.

"The place isn't propitious to prepare them," he said.

"Deign to follow me to my palace," Assan replied. "You'll be able to dispose of everything there, rest from your fatigues, find abundant nourishment, and only leave again heaped with my benefits."

Kaboul smiled. "In order to prolong your life, must I risk mine?"

"Accompanied by me, what have you to fear? Cover yourself with my cloak. Let's go along the Dumbrowitz; I live near the entrance to the city."

Kaboul followed him. A meal was prepared for the master of the house, and after Kaboul had composed his philter he presented it to his host, who took it confidently and sat down at table with him, in spite of his quality of Zingari.

Let us do justice to the fortunate Assan; assured of living for two centuries, his Anna immediately became the sole object of his thoughts. That long year of waiting still tormented him, but only by virtue of the impatience that he had to be happy, and not, as before, in the dread of not being able to raise his family.

He remembered the prerogative attached by Kaboul to his marvelous gift; rich with two hundred years of future, he had enough capital to sacrifice one to his mistress, and furthermore, he was eager to verify that Kaboul's promises were not deceptive. He therefore wished that the year of waiting would be effaced from his life and that the day of his marriage to Anna would dawn immediately for him.

His wish was scarcely formed than he experienced a kind of dazzlement, while the events of that year suddenly passed before him as, when lightning splits the sky, a thousand confused objects present themselves to our gaze and disappear instantly, or when wheels rapidly spinning on an axle appear motionless in their velocity. Anna was already in her bridal attire; the entire city was resounding with cries of joy and the roll of drums in honor of the daughter of the Prince of Walachia, and the bells of the Greek church, suspended, in accordance with custom, between two cypresses at the door of the temple, were announcing to the assembled crowds the approach of the newlyweds.

For Assan and for Anna the first days of the wedding were escorted by all the enchantments of amour and pleasure. If any importunate ceremonial came from time to time to interrupt those moments of delight, Assan had only to make a wish to find himself suddenly alone with his lover, liberated from vain etiquette. It was a few more moments removed from his life, but does one really exist during hours of ennui? Then again, Assan said, the early days of a marriage are so sweet that they merit exception.

But how happy he was, how intoxicated, when his young wife made him party to tender anxieties. She was tormented by a mild languor and bizarre needs. Assan understood that he was going to be a father, and no longer slept, he was so full of joy. At that time, the voivode asked him to travel on his behalf to the Sublime Gate; it was a matter of important affairs to communicate to the Reis-Effendi. He could not refuse that service to Anna's father, but could he abandon the woman who was about to render him a father?

This time, the sacrifice of the three months that the voyage would last appeared to him to be dictated by reason. He therefore made the wish, and the dazzlement arrived for a second time. The three months elapsed, and our sage, proud of having satisfied reason and nature, resumed thinking about his son. What would he do when he was born? It is not everything simply to be a father; it is necessary to fulfill the duties.

My poor son! He'll be named Assan, like me. My wife will love him more for that. I'm sure that he'll be a superb child. Dear Anna, she's going to suffer a god deal. I can't be a witness to her pains, I feel that keenly…my son and my wife, everything in the world most dear to me, between life and death! Let's abridge that time of ordeals; this time it's for the sake of pity, and humanity—and then I'll be able to embrace my son.

He took advantage once again of his prerogative, and his dear Anna gave both…to a daughter.

All his projects were thwarted. He needed a son, however, a little Assan. He occupied himself with that, employing, in order to satisfy his impatience, approximately the same means as during his first paternity, and finally succeeded. Assan II saw the light of day.

But a good father thinks of everything, and there never was a better father than Assan I. What would he do with that son when he grew older? Would he send him to the University of Padua, where he had been educated himself? No, he could never be separated from his son; he would confide his education to a reliable man versed in the languages of Europe and Asia, like the savant Asgleton, resident at the moment in Bucharest. Why should the honest Asgleton not take charge of it himself?

Between now and his son growing up, however, the scholar in question would doubtless have left Wallachia. That was a painful idea. Philip of Macedonia rejoiced so greatly because the gods had caused Aristotle to be born in his time, in order that he could confide his young Alexander to him. Asgleton was almost worth as much as Aristotle, and a few miserable years were not worth as much as something in which Philip of Macedon had rejoiced so much.

40

I shall immolate myself for my son, in order that he age seven years!

His family grew; he needed a larger palace and more spacious gardens. How could he accommodate himself to the slowness of the workers and that of the vegetation?

It was thus that, the master of his destinies, Assan sacrificed his present life in order to advance further and further into his future; from wish to wish, from dazzlement to dazzlement, he eventually perceived that his hair was going gray and that his wife was growing old. What had he done with his youth? He had spent it entirely hastening the moments that he dreaded.

A vast career is still open before him, but with another age, other passions take possession of his heart. It is necessary to offer to them again to aliment the good years; ambition arrives; he glimpses the road of honors and wants to travel it. One succeeds in that easily with time and money, and, to his misfortune, he is the master of his fortune and his life.

Already, everything he loved on earth has ceased to exist; even his son has succumbed to old age. Alone, Assan continues on his way, sustained by the ambitious hope of being voivode, as his grandfather once was. Finally, he obtains that fine title, but he receives with his appointment the order to raise troops and march in person with the hospodar of Moldavia against the Tartars of Boudziac, who have refused to pay a tax to which they are subject.

The new voivode, forced, in accordance with custom, to give the Overlord five hundred thousand Turkish piastres for his succession to the regency of Wallachia, found himself ruined; in order to undertake the fatal war he had to surcharge his subjects with more taxes and enroll them under his standards. Those new and painful occupations did not allow the moments to flow agreeably enough for him not to seek to abridge them: a dazzlement came to his aid, and he immediately found himself at the head of a superb army, half of which deserted the following day. Counting on his courage and on providence, he delivered battle regardless, and lost it. Summoned before the divan in order to justify his conduct, Assan went to Constantinople, where he was thrown into a dungeon and forgotten.

The unfortunate man, surrounded by lugubrious objects and guards with surly tones and forbidding faces, had plenty of time to make long reflections on his catastrophe.

I'm approaching the terrible epoch when my life must terminate, he said to himself, *but I've scarcely lived; perhaps I've sacrificed too lightly to my avidity for enjoyment numerous days that might not have been devoid of charms; for on that rapid route that took them away from me forever, I have sometimes glimpsed objects worthy of being regretted. Let experience render me sage henceforth; time is becoming precious to me; once returned to my estates, I shall be able to employ it for the happiness of my people, and my own; every hour will have its employment, perhaps its torments, but also its pleasure; I shall do good, I...*

Meanwhile, he added, *I'm a prisoner, crushed by the weight of a false suspicion; there's no point in clinging on to the present moment, the few happy days for which I hope can't be spent in this horrible cell; I sense the need to confound my accusers before the Sultan; so let the hour when justice will be rendered to me sound!*

So saying, he finds himself on his death-bed. A djinni covered in mourning veils, his forehead crowned with scabious and columbine, appears beside him; in one hand he is holding a trenchant blade, in the other tablets that he presents to him:

"Assan Corati, your two centuries are finished; you lamented the brevity of life, but when two hundred years were accorded to you, you sacrificed them foolishly in order to run after an illusory future that fled incessantly before you. Twice centenarian, see on these tablets the positive calculation of your existence. Since your encounter with the chief of the Zingaris, you have scarcely lived five years. Your hour has sounded!"

"Already!" cried the unhappy voivode, in a lamentable tone of voice. "Already! When I was making such noble plans for the glory and wellbeing of Wallachia! Wicked Kaboul! It is you who have caused all my disasters! Did I need your perfidious philter? Why did you not let me follow the common destiny of all men? I would have lived longer and more happily, reluctantly, it is true. But in sum, I would be dead with my Anna and before my beloved son. Cruel Kaboul! Wretched chief of the..."

Come on, my host, wake up!" the latter shouted at him, shaking him forcefully by the arm. Do Wallachian boyars have the habit of sleeping before a meal? Wake up, Assan Corati. Your maize soup is divine, but it's going cold."

And Assan opened his eyes wide in a fearful manner, looked around and, seized by astonishment, found himself back in his palace in Bucharest, situated on the bank of the Dumbrowitz, at table with the chief of the Zingaris, to whom he had just given hospitality.

"I'm not voivode, then?"

"No, but you could become one if the dungeons of Constantinople don't frighten you. At any rate, console yourself; you won't survive your son and you'll die with your Anna—who won't marry you, it's true, for another year. Well, my host, do you believe now that, thanks to thought, the hours can become centuries? Your dream hasn't lasted ten minutes, but you've accomplished, while it lasted, an entire existence."

"But by means of what spell?" said Assan.

"None," Kaboul replied. "The philter that you've taken was only composed of narcotic plants that were to stimulate your mind during the slumber of your body. I only wanted to put into activity the ideas that were already filling your head, and those that I took care to entertain there myself. The muttered words that escaped you during your dream informed me of my success. Thank Heaven if that lesson can persuade you that it is sensations that make life and prolong it.

"Noble occupations and sage pleasures can give you two centuries of existence, not I. Everything in you assuring and honorable and tranquil old age, enjoy the present, for it alone is certain. Don't hold your finest days in scorn, throwing them behind you disdainfully; bring the goal of all your projects closer, value time and make use of it, for life is made of it, and never forget that the future is a gulf into which the present will plunge. If one laments the brevity of life, one incessantly makes wishes to hasten its rapidity.

"You can see that in the matter of reasoning, a Zingari is sometimes worth as much as a boyar."

"Alas," said Assan, "it will be necessary for me to wait another year before marrying my Anna."

The Misalliance

(France)

Sua quisque exempla debet oequo animo pati.
Phaedrus.[12]

Julian was born in a village, and yet, without possessing the brilliant faults of the city, he was no longer a peasant. Adopted by a rich merchant of Touchy, in Auxerrois, educated in his benefactor's home until the age of eighteen, he had lived in ease, in repose, and in the hope of a fine future. His heart was not suspicious of Providence, imagining that that state of wellbeing would last forever.

Suddenly, his adoptive father, dragged toward ruin by hazardous enterprises and false speculations, was declared bankrupt, and fled abroad. Abandoned and left to fend for himself, Julian, conceiving a hated for a city in which the name of the bankrupt incessantly struck his ears, remembered the paternal cottage, and immediately set forth.

As he traversed the village of Ouaine, the place of residence of the Marquis de Vaudon, he saw all the peasants in festival garb, with joyful expressions, assembled outside the church. The betrothal was being celebrated of young Marie, the daughter of the Marquis, and the Comte de Vermanton.

That day, in accordance with custom, Marie, the sovereign mistress of her father's domains, dispensed justice and benefits at her whim. Julian presented himself before her in a

---

[12] "Everyone ought to endure calmly the example they have set for others." The last line of "Vulpis et Ciconia" [The Fox and the Stork] by the Roman Gaius Julius Phaedrus, who Latinized Aesop's fables.

supplicant manner. Marie welcomed him benevolently, listened to him with emotion, and, although he had not received any notion of agriculture or gardening—something about which she did not even enquire—he was immediately put at the head of the stewardship of the parks and gardens of the Seigneurie of Vaudon.

For a generous soul, the need to acquit a benefit is imperious. Julian was devoured by that ardent desire, which had become such a violent passion within him that it seemed to paralyze his other sentiments. Night and day, a single object occupied him entirely. If young Marie seemed to find pleasure in contemplating a flower, in respiring its perfume, he took no rest until that preferred flower was everywhere in her path, striking her gaze.

One evening, as she was walking in the park, she uttered a long scream. Julian came running. The foot of his pretty benefactress had been torn by a perfidious bramble, and Julian saw blood on her shoe. Three days later the brambles had disappeared from the Vaudon park; and, as Julian was no more able than anyone else to moderate his vengeance, all the plants armed with thorns or prickles—the holly, the bushes and the broom—were included in the same proscription.

The Comte de Vermanton was keenly interested in the accident that had befallen his lovely fiancée, but he held it against Julian for a long time that he had made an English garden of the park of Vaudon. That young lord, like all those of his class, thought himself obliged to like hunting passionately, which was then regarded as the most salutary exercise and the most noble amusement. In fact, it is salutary to make blood flow and to accustom one's eyes to the spectacle of carnage. It is the relaxation of heroes. The Comte might as well, he said, have gone to cut the throats of rabbits in the farmyard as go hunting in a bark without brushwood. He therefore did not pardon Julian for his fits of gratitude, and complained about him to the Marquis; but Julian naturally had a helpful defender in Marie.

It is only just that those who have made us commit a sin are the first to excuse it; but the Comte could not be persuaded of that at first. He found it strange that the daughter of the Marquis de Vaudon should lower herself to defending a valet. She explained her reasons, and they were good, but the Comte, whom the argument irritated, allowing his natural vivacity to carry him away, launched upon Marie and Julian an expression so insulting that she, stifled by tears, was unable to reply.

She ran to shut herself up in her apartments, wept at her ease, thought about the subject of the quarrel, and, for the first time, by virtue of the imprudence of the Comte de Vermanton, whom she loved, her mind paused complaisantly on the cares with which Julian had surrounded her since his arrival at the château. She recalled his face, which was handsome, and his character, which was good. She remembered that he had none of the manners of a peasant, and that idea excited her curiosity. She also remembered the softness of his gaze, and then she no longer wanted to think about him.

If the Comte had happened to pick a further petty quarrel with his fiancée on the subject of Julian, in the present disposition of her soul, I do not know what might have come of it, so incomprehensible is the heart of a woman; but it did not happen, and all was well.

Time passed, and everything resumed its ordinary course. Marie often withdrew, in order to dream or to read, to a small summer-house situated in the middle of the esplanade of the park. She seemed to please herself there better than any other place in the château. As it was uncovered on all sides, however, nothing defended her there against the ardor of noon, and she was constrained to absent herself from it when the sun was in full force.

Julian perceived that and, only consulting his devotion, he put a large number of gardeners and villagers to work, and in the space of a single night, immense holes were dug around the summer-house, and lindens and acacias, removed from their native soil, were transplanted there with all imaginable precautions. The following day, Julian was pleasantly repaid for his troubles by seeing Marie's astonishment at the sight of her cherished summer-house suddenly surrounded by shade and flowers.

The Comte de Vermanton murmured again; that clump of trees deprived some parts of the château of an admirable view, in his opinion. This time, the Marquis agreed. He thought the steward of his gardens very impertinent for having permitted himself to overturn everything without orders. To add to the misfortune, the newly-planted trees all died after a few days, and poor Julian, as the price of his attentive cares and his boundless devotion, was dismissed, without the person who was the continual object of all his cares and the cause of his misfortune daring to risk a word in his favor: a further contradiction of the feminine heart, but which my reader, if he has ever been in love, will find easily explicable.

Charged with giving Julian the order to depart, the Comte de Vermanton acquitted the task with such arrogance and harshness that the latter could not retain the expressions of his anger. The Comte, a young man full of impetuosity and vanity, was violently transported, and forgot himself to the extent of striking him. The furious Julian, beside himself, forgot himself in his turn, sized in desperation the gamekeeper's weapon, which was beside him, and hurled himself at the Comte, who, forced to think of his salvation, retreated precipitately, slipped, and fell into a vast channel that traversed the park of Vaudon, and into which the Ouaine stream discharged its waters.

Julian would be avenged, then! No: Julian was ready to punish an unjust aggressor, but nature and God, who puts compassion in the hearts of all men, summoned Julian to aid one of his fellows who was about to perish, and Julian dived into the water. With a muscular arm he struggled against the strength of the current, torn by a few fragments of rocks, his efforts and his search evidenced by the traces of is blood.

Finally, he reappeared at the surface; with one hand he had seized the Comte by his garments, with the other, while awaiting a liberating boat, he clung forcefully on to projections of the causeway. But his courage and his devotion were no longer sufficient; suddenly, his eyes became troubled; in vain he made one last effort to seize a vague object that seemed to offer itself to him. Soon, he could no longer see anything or feel anything, and a complete paralysis took possession of all his limbs.

When Julian recovered his senses he found himself in a dark place, where his gaze, still weak and dubious, could not distinguish any object at first. For a few moments, he thought he had woken up in another world. No recollection of his first existence struck his memory, love and hatred had been effaced from his heart.

Gradually, his intelligence returned; he examined the place where he was more attentively, and, raising himself up painfully on his bed, he parted the curtains that were intercepting the light. With some astonishment, he saw that he had been transported into a rich and beautiful apartment, which he recognized as belonging to the Château de Vaudon.

With even greater delight, he perceived in a corner, by the feeble light of a lamp, young Marie, occupied with her maidservants in preparing the linen necessary to bandage invalids. Her eyes seemed still to be swollen by tears, and Julian, in spite of his pains, who was beginning to awaken fully, regarded himself as the happiest of men in thinking that he might be the object of those touching cares and that some of those precious tears might have been shed for him.

The Comte de Vermanton as soon able to get up, and his first visit was to his liberator. As for the latter, his wounds were dangerous; an ardent fever agitated him at times and caused anxiety for his life. Every day, Marie lavished the cares of the most tender pity upon him, and every day, Julian was increasingly intoxicated by the sight of the person that he had initially only loved out of gratitude. In the moments when dolor seemed to give the poor invalid some respite, she deigned to converse with him in order to distract him, and every time, when she left him, she promised herself not to lend herself to any more conversations of that sort.

In one of those tender moments when Julian, forgetting the social distance that separated him from Marie, poured out his soul freely into hers, he confided to her the hopes and misfortunes of his youth. His self-respect—which one always has in the presence of the person one loves—must have suffered from some of those details, and Marie was grateful to him for it. But when he reached the terrible events that had deprived him of an adoptive father; when he reminded Marie that, without her, he might have remained devoid of support, with no shelter on earth, his voice was so altered that he could not finish his story. Marie, moved to pity, extended her hand to him tenderly; he took possession of it avidly, and their eyes, bathed with tears, immediately met.

Let us leave them weeping together for a moment, and occupy ourselves with what was happening outside the room of the interesting invalid.

Great events had just changed the political face of France. Two parties in an offensive attitude seemed only to be waiting for the moment to come to blows. A decree of the Constituant Assembly abolished the titles and the prerogatives of the nobility, and the Marquis de Vaudon, an ardent adherent of the new principles, had just renounced all his privileges gladly, and had had his coat of arms removed from that gate of his château, when the Comte de Vermanton came into his house.

"Monsieur le Marquis..."

"I'm no longer a Marquis, thank Heaven, my dear Vermanton."

"If that is the case, Monsieur, all our anterior engagements are broken; I take back my word, for the daughter of Citizen Vaudon cannot aspire to alliance with the noble family of the Comtes de Vermanton."

"Let your will be done, Monsieur; but you're going to cause a scandal that might turn against you one day."

"Adieu!"
"Adieu!"

"Come, my daughter!" exclaimed the Marquis, on seeing Marie traversing the apartment. "Sit down, my child. I'm going to afflict you, but I hope that you'll find enough strength in your affection for your father and in your wounded self-esteem soon to be scornful of the insensate who pretends to disdain us."

"Who are you talking about?"

"Your fiancé, Comte de Vermanton, is refusing to fulfill his oaths and renouncing your hand."

"Truly?" cried the imprudent young woman, launching herself out of her chair and throwing her arms around her father's beck. "He's renouncing me? Oh, so much the better!"

"I don't understand your delirious joy at all; it seemed to me that you loved him."

"Yes, I thought so for some time," she said, lowering her eyes, "but since I've heard him getting angry with you in the arguments the two of you have often had..."

"Good Marie!"

And, immediately running to rejoin her patient, with a smile still on her lips and her eyes shining with happiness, she said to him: "A great misfortune has just occurred."

He learned everything, and in his sympathetic transport, he also cried: "Oh, so much the better!"

However, Julian's illness took a disquieting turn. The excessive emotions that he felt every day irritated his wounds and inflamed his blood, and the fever no longer quit him. Until then, the doctor, in accordance with the habitual prudence of his profession, had carefully refrained from any pronouncement; finally, he declared the existence of a great danger.

There is alarm in the château; Marie, overwhelmed by dolor, no longer wants to quit Julian's room, and her tears and sobs have soon informed the latter of the love to which he has given birth and the peril that is menacing him.

It was in the middle of one of those cruel nights that, awakened with a start by pain, Marie's lover perceived her, on her knees at the foot of his bed. She was praying.

"I can see," he said to her, "that there is no more hope. Console yourself; there was no happiness on earth for me; if I had recovered my health it would soon have been necessary for me..." Then, suddenly interrupting himself, he cried: "Oh, if death equalizes everything...Marie, I'm going to die...no, you're not unaware..."

"Be quiet," she said, placing her trembling finger on her friend's lips. "Be quiet, I know everything."

Then, seizing the unfortunate man's hands and pressing them between hers. The chaste, good and tender Marie, with an almost solemn air, curbed her forehead toward that of the invalid, and deposited the first amorous kiss on lips already chilled by death.

"Now we're united!" she cried, and she fainted.

But Julian had only been condemned to death by his physicians, and nature overturned the sentence. The return of his health, the certainty of being loved, the political opinion of Marie's father, and the departure of the Comte de Vermanton, all seemed to be a presage of happiness for him.

Such tender hopes were not realized, however. Citizen Vaudon received Julian's proposal poorly. In vain the latter said to him: "We have the same principles; I think, as you do—and I have even more interest than you in thinking it— that all men are equal. Give me your daughter, then. You would be unworthy of the name of man if, for the few thousand écus you have more than me, the only difference that can exist between us, you sacrifice your child's happiness and mine. In the name of humanity, and reason..."

He was about to continue his eloquent speech when, in the name of reason and humanity, the Marquis took him by the shoulders and threw him out of the château.

The furious Julian wrote to Marie:

Your father is a barbarian; am I, then, less than him, to excite his scorn? I love you, you love me; what more is re-

52

quired to unite us? He criticized the conduct of the Comte de Vermanton; it was less insensate than his own. Woe betide parents whom honors or riches render deaf to the cries of amour and nature!

Marie was almost of the same opinion, but that was not sufficient. By an excess of misfortune, her father found the letter. He foresaw what the consequences might be, and, charged at that moment by the municipal authorities to furnish voluntary defenders to the fatherland, he put Julian at the head of the list.

Whether he liked it or not, poor Julian was now a soldier. What became of him? I don't know. Doubtless he did his duty, was brave, comported himself with heroism, and got himself killed. Let us not talk about it anymore and return to Marie, the principal object of this story.

Time, the great consoler, the great destroyer, the great magician, brought about many changes in the Château de Vaudon. The revolution was in progress, and in its bloody course crushed underfoot its own founders. The ex-marquis found himself the target of continual denunciations; he was reproached for the lukewarm quality of his republicanism, while the common folk were outraged on Julian's behalf. He thought he could ward off the storm ready to descend upon him by sacrificing his daughter, and Marie, an obedient victim, thinking that she was saving her father's life, became the wife of a man who only resembled Julian in his birth, and the Comte de Vermanton by the impetuosity of his character, but who, in those days, found himself at the head of the ruling party.

Alas, it was in vain that Marie's father had believed that he would find a defender in his son-in-law; an honest man, a true patriot, he had dreamed of the republic but could not conceive of anarchy. He was thrown into a dungeon. Another unfortunate was groaning beside him on the straw.

"Is that really you, Marquis?" exclaimed the Comte de Vermanton, for it was him. "By virtue of what change of opinion do you find yourself here?"

53

"My friend, I wanted to save the republic."

"And I the monarchy."

The same day saw them both perish on the scaffold.

Reader, close your eyes upon that disastrous epoch; let twenty years go by of troubles, glory and misfortune, and follow me within the walls of Paris. See, in this modest house, opposite that brilliant mansion, an affectionate mother listening to the laments and sharing the chagrins of an only son, her only friend.

That good mother in Marie; that good son is the tender fruit of her unfortunate marriage. Widowed and reduced to the most obscure condition, only subsisting on the labor of her son, whose success in the arts enables her to hope for a better future, she sees her present situation aggravated again by the deadly passion that her son Gustave has for the only child of a man whose fortune and considerable rank prohibits any hope.

Having succeeded by his merit alone in reaching the highest employments in his military career, the Duc de Stétin devoted all the moments of his glorious leisure to directing the brilliant education of his daughter Amélie. Gustave, chosen by him to initiate her into the secrets of drawing and painting, did not take long to conceive the most violent amour for his pupil. The Duc was informed of it and his pride revolted. Not content with banishing the artist from his house, he resolved to put everything to work to extract from Amélie's heart a nascent sentiment that made his patrician forehead blush with shame.

For her part, Marie, with the tender concerns with which a woman, and especially a mother, knows how to surround her words of consolation, sought to calm the impetuous spirit and excited heart of the young painter.

"My friend, my Gustave, where can an insensate amour take you? Can the son of a poor widow devoid of a name and a fortune aspire to the hand of the heiress of the Duc de Stétin? She loves you, you say, but my son, can love alone legitimate everything? See how many persecutions the father of your

Amélie has already brought down upon us. He will never consent to such a marriage; he cannot and ought not to do it. Gustave, your mother understands the extent of your chagrins, and shares them. The memories of my youth remind me of dolors similar to your; my heart was broken, like yours. Let my example stiffen you, and inspire you with the courage of resignation."

She was about to continue, but a valet who had emerged from the brilliant mansion opposite her dwelling handed her a letter. It was from the Duc de Stétin. He complained bitterly about the young man's conduct, deplored the inconvenience of such a proximity, and concluded by declaring that if the "vile seducer" did not consent to go away voluntarily and immediately, he would be able to constrain him to do so by means within his power.

In despair, trembling for her son, Marie was rereading that fatal missive again when the characters of a familiar handwriting reawakened in her heart a memory that was simultaneously very tender and very cruel.

She was thinking about that singular similarity when a second domestic came in and announced the visit of the Duc de Stétin. Gustave left, and the Duc soon appeared in person.

"Madame," he said to Marie, who received him with her face ruddy with dread and her head bowed, "I have come to know what your final resolution is. It's with regret that I'm afflicting you, Madame, but don't constrain me to take a severe course with you. Your son dares to love my daughter; more than that, abusing her youth and her inexperience, he has dared to make her love him! Fortune, name and rank, nothing stopped him!"

"Alas, Monsieur le Duc," Marie replied, who, recovered from her disturbance, had had time to examine him attentively, "if my son is guilty, I cannot pretend to defend him, but his amour is an involuntary sentiment and his youth is his excuse."

"An artist! Has he, then, been able to believe that such an alliance was possible?"

"At our age, Monseigneur, one can only listen to ambition and vanity; at his, one only consults one's heart, and the rank of the woman beloved is forgotten for her attractions."

"So, Madame, you approve of your son's conduct?"

"I approve of nothing, Monseigneur; I sympathize with an unmerited misfortune. I respect the established social order, but my son never had any intention of troubling it. Be his judge yourself. You have been his age, you have doubtless been in love; did you then only consult reason and social proprieties?"

At that moment, a sudden blush colored the forehead of the powerful man and betrayed the vivid emotions of his soul. He calmed down, however, and in a firm and decisive tone, he repeated: "Madame, your son loves my daughter; they cannot live in the same place; he must go away, he must go away! Oh, who knows whether he might not take audacity so far as to write to my Amélie!"

"I cannot deny it, Monsieur le Duc," replied Marie, trembling, "having surprised a letter..."

"A letter! He has dared!"

"Here it is," said Gustave's mother, then, after having taken from the drawer of her writing desk a carefully-enveloped letter. "Pronounce, then, on the fate of the man who wrote it."

And the Duc, after having opened it indignantly, read:

Your father is a barbarian; am I, then, less than him, to excite his scorn? I love you, you love me; what more is required to unite us? He criticized the conduct of the Comte de Vermanton; it was less insensate than his own. Woe betide parents whom honors or riches render deaf to the cries of amour and nature!

It was signed: *Julian.*

Astonished he raised his eyes.

"Marie! Marie, is that you?"

"Yes, Julian, yes, it's me; it's me whom you want to deprive of a son, of the only being on earth who loves me today."

"Let's not talk any more about misfortunes, let's not talk any more about refusals! The Duc de Stétin does not exist for you; it's Julian, Julian who has been able to make your tears flow, and who implores your forgiveness on his knees! Marie," he added, smiling, "might the daughter of poor Julian hope to be united with the grandson of the Marquis de Vaudon?"

The Benefactors

(Spain)

Omne dixeris maledictum,
cum ingratum hominem dixeris.
Cicero.[13]

Lopez only lived in a cottage, but it was situated under the beautiful sky of Andalusia, in the pretty kingdom of Jaen, at the florid foot of the mountains of the Sierra Morena, and his daughter Inésille, his only child, his good, his beautiful, his dear Inésille, lived with him. He did not regret anything of his past wealth except the ability to complete his daughter's brilliant education, interrupted by his misfortunes.

"Inésille," he said to her, "in the time of my prosperity I often did good deeds, and no one came to my aid; generosity only rarely inhabits the human heart."

"The large number of ingrates would seem to prove the contrary," Inésille replied.

"Ingratitude would be less common if one were better able to place one's benefits, but rich and powerful men, incessantly surrounded by valets, flatterers and schemers, are unable to pierce that slavish crowd in order to bring to virtuous indigence a noble benefit that would assist without debasing. One ought, before obliging, to know whom one is obliging."

"One listens to one's heart and is deceived; that is what you have often done yourself."

"I was wrong…!"

---

[13] "When you call a man ungrateful, you have exhausted the vocabulary of reprobation."

He was about to continue when a clap of thunder was heard; a violent storm was in preparation, and Lopez, immediately forgetting benefactors and ingrates, ran to open the main gate of his courtyard, in order that travelers, surprised by the squall, could find a shelter beneath his hangar, in anticipation of the torrents that were already beginning to flow in all the ravines of the mountain.

A brilliant carriage, harnessed to six mules, suddenly came in. Don Fernand got down from it, had his mounts and his valets placed under the hangar, and presented himself at the door of Lopez's cottage.

Inésille opened the door, and Don Fernand was greatly astonished to encounter under the thatched room a figure so slim and features so distinguished. The noble aspect of Lopez seemed no less surprising. His astonishment, his pressing questions and the interest he seemed to take in their situation engaged the latter to tell him about his misfortunes. Fernand listened until the end with a profound attention.

"By the sword of the Cid!" he exclaimed, with tears in his eyes, "I thank my divine patron for having led me to this dwelling; thanks be rendered to Heaven as well as the storm! Lopez, I am rich and my heart is sensible; you will not refuse the offer I'm going to make to you. Sooner or later your fortune ought to be returned to you; deign to be my debtor..."

"I don't desire anything for myself," said Lopez, "but my Inésille, still in the flower of her youth, has been deprived for a long time of the useful seeds of a salutary education, the caresses of a companion and the cares of a mother—for it is those cares that the most affectionate of fathers cannot replace."

"I have an aunt," Fernand replied, "Who lives in Cazorla with her two daughters, both very close to the age of your Inésille. That family, in which you will find an inexhaustible kindness united with an enlightened religion, a solid and varied education, deprived of the gifts of fortune, only lives on a modest pension that virtue, humanity and relationship impose the duty upon me of providing. Cazorla is situated not far from here, on the banks of the Vega, in a delightful location; go yourself on my behalf to find my noble relative and confide your daughter Inésille to her..."

Lopez did not let him finish, seizing his hands and watering them with tears of gratitude.

Son, Inésille, conducted by her father to the home of Fernand's aunt, received the most amicable and affectionate welcome there, and Lopez, disabused of his prejudices in regard to men, returned to his cottage content with himself and others, promising himself not to calumniate the human species any longer, and to go and see his daughter often.

One day, he was thinking about Fernand and his delicate generosity when, on parading his gaze sound his habitation, he saw, on a tree that was not very tall, a poor little orphan dove, scarcely covered with a light down, and which, as if abandoned by nature entire, was filling its deserted nest with soft lamentations.

At the same moment, from the summits of the Sierra Morena, a bird of prey—it was a vulture—deploying its immense wings, directed its flight toward the plaintive dove-chick, and soared for some time over the tree that sustained its cradle.

Lopez was already seeking the means to rescue the innocent chick when he thought he perceived that, at the sight of the vulture, the little dove, ceasing its lamentations, seemed to be frolicking joyfully in its nest and extending its open beak toward it.

Indeed, he soon saw the terrible bird descend slowly, charged with precious booty, toward its young protégée, and lavish an appropriate and choice nourishment upon it, with a care and attention unknown to vulgar vultures.

"O marvel!" cried the worthy Lopez. "How great my injustice and my blindness was! I refused to believe in benevolence, and it even exists among vultures!"

He never wearied of contemplating a spectacle so touching, and every day he came back in order to contemplate it again. It was a subject of innumerable reflections for him; he took pleasure in seeing innocence grow up under the wing of strength, the weak assisted by the powerful. Soon, his ideas, by virtue of a natural connection, took him back toward Cazorla, where his sweet Inésille was also living happily under the protection of a rich man, a power in society, and he went home blessing Don Fernand and the vulture.

Already, the genteel dove-chick was beginning to cover itself with silvery plumage; already, from branch to branch, it was trying out its timid flight in its natal tree; its hardened and sharpened beak was already seizing aliments with facility.

One day, the vulture came to bring its customary nourishment; it examined its ward attentively, found it fat and appetizing, as it wanted it to be, and devoured it.

Lopez witnessed that, and he remained "astounded and perplexed," like Gargantua at the death of his wife Badebec.

"Mercy!" he cried. "What do I see?"

The worthy man was astonished that a vulture was eating a dove, when the contrary alone would have been supernatural.

But the idea of his daughter immediately returned to his memory.

My Inésille, my dove, he said to himself, *is also under the protection of a vulture, a great lord, in sum, a man of prey. Oh, let us not lose a moment...*

An on the way, he repeated to himself a hundred times:

One ought, before accepting a benefit, obtain good information regarding those who are according it to us; protectors and the protected ought only to adopt one another after mutual investigations.

And so saying, he arrived out of breath in Cazorla and ran to the house where his daughter lived...alas!

The Sorcerer's Child

(Sweden)

If human beings arrived at the point of perfection of which they think themselves capable, their relationship with the rest of nature would immediately cease.

(Aristotle, *Rhetoric*, vol. 3, ch. 1)

The celebrated necromancer Maugis left a part of his secrets to one of his disciples, named Sirvax, who soon astonished the astrological schools of Seville and Toledo by his profound knowledge of the double magic, and especially by the audacity of his attempts.

"The transcendent and sublime science that we glory in cultivating," he said one day to the initiates of Hermes enclosed with him in the cavern of Salamanca,[14] "will never attain the summit of the luminous column as long as human senses, the only instruments by means of which we analyze and decompose objects, have not arrived at a more exquisite delicacy of their own accord. In the great work, God has taken hazard as his aide; he contented himself with dispersing the seeds of human creatures over the globe, matter has done the rest.

---

[14] A legend popularized by Miguel de Cervantes alleges that the Devil once taught necromancy in the Cave of Salamanca, which had previously been the crypt of the Church of Saint Cyprian. Maugis is the name of an enchanter featured in more than one *chanson de geste*, including the story of the four sons of Aymon; that and the fact that the events of the story predates the founding of Stockholm suggests that the story is set in the eleventh century.

"Different combinations of metals and primitive earths formed the envelope of the first individuals, and produced the existing varieties of our sickly race. The same seeds formed black men and white, Circassians and Laplanders; but the blind instincts of brute matter have diversified their forms and enclosed the celestial rudiment of human beings in a narrow and uncomfortable prison, where their reason and senses cannot develop. Hazard, in sum, has paralyzed the initial jet of supreme intelligence.

"Since that time, children have been born with the infirmities of their parents, and the sciences threaten to stop at the barrier that the weakness of our organs opposes to them. I want to open a limitless route to genius and reason, and give human thought, not a wretched dungeon for a dwelling, but a vast palace where it will reign without shackles."

A slight murmur rose up in the assembly; but Sirvax, raising his head proudly, cried: "I have spoken! A new family of beings, nobler and more perfect than us, will owe its existence to me. And who will oppose that? Does not the sun shine now as in the first days of the world, and will the great Maugis have left his sublime and mysterious science to his pupil in order for it to remain slavish and sterile in his power?"

Entirely devoted to his project, he soon left Spain and retired to one of the numerous deserted islands that cover Lake Meler. Sweden, rich in metals and mineral products, seemed to him to be the land most appropriate to the experiments that he was meditating.

Several years went by without any one hearing mention of him; then, suddenly, the rumor spread that, by the power of his art, a man had been born without having been conceived in the womb of a woman. Curious to verify such a phenomenon, I embarked on the Baltic, went up the Meler, and, after leaving left behind me the enormous rocks on which Stockholm has since been built, I visited almost all of the islands covering the surface of the lake, and finally discovered the one on which Sirvax lived with his magical child.

Sirvax was on the shore; on seeing me he took on an expression of sadness and constraint that astonished me.

"Well," I said to him, "you've succeeded, then?"

"Yes," he replied. "He's alive, he thinks and he speaks; you can see and judge for yourself. " And his brow darkened again. He seemed to head for his habitation then, and I followed him, heaping him with questions.

This is what I can remember of his replies:

"Twenty times human ashes, dessicated bones and the black liquor of old sepulchers passed through my crucibles, decomposed by me. The envelope of human beings is the same as that of pebbles.

"The *magicum carmen* is the deposit of the high sciences; but the sciences are mothers of the truth that enlightens us and the pride that leads us astray. I had noticed on the island of Malta a rock struck in the three sacred epochs of the day by the sun's rays, to which it doubtless owes its existence, for light made the world. I detached fragments of it, which, crushed and mixed by me with the purest gaseous fluids, took on form...

"Alas, it is necessary to admit that the proportions and the arrangement of human organs also reveal a sublime intelligence; I suspected as much and I blasphemed. I spent five years of my life trying to alter the dispositions and give my work more perfections and harmony in its movements; I did nothing but err for five years. The arms have to be placed thus in order to protect the sources of life contained in the breast, to bring before the eyes the objects that they need to contemplate and to the mouth the nourishment that it must receive.

"The last-named function satisfying the need that is felt most imperiously by humans, the organ of smell needs to be placed directly above that of nutrition, in order to savor even before the palate; and the eyes, active sentinels, also need to survey the materials offered to the mouth in order that no hostile body slips inside unknown to the sense of smell.

"But if I have been forced to respect those principal dispositions of the human body, I believe that I have at least found the means of improving them by complicating them. To the natural means of human respiration I have added to mine aspirant arteries like those of birds, and stigmata imitative of those of insects, in order to give his blood a warmth and activity that that his thoughts ought to feel. Our feeble eyes cannot distinguish forms and colors at too close or too great a range; his have such an extent that three leagues of distance does not impede them. Finally, I have given his senses such a development that I ought to expect anything of a reason directed by such motors."

"But how," I said to him, "after having planned all the mechanisms of that body, were you able to make life enter into it?"

"That is the secret of my art," he replied. Then, unrolling before me a long parchment covered with Oriental characters, and indicating them to me with his finger, he said: "The blood of a young bull stifled at the moment of its first amours, and the liquor of euphorbia and henbane, extracted at a certain time, would have been sufficient in combination to enable the intervention of the aid of the demon, but the demon was not a guest worthy of such a lodgment. I was able to constrain one of the intelligences that inhabit the mixed worlds to come and inhabit and direct my material creation."

Sirvax suddenly stopped at that point in his discourse, and then, with a long sigh and resuming his thoughtful expression, he went on: "In any case, you can judge for yourself; but let's be silent, we're approaching the place where he reposes, let's beware of waking him up too abruptly."

I was gripped by a sort of terror that I could not explain, as if alerted by instinct to an imminent danger. Although the sound of our footfalls was barely audible, a muffled and prolonged groan greeted us immediately. Then, a deformed and gigantic being appeared before me, raising with difficulty an enormous head that was balanced on broad shoulders. His eyes, yellow and earthen in color, seemed only to dart oblique glances; his skin, pale and dull, was not colored by the movements of blood; and his hair, or rather his mane, of a grayish hue, scarcely hid two large ears, which, fashioned like shells, shared with those of hares the property of rotating in the direction in which a sound was audible.

"Who comes to trouble my repose?" he cried, turning haggard eyes toward us. "Is the day not made for sleeping?"

"Be quiet, Mudloch," Sirvax said to him, his forehead covered with a sudden blush. "What use do you make of your reason? Have I not already proven to you that only the exquisite sensitivity of your sight, until now, has opposed your being able to support the rays of the sun like other men?"

At this point the sorcerer's child seemed to be seized by frenetic transports. "False reasoning," he said to him. "You raise your voice with such force that my ears are torn by it. The daylight only gives birth to darkness, your mind only gives birth to lies."

Having said that, he turned his back on us, without even perceiving my presence, and he went to lie down again on an enormous pile of heather.

"His senses still abuse him," murmured Sirvax. "Time will rectify that, but what keen senses of smell and hearing! In darkness, what surety of gaze! He senses the opening of a flower on one of the neighboring islets; he can hear the sound of a falling leaf fall six hundred paces away; and he can hit a nightingale with an arrow at a distance that scarcely permits us to distinguish the tress on which the bird is perched."

Toward dusk, Mudloch came to knock on the door of Sirvax's habitation and demand his breakfast.

"My friend," the latter said to him, moderating the tone of his voice, "the evening meal is not a breakfast; we're about to have supper, come and eat with us."

"Breakfast is breaking a fast," replied Mudloch, "my night has just gone by, the day is commencing, and I've come to take my first meal. Cease, then, incessantly trying to make me adopt words that are contrary to my ideas. The senses are the organs of the intelligence, as you have told me yourself; you'll agree that mine have a perfection that yours cannot attain; my reason is therefore superior to yours; admit the insufficiency of your means, serve my breakfast, and have breakfast with me if you think it appropriate."

An enormous Halland salmon was set before him, but, having tasted it, he quickly pushed it away, complaining about its excessively strong flavor. I ate some; it seemed almost insipid to me.

However, I was able to attract the confidence of Mudloch by not opposing him in any way. After the meal I accompanied him, almost groping, in his nocturnal course. For three entire nights I became the companion of that man of darkness, about whose existence I wanted to know. His sight had a prodigious range, but the intermediate spaces escaped him; he could only see what he could not touch. The perfume of a flower seemed to give a dolorous quiver to his entire body, and the slightest sound held his mind in suspense.

In accordance with his senses, he conceived space, number, shape and movement, but occult causes, the possible, instinct, the future, and the sudden revelations of the soul all escaped him. His thought did not launch forth beyond a cold reasoning based on external sensations. His organs enclosed all of his intelligence, abused by them. His was a body that lacked a soul, a reason deprived of instinct. Without foresight, without enthusiasm, without imagination, disinherited of his divine part, of ideas coming from the heavens, he was the human being as Locke has since presented him to us, he was the man of science—in sum, the man of man.

"What do you think of him and me?" Sirvax asked me, one day.

"I think," I replied, "that in order to complete your work, you need to make a new world for your new man, but never hope to see that earth of your creation shaded by the branches of the tree of genius. Reason alone does not invent or discover anything; your Mudloch is deprived of any species of imagination, and even in the physical sciences, it is by means of that faculty that one arrives at the highest truths. One begins by inventing, and when, by experiment and reasoning, the means of verification, one has succeeded in giving bases and supports to one's theory, one believes that one has discovered it. One has created it.

"Instinct and imagination, in human beings, are like memories of a prior existence, and the emanations of a world of light that humans doubtless once inhabited; they owe to one their natural beauty, to the other the extent of their genius and preeminence over the other beings of creation. Your Mudloch, the son of matter, cannot possess either of those two sublime faculties."

While I was conversing thus on one of the shores of the island with Sirvax, who was seeking to combat the disadvantageous opinion that I had conceived of his favorite, we saw a small vessel approaching the strand, from which several men and a young and beautiful woman soon emerged. Sirvax seemed desolate at this further increase in the population of his island.

"On the contrary," I said to him, "thank Providence; it has sent you today the surest means of testing the human sentiments to which the child of your art might be susceptible. The sight of a woman ought to act immediately upon his heart, and develop emotions thus far dormant there."

We went to meet the disembarked newcomers, and Sirvax recognized them as some of his friends from Salamanca, curious, like me, to verify the reality of his promises.

Nightfall soon brought Mudloch to the sight of the young woman. He gave no evidence of attraction or surprise; his heart remained cold, his face impassive, except that his scornful gaze seemed to reproach her for being the weakest of the individuals surrounding him.

By means of their multiple questions, our philosophers from Salamanca had soon obliged Mudloch to explain the theory of his sensation himself. At first they all seemed very surprised by the eccentricity of his ideas, but when he came to invoke the superiority of his organs over those of other humans, he cited in his favor the axioms of their own school, *intellectus in sensu*, several of them began to doubt.

However, it still seemed difficult to them to admit that the day was consecrated to sleep and obscurity. One of them said: "It's during the day that birds sing and flowers open; the sun is the torch of nature; everything that vegetates or respires is reanimated, vivified and guided by its light."

"Absurd sophisms!" cried Mudloch. "The feeble light of day can suffice for your weak sight, dazzled by the luminous glare of night. The sun dispenses heat, the moon dispenses light; heat dilates the fibers of the body, enfeebles ideas and invites repose; who can deny those incontestable verities? Night reanimates the flowers that the sun withers; it is during the night that they exhale all their perfumes, that myriads of moths, more numerous than those of the day, flutter around them; it is during the night that the nightingale sings, that the races of the most noble among the birds agitate; do not the bear, the wild boar, the anteater and thousands of animals wander by night in our forests? By what right do you judge by yourselves? Do the osprey and the owl not have eyes as good as the warbler and the finch? Do you dare to compare your sight with mine? Abjure ancient errors, therefore, the moon alone is the torch of nature; everything that breathes is reanimated, vivified and guided by its light."

The balance was beginning to tip strongly in favor of the new speaker. The discussion was then taking place in obscurity, and our sages were no longer astonished that they could not see. The magical influences of the moon and darkness on the minds of mortals and the guests of tombs were retraced in their thoughts, and were reinforced by the theories of the motherless man in favor of the night. Sirvax, in whom pride had already subjugated reason, appeared triumphant, and addressed his colleagues:

"Perhaps my promises will be accomplished," he said, "and a new era is commencing for science; let us not hasten our judgments; let us examine before deciding. I shall try to see it in the night, insofar as my feeble means permit me to do so. It even seems to me that my eyes, less abused, can distinguish objects in the obscurity that surrounds us..."

And while that cabalistic family was arguing thus in favor of darkness and sensual intelligence, the young woman, who had retired at the beginning of the evening, came back in, carrying a blazing resinous pine branch.

Mudloch, dazzled and furious, had got to his feet, raising a threatening gesture toward her, when Sirvax threw himself in front of him. "What are you doing, raising a hand to a woman?"

"What is a woman?" said the monster. "What! Is this the companion of man about which you have spoken to me? If that is so, this woman is mine..."

"What is he saying?" cried all the spectators of the scene simultaneously, gripped by terror.

"She cannot belong to you," added the disciple of Maugis. "Society imposes laws upon us, which must be respected."

"What does society matter to me?" said Mudloch, roaring with fury. "I only know the laws that my senses, the organs of my reason, impose on me."

"But does this woman love you? Can she love you?"

"I do not know love and do not require it. Does the inhabitant of forests talk about love when he retains his indocile companion beneath his claws? Society! Love! Barbaric words invented to paralyze reason and strength! She is mine, I tell you; the countries from which you come must produce others for you, but, alone of her species on this island where I was born, she is mine!"

And, with his eyes filled with a somber gleam, and his mane bristling, with convulsive movements, he advanced toward the pale and dying creature. I leapt toward her and took her in my arms, while Sirvax, taking possession of the blazing pine branch, which she was still holding, presented it to the monster's face and forced him to retreat before the light.

We succeeded in calming the young woman's terrors, and were seeking a place where we could shelter her from further attempts by Mudloch until daylight, when we perceived that Sirvax had not returned to us. Anxious about his

70

fate, we resolved to go in search of him, equipped with weapons and torches.

Shrill cries soon guided us to a part of the island where the unfortunate sorcerer, chained to a tree, was being heaped with maledictions and blows by the child of his art, who was reproaching him for raising an obstacle to his natural and reasonable desires. Seeing us armed, Mudloch seemed frightened and tried to flee. We stopped him in order to reproach him for the infamous treatment to which he had subjected his benefactor and the author of his existence.

An infernal smile appeared on his lips. "What do I owe him?" he said to us. "Has he created me for my benefit? What pact was I able to conclude before being born? I have served his projects in making use of his gifts; what more does he demand? Is he not obliged to me? He is triumphant today, since he sees that my reason has sufficed to convert yours, and that my strength has vanquished his. But for you, he would be subject to the punishment that any being deserves who is in contradiction with himself, any being cruel enough to harm his own work, to stop the effects of which he is the first cause. He knows my will now; he knows my strength and my skill; let him satisfy me or he will tremble!"

As he finished those words he plunged rapidly into the darkness, and disappeared.

"See, then, the results of the superior reasoning on which you want to found your new science," I said to Sirvax. "Believe me, let us abandon his fatal island as soon as possible, and let us leave that beast with a human face, that veritable lycanthrope, to bury his barbaric intelligence in this solitude."

He resisted, but we dragged him toward our boats, still moored to the shore.

"No!" the unhappy sorcerer soon cried, detaching himself from our arms. I want to see him again! He's my son! He's my work! He's doubtless already repenting..."

As he finished speaking, frightful laughter burst forth from a great distance behind us. Sirvax had just fallen at our feet, pierced by an arrow.

We forgot all the danger in order to surround him with the most tender cares, but his blood was escaping in floods; his wound was mortal, and he ordered us himself no longer to think of anything but our own safety.

"Have I been punished for having dared too much? Is it, then, for our wellbeing that nature has placed limits on our senses and covered her designs with a veil of bronze?" he said, gazing at the ground. Then, after a moment's silence: "I divine…God be praised!" And he exhaled his last sigh.

Gripped by horror and pity, we quit that bloody shore, and my companions soon returned to Salamanca, to frighten with the story all the disciples of Hermes who, since Sirvax's supposed success, were no longer occupied in anything but making men and correcting the imperfect works of God.

It is said that Mudloch succeeded in traversing the Meler, that he traveled through several countries, always at war with the protective laws of society and the mildest instincts of nature. Finally, weary of others and himself, he wanted to visit the rocks of Malta from which he had been drawn, and ended his days voluntarily there, without remorse for the past and without hope for the future.

His body was not subject to the effects of carnal dissolution; by virtue of a singular phenomenon, it returned to its primitive state, while conserving its hideous and terrible form; and the Maltese still show travelers that petrified cadaver, separated from the rock, suspended over the abysms of the sea, which is commonly known by the name of *il fratre impiccato*.

It is also said that, in the course of his errant life, he became a father, and that his monstrous race acquired a rapid increase. The same reports certify that from him is descended the host of men who mistake darkness for light; those beings deprived of instinct and imagination who glorify themselves in enjoying a mechanical reason, a mineralogical sensibility; the multitude of atheists, of materialists who, doubtless deprived of a soul like the author of their origin, are obstinate in refus-

ing one to other men. People say that; I have difficulty believing it.[15]

Sethos and Cleophas

(Greece)

> *On the edge of a spring or the banks of the Ganges, one*
> *can always fill one's cup and satisfy one's thirst.*
> (Indian philosophy)

In Hermionida, not far from Mount Pronos, lived two friends, Sethos and Cleophas. A field cultivated by their hands, and a modest income derived from a quarry situated on the isle of Calauria, composed their entire fortune. Nevertheless, they blessed the gods, and, if one feels happier the more one loves, Cleophas was the happier of the two, for Sethos only loved Cleophas, while the latter combined with his tenderness for Sethos the most ardent amour for Cleone, his friend's sister.

Who could believe that, with so many reasons for being content with his lot, he dared to form the project of separating himself from those who were so dear to him?

"What is fortune?" Sethos said one day. "Does the moderation of our desires render us as rich as Pericles of Athens himself?"

"Yes," Cleophas replied, "but my marriage to your sister with diminish our ease."

"While augmenting our happiness," Sethos replied, "for is not seeing oneself live again in charming little beings full of innocence and candor one motive more for rejoicing? And do the gods not watch over cradles?"

"But Sethos, it is necessary to foresee misfortunes, yeas of sterility, bad debtors, old age and infirmities. Listen; dreams are rarely deceptive, and last night, my uncle Polycletus of Thassos appeared to me; after having reproached

74

me for my scant ambition, and offered to associate me in the considerable commerce he makes in Athens, he set before me rich carpets from Carthage and Miletus, ivory from Libya, furs from Cyrene and Panticapea. The sight of those riches inflamed my gaze, and when I woke up, a forceful sneeze—a presage of good luck,[16] as you know—came to support my uncle's pleas, so to speak, with the opinion of the gods.

"I shall, therefore, depart for Athens. We need so little more to be perfectly happy; my petty fortune will soon be made, and then I will come back to this place, never to leave you again."

He did, in fact, leave. Poor Cleone, whom he had tried to convince of the necessity of his voyage, wept and hid her tears; ad when, in order to see him embark, they went past the temple of Ceres Thermesia, Sethos embraced him ardently, and said to him in a voice choked by sobs: "Friend, I attest by the goddess that is presiding over your departure that from this moment on, in order to abridge the days of our absence, I too will run after fortune. The first of us who attains it will stop the other in his course, and we will no longer think of anything thereafter but living for happiness."

The vessel drew away. Sethos and Cleone, motionless and silent, followed it with their eyes for a long time, and when they lost sight of it, they threw themselves into one another's arms and recommenced weeping.

Polycletus welcomed his nephew with amity, and showed him the riches and monuments of Athens, taking him successively to the temples of Theseus, Minerva, Apollo Patroos, the Propylaea, the Odeon, the Cynosarges, the theater of Bacchus, etc. At first Cleophas saw these marvels without astonishment; raised in an almost savage land, his taste was not yet sufficiently formed to sense and appreciate the products of the arts. The pleasant memories that he had of Hermionida still embellished that country so much in his eyes

---

[16] Author's note: "The Egyptians had a similar belief in this matter."

that it seemed to him that the sublime temple of the Parthenon could scarcely equal that of Ceres Thermesia, and that the Minerva of Phidias ought to inspire less respect than the statue of the god Pan sculpted in wood near the promontory of Bucephalus. Oh, how far the Cephise was from having the soft murmur of the waves of the Hylicus!

Gradually, however, his eyes became accustomed to distinguishing those pure and suave forms, masterpieces of the Greek chisel; the rich colonnades of the Parthenon reappeared before his gaze more exercised, in all their majesty full of harmony. He admired, and was even impassioned by, sculpture and painting, frequented artists' studios, judged their works highly, and, like all the opulent youth of Athens, took sides violently for or against Parrhasius or Zeuxis.

Meanwhile, Polycletus, the custodian of Cleophas' petty fortune, had augmented it considerably by making use of it in his commercial enterprises; but the latter's ideas had grown in the same measure as his treasure. It was no longer in the simple habitation of Mount Pronos that he was to find happiness with Cleone; it was in an elegant retreat situated on the banks of the Ilissus, decorated by a pupil of Phidias with marbles of Marpessa or Pentelicus. He therefore prolonged his sojourn in Athens, even occupying himself in an employment in Polycletus' business, and satisfying at the same time his desire to enrich himself and to improve his knowledge of the arts.

Among his new friends there was one almost as renowned as Alcibiades for the elegance of his manners and the richness of his garments; he inspired in Cleophas a taste for luxury and pleasures, and soon introduced him into the seductive societies in which everything that Athens contained of the powerful and the illustrious among the youth, and even among men of war and philosophers, assembled around the beautiful Ionians attracted by Aspasia to Attica, to soften and corrupt mores.

The first time he had access to those sumptuous palaces and was a witness to those piquant conversations, alternately full of enjoyment, wit and philosophy, his thoughts went back again to Sethos and Cleone; he would have liked to see them, drawn into those brilliant circles, enjoying the same pleasures and the same surprises as him. Soon, however, he pictured the good Sethos, with his tunic and coarse woolen cloak, and the candid Cleone, with her head covered by a that woven from linden fiber, in the midst of those men clad in crimson and silk, and those elegant women whose curled hair inundated with yellow powder was disciplined by rich headbands or imprisoned in golden nets, and he sensed within himself, with a mortal displeasure, that the sight of his friends would then cause him nothing but shame and confusion.

Insensibly, he adopted the mores and habits of the young men he frequented the most; he became accustomed to regarding wealth as the first condition of happiness; he gave the name of amity to the complicity in debauchery that he contracted with young insensates that he scarcely knew. Already, without the memory of Cleone being entirely effaced from his heart, his brutalized reason almost revolted on thinking that a young woman with no other means of seduction than her beauty, her frankness and her amour, might have conquered a disciple of Alcibiades and Aspasia.

In the meantime, Polycletus died, leaving his only son considerable wealth and Cleophas the enormous profits that he had made for him during his sojourn in Athens. Cleophas did not forget then that a sacred engagement recalled him to Hermionida.

But the month of Anthesterion is approaching, he said to himself, *it will bring back the great feast of the dead, and I ought to ender new honors to the memory of my uncle and my benefactor; it's a duty prescribed by nature and gratitude.*

He therefore stayed on in Attica, and, in order to distract himself from his recent dolor, he opened his house to the idle crowd of his companions in pleasure; there were son nothing but dances and feasts, and the sober Cleophas, who had once only nourished himself on the produce of his hunting, the fruits of his garden and the honey of his bees, lying on a voluptuous bed in the midst of numerous guests, cup in hand, crowned with ivy or flowers, saw his table covered with the most sought-after dishes: sardines from Phalera, oysters from the Lucrin Lake and Kalamata olives.

The birds of Phasis, roe deer from Melos, locusts, held in such high esteem by the Athenians, the dorado, the xiphias and the eel of Lake Copais, seasoned with cumin, seemed to him to be scarcely worthy of appearing before his guests, who got drunk with him on the wines of Thassos, Mende, Chios, Corcyra and Lesbos. When the meal was over, after having traveled the route to Piraeus and the interior Ceramicus in a chariot harnessed to four white horses from Sicyone, he came back and gambled, often happily, large sums of money at dice or knucklebones.

Soon, however, he felt the need to reform his luxury; gambling was no longer favorable to him; his false friends, after having borrowed large sums of money, no longer saw him; malicious gossip took possession of his faults to make shameful vices of them. The Neocora of the temple of Theseus, whom he had refused to admit to his feasts, accused him loudly of impiety toward the household gods, for having asserted that a man is only endowed with one body and one soul, and that the simulacrum does not inhabit the gate of hell any more than the shade watches over the sepulcher. He was a foreigner; he sensed then that he was devoid of protectors and friends; and, after hastily assembling the paltry debris of his fortune, he fled Athens.

Having embarked at Piraeus he soon reached the island of Aegina, and as he descended from his ship he saw a man in the harbor who was getting ready to board another in order to go to Athens. It was Sethos. Cleophas, drawn by his heart but retained by his shame, did not know whether he ought to show himself or hide from his friend's eyes, when the latter perceived him.

"I was going to search for you!" he exclaimed. "The gods have finally brought us together, in order not to separate us again. My friend, my brother, my Cleophas, let us bless again those gods, who seemed to want to console me for your absence by redoubling their benefits."

"It's for me alone that they have reserved their rigors; I'm ruined, Sethos."

"Oh well, no matter, friend; I'm rich, rich enough for two of us. I sold the quarry at Calauria, with the money I greatly increased the extent of my land, and Ceres has blessed my labor. In sum, I'm rich, and I was going to join you in order to share my wellbeing with you."

"I can't accept your benefits, Sethos; you're rich and I'm poor; equality has ceased to exist between us and I won't abuse the generosity of your heart. In the name of our old friendship, though, accord me a place next to you; make me the steward of your property, When, by means of my industry and my labor I believe that I have rendered you a few services, only then will I dare to ask you for the hand of your sister Cleone."

"Your mind is going astray, dear Cleophas; what fortune do you suppose me to have, then, to implore me for the stewardship of my properties? Can you think that I would have waited until now to recall you to my side? I'm rich as Sethos can be rich; I have an income of a thousand drachms."

"A thousand drachms!" exclaimed Cleophas. "And you rejoice in your wealth! And I, who still possess at least twice as much as that, thought that I was in poverty! A thousand drachms, Sethos! That has just revealed the extent of my misfortune to me. It is my vices that make my distress; it is your virtues that make your opulence. Faithful to friendship, moderate in your desires, you are still the good Sethos of Hermionida; but the splendor and the pleasures of Athens have withered my youth, corrupted my heart and increased the scope of my needs without adding to my happiness. I have not been able to appreciate either friendship or fortune, and I possessed both of them! But I possess them still; Sethos, you shall be my guide, my model; and I finally understand today that a desire repressed, an evil penchant vanquished, add more to our wealth than a thousand silver drachms."

The Poet of Hellas

(Modern Greece)

Youth is all flame, all discourse. How often its actions do
not match its promises!"
(Pierre Charron, *De la sagesse*.)

Stultum est imperare coeteris, qui nescit sibi.[17]
(Pubilius Syrus.)

May I only live long enough to see the Acropolis,
the Propylaeas and the Parthenon of Athens
snatched from the barbarians!
(Christian Muller, *Voyage en Grèce*, 1822)

A favorable opportunity was presented to me to visit the
fatherland of Aristides and Pericles, and I seized it eagerly,
delighted to be able to contemplate once again that cradle of
the arts and civilization, that vast hearth of glory and genius,
which seems to have been exhausted in propagating its fecund
enlightenment around it.

I arrived in Attica, provided with a letter of recommen-
dation for the sage Rosli, one of the most distinguished citizens of Athens, of the archontic family. He had been praised
to me as a poet and philosopher, and experience soon con-
firmed the veracity of those apologists for me. My faithful
guide in all my investigative expeditions, Rosli revived with
all the power of his historic memories and the force of his im-

---

[17] "It is against reason for a man who cannot command himself to command others."

agination, the mutilated remains of a splendor that had once dazzled the world, and which we perceive lying in the dust.

Palaces and cottages, partly constructed with the debris of ancient monuments, came to interest our sight by the mixture of different orders of architecture in combination. All the times, all the authors and all the masterpieces confounded pell-mell in those bizarre constructions pleased the imagination even while saddening it.

"The fronton of that house is by Phidias," Rosli told me. "The foundations of that tower belonged to the Romans, and the heavy wings with which it has been overloaded recall the degenerate taste of the Low Empire, to which the modern plasterwork of the Turks has been added. But Damophon made those architraves, and these elegant pilasters were traces by Dinocrates. Here, the columns of the temple of Apollo sustain the portico of the Aga of janissaries, and these statues, removed from the altar of Diana, serve as the ornament of a Pacha's harem."

One day, I urged him strongly to satisfy my curiosity and the interest he inspired in me by initiating me into the secret of one of his poetic compositions.

"I consent to that," he said, "but let's avoid gazes, for poetry is proscribed here as the sister of liberty. Bards can sing the praises of their heroes dead on the battlefield, but our heroes die on scaffolds, and sometimes to the maledictions of those they wanted to liberate. I'll tell you the misfortunes of young Oswali Nicetas, who sacrificed by turns his fatherland to his mistress, and his mistress to his fatherland: a weak child, worthy of pity, although culpable toward amity and amour, and who abused tyranny and liberty equally."

We sought solitude and shade, and we went to sit down under the honeysuckle arbors that crown the heights of the ancient Lycabettus. In front of us the fields of Attica deployed the beauty of their location and the richness of their soil. Mount Hymettus, which limited the horizon to the east, seemed to be covered in flaming vapors; at its feet the Ilissus meandered gently, deprived of its strength and its splendor, like the walls that it once washed. Behind us, the gardens that recalled Academus, and above all Plato, were dominated by the steeples of Saint Euphemia, built on he celebrated hill where Sophocles' Oedipus found the recompense for his virtues and the end of his misfortunes. Gilding with its oblique rays the temples of Jupiter, the Mohammedan mosques and the Christian churches, the sun, sinking toward the western horizon, was still giving nature the sentiment of life and fecundity. Rosli paraded his gaze over that delightful tableau for some time, sighed at the sight of the crescent that surmounts the summits of public monuments, and intoned these songs.

OSWALI NICETAS

Wake up, daughters of Greece, wake up, for it is necessary that your mouths repeat to your lovers my songs of liberty. Wake up, women of Athens, and wake your sleeping husbands; listen to my songs, for your children must fight one day for liberty.

Unfortunate Nicetas, last descendant of Thrasybulus, fatal to tyrants, the sun of Athens had shone upon your cradle, and your footsteps, still young, were imprinted in the snows of Germany. You went to demand that nourishment of the soul, education, the noble pedestal that raises us above others for the good of all. You knew that science and virtue are the nurses of liberty, and that ancient Mytilene, in order to prolong the slavery of the vanquished, only imposed ignorance upon them.

You came back among us, doubtless too young; however, the sacred fire of the fatherland was already burning in your heart. You saw Greece again, no longer as the Muslims had made it, but such as it once was, such as you wanted to see it reborn; the ashes of its heroes quivered underfoot. Before you, in your dreams of glory, as if by enchantment, stimulated by noble memories, Piraeus recovered its formidable walls, the Parthenon rose majestically on its broken columns, and the ancient gods of Hellas came in a host to repopulate their deserted temples.

For you, the isle of Cerigo was still Cytherea; Castri and Japora still took pride in the names of Delphi and Parnassus; the mountains of Telo-Vouni and Vulcano, and the rivers Keuzler and Sart, conserved their ancient and harmonious names of Hymettus and Ithomus, Scamander and Pactolus.

Nicetas found his childhood companions accustomed to the yoke, submissive almost with resignation. At the sight of the crescent they curbed their humiliated brow, and without shame and without fury stopped in an attitude of respect or dismounted at the sight of a janissary.

"Cowards!" Nicetas shouted at them, indignantly. "Infidel to our forefathers, will you cast your liberty incessantly at the feet of tyrants?"

And they replied: "What is a tyrant? What is liberty?"

In the midst of the dances and panegyrics of Athens, when the rose and the cornflower crowned their head in order to chase away the annoyances and the memory of oppression, the words of Nicetas fell upon them like thunderbolts.

"Joyful children of a dying mother, will you never avenge her? Can you not at least hide the dagger of Harmodius under your flowers? You crawl, vile Hellenes; you crawl while forgetting that God has given the reptile a dart to take vengeance on the superb foot that crushes it."

Only young Lambros understood Oswali. Issued, like him, from the most illustrious family of Livadia, he could no longer support the reproaches of his friend and relative.

"Silence," he said to him one day, taking him aside. "Achmet, who governs Athens, anxious for his power and fearing revolt, has not yet dared to be cruel enough for anyone to be able to support us in this place. Let us address ourselves to more unfortunate Greeks. I know where to find them. The purest water becomes stagnant in stillness. I'll depart; soon you'll see the torrent descend from the mountains of Epirus.

Oswali hugged him.

"The islands of the Archipelago," Lambros said to him, "have been waiting for a long time for a determined leader; visit them; the sea and the mountains are the last refuges of liberty. Before the feast of Athanasius has succeeded that of Saint Dimitrius, the liberating cry, departing from the Chimariot mountains, will have resounded on the shores of Smyrna."

He spoke; like the rapid stars that furrow the clouds, which stupid Muslims believe to be flaming arrows launched by the hands of angels, Lambros crossed the plains of Thebes and the gulf of Lepanto; the echoes of Pindar were revealed in his voice; the Christian populations of Albania and Chaonia were visited by him, in spite of the countless perils with which spiteful nature and the vices produced by slavery surrounded him.

Butrinto, where the lyre of Ovid and Virgil sang, in which the ashes of Hector and the unfortunate Medea sleep, calumniated by Euripides for money, appeared to Lambros in all the splendor of its debris. It was in the midst of Acropolises built by the Romans and the fallen temples of ancient Greece that Lambros cried: "Companions, the unknown voice that once, having emerged from the rocks of Paxos, brought you the news of the death of the Savior, is resounding again today in the woods of Zara and the gorges of Cormovo, to announce the imminent dawn of our deliverance."

Everyone respired joy in Delvinaki, for the shepherds of Thesprotia had been able to remain free in the midst of the general servitude. The maidens of Epirus, clad in white, their heads and breasts crowned with saffron-colored scarves, were devoting themselves to the long evolutions of the Romaic dance when Lambros, carrying a broken and bloody cross in his hand, launched himself into the midst of the dancers, shouting: "To arms, sons of Epirus! To arms! Only the independence of all can consolidate yours. The oak that stands solitary on the crest of the mountain is soon felled by lightning or the hurricane."

He traveled all the cantons of Livadia and Epirus in turn, escaping the emissaries of the Turks under a thousand disguises. The inhabitants of Zagori, Parga and Souli, the republicans of Acroceraunia, the Toxide mountain men and valorous

Mirdites, so distinguished among the Albanais[18] by their courage and their devotion to the Christian cause, promised him

---

[18] Author's note: "The Albanais, called Arvanites by the Greeks and Arnaoutes by the Turks, originally Schetechips or Schypetars, as François Pouqueville seems to prove in his magnificent work on modern Greece, from which some of the following details are taken, are divided into four numerous families, the Mirdites, the Toxides, the Japys and the Chamydes. The Mirdites, having remained faithful to Roman Catholicism, valorous soldiers of Scanderbeg, defended their religion and their liberty for a long time against the prophet's warriors, whom they forced to flee before the holy banner of the virgin of Orocher. Afterwards, they appeared to recognize the right of suzerainty of the Great Lord, but on condition that, exempt from the shameful tribute of capitation, they lived freely, masters of their land, and that their religion would be respected, advantages that were accorded to them with the intention of depriving them of it as soon as the opportunity arose. But that generous tribe remained armed in order to defend those glorious prerogatives; and after the first Muslim transgressions the reprisals were so terrible that the satraps preferred to have them as friends rather than enemies. Of robust constitution and a noble and severe physique, the Mirdites dressed in a white saie that did not surpass the knee and which, secured round the waist by a broad belt, gave them a considerable resemblance to ancient French crusaders. Their women, similarly raised in the midst of dangers and always on the defensive, only went abroad armed with pistols and followed by dogs ready to defend them at the approach of a Muslim.

The Toxides, adroit sharpshooters, as they had once been skilful archers, formed the most beautiful race of the region, and their elegant costume, borrowed almost entirely from the ancient heroic costume, added to their natural beauty. Shod in cothurnes, the body swathed in a toga, allowing the chlamys to extend over their broad shoulders "if they had worn helmets and the plumes mingled with their fine hair, they might have been mistaken for the soldiers of Achilles and Pyrrhus." Less free than the Mirdites, but enjoying more ease and a less agitated life, the Toxides had some of the advantages of civilization, and but for the frequent vexations of the Turks the valleys of the Tomoros might perhaps have seen flourishing and industrious towns inhabited by the most beautiful people n earth.

The Japys, retired behind the rocks of the Acroceraune, living amid arid mountains, possessed nothing but a savage liberty, and like the indigent soil that nourishes them, are thin, wan and hideous. Only subsisting on rapine, in the midst of profound obscurity, they are able distinguish their prey and seize it. Continually at war with their neighbors, the sudden presence of a Japys causes cries of alarm on all sides, which attracts danger and often death. They all prefer to dwell in dark lairs, however living in a state of poverty and degradation, rather than descending into the plains where the Turks, who fear such skill and courage, offer them abundance and pleasure in exchange for liberty.

Beauty, luxury, fertility and independence all seemed to combine to heap the fortunate Chamydes with the greatest benefits; they had been able to preserve their hearts from the approach of poverty and the Ottomans, but the treason was introduced therein after the ferocious Ali Pacha, and the race of Chamydes was almost entirely exterminated.

Such are the four great Albanais families inhabiting Epirus and Macedonia, and whose populous tribes are disseminated in the Peloponnese, Livadia and a few islands in the Aegean. Strangers to territorial distinctions, they are classified according to their respective languages: the guegaria (the Guegues, now Muslims, were once the companions and brothers in arms of the Mirdites; they no longer have any relationship to them than that of language), the toskaria, he japouria and the chamouria, related to one another by a common type, like the Dorian, Ionian, Aeilian and Athenian dialects, being

aid and succor. Even the brigands of Caulonia ran to him. "Nourish our families," they said to him, "and make use of our arms for such a fine cause. Our mores are in horror, it is said; woe betide those who have given them to is! Here, theft and murder are merely reprisals; render us better; slavery only engenders crimes; virtue is liberty."

He disdained those common mortals, worthy of their fate, who were only able to groan beneath the master's rod, like the volcano of Chamoussi, which has troubled the air for a long time with its long rumbling and obscured it with black smoke, but whose next eruption is still awaited. His glorious companions were distributed in bands, and they all took various roads heading for Livadia, the meeting place, after which the Cauloniates had prognosticated victory by consulting the shadows cast by a ram's bones presented to the flames of a fire.

Almost a year had gone by during Lambros' holy mission. He hastened to send a messenger to the Archipelago, to the man he regarded as the true chief of that noble enterprise.

Lambros put all his hope in you! Where were you, what were you doing, Oswali Nicetas, you who, by your grace, your courage and your eloquence, rose above your rivals, as the snowy peak of Kamila rises above the other summits of Pindar? Where were you, what were you doing, Oswali Nicetas?

A curse upon him! A curse upon his family! The torch that lit the fire has been extinguished while it deployed its wings of flame! Beautiful Hellas, continue weeping, weep forever; your beloved son has betrayed you; he has despaired of you, he has forgotten his oaths. A curse upon you, Oswali Nicetas!

---

only a marked nuance in the language of the four primary populations of ancient Greece. (X.)" The book by the diplomat François Pouqueville from which this information is derived is the three-volume *Voyage en Morée, à Constantinople, en Albanie* (1805)

The shores of Chios had received him, a worthy competitor of Lambros. His heart still full of great projects, he visited the first families of that populous and flourishing island. Luxury, commerce and the love of profit covered oppression with a brilliant mantle there, and seemed to lessen its weight. Again he thundered, and went unheeded; cold reasoning replied to his cries of glory; the obstacles chilled his enthusiasm; pleasures surrounded him; he lowered his gaze upon them. In that crisis of weakness and hesitation, amour appeared armed, and the fatherland was forgotten.

Aglaia was the most beautiful of the daughters of Chios, and yet, although she was Christian and Greek, a Greek Christian would have blushed at giving her the title of wife, for her mother had been seduced by an enemy of Christ and the blood of a Muslim ran in her veins. Her dark and voluptuous eyes respired Asiatic softness; her light figure and blonde hair recalled the beauty of the virgins of Morea; her talents, and even her adornment, attested further to her duel origin. The gold of Venice and the pearls of the Orient decorated her head alternately with the turban and the flammeum; her fingers, like those of the women of the seraglio, after having borrowed a light vermilion from henna leaves, wandered over the harmonious zel or caused the kanoun to resonate beneath an ivory key. Bizarre and charming young woman, woe betide anyone you love! Alas, woe betide you, for it was Nicetas!

He was walking one day in along the bank of a spring where the white Anaraide received the simultaneous homages of the Greeks and the Ottomans.[19] A piercing scream was heard; Nicetas ran to the aid of a young islander who was

---

[19] Author's note: "Whatever their religion, the inhabitants of Greece offer a kind of worship to the genii of springs, which they no longer call laurents or naiads but anaraides, and no traveler would dare to slake his thirst at a spring without depositing in tribute either a branch or a flower in a niche hollowed out expressly to receive those offerings to 'the good demon.' (X.)"

struggling in the arms of a vile rapist. At the sight of a Greek he cried: "Slave, get away or your death will expiate your insolence," and was already raising his arm to strike. A dagger-thrust was Nicetas' response. But that enemy blood, the first to redden the blade prepared for liberty, only ensured the triumph of amour. Like the lake of Dgerovina, whose waves swallow whatever floats on their surface, amour extinguishes and absorbs any other sentiment. The friend of Lambros did not take long to experience it.

An Osmanli had fallen under his thrust; his life was in danger. Aglaia offered her liberator a refuge under her mother's roof. There they were both intoxicated by poisons drawn from a gaze or a smile. There, spending all day on his knees, he repeated with her the amorous scolia of Hellas, or learned from her the emblematic science of the women of the Orient that gives a language to every flower. Soon, in an expressive silence, it was only necessary for him to present her with a lotus branch to speak to her about her beauty, a stem of peachwort to tell her: "I love you." It was thus that his republican soul unwound under the breath of amour, like the lyre of the poet under the inflamed vapors of the simoom.

A deceptive rumor of the death of Lambros reached Nicestas' ears then, and the last impulses of his patriotism expired with the hope of seeing his friend again. Meanwhile, the storm was gathering around him; the vengeance of the Pacha of Chios threatened to brand him as a murderer; his retreat was on the point of being discovered when Aglaia's mother sensed the last drop of her life escaping from the eternal clepsydra.

"My children," she said to them, you love one another, and God cannot reject your love, for your religion is the same. Between the hands of a dying mother, swear to be united with one another and I shall die content. But you both have need of a protector. Take this ring; go find Achmet, now Pacha of Athens, and tell him that the one..."

She tried to go on, but death prevented her from so doing.

Aglaia was Achmet's daughter; he welcomed her affectionately; but he saw in Oswali not his daughter's liberator—does the heart of a barbarian feel gratitude?—but a glorious scion of Greece that a fatal passion delivered entirely to his perfidy. Illustrious family of Canzianes and Nicetas, will you become the ally of a son of Othman? O my verses, launch forth with the rapidity of Arnaute's arrows! Only leave a sight trace on the target you are about to attain. Will it be necessary for me to eternalize the bounty of a Greek?

In the oppressor of his homeland, Nicetas only saw your father, unfortunate Aglaia; he believed that by his cowardly devotion he was ensuring your wedding, and thought to arrive at happiness by perjury. No, his wishes would be deceived, and the nuptial crown would never be suspended from your paneling between the revered images of the saints.

Meanwhile, the storm was growing. A slave mounted on a horse covered with sweat and dust stopped outside Achmet's palace. There the horse collapsed and died of its fatigue, and the slave ran into the Pacha's apartment, crying: "Vengeance! Achmet, a troop of brigands, after having ravaged Livadia, is heading for our walls. Vengeance! To the sound of the simandre and the siankos they are summoning the poor and the rebellious to murder and pillage.[20] Vengeance! Vengeance!"

Achmet armed himself and his janissaries surrounded him. Even Oswali, Oswali Nicetas, the friend of Lambros, at the head of a Christian legion of Armatolis, ran toward the perils in which he believed that he would find glory.

Beyond the rocks of Sandli, in the valleys of Aspa, the rebels dare to deliver battle to Achmet's troops. Three times the soldiers of the tyrant of Athens are defeated and dispersed;

---

[20] Author's note: "A simandre is an iron plate that Greek Christians strike with a hammer in order to replace the use of bells, which is forbidden to them by their masters. A siankos is a large seashell, common in the Mediterranean, from which sounds are extracted similar to those of a trumpet." (X.)"

three times Oswali brings them back to combat, and finally to victory. But when he plunges furiously into the heart of the enemy battalions, a strange object strikes his gaze; it is the cross of the savior; a cry resounds in his ears; it is that of liberty; a warrior advances to fight him; it is Lambros!

His crime is revealed to him. He has just broken the sacred tree that he planted himself; his eyes darken, his head is bowed, the blade escapes from his hand; he falls in the midst of his victorious Armatolis, murmuring: "Liberty!"

The generous sons of Albania showed themselves worthy of the cause they had embraced; not one of them laid down his arms; all of them died in the place where they had chosen to fight, similar, after their fall, to a forest of pines uprooted by a storm. People still point, in the middle of the rocks of Sandli, to the precipice into which the Cauloniates hurled themselves rather than surrender, with cries of liberty. The Osmanli have called it "the Tomb of the Brigands," but a time will come—perhaps it is not far distant!—when, from the valleys of Aspa and Zenarul, the traveler, on raising his eyes toward those rocks, will find there, written in letters of gold: The Tomb of Heroes.

Lambros, disarmed and captive, had fallen into Achmet's power. Nicetas implored mercy for him, but his hope, his prayers and his tears only excited the tyrant's smile. He fell to his knees determined to save his friend; he got up determined to avenge him. A new conspiracy was woven in Athens; but desperation alone presided over it; a few Toxide mountain men, escaped from the carnage of Aspa, a few Armatolis, enthused by the valor of their leader, swore to support him. Nicetas only spoke of vengeance, not daring to speak of liberty. Was it worthy of the man who wanted to reconquer it by a crime?

In the middle of the night, his companions are to surprise Achmet's guards and kill them. When the drums of the seraglio announce the tenth hour, profiting from the security his presence inspires, he heads for the Pacha's apartments armed with a dagger. It is blood that he had come to seek; it is the blood of Aglaia's father, but that idea does not stop him, for the deliverance of Lambros depends on the blow he is about to strike.

The signal agreed by the conspirators will be heard before long, and Nicetas, in the darkness, is still wandering in the long vestibules of the palace. He fears having gone astray in the darkness, when a faint light appears at the end of the corridor; a woman is carrying it. It is Aglaia. At the sight of Nicetas' shadow vacillating between the columns she utters a cry of fright. "Silence!" says the latter. "Where is your father?"

"God! What fury is imprinted in your gaze!"

"Where is your father?"

"Why that dagger? Do you intend to attempt Achmet's life, the life of your Aglaia's father?"

The signal of the conspirators is heard, and Oswali thinks that he can already hear the janissaries' cries of death.

"Get back, daughter of Achmet, get away!"

"What is that noise? What are those clamors? Nicetas, I will not leave you."

"Flee me, I tell you; Achmet's blood is in your veins."

The cries are redoubled in the palace; the moment to strike has come, and the numerous footfalls of armed men seem to be heading tumultuously for Lambros' prison; but Aglaia, mute and motionless, with tears in her eyes, is still placed between her father and her lover. Oswali pushes her away, but the arms of the daughter of Chios open again to enlace him.

"Daughter of Achmet," he cries, finally, seized with a convulsive fury, "cause of my eternal shame, the only bond that links me to tyranny, the only barrier that separates me from liberty, fall and let Lambros be free!"

The homicidal steel plunged entirely into the body of the young Greek woman; she utters a groan, goes pale, and succumbs, but her arms, stiffened by death, still surround her murderer. Thus a dove of Smyrna, wounded by a cruel master and dying, still directs its flight toward him in order seek its last refuge in his bosom.

The death of Aglaia was a needless crime; Nicetas' companions had already been vanquished. He was caught in the presence of his victim, still covered in blood and uttering lamentable cries. The next day, his head, separated from his body, and his mutilated hands, were suspended at the door of the palace, objects of horror for the Greeks and for the Muslims, who repeated together: "A curse upon you, Oswali Nicetas."

Liberty, similar to the Persian tree that sees its crimson flowers fall and renew themselves incessantly, you will see your fallen defenders replaced by other heroes, still desirous of dying for you. Has your blood not yet flowed sufficiently over your altars? Will the great day not soon dawn when we shall see you descend among us again? My lyre is dedicated to you; may it teach Greece to merit your favors by dint of virtue.

Sons of Hellas, it is necessary to fight with the lyre and weapons, like the immortal Riga. Strike, heroes! Strike and die; the poet will conserve his concerts for you. You, son of Pindar, think of the eternal glory, think of the eternal shame; the voice of the sirens resounds, strikes the air and faded away; the voice of the muses has echoes in posterity. Let the oppressor of your fatherland pass with the noise, the glare and the traces of lightning; but let your lyre remain mute in his passage; let your sublime chords prepare the day of the awakening. Speak of Lambros, delivered from Achmet's irons, revealing his existence by the exploits of Tchesme and Coronea; sing the praises of valor, virtue and liberty; sing again, sing above all the praises of the heroic liberators!

Rosli fell silent; he stood up abruptly and his eyes, with a terrible gaze, suddenly turned toward the red flag of Islam that floated over the Acropolis of Athens. A festoon of honeysuckle, detached from the arch of the arbor, was suspended over his head and had just crowned him; embalmed breezes agitated the groves of larches and olives and the laurel- and rose-bushes around us; and in the state of mind in which I found myself, the gradually-increasing murmur seemed to me to be an assemblage of confused voices, which, emerging from the ruins and tombs of Athens, spoke to us of glory, amour and liberty.

At that moment, the sun, swimming in a sea of fire, plunged over the horizon, and its final rays, attaining the summits of Lycabettus, were reflected in Rosli's face, imprinted with all the characters of a celestial inspiration. Moved by what I had just heard, surrounded by eloquent ruins and ancient memories, I seemed to see the god of daylight, the god of verses, Apollo, still communicating poetic genius over his destroyed temples, to the last priest of the Muses.

The Arinzes

(Siberia)

> I had only to pass by; he was already dead.
> (Racine, *Esther,* act III, scene IX)

I had visited Siberia before, at a time when the southern provinces of that vast country offered to the eyes of a traveler an active and abundant vegetation, numerous cities and a free population of warriors.

The nation of the Arinzes, or Arinthes, was elevated over all the others in those fortunate climes as much by the wisdom of its legislators as the antiquity of its institutions. It was among the Arinzes that the cult of shamanism was born, which still exists, albeit disfigured, among certain Siberian populations, and which, propagating in the Indies, China and Japan, gave birth to Lamaism and Brahminism—which, in their turn, saw their dogmas borrowed by the Egyptians and the Greeks. Even the Druids might well have been only the disciples of the first Shamans.[21]

---

[21] Author's note: "We do not pretend to adopt Jonathan's opinion on this great question entirely; it would, however, be easy to bring forth considerable evidence in favor of our author if the argument did not require excessive development. Under the names of Ghermans, Sarmans and Sanaeans, it was doubtless the Shaman priests that Strabo, Clement of Alexandria and Porphyry wanted to designate, recognizing the great antiquity of their doctrine.

"The name "Shaman," according to Thomas Hyde, an Academician of Saint Petersburg, is derived from a language unknown today, which was probably the Arinzian language.

The glory of arms had served to transport their religious philosophy afar. The heroes of Arinzia, of which the name alone caused the hordes of Asia to tremble then, after having augmented the power of their fatherland by numerous conquests, had transplanted its colonies all the way to the heart of Persia. One of them had even crossed the Ural mountains and traversed the northern part of Europe in order to found Arinthoz under the sky of Gaul.[22] I visited that great people in the height of its splendor; I quit it marching to new prosperities.

A few centuries went by, and my continual journeys brought me back to the same lands again. The people and the climate, everything had changed. I searched for the nation of the Arinzes and no longer found it. I learned that its glory was eclipsed, its legislators forgotten, its warriors vanquished. Expelled from its destroyed cities, it had seen the savage Ostiaks and the barbaric Tunguses fighting over its miserable debris and exterminating it, like bands of ferocious hyenas.

The Brahmins who do not deny that they owe their science to those ancient philosophers, have borrowed from them the doctrine of metempsychosis, as well as the Lamaists who have consecrated it in the person of their divine pontiff, the High Lama, whose existence they believe to be eternal, in a succession of different human forms, Bouddhou, or Bodda, the god of the Shamans, whom we rediscover in the story of "Contradictions," must be the Bed of whom Saint Jerome speaks; *bod* signifies "divine" in the ancient languages of the Orient, and M. Stollenwerck, in his historic research on the principal nations established in Siberia, seeks to prove that the famous Xaca, named Fo or Bo since his apotheosis, and is said to have been born 1017 years before Christ, is none other than the god Bouddhou. (X.)" The work cited, *Recherches historiques sur les principales nations établies en Siberie* (1801) is actually a translation of a 1768 work by Johann Eberhard Fischer.

[22] Author's note: "Arinthoz is today a small town in the Franche-Comté."

I was told that a few Arinzes, however, had found refuge on the banks of the Yenisei, in the midst of the Katschintz Tartars. Alas, even in the bosom of that hospitable horde, their descendants had suffered a slow destruction. Only one man remained of that great nation—one alone!—and he was very old.

When I came to talk to him about the ancient splendor of the people of which he was the issue, surprise and tenderness seemed to take possession of him. His eyes moistened with tears; he took my hand and kissed it.

"Blessed be the man who caresses my ears again with the sweet name and the glory of my ancestors," he said. "Alas, I was only born to mourn their woes, and the fatherland that I never knew."

He went on: "Its destinies, at least, are not unknown to me; my father, instructed by his own, told me in his turn about the great actions of our heroes and the divine songs of our poets—for what people has ever shone more nobly with the double glare of the arts and war! The shores of Baikal, the banks of the Anadyr, and the summits of the Altai Mountains, crowned with a vast forest of cedars, resounded then with our cries of delight and the noise of our exploits!

"The Anadyr! The Altai! How sweet is it to pronounce those words, with which the long conversations of my father pleased my imagination. Today, my mouth alone still articulates the sounds of the Arinzian language, the most beautiful and the sweetest of all languages, and my memory alone still conserves a few faint memories of so much power!

"Stranger, who seems to be interested in the destinies of the great nation, deign to be the depository of what remains of its antique glory; thanks to you such a vivid splendor, so many great deeds and so many illustrious names, might survive a poor old man, and enable generous hearts still to palpitate when I am gone. My memory, which is tottering, can repose on yours. I render justice to my generous hosts; I have sheltered under their tents, I have armed myself at the fires of their hearths; I have slaked my thirst on the milk of their mares; but

97

they have never been able to listen to me, and my stories humiliate their pride.

"Stranger, I am old and I feel weak; I need to reassemble my ideas and repeat within myself so many various destinies and events. Come back and visit me tomorrow."

I was exact at the rendezvous, but the old man was dying. Pale, his hands icy and his sight almost extinct, he was lying in the middle of his cabin, in a long narrow box similar to a coffin—a kind of bed common in those climes. He appeared to recognize me, however, and he made an effort to speak to me; but his voice refused to render his thoughts. Gripped by regret and pity, immobile before him, I watched him struggle against death for some time.

That spectacle was both imposing and terrible for me. I had seen more than one life extinguished, but in this case, I was witnessing the complete annihilation of a nation. With that frail old man, an entire people seemed to be descending into the tomb: heroes and poets who had doubtless had shed their blood, and sacrificed their repose and their happiness in order to conquer, in human memory, a name that they believed to be immortal; a harmonious language, sage institutions, discoveries, perhaps precious for humanity; great deeds, great triumphs, great catastrophes; the hope of virtue, of power, of vanity—everything was annihilated with the old man's last sigh.

No monument elevated by the nation of the Arinzes is standing in the country that it had submitted to its laws; the memories of the peoples once vanquished by it have conserved nothing of the glory of their former conquerors; nothing, in sum, except this paltry manuscript, remains to attest to its passage on the earth.

Good and Ill Fortune

(France. etc.)

Oftentimes the little things make the fortune of the great.
(Charron, *De la sagesse*.)

I am inclined to believe that there are men hidden
in the crowd who are greater than those we see appearing
on the world's stage and who attract the eyes
and admiration of all.
(*The Spectator*, XL)

The insults of my fortune have made those
of my reputation...
Merit is only judged by prosperity.
(Théophile de Viau, "Epistre au lecteur.")

Whatever my fate or my destiny might be, then,
my deliberation is to serve both, in default
of which I remain inert and futile.
(Rabelais. Prologue to the *Book of Pantagruel*.)

Toward the end of the year 1749 two carriages were rolling noisily, in close proximity, along the road from Paris to
Versailles. The first was the public coach, which only had one
passenger, Monsieur Pigafet, a man of merit; the second was a
brilliant carriage harness to two superb and vigorous horses,
drawing rapidly toward the seat of power the Comte de M***,
renowned throughout Europe for his talents, his opulence and
his singular adventures.
The noble chargers were on the point of overtaking and
leaving far behind the paltry nags for hire, but the two axles

touched, and the impact was so violent that the public coach, its driver, its horses and its sole passenger were thrown pell-mell into the middle of the road.

In his fall, Monsieur Pigafet injured his right hand. The Comte de M***, naturally benevolent and sensible, offered him all his apologies, his regrets, and a place in his carriage for the remainder of the journey. The coachman was compensated for his misadventure, and, as soon as he arrived in Versailles, the Comte summoned a surgeon, who bandaged Monsieur Pigafet's sprain.

The latter touched by his new host's continual attentions and the chagrin that being the cause of his slight accident seemed to cause him, thought that he ought to reassure his conscience, and certified to him that the collision of the two carriages ought not be attributed to the impetuosity of the horses or the clumsiness of the driver but to the tenacity of his evil destiny, which always placed a ditch near to his objective or a reef close to his port.

"My journey from Paris to Versailles was to destroy or realize a great hope," he said, "I was reaching the goal, I fell into the ditch; I should have expected it; everything is in the order of things, and it is truly already too much honor for me to see a noble count among that causes of my thousand and one catastrophes. Once, a paltry spaniel caused me to lose the object of my amours; a witticism might have closed the doors of the Académie before me, and a mere insect has, so to speak, overturned a throne for me..."

Astonished, the Comte de M*** stared at Monsieur Pigafet. The latter, however, seemed to be speaking calmly and simply; his gaze was tranquil and assured; nothing, in sum, gave evidence of any absence of reason. His host, whose curiosity was keenly excited, testified to him again all the interest he had in his fate, sought to dissuade him from the sinister presages that he took from his latest accident, and concluded by begging him to acquaint him with some of the surprising adventures of which he appeared to have been the victim.

Monsieur Pigafet who, to judge by his preamble, seemed to be as ready to talk as the Comte was to listen, did not have to be asked twice.

"Paris saw my birth," he told him. "My father, an honest man but systematic, having discovered in me some aptitude for intellectual labor, thought to ensure my future happiness by enabling me to acquire superficial notions in a great many arts and sciences, convinced that the varied knowledge in question would render me capable of choosing an estate in harmony with my genius and my faculties.

"The progress of civilization among peoples, nascent societies gradually consolidating themselves amid the troubles and excesses of barbarity, the voluntary brake that is imposed of its own accord—all the benefits of legislation, in sum—struck my imagination forcefully. I studied law, and soon qualified as an advocate.

"I had already acquired a certain reputation among my colleagues when I was summoned to the Châtelet to plead a cause, of the rightfulness of which I was intimately convinced. My antagonist, a man named Bernard, a bungler if ever there was one, who veiled his ignorance and his conceit beneath a false air of modesty, announced in an ill-assured voice a very bad speech, although it would doubtless have been made better by someone else. His voice became so quiet in the course of his reading that it ended up being completely inaudible, and individual conversations were established among the public, the court, and even the tribunal.

"I spoke in my turn; people lent me the greatest attention but, in the heat of improvisation, a violent gesture that I made disturbed my wig, and gave me such a grotesque appearance that unanimous laughter burst forth from all parts of the hall, further augmented by the clumsy efforts that I made to repair the disorder of my wig. Not only did I lose my case, but every time I reappeared at the bar, the same laughter seemed ready to welcome me when I mounted the podium. I became discouraged and quit a career in which an equivocal gesture had sufficed to compromise the rights of a widow and an orphan.

"The physical and mental study of human beings had always had many attractions for me; a part of the natural sciences was not unknown to me; the medical theory in vogue seemed to me to be susceptible of receiving important ameliorations. I devoted myself to it ardently; I compared Hippocrates, Galen and Avicenna with the moderns, and I thought I perceived that the sublime science, in losing its simplicity, had degenerated in the hands of doctors to theriac and elixirs. I dared to combat inflammatory disorders with water, diet and bleeding; I even dared to proscribe quinine, then in its apogee. I made countless enemies among apothecaries, wine-merchants and my colleagues, but, proud of the unexpected successes I obtained, I pursued my course audaciously.

Summoned one day to consult with a newly-qualified doctor, I recognized him as my former antagonist, the ex-advocate Bernard. He too had become a physician. Not at all of my advice as to the manner of treating our client, he declared him to be a dead man if I had my way. The patient gave me his confidence, and was proved right, for his convalescence was complete when, having eaten grapes on my order, an accursed pip that stuck in the esophagus caused him to make such efforts to dislodge it that he was struck by apoplexy and died on the spot,[23] to Bernard's great joy, who extolled his prediction everywhere, and what he called the fatal consequences of my theory.

"My reputation suffered from it; his gained thereby. In cabarets and apothecaries, the clamors against me recommenced. In vain I proved that only the unfortunate grape pip had destroyed the beneficent effect of my treatment; people pretended not to hear me. To complete the misfortune, Lesage's *Gil Blas* appeared at that time, everyone thought he recognized me in Doctor Sangrado, everyone gave me that nickname, and ridicule completed what hazard had com-

---

[23] Author's note: "The event is not implausible; a grape pip caused the death of Anacreon, and the dear Hababah of the Caliph Yazid II."

menced. I was discredited. With me, I dare say, fell the nascent edifice of the veritable art of healing.

"In France, a nickname is often more harmful than an evil deed. The wound made by the weapon of ridicule only scars over beneath other skies, in other climes. After having liquidated my petty fortune, I resolved to make the most of myself, and I exiled myself voluntarily from my jeering homeland.

"Commerce, the bond of peoples, the father of civilization, the perpetual source from which all life's pleasures and comforts flow, is a subject worthy of the highest meditations. *In spite of the scorn that petty people with grandiose airs or grandiose names affect to attach to it*, I said to myself, *it is in order to extend or protect it that almost all wars are undertaken, that kings risk the security of their thrones and the blood of their nobilities, that diplomacy redoubles genius and cunning, that the industrial arts are improved and an eternal correspondence of competition and activity is maintained throughout the civilized world; I shall therefore become a merchant.*

I established myself in the Antilles, to which I transported the productions of French manufacturing; I sent the products of the Antilles to France, with the exception of quinine; for, superior to Coriolanus, I did not want to harm my ingrate compatriots. My commercial exchanges succeeded beyond by expectations; within a few years, my funds, multiplied tenfold, permitted me to see again, at the head of an honorably acquired fortune, the cherished places that had given me birth, and to brave the quips and gibes of my former rivals.

"Hoping to add further to my wealth, I employed the greater part of my capital in the purchase of a cargo of Indian fabrics, then widely employed in Paris, and set to sea with it incontinently, nursing the most optimistic projects of happiness. The crossing was untroubled, but on disembarking in the port, I perceived that almost all my merchandise had been perforated and eaten away, through and through, by a little worm that had introduced itself into the bales. I was ruined.

"The next day, another vessel arrived, chartered by the same Bernard, who was to pursue me everywhere, carrying the same goods; it had nothing to fear from competition, and for the third time, he profited from my disaster.

"Despair took hold of me. A Russian general, with whom I had returned from the Antilles, advised me to travel in order to distract myself, and even proposed to accompany me to his homeland, where, he said, I could not fail to find an advantageous employment, in view of my extensive knowledge and the protection that his government willingly afforded to the French. I accepted his proposal, and departed for Saint Petersburg, where I was soon in communication with the most powerful men in the court. I requested a position in education, the judiciary or the administration, but there was then much talk about a war with Sweden, and the reply was incessantly made to me: 'We need soldiers not scholars…we need soldiers, not judges…we need soldiers, not civil servants.'

"I went to find my friend the general, who took me on as his aide-de-camp. The war broke out. I distinguished myself in several very lively conflicts, and was fortunate enough to save the life of Marshal Lacy during the Wilmanstrand affair.[24] From then on I had in him a declared protector, and I glimpsed the hope of acquiring a name in a military career. I was in command of the corps that was the first to penetrate Aland Island, and the Empress Elisabeth, when peace was concluded, deigned to write to me to express her contentment and announce my appointment to the government of Astrakhan.

"Events succeeded one another under the most favorable auspices; I was no longer ambitious for anything but the honor of being commander-in-chief in an action sufficiently important to prove my capacity and give me a rank among the illustrious warriors of the North. The opportunity did not take long to present itself. The famous Thamas Kouli-Kan, the

---

[24] The Irish-born Russian commander Peter von Lacy fought a battle near Wilmanstrand in Finland at the outset of the war between Sweden and Russia in September 1741.

usurper of the throne of Persia, suddenly covered the shores of the Caspian Sea with his troops. A considerable corps of independent Tartars stimulated by him was threatening the banks of the Volga. I marched to encounter it at the head of old troops proved in the war against Sweden, reinforced by the worthy Tartars of Circassia, who came to implore the protection of Russia.

"The chances of success did not seem to me to be in doubt. Thamas was still far away; I had for adversaries not soldiers but undisciplined brigands commanded by inexperienced leaders. However, not allowing myself to be dazzled by appearances so brilliant, I summoned all resources, all tactical ruses to my aid. I disquieted and fatigued the enemy forces by false marches, I abused them by means of false reports, and chose the most advantageous position for the attack, after having set up a powerful ambush on their flank, which was to provide a diversion if they obtained an initial advantage, or crush them in a retreat.

"Well, Monsieur le Comte, would you believe it? I was defeated. In the midst of the action, when the enemy battalions were already breaking away to flee, a north-easterly wind suddenly carried toward our ranks a dust so dense and hot that they were blinded, and were no longer able to distinguish their allies from their adversaries. The Circassians and the Russians collided with one another; the enemy troops, recalled to the battle by the advantage of their position, vanquished us without difficulty, after having destroyed—I don't know how—the ambush I had prepared so cleverly.

"Thus, the hope of a great name, the confidence of an Empress, the fruits of several years of glory and dangers, were all taken away from me by dust! Dust nullified the superiority of my troops, the sagacity of my measures and the efforts of my tactical foresight. But judge, most of all, my astonishment and my indignation when I learned that those wretched vagabonds, my vanquishers, had been commanded during the battle by that eternal Bernard, whom I encountered everywhere in my days of mourning.

"I shall not explain to you by what hazard he found himself in Asia, the leader of a horde of bandits; I don't know it. I scarcely had time to occupy myself with him at the time; I was only thinking about myself. The government of Astrakhan had been taken away from me; fearing something worse than disgrace, I hastened to return to Europe in order to reach France promptly. But my destiny had to be accomplished; a new misfortune awaited my in Germany; I fell in love there.

"You will not demand that I explain to you how a young, beautiful, coquettish and romantic woman had the art of turning my head, by alternately affecting with me a tone of sentiment or an attitude of chilly reserve. By dint of cares, tenderness and sacrifices of all genres, I believed that I had finally succeeded in disarming her rigor. One day, in a delightful tête-à-tête, she deigned to let me glimpsed that I was not hated; I knew that only the pathetic pleased her in amour; I was strongly smitten, I became fluently eloquent; I begged, I implored, I wept, and I was already seeing her softening progressively when, to but the seal on the delirious scene, I thought I ought to fall at her feet, and clumsily put my knee on the paw of her favorite lapdog, which yapped and bit me. The pathos stopped there; the beauty emitted a loud burst of laughter that was a formal dismissal for me, for she respected herself too much to give herself to a lover who made her laugh, and thus dishonored her entirely contemplative and thoughtful life.

"As you can imagine, Bernard, the vulture incessantly attached to his renascent prey, could not be far away, in order to profit from my new defeat, so I discovered that he married my vaporous beauty a short time after my departure. My amour, however, was no less true for being irrational; the appetite for retreat and to see France again had quit me; I felt an ardent need for new emotions that might extinguish, or at least diminish, the regrets that I could not help experiencing for the object of my stupid passion. I learned that a new colonial company was being organized to exploit the coasts of Guinea from the River Volta as far as Jackin, and I was soon part of the crew of the first vessel setting forth on that expedition.

"After having spent some time in the fertile kingdom of Juda, perceiving that my companions, who had appeared in my eyes until then to be new Argonauts destined to bring the benefits of civilization to barbarian populations, were only interested in the slave trade, I wanted to try to realize myself the honorable intentions that I had so generously supposed them to have. I traversed the territory of Ardra and plunged further inland. The first Africans I discovered in that excursion fled at my approach as if frightened by the sight of me, but they soon came back in greater number, surrounded me, uttering shrill cries, tightened the circle round me, seized me, tied me up and took me to their chief. I was in the kingdom of Dahomey, which had not yet received the visit of any European.

"The great Dahomey, the king of the land, appeared almost frightened by the sight of me himself; he remembered however, as I learned subsequently, that his ancestor Trudo Audati,[25] the hero of that part of Africa, had often told him that in his day, men of a white color had fallen into his power in the course of his conquests. That idea reassured him and I found myself well placed in consequence, for he seemed more disposed to take me for a demon than a man.

"In a matter of months, thanks to the few words and rules of which the jargon of savage peoples is composed, I was in a position to converse with him. Initiated by me into the mysteries of the civilization of our marvelous Europe, he took me in affection. A terrible malady from which I saved him by means of water, diet and bleeding, advanced me even further in his good graces; I became his intimate counselor. I hoped to be able, one day, to be finally regarded as the legislator of those unknown countries. That idea pleased my imagination, and everything was put to work by me to destroy in Dahomey the

---

[25] Trudo Audati or Agaja, was King of Dahomey (now in Benin) from 1718-1740, when his son Tegbessou succeeded him, ruling until 1774, but the latter appears to have been replaced in the present story by a fictitious monarch.

atrocious customs and superstitions with which the people of the African continent are infected.

"The king, endowed with great reason and an excellent nature, sometimes seemed to enter into my projects, but his belief in his fetishes, the power of consecration that time gives to the most absurd things, opposed continual obstacles to my philanthropic views. I triumphed in everything, however; slaves ceased to be immolated on their master's tomb along with his most cherished wives; human victims were no longer offered to deformed gods of stone and wood; punishments, proportional to faults, were no longer crushing and no longer confounded crime with error; armies were recruited without devouring the active portion of the population; and agriculture, once confided to weak and sickly women incapable of sustaining such labor for long, became the prerogative of men, who no longer dared to believe that laboring the earth and thinking were occupations unworthy of them when they saw ease and pleasure succeed poverty and ennui everywhere.

"Good effects following my good advice rapidly, the king caused the marks of gratitude and affection that his people showed him for the unexpected changes to rebound on me. He wanted to associate me with his power, and unanimous acclamations welcomed the proposal that he put to the elders of the nation. It was only a matter of proceeding with my installation. Since time immemorial, the coronation of the kings of Dahomey had consisted of parading them before the people and the army mounted on a superb white elephant, one of the fetishes of the country, in accordance with the movements of which the priests prognosticated the splendor and duration of the nascent reign.

"Advice to legislators! I had believed it necessary to respect a few ancient prejudices of the country. I elevated my new laws on the foundations of the old ones, and when I was about to attained the goal of all my endeavors, all my troubles, the old bases were suddenly shaken, and overturned the new edifice.

"An *insondo*, a wretched insect about the size of one of our ants, and the most redoubtable enemy of the elephant, had slipped into the trunk of the one that was to carry me in triumph.[26] The animal, irritated by sharp stings, first gave signs of impatience, which excited the astonishment of the people, but soon the violent pains that it was feeling brought its fury to the highest degrees; it uttered frightful clamors and ended up breaking its large head on nearby rocks.

"I had been extracted from the danger that threatened me, but another no less great still awaited me. The priests declared me to be unworthy of the throne and of life; the prosperity of the state as compromised; my innovations had aroused against me the shade of Trudo Audati and the mortal gods of Dahomey. The king loved me; he owed me his life; but the death of his fetish alarmed his superstition. He hesitated for some time, but in the end, gratitude prevailed and he limited my punishment to exile, after having a forceful bastinado administered in order to acquit his conscience.

"A mite that was multiplying its race in the piles placed in the bosom of the Adriatic posed more dangers to formidable Venice than all the kings in Europe in league against her; a mite precipitated me from the throne and might have changed the destiny of an entire continent...

"I learned subsequently that the people of Dahomey regretted me; they sent people to search for me all the way to the kingdom of Juda, but I had quit the coasts of Guinea. Believing that they could readily replace me with a man of the same color as me, they made proposal to one of the Europeans they encountered on the coast; he accepted; the services that I had rendered were attributed to him; he was heaped with riches and honors. It was Bernard. If I had loved vengeance, I would have rejoiced in that accident, which placed my ingrate subjects in the power of a schemer devoid of capability.

---

[26] The insondo, and its alleged habit of crawling up the trunk of an elephant and driving it mad, can be found in Diderot's *Encyclopédie*.

"What can I tell you, finally, Monsieur le Comte? I came back to France. I became an author, hoping to find in the labors of the intellect the repose and happiness after which I had sighed for such a long time. I believed that I no longer had to deal with anything but posterity. How my contemporaries disabused me! A very interesting work that I composed, on the mores, customs and politics of the barbaric kings of Africa, was regarded by the censor as a satire against several European sovereigns. The work was banned, the author was nearly sent to Bicêtre or the Bastille.

"I needed glory, however; unable to be a great physician or a great general, I desired at least to see myself inscribed on the list of the forty immortals; I gave birth to a tragedy. By dint of cares and pains, I succeeded in having it performed; a joker in the stalls caused the third scene to fail with a remark, very facetious, it is true, but hardly conclusive against the merits of the play. In the meantime, Bernard, on his return to Paris, was modestly enjoying there a high reputation as a man of war, a savant jurisconsultant and a philosophical traveler.

"Wanting to repair, as much as possible, my theatrical check, I tried to assemble around me a few men of the world and several renowned litterateurs, in order for them to witness a reading of my drama. A dancer at the Opera, kept by Bernard, gave a great supper that same evening; my colleagues the authors were invited to it, and I only had for an audience a few young dandies and a few old Regency roués, who listened to me while simpering, grimacing, yawning and falling asleep, ratified the public verdict, and unanimously declared my play detestable.

"I was not discouraged; an epic poem was the fruit of that poetic resignation. No publisher wanted to print it; my reputation had gone before me, and I learned as I emerged from one of them that Bernard had just been elected to the Académie, bringing to that illustrious society no other literary entitlements than a quatrain in honor of the aristocratic and pretty lady that Marie-Thérèse deigned to call 'my friend and good cousin.'[27]

"After having exercised all professions with some talent and a great deal of probity, I thought I divined that scheming mediocrity alone had the right to success. Had not a man of that species collected the fruit of my talents and my endeavors in the four continents of the world? I was growing old; I felt the need to ensure my future. Not without difficulty, I decided to follow the common route. A serial solicitor, I frequented the antechambers of great men, writing articles for them and 'verses to Chloris'[28] for their mistresses; I made friends in the press, in the ministries, and even the king's wardrobe. Finally, I had found zealous protectors; all the necessary steps to obtain the employment I solicited had been taken; the road to the court was smoothed before me; it was only a matter of presenting my petition to the king; it therefore appears very natural to me that the hand that was to draft and sign it should suddenly be struck with impotence.

"I foresee my fate and don't want to complain of it. The collision of our vehicles has doubtless overturned with me, in the middle of the road, the entire result of my assiduity toward the great, and my little verses to Chloris; but this time let my accursed destiny be praised for it. It would be too painful for me to think that the only reprehensible action of my life would be the only one that allowed me to achieve success. There is no little check from which great good does not result when viewed from a higher altitude.

"If my various catastrophes have harmed my fortune and my reputation, fragile and perishable goods, at least they have developed my soul, enlarged the sphere of my intelligence by constraining me to exercise my mental strength in different genres and among different peoples; they have taught me only to lavish my esteem and my disdain in accordance with a profound knowledge of men and things, and not on vain appear-

---

[27] The reference is to Madame de Pompadour.
[28] This phrase originates from *Don Quixote*.

ances. For there must exist in the world many people of merit and talent whom unfavorable circumstances and unfortunate hazards have thrown, like me, into the obscure ranks of poor and unknown beings.

"The glamour of great titles and great reputations will no longer impose itself upon me. Such little things are sufficient to elevate or destroy human glory, and I have so often experienced that! Did not the form of Cleopatra's nose, as Pascal has observed, cause the fortune of Augustus, the doom of Antony, and change the face of the world? According to the Academician Duclos, the bugs that tormented the conclaves of Rome often triumphed over conspiracies and seductions, and had Popes appointed whom but for them, would never have been elected. A child playing in an optician's shop, enabled the discovery of myriads of suns and new worlds, and prepared, without suspecting anything, the illustriousness of Simon Marius, Galileo and twenty other great astronomers. A falling apple demonstrated the laws of the universe to Newton, and perhaps revealed to him the full extent of his own genius.

"As for me, who seems to have been cast upon this globe in order to prove the influence that can be exercised on the destiny of man, the master of the world, by all those subaltern and scorned causes—a false gesture, a nickname, a grape pip, a worm, dust, a lapdog, an insect—have they not closed before me twenty routes that lead to glory or happiness?

"I could have become a fatalist, but I don't want to be, and I never shall be. A thousand times insensate are those who refuse to believe that an immense thought presides over the existence of those infimal beings, imperceptible but important cogs in the great mechanism. The harmony of the universe is only maintained by dint of apparent irregularities. I shall not cry 'All is well!' but I will say: 'Nothing is useless or despicable.' An atom takes on importance by virtue of its position, as the figure zero does in mathematics; everything has its power of action, everything can become a lever in its turn, everything has been produced in order to maintain the eternal reaction of good and evil, which alone gives movement and life to creation."

Monsieur Pigafet fell silent.

After having listened silently to his long philosophical tirade, The Comte de M*** said to him:

"Your story has interested me keenly, and has surprised me more than you can imagine. Your great intelligence, however, Monsieur Pigafet, does not appear to have enabled you to comprehend as yet that if unmerited misfortunes can be attached incessantly to a man without causing him to wilt, fortune often also smiles on men, perhaps unworthy of it by virtue of the poverty of their means, but incapable of seeking to secure it by intrigue or baseness. I am Bernard, the Bernard who profited from your disasters without having caused them, who was sometimes your rival but never your enemy, who succeeded in acquiring a great reputation without having sought it, honors without loving them, and does not have to blush at his prosperity any more than you do at your misfortune."

At this point Monsieur Pigafet made a movement to interrupt the Comte de M***, or Monsieur Bernard, as one might prefer to call him, but the latter, after having implored his silence by means of a gesture, continued thus: "I shall, in my turn, tell you the story of the principal events in my life. I shall be brief, my story only being the complement to yours.

"It is good to follow one's particular vocation in the choice of an estate, but as I had never had a particular vocation for one thing rather than another, I only consulted my father's taste, and became an advocate to give him pleasure; but if I was devoid of eloquence, I was not devoid of good faith, and I soon sensed that the gifts of an orator had been refused to me by nature. From that came the timidity, anxiety and weakness that struck you so forcefully during my first speech. The accident of the wig caused me to take part in the general laughter; doubtless I was wrong, but one is not always master of oneself and your figure really was very comical.

"The unexpected success that I obtained before that tribunal did not blind me, however, for, a few days later, one of my uncles, a rich physician very much in vogue, having proposed to make me his sole heir on condition that I inherit his clientele along with his fortune, I became a physician for my uncle as I had been an advocate for my father. I knew just enough of that art to put on the doctoral robe.

"I knew what I had learned and nothing more, and any innovation appeared to me to be sacrilege. Judge how indignant I must have been to see you touch the holy ark of routine; I launched my prediction of death like an anathema; the grape pip made me triumphant. That did not blind me either, for, my uncle having died in the interim, I inherited his fortune, abdicated his responsibilities and resolved to spend my life pleasantly doing nothing, the sole objective of my slothful ambition.

"My steward, an upright man for his estate, invested my funds in commerce, and made the most of them for both of us; I had my share of the profit and refrained from complaining. Your corrosive worm might have aided the sale of my merchandise but, no complicity being admissible on that point, I shall not advance anything for my defense.

"Eventually, as the years passed, idleness began to weigh upon me; I resolved to travel the world in order to distract myself. Reading a few veridical voyagers and a few inspired poets had told me that the Orient is 'the empire of roses and beauty.' I have always loved beautiful flowers and beautiful women, and I set forth for Persia, having reread my voyagers, my poets and the *Thousand-and-One Nights*, in order to inform myself of the mores and customs of the countries that I was about to travel.

"I saw very few roses and no women there, but on the contrary, a general poverty and terror painted on all faces, continual massacres between the Uzbeks and the Persians. Kouli-kan, otherwise known as Nadir Shah, was then at the height of his glory, and I fled before his arms, which ravaged everything in their passage. I arrived among the independent

Tartars, who wanted at first to cut off my nose and ears; but having perceived on the left side of my face a small mole, regarded by them as a certain presage of good fortune and success, they changed their minds and appointed me commander-in-chief of the troops they were gathering to support Nadir's efforts against the Russians.

"My dear Monsieur Pigafet, you know as well as I do how things worked out, but what you don't know is that, born with a character not at all bellicose, as soon as the battle started, I thought about nothing but my own safety and turning tail. A portion of my troops, full of confidence in my mole, followed my every movement and plunged after me into a little wood of palm trees where, by the greatest of hazards, we discovered your superb ambush, which we did not expect. Its soldiers had lowered their arms when the frightful dust that rose up constrained us to turn round; we then found you in the greatest disarray, fighting against one another. After having left you to it for some time, we finished you off easily, and I was carried back in triumph by my Tartars, enthused by my courage and my mole.

"I had my share of the booty, but, weary of glory as I had been weary of repose, I quit my Tartars in order to visit northern Europe. In Germany I did indeed marry a charming woman who only became amorous of me because I was a Frenchman. Your abrupt rupture with her had caused talk, malicious gossip threatened to take possession of that affair, and frightened her, but you had only stayed for a short time in the region where she resided. She lived a solitary and retired existence; few people had witnessed your liaison; she thought, in giving her hand to one of your compatriots, to take advantage of your adventure; your cares and assiduities would be attributable to me. So, spared the long proofs to which she had subjected you, I replaced you immediately, and our marriage gave the impression of a reconciliation. She died; I missed her, for, in spite of her defects, she had an excellent heart.

"For a few years I furnished considerable funds to the colonial society whose projects had disappointed you so greatly. I had a new need to emerge from my repose; this time I was no longer in search of a land of roses and beauty; I went to Africa to put myself at the head of the vast enterprise of Guinea. Our affairs prospered there and might have grown further, for, according to certain accounts, we knew that immense gold mines existed in the interior. But how could we penetrate the lands of those mostly anthropophagous barbarians?

"I was thinking about that when I was suddenly approached by the delegates of the great Dahomey, who, after inspecting the color of my face, asked me to follow them. I was not about to let such a fine opportunity escape me. The descendant of Trudo Audati welcomed me with the most ardent demonstrations of joy and amity; he offered to have a thousand slaves immolated in my honor and to give me six hundred native women for my seraglio and to effect my circumcision. I thanked him for so many fine things, and told him that bloodshed did not honor anyone, that he had far too high an opinion of me if he thought I needed six hundred mistresses, and as for the final article, I begged him to dispense me of it.

"He replied, very politely, that my humanity and modesty pleased him, but that he had two thousand wives himself, without that involving any requirement. He asked my name, and when he heard it, I believe I saw him prostrate himself before me, because Berr-nahr, in the Alghemi language, much used in Dahomey, signifies 'most divine.' We became the best of friends; he still liked you, and charged me with reviewing your laws, slightly discredited by the accident of the insondo. I only changed the text, but it was necessary to give proof of capacity. I reassembled them and caused them to appear new under the denomination of the Code Bernard or Berr-nahr, which gave the people the best opinion of me.

"Finally, after having taken advantage of my power to enable the exploitation of the gold mines of Dahomey, heaped with wealth and honors, escorted by the blessings of the entire population, I quit Africa to return to France.

116

"On my return to Paris I became an object of general curiosity; I was the modern Cicero or Hippocrates, he hero of the Volga, the Lycurgus of Africa; it's true that my fortune was immense. As you can imagine, I had a great many friends, who talked about nothing but my intelligence and my talents, and I allowed myself to be seduced by the flattery. Protectors presented themselves on all sides; they told me that an ex-king of Dahomey ought to be at least a Comte in France, and I bought the comté of M***. My friends told me that a high social position required a mistress at the Opéra, and the same social obligation forced my dancer to invite men of letters to her suppers. The latter persuaded me, in their turn that good form demanded that a great lord like me was in the Académie; I had written, I don't know how, a quatrain for the Marquise de P***, and I was an Academician.

"That, my dear Monsieur Pigafet, is how, without any intrigue or conspiracy, led by fortune and hazard, borne by the subaltern causes that made your misfortune, further assisted by my mole, my name, that of my homeland, the color of my face and my dancer's suppers, I achieved such great prosperity honestly. Always in your wake to collect the debris of your shipwrecks, I would always have been disposed, however, to bring you aid and assistance if had been informed of you existence and your misfortunes. You ran after fortune and glory, which ran after me; let us hope that from now on, they will place their favors better, and that, far from harming you, I will only find myself near to the objective with you in order to keep you away from the ditch, close to port in order to warn you about the reef."

And the two of them embraced, as if to reconcile their contrary destinies. Monsieur Pigafet was ashamed of the unjust opinion that he had thus far had of such am honest and sympathetic man.

"What motive brings you to Versailles?" his new friend asked him, eventually.

"I have the word of the minister," the latter replied, "for the newly-vacant position of Councilor of State."

At these words, Comte Bernard seemed distraught. "The position of Councilor of State!" he exclaimed. "Alas, it was granted to me this morning by the Minister himself."

And Monsieur Pigafet replied, tranquilly: "I should have expected it; it is entirely in the order of things."

Tam-Garai, The Good Banian

(Hindustan)

Glory is only the shadow of virtue; the former
cannot exist where the latter is not.
(Maxim extracted from the Indian *Sama-Vedam*)

Before the Tartars, the Moguls, the Marattas and the
English had conquered and oppressed by turns the most beautiful oriental lands of India, the kingdom of Gujarat was regarded as the nurturing soil and the richest province of that
vast peninsula. A young rajah, full of audacity, valor and brilliant qualities, had just succeeded his father there. Sovereign
of a great people, a fertile land, counting a tributaries the kings
of the Deccan, Jaisalmer and Chittoor, ambition did not take
long to take possession of him; he wanted to surpass Alexander by his conquests, Mariadiramen by his equity; he was even
almost ambitious for reverses, in order to show himself to be
the equal in that of Porus. The most learned Brahmins of Benares and the most celebrated poets of India were summoned
to his court in order to celebrate the exploits that he was plan-
ning and the virtues that he was going to have.

He doubled the number of his soldiers, dressed them n
magnificent costumes, and resolved to pass his entire army in
review personally, in order to dazzle his people.

Between the mountains of Bollodo and the gulf of Gujarat there is an immense plain bordered by a double row of
palm trees and sandalwood trees. It was there that the young
prince's troops were gathered from all parts of the realm; it
was there that the inhabitants of Baroche, Cambay, Bagodra,
etc., crowded together, avid to enjoy such a noble spectacle
and the presence of their sovereign.

The army lined up in good order on the shore of the gulf, and the royal cortege soon appeared. Two thousand rajputs, or sons of noblemen, formed the advance guard. They were all clad in baftas—muslin strips wound around the body—of the finest cotton, garments of striped silk and gold and silver brocade, each holding one of the renowned bows fabricated in Multan or a lance or ax from Kabul. To the rattle of all those instruments of war, covered by a scarlet cloak, his forehead and breast charged with diamonds from Somelpour, Golconda and Visapour, the prince appeared, mounted on a white elephant, richly harnessed and radiant itself with precious stones from Pegu and the island of Ceylon.

Our young hero, proud of a luxury and splendor that he regarded as the forerunners of glory, was already seeking to read in the eyes of his subjects the impression that he had produced when he perceived that the people, rather than launching themselves toward his escort in order to enjoy the delight of contemplating him at closer range, seized by a sudden vertigo and an increasing agitation, were retreating toward the groups of trees that garnished the edges of the plain.

A frightful panther, emerged from the mountains of Bollodo, was the cause of the tumult and the general alarm. Intimidated by the multitude that hastened to recoil from its approach, it was advancing slowly, its mouth agape, through the large gap that terror opened up before it, when a wretched old man, who had thus far stood apart—he was a halalkhor, a despised caste equal to that of pariahs—found himself alone, separated from the other Indians, because, in spite of the imminence of the peril, he had not dared to soil with his impure contact the noble fellow citizens that surrounded him, trembling.

The monster bounded toward the old man, roaring with joy, already getting ready to carry him away to the mountains. Suddenly, a man emerged from the crowd, boldly cut off the panther's retreat, constrained it to let go, and audaciously plunged his arm into the open maw. In vain, the furious animal, panting with rage, his eyes bulging, reared up and plunged its iron claws into his sides; the Indian resisted, struggled, stifled it and threw it on to the sand, dying. The people uttered a cry of joy and astonishment, above all on recognizing in the vanquisher of the panther the good Banian, Tam-Garai, who had previously dissipated all his fortune in assisting the poor of Gujarat.

When calm was reestablished, the young rajah, costumed as a warrior and mounted on an Arab charger, which he caused to prance skillfully, went along the ranks of his soldiers, promising all of them triumphs and honors. The people admired his grace and his dexterity, and the magnificence of his army, but, incessantly distracted by a recent memory, their eyes turned anxiously toward the mountains of Bollodo.

The departure was announced for the following day. The royal tents were set up on the shore; aromatic herbs were burning in all directions, fires were distributed over the plain, the Brahmins drew the benedictions of heaven down upon a king who was the hope of Hindustan, and the poets of the court intoned the noblest songs celebrating his ease in the art of equitation, the sparkle of his diamonds, and even his generosity, doubtless in the intention of provoking it.

Having returned to his tent, intoxicated by incense, dreaming about the execution of his vast projects, the king decided to examine for himself the marvelous impression that the brilliant display of luxury and power must have left in the minds of his subjects. Clad in the simple costume of a rajput, he headed toward the long grove of sandalwoods and palms where the people had hastily constructed shelters in order to pass the night therein.

Groups had formed everywhere; the conversation seemed lively and animated. He approached some of them, and the name of Tam-Garai was the only one that struck his ears. People were questioning one another with interest regarding the condition of his wounds; they were commenting on the excess of his devotion to save the life of a wretched halalkhor. Everyone had seen his combat with the panther and everyone, recounting it with different circumstances, was competing to magnify the size of the monster and the audacity of the combatant.

Indignant that, on the day of the great review, people dared to talk about such things, the king mingled with other groups. In those people were recalling with admiration the banian's good deeds. During a year of famine, he had nourished at his expense more than a thousand poor people; by means of the secrets that he had discovered and revealed in medicine, he had saved the lives of an equally great number. Incessantly, the name of Tam-Garai, repeated from mouth to mouth, came to fatigue the attention of the king and wound his pride.

He withdrew, summoned to his tent a Brahmin who had tutored him, and whose frankness and virtues he respected. The sage listened calmly to the result of is nocturnal excursion and replied to him: "Luxury and magnificence dazzle the eyes momentarily and are effaced; the remembrance of a fine deed remains in the memory of the people."

The prince meditated on that, and after a brief silence, he said: "Well, then, I shall do fine deeds!"

His favorites arrived; bayaderes and acrobats were summoned, and in the midst of feats of agility and voluptuous dances, a part of the night was spent chewing betel, and drinking arak and toddi liquor.[29]

On his return to Gujarat—now Ahmedabad—the capital of his estates, the king, more avid than ever for glory, sought some means that he could employ in order to accomplish the fine deeds that he was meditating.

It is finer to triumph over a people than a panther, he said to himself. *War alone can render me illustrious.*

He immediately enquired of the minister charged with the finances of the realm whether the rajahs of Jaisalmer and

---

[29] Author's note: "Betel is an amalgam of areca nuts and quicklime enclosed in a leaf of piper-betel, a sarmentous plant of the pepper genre; arak is a spirituous liquor extracted from sugar case; toddi is a species of palm. (X.)"

the Deccan had paid their tributes in full; he was told that two hundred thousand gold rupees had just arrived in the treasury on their behalf. The prince was mourning an exactitude that took away any pretext for invasion when someone came to tell him that the city was in consternation. The little rivulet of Lambremetti, which traverses Gujarat, and the alternate drying out and flooding of which were public calamities, had broken its banks and almost submerged the house of a rich merchant built on its bank.

A woman and a child were alone in the habitation; they had been seen on an elevated terrace vainly imploring help by means of their gestures and cries. The flood, which was extending further had almost reached them and was threatening to engulf them, but the rain-fueled torrents that had swollen the river bed were imparting such turbulence to the waves, especially in that location strewn with rocks and new buildings, that no one dared to risk certain death in order to save the lives of the unfortunates.

The king, surrounded by his court, arrived at the site of the disaster, waving a large golden cup of inestimable workmanship, enriched by the most beautiful diamonds of the crown.

"It belongs to whoever will save them!" he cried.

A murmur of approval was heard round him, but none of the spectators attempted to merit it, and the king was making it shine again to all eyes when a man was perceived following the rapid current of the Lambremetti in a little junk, and who, in accordance with the custom of the Indians, was plying the oar with his foot while his hands served him as a point of support, trying to steer in the direction of the unfortunate victims.

The frail boat was soon carried on to the reefs, broke up and disappeared beneath the waves along with its pilot. The latter, an intrepid swimmer, triumphed over that peril; armed with an ax, he launched himself from rock to rock, and removed a few pieces of wood from a building, which he tied together sturdily with cords of every kind that were thrown to him from the height of the terrace. The mother and her child descended on to that raft and were firmly secured to it by their liberator. Delivering them to the current, he gave them further protection from its impetuosity by means of a rope that he held taut while swimming behind them. Finally driven into an inlet of the river, they returned to solid ground there, safe and sound.

The people, running to met them, made the air resound with their acclamations, and immediately took the savior of the interesting family to the king. It was Tam-Garai. The young prince blushed on hearing him named.

"Here," he said, presenting the cup to him. "This is the recompense for your courage."

"I cannot accept it," the Banian replied. "In Brahma's eyes, would take away the merit of a good deed."

"But do you not think," replied the astonished king, "that if you had died in that perilous enterprise, everyone would have thought that only the hope of recompense had drawn you into it?"

"What does the judgment of men matter to me? I saw the danger that two of my fellows were in, and I only consulted my heart."

"No matter; I know that your prodigal benevolence has caused your ruination; I will take charge of reestablishing your fortune."

"Heaven has provided for that, Prince; a rather considerable sum that I had previously lent has been returned to me this very day."

There was no talk in the court of anything but the generosity of the king, who had sacrificed the most beautiful of his cups to save two of his subjects; among the people there was no subject of conversation but the noble devotion of Tam-Garai.

The rajah said to his Brahmin: "Are you content with me, Father?"

"Yes," replied the latter, "your action was noble, but that of the Banian will efface it, for you sought a glory without peril, while he confronted a peril without glory, in order to obtain a disinterested triumph."

A few more months went by in the preparations for the war whose objective even the king of Gujarat could not define. He loved justice too much to invade the neighboring states and drag his subjects into such terrible hazards without a pretext. While awaiting a favorable circumstance, he supervised personally the completion of a superb palace that he had built in the middle of the Meidan, or public square, of Gujarat. He had arranged everything and anticipated everything in order that if death overtook him during his conquests, that superb monument would be sufficient in itself to make his name pass to posterity.

When it was entirely constructed, he asked the truthful Brahmin: "What are the people saying?"

"Prince, there is no talk of anything but the good Banian's cistern."

"What? What's that? What cistern? What do you mean?" cried the prince, in a sudden fit of temper.

"I mean," the Brahmin replied, tranquilly, "that, wanting to diminish as much as possible the dangerous effects of the inundations of the Lambremetti, and simultaneously guard against water shortages being felt in Gujarat when the bed of the stream is dry, as it is at present, Tam-Garai has had a vast cistern constructed at his expense, which, by means of subterranean conduits, receives the superfluity of the river during the rainy season and conserves it for times of drought."

"But my palace!" said the prince, in a distraught voice. "What are the people saying about my palace?"

"The people think that you will be magnificently lodged therein."

"Do they dare to put in the balance the most beautiful monument in Hindustan and a paltry cistern?"

"King of Gujarat," the Brahmin said, raising his voice, "the people can only estimate you by the good that you do them, and monuments only have value in their eyes by virtue of their utility."

More than twenty poems, in great, well-cadenced verses, appeared then regarding the palace in the Meidan, the marvel of India, but the rajah only listened to them with annoyance, for the people had composed a little ditty in honor of the Banian, devoid of artistry and with, which began with the words: "Oh, the good Tam-Garai! May Brahma watch over Tam-Garai!" And those fatal words often reached the sovereign's ears.

One courtier, more clear-sighted than the rest, perceived his sadness and divined the reason for it. He threw himself at the prince's feet, put his right hand on his breast, put the other on the ground and brought it back to his head, crying: "Justice! Justice in the name of Brahma! Justice in the name of the people!"

The young rajah, who was not unaware that equity is also a means of arriving at glory, and who had desired for a long time an opportunity to eclipse by means of a solemn judgment of Mariadiramen, the Solomon of India, ordered the courtier to explain himself.

"Prince, an infamous individual, a heresiarch, imbued with the frightful principles of the Agama, dares to preach publicly the equality of conditions among men."

"What is his name?"

"Tam-Garai!"

The Banian, summoned to appear before the king, was convicted of having frequented indifferently individuals of all castes, of having suffered the contact of a halalkhor without being purified subsequently of that pollution, and, as an adherent of the Agama, he received the order to exile himself from the realm. Even the good Brahmin dared not speak in his defense, because it was a matter of an affront to religion, and, moreover, the king had declared that, in order to appease the wrath of the gods, he would have a pagoda constructed in their honor in Gujarat that would surpass in its splendor those of Juggernaut, Multan and Kalamma.

The prince is recognizing the wisdom of my advice, the Brahmin said to himself. *He is coming back to useful monuments.*

It was then, above all, that all lyres were set in motion to inform posterity of the equitable judgment of the rajah of rajahs of Gujarat.

The people only responded to all those praises by singing their favorite song: "Oh, the good Tam-Garai! May Brahma watch over Tam-Garai!"

The prince, who already believed himself to have been immortalized by the songs of his poets, by the splendor of his palace and the paternal moderation of his sentencing, finally rid of the only rival who disputed the admiration of his people with him, resolved to add to his illustriousness what it still lacked. For a long time the Sanganians and the Warrels had been infesting the coasts of the realm with their piracy; it was agreed that they should be exterminated, but that required the organization, at great expense, of a formidable navy, and the people were already complaining about the number of taxes.

"Double them," said the courtiers. "Camels are only docile when they are laden."

The king listened to them, and alienated himself entirely from the spirit of the nation.

After long preparations the army set forth. In order to embark in the gulf of Gujarat, it had to traverse the weak towns of Kowlis, destroy those populations of brigands, depose the queen of Sangania from her throne, and then take possession of the sea from the point of Diu all the way to the Malabar coast, forcing the Warrels to surrender their weapons and vessels to the conqueror.

The Kowlis, taken by surprise, only put up a feeble resistance. They were defeated, destroyed or delivered to slavery. The king, leading as a hero, shared all the perils of his soldiers, immolated the chief of the enemy bandits with his own hand and accounted for two elephants killed beneath him.

The defeat of the brigands was followed by three days of rejoicing, after which the victorious rajah ordered the embarkation. Scarcely had the signal for departure been given, however, than a vessel was seen to enter the gulf, sent by the Warrels and the Sanganians.

The delegates of those peoples prostrated themselves before the king, and one of them expressed himself thus:

"Rajah of rajahs, for a long time war was our only profession, and our only resource; more than once we have proved by our resistance to the united forces of your father, the kings of the Deccan, Cambay and Balaghat, that our submission only depended on our will. *Live by combat* was, for a long time, our only law, but times have now changed. Other needs have made themselves felt among us; the cause of that is too beautiful to remain hidden, and this is it: a merchant junk, captured by our Sanganians, included among its passengers one of your subjects. He was about to submit to the common fate of all our prisoners,[30] when a few former inhabitants of Gujarat serving among us recognized him and implored our queen for mercy on his behalf.

"Astonished by the pompous account that was given of his virtues, she desired to see him; the sage's words bore fruit in her heart. Soon, by virtue of his advice, everything around us took on a new face; our numerous captives, returned to a milder existence, utilized and appreciated in accordance with their talents, caused to blossom suddenly in our savage retreats the arts necessary to life. Ceasing to intoxicate themselves incessantly with bhang,[31] the devouring liquor that, exciting their imagination, bore them to ferocity, our compatriots resumed the character natural to Indians.

"Gradually, our disarmed vessels attempted a few exchanges with neighboring peoples; commerce entered our ports. Our lands, left uncultivated by our insouciance, were

---

[30] Author's note: "Immediately after taking prisoners, those people cut their Achilles tendons in order to make it impossible for them to escape."

[31] Author's note: "A mixture of opium and henbane." It is actually a preparation of cannabis,

rendered to fertility; ease and pleasure ameliorated our mores. The Warrels, our eternal companions, sensing that sudden revolution themselves, adopted its consequences. A few hardened hearts and malcontents sometimes sought to return us to our primitive state, but the virtues of our new legislator and the firmness of the queen imposed silence on them.

"A change so extraordinary, so marvelous, was the work of a few months and a single man, so the Sanganians and the Warrels now repeat in chorus the song of Gujarat: 'Oh, the good Tam-Garai! May Brahma watch over Tam-Garai!'"

At that name, the prince lowered in head in consternation. The delegate went on:

"Do not trouble the happiness that we are beginning to enjoy; any pretext for war has ceased among us; the vessels captured from your subjects will be returned. Allow our prosperity to increase and, in due course, you can fix yourself the tribute that we will pay as compensation for your unnecessary preparations for war.

"Accept these hostages, guarantees of our faith," the delegate said to the rajah, presenting two of the sons of the queen of Sangania, "let them learn from you the art of rendering peoples happy. How could they not practice virtue under the eyes of the man who counts among the number of his subjects a Tam-Garai?"

"Tam-Garai!" cried the young king, raising his head, inflamed by chagrin and fury. "Will that name pursue me everywhere? Will he incessantly triumph over me, destroying my noblest hopes? Will it be necessary for me to renounce conquests, and glory, my sole passion, because a Tam-Garai exists?"

The veridical Brahmin was beside the monarch, and it was no longer a matter heresy and the Agama. "If you love glory," he said to him, "moderate yourself, and do not render foreigners witness to your weakness. Accept the Sanganians' proposal; a treaty is worth more than a victory. It is finer to vanquish by means of words than by arms, and persuasion is better than conquest."

"So the Banian is greater than me."

Nevertheless, the conqueror of Kowlis returned to his capital carried on a superb Tatta palanquin by the foremost lords of his court. However, the shrill sounds of the trumpet, the racket of drums, the cries of the soldiers and the songs of poets did not prevent him from hearing a few voices still murmuring: "Oh, the good Tam-Garai! May Brahma watch over Tam-Garai!"

Left alone with his Brahmin, he said to him: "Father, explain to me, in sum, how it is that a miserable subject of an almost scorned caste, without an army, without treasures, dragging out his existence alternately in poverty and exile, has been able incessantly and advantageously to compete with me, the rajah of rajahs, a king the son of kings?"

"My son, it is because you have only loved glory; the good Banian loves virtue. The latter does good to everyone, is useful to everyone; the former only satisfies the vanity and ambition of a few. If you want to be veritably great and leave posterity a durable and respected name, never forget the precept of the Sama-Vedam: *Glory is only the shadow of virtue; the former cannot exist where the latter is not.*"

A few confused ancient traditions give reason to think that the Indian monarch, of whose reign we have just given a sketch of the early years, died at a very advanced age, after vast conquests that rendered him sovereign of all the lands between Chittoor and Golconda, all the way to the mountains of Orixa. At the end of the last century, however, I traversed the ancient kingdom of Gujarat, now a province of the Marattas. No one has conserved the memory of so many exploits; the very name of that prince is completely unknown, while that of Tam-Garai is repeated with veneration throughout the Oriental peninsula. The beautiful verses composed in honor of the rajah have suffered the fate of the hero they celebrated, but, from the mountains of Bollodo to the coats of Malabar, people still repeat the song of the good Banian.

The Two Coins

I will speak, but will anyone believe me?
(Francis Bacon, *Sophisms*)[32]

Everything in nature has its language; horses and donkeys have sometimes been endowed with speech; I take as witnesses Homer and Scripture. Monsieur Dupont de Nemours knows the different dialects of various species of birds;[33] even rivers have raised their "loud voices." Distinctly articulated sounds have emerged from rocks, and it is probable that stones, the hearing of which was keen enough to be sensible to the charms of Orpheus' lyre, might communicate orally between themselves. I shall therefore disregard the clamors of the incredulous and relate naively the singular conversation that I overheard one day.

Pensive and solitary, I was walking in the vicinity of Paris; there, my arms folded over my breast and my head bowed, I was allowing my mind to wander and had abandoned myself meekly to the charm of my reveries, when a silvery voice suddenly struck my ears. I turned round and saw nothing; I listened again, and again I heard the soft voice, but I wanted to know its origin in vain.

By dint of research and attention, I finally perceived that the soft and silvery voice, either by virtue of magic or miracle, was coming from...where? Shall I say it...?

From my pocket.

---

[32] The citation does not appear in the standard English version of the sophisms explored by Bacon in *De augmentus scientiaum* (tr. as *The Advancement of Learning*).

[33] The naturalist Pierre Dupont de Nemours (1739-1817) published a supposed dictionary of the language of crows in 1807.

Yes, from the pocket of my waistcoat.

I am no more credulous than anyone else; I doubted it for a long time, but it was necessary to yield to the evidence when a second voice replied to the first. What, then, were the interlocutors? Only two silver coins, one of five and the other of six francs, were furnishing the interior of that pocket for the moment. My suspicion had to fall on them, and my suspicion soon became certainty when I distinctly heard the following dialogue:

"By what hazard do I find you here, my dear? Blessed by the gods that have reunited us, the gods from whom you and I are perhaps descended, for they were once made of gold and silver."

"You could not have been more knowledgeable had you been a medallion," replied the other.

"My small education will not astonish you," replied the first, "when you know that, born under the reign of Louis XV, whose effigy I still bear, I have belonged in my time to the finest minds of that century. I have passed from the pocket of Helvetius to that of Crébillon fils; even those of the likes of Voltaire and Diderot were open to me, and it is in the society of those illustrious men that I have acquired the little that I value mentally. But my dear, take me out of my embarrassment; great gods, how your face seems to me to have changed! Without your voice, it would have been impossible for me to recognize you, so much difference have a few years brought to your features."

"No one is master of his destinies," replied the five-franc coin. "By turns republican, imperial and royal, my head sometimes covered with the bonnet of liberty, or circled by the laurels of the empire, I have incessantly and involuntarily changed form and served all the governments that have ruled France in the last thirty years. If you have cultivated the sciences and literature, less fortunate than you, I have only been able to devote myself to politics, having almost always belonged to statesmen."

"Oh, my good friend," cried the six-franc piece, "how pleasant it would be for me to hear your story! We're alone; our possessor does not seem to be disposed to separate us very soon; the moment is favorable."

"You first," said the other. "I am the younger and I ought to cede the floor to you."

The coin contemporary with the likes of Voltaire and Diderot was savant and talkative, and did not have to be begged.

"I owe my existence to the casting that the minister Argenson[34] ordered in 1718, with the bars of silver furnished to the Regency by the businessmen of Saint-Malo. Alas, misfortune was to assail me upon my entry into society. I only saw the light in order, like my peers, to be subject to the most unjust persecution.

"I shall explain. It was in those days that the famous Law had the Regent adopt his ruinous system of finances. In order to have recourse more easily to his paper money, he thought himself obliged to discredit us in public opinion; hence the vexation of which we were so long the target. At every moment a new edict arrived to put in doubt our rights and our value. Eventually, after long fluctuations, victory remained ours; Law was shamefully expelled from France and, after having been the richest man in the state, he died in poverty in Venice—a just punishment for the countless affronts that he had made gold and silver suffer.

---

[34] René-Louis de Voyer de Paulmy, Marquis d'Argenson (1694-1757) was the councilor of state who tried to sort out the confusion caused by the application of the monetary theory of the far-sighted and pioneering Scottish economist John Law (1671-1729). He later was appointed Controller General of Finances during the Duc d'Orléans' Regency, founding the Banque Générale, which issued the first French paper money; he also promoted shares as a form of wealth—which, unfortunately, enabled a speculative inflation that caused a financial collapse.

"I shall pass over in silence the time when, put into circulation in commerce, I traveled through a thousand strong-boxes, twenty seaports, always in activity, passing from hand to hand, from bag to bag, incessantly presented, accepted, exchanged, piled up, borrowed, lent or stolen, and not even having the leisure, in my brief stations, to make a few philosophical or mental observations regarding my numerous possessors. Heaven took pity on me, and soon, far from commerce and merchants, I resided in the Marais in Paris.

"My new master, a good bourgeois, a partisan of antique mores that he maintained as much as he could in his family, was old, rich, thrifty, sober and tidy within his house, admonished his wife, gave advice to his daughter, wore a rectangular wig, was always talking, rarely reasoned, never laughed, and yet, a secret lover of the fine arts, sometimes slipped out of the house to go and render homage in the common temple—the Opéra, that is.

"However, either by virtue of fatigue, organic weakness or, more likely in order not to deviate from the established usage, sleep seemed to enter his box with him and take possession of his senses, until dance tunes suddenly arrived to extract him from his lethargy. Then he opened his eyes and ears wide, embraced with his gaze the goddesses and nymphs who had come to display their charms, graces and divinity to the eyes of the public.

"One of them seemed to occupy him exclusively; he followed her with his eyes, mimed all her movements, held his breath when she danced; and when she had disappeared, whether in a chariot or a cloud, he uttered a deep sigh, picked up his cane and hat, went home, admonished his wife and gave his daughter advice.

"One day, he adorned himself, admired himself, adonised himself and went directly to a superb town house, had himself announced, and found Venus or Calypso in a negligee, a thousand times more seductive than all the adornments of Olympus. He tried to speak, but his tongue was embarrassed; unable either to preach the ancient virtues, make admonitions or give advice, he stammered, became anxious and disconcerted, and then, by virtue of an instinct then rare in the bourgeoisie, he replaced expression by gesture, plunged his hand noisily into his pocket, where I was lodged with several companions; we rendered a sound that instantly seemed to speak for him, and even to lend his silence a seductive eloquence.

"The beauty who, by virtue of the angularity of his stature, the clarity of his speech, his cane with a golden pommel and his energetic gesture, mistook him for a man of finance, began to soften confidently; he saw that and, falling at the feet of the goddess, showed her a handful of écus minted in Tours. But she doubtless only cared for gold. Whether out of scorn for us, or because the grotesque face of her old gallant stifled her natural sensibility, she uttered a long burst of laughter and, striking the hand that was holding us pell-mell rudely from below, caused us to fly into the middle of the apartment, or roll under the furniture. Ringing for her servants, laughing more uproariously and having her aged adorer thrown out was for her the work of a moment.

"She was still laughing when a brilliant musketeer came in noisily. We were lying scattered here and there on the parquet. The indifference and offensive scorn with which she seemed to overwhelm us, to which we were certainly not accustomed, caused my indignation to rise to the highest degree, for, without being a Spanish doubloon, everyone knows what he is worth. My ruffled self-esteem, however, did not prevent me from hearing the following colloquium:

"'Well, my lovely friend, why these noisy bursts of laughter? Are you reading the farces of Voltaire or the tragedies of La Harpe?'

"'My dear Dorat,[35] how opportunely you arrive.' (Laughing.) 'The most inconceivable, most comical story! Laugh, then!'

---

[35] The musketeer and poet Claude-Joseph Dorat (1734-1780) contrived to attract the hatred of the *philosophes* and their en-

"'I'd like nothing better; but I still need to know...'

"(Laughing.) 'A character from a play, my dear Dorat; a charming character!'

"'But, in sum...?'

"'Two huge eyes...écus...the most singular face! Laugh, then!'

"'I'm waiting...'

"(Laughing.) 'It's charming! It's divine! I'm dying of it!' (Suddenly becoming serious again.) 'An imbecile, a boor, a specimen who has permitted himself to fall in love with me.'

"'I don't see, thus far, any thing inconceivable in your story, nothing but what is quite natural.'

(In a forced manner.) 'Who dares to offer me silver! Me! Does he take me for a woman devoid of morals? For a cheap whore? Silver!'

"'That's frightful; it's almost lacking respect for you.'

"'So I had him thrown out.'

"'Of course, beautiful lady. Speaking of silver, that reminds me that yesterday, with the marquis, we had an orgy.'

"'An orgy! You don't say!'

"'What do you expect? I have vices, you know, my dear friend.'

"'You have no need of them, with five mistresses.'

"'No! On my honor, I love no one but you; but you weren't there; I wanted to distract myself. Pezay[36] ragged me into playing lansquenet; I gambled; I lost; I owe twenty-five louis, on my word, which is sacred.'

"'You don't doubt my amity.'

"'I've had more than one proof of it.'

"'But my dear Dorat, a luminous idea! My old ape will pay a part of your sacred debt. Look on the parquet.'

---

emies alike, in spite of his relentless self-promotion. He published *Les Baisers* in 1770

[36] Alexandre Masson, Marquis de Pezay, a soldier and poet, pictured in company with Dorat in a well-known engraving.

"'Écus! Where the devil do you put your funds? Come on, quick, help me.'

"And there go our musketeer poet and his generous friend, finally deigning to take notice of us, searching for us in the nooks and crannies, and assembling us in haste. The beauty completed the twenty-five louis, and our new master quit her, swearing that she combined the charms of Ninon with a soul a thousand times greater than hers.

"We expected to pay that sacred debt. Nothing of the sort. *Les Baisers* had just appeared; half the sum was employed in warding off the severity of a critic, a sort of literary Themis who is well aware of how to make use of his balance; the other half, destined to pay the expenses of vignettes, culs-de-lampe, etc., and of which I was a part, went to the publisher, who immediately took us, in fine company, to the home of the author of *Zaïre*, from whom he had just bought a little satire for a rather large sum. Thus Dorat ruined himself in order to be immortal, while Voltaire enriched himself while immortalizing himself.

"I shall not dwell any longer on things interesting for me alone, and I'll hasten to get to the point.

"The era of my misfortunes was already advancing. The Revolution was prepared, ripened, and finally burst forth, and in its bosom, I saw a considerable mass of new paper money, which caused us to suffer for a long time the fate to which Law had once made us suffer. But that was only the prelude to greater misfortunes. The nation that we had served and enriched for so long seemed to repudiate us; a new monetary system was established, and every year, a considerable host of us, sent to the foundry, lost their faces and their existence there.

"I remember that, in those days, by the greatest of hazards, I belonged to the respectable widow of the good bourgeois who admonished his wife and gave advice to his daughter. Appointed, since her husband's death, the Dame de Charité of her arrondissement, the worthy creature acquitted the duties of her responsibility marvelously, visiting attics and

137

hovels, taking with her consolation, hope and forgetfulness of dolors.

"One day, she included me in the number of her alms, and we soon arrived at the top floor of a house, in an obscure redoubt into which just enough daylight penetrated to allow the perception on a camp bed of an unfortunate woman in a state of destitution difficult to imagine. Our presence seemed, for a moment, to make a radiance of joy appear in that discolored face, on which dolor and poverty had imprinted their destructive seal. My mistress separated herself from me then in favor of the unfortunate woman, who received me with all most expressive marks of gratitude. She kissed the hands of her benefactress, and kissed me, staring at me with astonished eyes moist with tears.

"Imagine my surprise when I recognized that miserable creature, so poor, so disfigured and so abandoned, as the brilliant dancer who had once received me with such cheerful and scornful disdain when I had been offered to her by the husband of the good woman whose hands she had just kissed!

"I only emerged from the hands of Dorat's generous friend to enter the coffers of an Israelite, a great miser, a great second-hand dealer, a pawnbroker, who, passing a defaming file over my face, mutilated me in a cowardly manner and forced my new masters to mistake for an outrage of time what was only the effect of his sordid avarice.

"A short time afterwards, the thunderbolt fell on our heads. The government of the day, forgetting all divine and human laws, caused our value arbitrarily to depreciate. Since that time, an object of scorn, bearing a title that I cannot justify, I have seen my numerous possessors only keep me with anxiety, incessantly exchanging me; and I have only known joy when fate placed me next to you. In sum, I'm awaiting the fatal day when, designated for melting down, I shall necessarily be deprived of this form and this royal effigy, which I have conserved faithfully since the day of my creation. If anything can soften my bitter regrets, however, it is the hope of then being counted among the number of your peers."

At that point the six franc piece stopped speaking; the five, after having thanked him, began thus:

"It was in 1793 that I was born, in the midst of France's civil strife. The Legislative Assembly made an appeal then to the people, who were soon seen, imitating Cincinnatus and Fabricius, abjuring self-interest and luxury, carrying their gold and silver jewelry and vessels to the Mint. I owe the light of day to that patriotic impulse.

"Alas, I confess to you that I did not remain faithful, like you, to my original imprint. Each of the governments that succeeded one another then changed my form and figure. The Legislative Assembly, the Convention, the Directoire, the Consulate and the Empire saw me ornamented with their legends and attributes by turns, and, whether by weakness of character or the irresistible force of circumstances, I became what people called a frank weathervane.[37] There was even a moment when I found myself, like many other honest folk, belonging to two parties at the same time. Yes, during year XIII, while I bore the emblems of the expiring republic on one side, on the other I presented the face, the new name and the new title of its destroyer.

"Without boasting, I can say that I played a certain role in public affairs then. My companions and I, spread in profusion among the people, were forming their sentiments, exciting their amour and preparing their enthusiasm. I would never finish if I wanted to recount to you all the services that I rendered to the government that had just been established. Our presence alone, as if by enchantment, caused the masks of false lovers of liberty to fall; I saw those Brutus financiers immediately quit the severe physiognomy then *de rigueur*, abjure the rudeness of equality in order to try out protective smiles and the reverence of the court.

"At that time, I belonged to a rich arms manufacturer, who, although of a very plebeian nature, had the mania of an-

[37] The pun embodied in *girouette franche* [frank weathervane] only translates marginally.

cestry to the highest degree. Portraits of all his bourgeois ancestors, classified in order of birth, were proudly plastered over the walls of his apartment when the revolution burst. Fearing for heads so dear, which, in truth, were almost all white-powdered, a certain sign of feudality, he thought that the only means of warding off the proscription that might fall upon them was to cover them prudently with the insignia of liberty. A painter was immediately summoned; in the place of a rose, my master had a large cockade traced on his grandfather's cadogan, in spite of to enormous baskets that revealed the anachronism of the cockade. His father was decked in a Phrygian bonnet, in spite of his purse and pigeon-wings, and his uncle, a curé when he was alive, and consequently more imminently in danger than the others, was armored, booted and spurred; a dragoon's helmet covered his tonsured head, and a bushy moustache shaded the lips from which nothing had once emerged but words of peace.

"But the new political change of 1804 arrived to prescribe further family metamorphoses to my worthy master. The monarchy seemed to want to be reborn. Suddenly appointed a baron, he began blushing at his father's Phrygian bonnet. Perhaps the painter would have come back to destroy his own work, and who knows, by means of embroideries, sashes and crosses, to make comtes, marquises and commanders of Monsieur le Baron's plebeian race. The dragoon curé would have been, at the very least, promoted to the rank of cardinal; but amour decided otherwise.

"A daughter of an ancient house pleased the arms manufacturer who, thanks to his fortune, obtained her in marriage. From then on, entirely renouncing his ancestors, he replaced them with his wife's, which he had painted at his expense. One day, however, by virtue of a residue of affection that he could not vanquish, so durable are first impressions within us, all his ancestors were remade in silhouette, and while the noble part of his family occupied his sumptuous apartments in the city, the entire plebeian part went to cover the walls of the Chinese pavilion of his country house.

"Monsieur le Baron, governed by his wife, did not take long to dazzle the capital with the luxury of his houses and his carriages. Madame la Baronne loved to shine. But the ex-arms manufacturers perceived that the expenses exceeded his income; he talked about economizing; the Baronne, who did not like those abject means, took charge of reestablishing equilibrium in his finances without changing the ordinary order of his house.

"A new pleasure was added to the numerous pleasures that people already enjoyed in the town house; a superb roulette table was established there. Gradually, the fashionable young people disdained dancing, music and the seductive tableau of groups of elegant women distributed in the drawing rooms. Access to the house became easy for strangers and it was eventually transformed into a veritable gambling-den. You're going to learn, my dear, how heaven deigned to make use of me, a poor weak creature, to change the brilliant face of that house and punish Monsieur le Baron for the poor use he made of his wealth.

"In the middle of a magnificent fête that was being given in the house, a poorly-dressed man presented himself. 'Does Monsieur le Baron recognize me?'

"'I have a confused idea...'

"'I'm your relative, Monsieur le Baron: Gaspard...'

"'Lower your voice.'

"'Son of...'

"'Lower, I tell you. I recognize you, but I'm importuned here; please follow me.'

"And he led him into the principal pathway of the garden. 'What can I do for you, Monsieur?'

"'Help me to get out of an embarrassing situation, like a good relative. I possess a few talents; I have activity...'

"'That's sufficient. Leave your address with my concierge; I'll give the matter some thought.'

"'I had a place, Monsieur le Baron; I lost it, and your protection...'

"'Adieu; Madame is doubtless becoming anxious about my absence; I'll rejoin her.' And, drawing away, he seemed to offer his hand to cousin Gaspard, who, seeing nothing in that gesture but a sign of amity, seized it eagerly, but soon withdrew his own hand on feeling a few coins, of which I was one, escape the baron's.

"Cousin Gaspard's movement of pride caused us to fall in the middle of the path. 'Keep your alms!' he exclaimed, and he ran precipitately through the gates of the house, while the baron, ashamed and indignant, went back in, and only calmed his chagrin on seeing the baize of the roulette table covered with gold and silver, and his croupiers' rakes bringing back to the coffers enough to pay the expenses of twenty fêtes similar to the one he was giving that day with so much ostentation and generosity.

"Among the gamblers that fortune was betraying at that moment was a young provincial heir recently disembarked in Paris with his treasure. Introduced to the baron's house, he had contracted the fatal passion of gambling. Chance had been so deadly for him that very day that, having seen his entire paternal inheritance slip though his fingers, consumed with shame and regret, prey to despair and misery, he tore himself away from that fatal place, where avarice and cupidity had held them in their eagles' claws for several hours. Turning over sinister projects in his head, he went through the courtyards of the house and launched himself into the gardens...

"Still lying in the path where the Baron and his cousin Gaspard had disputed the honor of abandoning me, I immediately offered my sight to the unfortunate young man. He stopped, and seized me. A gleam of hope shone in his face. Admire with me, my dear, the profound sight of Providence; I had doubtless just saved the life of my new possessor; he was about to owe me a fortune ten times greater than the one he had just lost. Alas, he was not to enjoy all the wealth that I returned to him for long!

"Unperceived for some time in the midst of piles of gold that surrounded me on the fatal baize, I eventually saw heaped upon me a considerable number of coins, the unexpected result of a combination crowned with the most brilliant success. My young master multiplied his stakes audaciously, broke the bank and ruined the Baron almost completely.

"Avid for new emotions, the unfortunate fellow frequented public gaming houses, and was reduced in very little time to the state of destitution from which I had extracted him so miraculously; by a great hazard I still belonged to him. One evening, he liquidated the little that remained to him, tempted fortune one last time, lost, and the following day I found myself in the drawer of an armorer in the Rue Saint-Honoré.

"Thrown for a long time, like you, into commerce, received in the establishments of our strongest bankers, I was able to observe the rich bourgeoisie of today, so different from the god bourgeoisie of old. How mores have changed! How far your madman of the Marais, who gave advice to his daughter and admonished his wife, is from the rich men of the Chaussée-d'Antin, full of frankness and generosity, who do not give their daughters and wives admonitions or advice, and who, far from going hypocritically to offer silver to our Venuses of the Opéra, openly protect the god of the fine arts and maintain his priestesses openly!

"Soon subject to a further metamorphosis at the Mint, I only came out to enter the house of a senator, a great man at court, a great orator in secret council, who filled twenty positions at the same time worthily, loudly prognosticating the immortal duration of the new reign while accumulating savings.

"However, great political events came to change the face of France; the ancient throne of our kings suddenly replaced the European throne with which an illustrious conqueror had crushed the republic and disinherited the monarchy. I immediately went, by Monseigneur's order, to live in the strong-box of a political writer, who was then protecting with his pen all the excellencies who had fallen or were still to fall.

"France, in that epoch, being invaded by foreigners, my companions and I played a very important role in democracy.

In a slight excursion made outside the capital's walls, I fell into the hands of Cossacks. It was in the belt of one of them that I found myself enclosed with a large quantity of foreign coins, such a roubles, imperials, griwnas, florins, ducats, fredericks etc., whose jabber I could not understand but who all seemed to me to have arrived in our common prison in a violent manner. I was already despairing of ever seeing the sky of my fatherland again, but on the eve of the capitulation of Paris—O shame of France!—I emerged from the ranks of the enemy army and reentered the capital furtively in order..."

The five-franc coin was at that point in its narrative, and I was still listening with sustained attention, when I suddenly felt myself grabbed by the collar. I raised my eyes. I perceived before me a man half city-dweller and half-peasant, half-bourgeois and half-soldier; he was brown-haired, tall, strong, and armed with a long saber. In sum, he was a gamekeeper, since it's necessary to call him by his name.

Throughout the conversation of the two interlocutors I had not perceived that for half an hour, I had been walking on cultivated ground, where my feet had trodden two asparagus plants, and crushed a rectangle of nascent beans. I was caught *in flagrante delicto*, with my feet on the beans. It was necessary to pay for the damage; to my great regret, one of the conversationalists went that way. It was the younger one.

Let that be a warning to distracted people who go to dream in the fields without thinking about asparagus plants and gamekeepers.

Ambitious Bébut

(Persia)

Listen to this true story, and see where ambition leads
(Hafiz, Persian poet)

In one of the outlying districts of Ispahan, under the reign of Abbas I,[38] a poor jewelry worker lived who was known in the neighborhood as Bébut the Honest Man, for numerous examples of disinterest and probity had earned him that fine title.

Chosen as an arbiter in all quarrels and all debates, his decisions were almost always respected, like those of the kazi himself. Laborious, active, intelligent, and esteemed by everyone, Bébut was happy, and amour also came to add to his happiness. Smitten with the beautiful Tamira, his employer's daughter, he was loved by her. One idea, however, troubled his felicity; he was poor, and Tamira's father would never consent to accept a man without a fortune for a son-in-law. Bébut therefore often thought about means of enriching himself, and his thoughts turned incessantly in that direction. Insensibly, without him perceiving it, ambition came to take the place of a milder sentiment in his heart.

In the midst of a festival of the harem, the great Shah Abbas having carelessly trampled underfoot the royal spray known as the jigha, a mark of sovereignty among Muslims, Bébut's reputation determined the officer in charge of the prince's jewels to confide the repair to the honest jeweler. The latter, delighted by the confidence that he inspired, promised

---

[38] Abbas I (1571-1629), known as Abbas the Great, was Shah of Persia from 1588 until his death.

himself to do everything possible to justify it. However, holding the richest gems of India and Persia in his hands, it was impossible that his ideas of ambition would not come to assail him with more force than ever.

Only one of those numerous diamonds would make my fortune, he thought, *and that of Tamira. I'm incapable of abusing my position, but if I did abuse it, would Abbas be any less rich and powerful? He would have made the happiness of two of his subjects, without suspecting anything. Another man in my place would find, in such work, an opportunity to put a treasure aside, but I would be content with a single one of those diamonds. It would be very bad, I admit, but I would replace it with a fake diamond, cut and mounted with so much artistry and skill that the value of the work would surpass that of the material. It would be impossible to perceive the substitution; God and the Prophet would see it clearly, I know, but in order to expiate the sin, which I would strive to render unique in my life, I would subsequently undertake a pilgrimage to Mashad, or even to Mecca, if remorse tormented me too much.*

It was thus, by means of *buts*, that Bébut the Honest Man succeeded in tranquilizing his conscience. The diamond was removed, replaced by a fragment of crystal, and he jigha appeared more brilliant than ever to Abbas' courtiers, who, only speaking to him with their foreheads in the dust, had scant leisure to examine the gleam of the stones.

One day, at the spring equinox, the leader of Abbas' followers, in accordance with Persian custom, was sitting at the gates of the palace, rendering justice publicly to all his subjects. An artisan from the district of Julfa cleaved through the crowd and prostrated himself at Abbas' feet and asked him for justice. He accused the kazi of having been courted and having condemned him wrongly.

"My adversary and I," he exclaimed, "initially had recourse to the decision of Bébut the Honest Man, who had judged in my favor."

The Shah asked who this Bébut was who enjoyed such a good reputation in the district of Julfa, and he summoned the kazi. After having examined the affair maturely, the monarch declared that he was of the same opinion as Bébut the Honest Man, and ordered the kalantar, the governor of the city, to bring him immediately.

When Bébut saw that officer and his escort stop in front of the shop where he was working, a sudden shudder ran through all his limbs, but it was worse when the latter, on behalf of his sovereign, enjoined him to follow him. He was ready to present his head, in order to dispense with any vain ceremonial, thinking it certain to be terminated by a stroke of the scimitar, but he put off his anxiety and went with the kalantar.

Having arrived before Abbas, he dared not raise his eyes, for fear of seeing the fatal spray and the impostor diamond depose against him. Almost dying, he thought he could already hear the grim rikas—the Persian royal guards—approaching, armed with their redoubtable axes.

"Bébut, and you, Ismael-kazi," Abbas said to them, "Since, of the two of you, it is the jeweler who renders justice better, let him fill the place of judge alone, and you, Ismael, succeed him in his employment. May you acquit his work as well as he will acquit yours."

The sentence was carried out punctually, and I have been assured that Ismael became thereafter an excellent jeweler.

Bébut-kazi, for his part, took possession of his responsibilities. His ambition ought to have been limited subsequently to becoming the husband of Tamira and living virtuously. The request for marriage was soon made and soon accepted. Bébut therefore believed that all his wishes had been fulfilled, and he was forming the most pleasant projects, when the kalantar of Ispahan presented himself before him. Still full of the alarm that the lord's first visit had caused him, he received him with more confusion than politeness, and asked him what had brought him such an honor for the second time.

The kalantar replied: "When I came to transmit the order of the magnanimous Abbas to you in your employer's house, I saw the beautiful Tamira there, with the eyes of a gazelle, a rose of Ispahan as brilliant as the azure campac that only grows in paradise; her gaze had the magical effect on me of the seal of Solomon, and I resolved to take her for my wife. I went to her father's house this morning, but his word is engaged to you, and Bébut-kazi is the sole obstacle to my happiness. Listen: I possess great wealth, and I have powerful friends; cede your rights over Tamira to me, and before long I will have you appointed divan-beghi; you will be the chief sovereign of justice in the city, the foremost in the world; furthermore, I will give you for a wife my own sister, formerly the nightingale of Iran, the dove of Babylon. I shall leave you to reflect; I shall come tomorrow to seek a response."

The new kazi was astounded.

To cede my Tamira to him, he thought, *in order to marry his sister, perhaps old and shrewish, is to exchange a pearl of Bahrain for one of Mascate; but he is powerful; if I don't consent to it, he'll cause me to lose my position, and I need my position. Perhaps I would sacrifice it again in order to possess Tamira, but if I cease to be kazi, her father might take back the word he has given me. I love Tamira more than anything else in the world, but it is necessary not only to think of oneself, and it would be more glorious for her to become the wife of a kalantar than a poor little kazi. Well, I shall sacrifice myself for her happiness. I shall regret her all my life, but...but...I shall be the divan-beghi.*

If Bébut the Honest Man, carried away by a nascent cupidity, had thought he was committing his first sin in favor of amour and not ambition, he ought to have been disabused when, his two rival passions having just collided within his heart, he could only banish the former. So, from that moment on, losing the esteem and confidence that had surrounded him thus far, when he had more need of it than ever, he was designated by the name of Bébut the Ambitious.

Still unaware that the higher one rises, the more difficult virtue becomes, he still promised himself internally to edify by his conduct the entire body of the magistracy of Ispahan that now dominated. Not only would he go to Mecca to visit the black stone, the temple of the Kaaba, and purify himself in the waters of Zimzim—the miraculous spring that God had once caused to emerge from the earth in favor of his sons Agar and Ismael—but he would distribute to the poor a double zekath,[39] and strive to reconquer by dint of equity the fine nickname awarded by the public to the jeweler of Julfa.

The first judgments that he rendered in the quality of divan-beghi felt the effects of that noble resolution, but an unfortunate affair that followed demonstrated to him the verity of the assertion in the *Shah Nameh*,[40] the poem by the celebrated Firdaussi: "Our first sin, similar to the fecund poppy of Aboutige, gives rise to numerous seeds, which sow bitter and venomous plants for us all along the road of life."

The royal spray of Shah Abbas broke again and was incontinently confided to the care of a former colleague of Bébut's. The work of the jeweler being subjected to a severe examination, it was perceived that a very fine diamond had been removed from the jigha and replaced fraudulently. The unfortunate jeweler was arrested and dragged to the tribunal of the divan-beghi. The ambitious Bébut saw that he was doomed if he did not hasten to put an end to the procedure; he pronounced himself, against the innocent accused, the punishment due to his own crime, and the sentence was carried out immediately.

---

[39] Author's note: "The Persians call 'zekath' the tithe of alms that, according to the Koran, they ought to distribute to the poor."

[40] Author's note: "Shah Nameh means 'royal book'; it was composed by the order of Mahmoud the Gaznevide, and contains in 60,000 distichs the history of the ancient kings of Persia. (X.)"

He soon sensed that a man like him was unworthy to render justice to his fellow citizens; it was no longer a pilgrimage to Mecca that he needed to appease his remorse; his ambition demanded for his conscience the distractions of luxury, splendor and grandeur. By means of exactions he amassed large sums of money; by means of presents he was able to render himself favorable to the most influential members of the Divan, was appointed Khan of Schamachia, and passed from the modest honors of the judiciary to the turbulent honors of a military government, a mutation very common in Persia.

Abbas then assembled his forces to march to the conquest of the province of Kandahar and subjugate the Afghans,[41] who have since imposed their laws on his descendants. It was in the midst of battles that Bébut the ambitious was able to distinguish himself to that other ambitious man, an indefatigable conqueror, whose immense insatiability, fortune, with all its favors, could not slake.

The Khan of Schamachia showed such a great devotion and such blind obedience to his master that the latter, delighted to find a man such as all despots need, admitted him to his privy council; for, not knowing any will but his, only thinking as he did, having no opinion but his, was what constituted an excellent counselor in Abbas' eyes.

That monarch, the vanquisher of the Kurds, the Georgians, the Turks and the Afghans, returned in triumph to Ispahan, which he had made the capital of his estates, intending to enjoy the fruit of his vast conquests there, peacefully, in the midst of the brilliance of his glory. But does the heart of an ambitious man ever know repose? The greatness of the sovereign crushed the people; Abbas sensed that. Powerful but detested, he trembled in the depths of his palace.

In the usual vein of Oriental politics, introduced into Europe in recent times, he resolved to provide a diversion for

---

[41] Abbas seized Kandahar from the Mogul Emperor Jahangir in 1622.

those general hatreds, which, in accumulating toward a single point, were compromising the security of his throne. In that design, he established numerous colonies in his principal cities, drawn from the vanquished nations, which, by virtue of their privileges, excited the murmurs of the original inhabitants of the cities.

Two immense factions were soon organized under the names of the Polenks and the Falenks; Abbas took care to maintain their rivalry, to stimulate it and moderate it by turns in order to deflect their minds from the actions of his government. Bloody conflicts sometimes erupted; they were suppressed until the day of the Shah's birthday, when he finally permitted them to come to blows as a sign of rejoicing; and when, armed with sticks and stones, they had strewn the streets with the dead and the dying, the royal troops suddenly appeared and, proclaiming the end of the amusements, chased the Polenks and the Falenks home with saber thrusts.

Reassured with regard to his people, however, the great politician soon trembled before his court, and then his family. Of the three sons that he had, two had been deprived of sight on his orders, declared in consequence, according to Persian law, incapable of reigning, and confined to the castle of Alamut.[42] One alone remained to him; that was the noble and generous Safi Mirza, the love of his father and the hope of the people.[43] His brilliant qualities did not take long to become fatal to him.

Abbas was thinking anxiously one day about the value and the popular virtues of his son when the young prince appeared and threw himself at his feet, handing him a letter that he had just received. In the letter, without revealing their

---

[42] Author's note: "Which is to say, 'the Castle of Death.' It was situated in the Mazanderan (the ancient Hyrkania) and had been the residence of the Old Man of the Mountains, the prince of the Assassins. (X.)"

[43] This is anachronistic; Abbas ordered Safi Mirza killed in 1615, before taking Kandahar.

names, great men of the kingdom, only supporting a tyrannical and cruel government impatiently, proposed to put him on the throne and took responsibility for clearing the path to it for him. Safi Mirza, indignant at a project that tended to render him a parricide, declared everything to the Shah and put himself entirely at his disposal.

Abbas embraced him, heaped him with caresses and, sensed his affection for him increase further. From that day on, however, his anxieties increased; he fell into such great perplexity that he lost sleep. In order to attain the conspirators he caused a large number of innocent men to perish under torture, and at every execution, sensing that he was rendering himself even more odious, he feared that his son, solicited again, might not rediscover the same virtue.

That state of trouble and terror becoming insupportable to him, he finally resolved to free himself of it at any price. A slave received the order to kill the prince; he refused to obey and offered his head.

"Have I no one around me to eat my bread and salt, then, but ingrates and traitors?" Abbas cried. "I swear by my saber and by the Koran that the man who rids me of Safi Mirza will be heaped by my benefits."

The ambitious Bébut presented himself and said: "It is written that what the King wants is always good; your will is sacred for me; I will obey."

He went to find the prince immediately, and, having encountered him as he was emerging from the bath, accompanied by a single akhta, or valet, he drew his sword and presented the royal order to him.

"Safi Mirza," he said, "resign yourself; your father wants you to die."

"My father wants my death!" cried the unfortunate prince, dolorously. "What have I done, then, to merit his hatred? But let his will be done."

And Bébut laid him dead at his feet.

In order to pay him for his crime, Abbas sent him the royal jacket known as the calaste and immediately appointed him etimadoulet, or prime minister.

Paternal love soon reclaimed its rights, however; remorse had the same effect on Abbas as terror, and during his long nights, the bloody shade of his son came to dispute the slumber and repose to which he had sacrificed him. Clad in mourning dress, the master of the Persians drew away from the pleasures of the court and, for the rest of his life, did not distinguish himself in his adornment from the least of his subjects.

One day he summoned Bébut, and the latter found him standing on the steps of his throne, entirely clad in scarlet, his head circled by a red turban with a dozen pleats—in sum, in the costume that the kings of Persia put on when they are preparing to announce a death sentence. Bébut shivered on seeing that.

"It is written that what the King wants is always good," Abbas said to him. "Give proof of obedience today, then, as you did before. You have a son, Bébut; bring me his head!"

Bébut tried to speak...

"Bébut-Etimadoulet, Khan of Schamachia, is your ambition slaked then, for you to hesitate to satisfy me? Obey! Your life depends on it."

Bébut came back carrying the head of his only child in his hand.

"Well," Mirza's father said to him, with a frightful smile, "How do you like it?"

"Alas," replied the unfortunate Khan, "judge by my tears; I have given death by my own hand to the being that I cherished most on earth; be satisfied. On this day only I have cursed my fatal ambition, which had submitted me to such an obedience."

"Go," the monarch said to him; "now you can judge the dolor that the death of my son, massacred by you, has caused me. Ambition has made us the two men with the most to la-

153

ment in this empire; but console yourself, Bébut: in that respect you resemble your sovereign."[44]

---

[44] Author's note: "A king coldly ordering one of his subjects to cut off the head of his own child and being obeyed is such a monstrous thing that it might seem beyond all plausibility if numerous examples did not support it. In this fact, which we would regard as a horrible exception, Jonathan is only depicting the common mores of a court in which tyranny and all the crimes it engenders have stifled natural sentiments. I will cite as proofs a few examples taken from the reign of Safi I, the successor of the great Abbas and the son of the same Safi Mirza mentioned in this story.

Shah Safi, after having killed several members of his family with his own hands—for there was no official executioner in the Persian court in those days; the sovereign often carried out sentences himself or charged the first person he saw with the responsibility—resolved also to get rid of the three sons of Isa Khan, his uncle, and after the murder he had the three bloody heads served at the table of the father and mother. The latter was at first nonplussed by that horrible sight, but soon threw herself at Safi's feet, kissed them and said to him: 'All is well; may God give the King a long and glorious life.' Isa Khan added that, far from such a spectacle causing him displeasure, if he had been able to suspect that Safi desired the heads of his children he would have made it a duty to anticipate his orders and bring them to him personally.

Shortly thereafter, Shah Safi had the grandmaster of his guard put to death by one of the officer's intimate friends, who nevertheless accepted the commission. Having then sent for the victim's son, he asked him what he thought of his father's death. 'Let no one mention my father to me!' cried that monster. 'I only recognize my sovereign as a father. May he be blessed in all his actions!' Those people loved life so much!

Chardin and Tavernier are full of similar facts, which prove the extent to which the words 'crime' and 'virtue' change value and meaning from one reign to another, only

Abbas received from his people the nickname of the Great; Bébut the Ambitious as soon only known under the title of Bébut the Infamous.

It is said that the latter died not long afterwards, stabbed by the son of the unfortunate jeweler whom he had caused to perish so unjustly when he was divan-beghi. Thus, verifying the observation of the poet Firdaussi, his first sin, the mother of all the others, let him to the common punishment.

---

applying to actions in accordance with the character of the sovereign. The ambitious man, once on the road to shame and honors, was constrained to complete his entire course, like the initiates of the mysteries of Isis who could not retrace their steps. In those royal lairs where humanity was treated as the crime of *lèse-majesté* and pity as sedition, it often required twenty crimes to be absolved of one good deed. Thévenot reports that when a young akhta of Safi turned away in order not to see the head of a Persian lord hacked into little pieces, the Shah said to him: 'Since you have such delicate sight it must be useless to you,' and had his eyes plucked out. (X.)"

The references are to the Anglo-French voyager Jean Chardin (1643-1713), who published a ten-volume account of his travels in Persia and neighboring regions; Jean-Baptiste Tavernier (1605-1689), who published his *Six Voyages* at the behest of Louis XIV in 1676; and the scholar Melchisédech Thévenot (c.1620-1692), who published a collection of translations of voyages of discovery in 1663.

The Fisherman of Ormus

(Persia)

Two sorts of people are insatiable:
those who seek knowledge
and those who run after riches.
(*Mélanges de littérature orientale*, vol. II p. 290.)[45]

I have sought happiness in glory and in opulence;
they are precious stones that only shine brightly
at a distance, and which anything can tarnish.
(Nabi Efendi, to his son.)[46]

Bébut did not yet have any nickname but the Ambitious, and he was conversing one day with the king, who, in a fit of familiarity, had deigned to permit his prime minister to sit at his feet on a rich Siston carpet while, lying on a sofa, he was placidly finishing his siesta, respiring perfumed essences, chewing a Bactrian onion and smiling at his favorite's words.

Suddenly, Kel-Anayet, the great Abbas' jester, came into his apartment, bizarrely coiffed in a pointed delbend[47] and clad in a long blue robe. He went straight to the ambitious minister, bowed profoundly before him, his arms folded over his breast,

---

[45] *Mélanges de literature orientale* (1772) was a collection of translations by Denis Dominique Cardonne.

[46] Yusuf Nabi's advice to his son Aboul Khair, dating from the seventeenth century, was published in volume form in French in 1857, but had presumably been sampled in periodicals previously.

[47] Author's note: "The delbend is the Persian turban; some are so large and so wide that they weigh up to fifteen kilos."

and asked him humbly for permission to kiss the hem of his robe.

"Scatterbrain," Abbas said to him, "why address your homage to Bébut rather than your master?"

"I'm a fool by profession," replied Kel-Anayet, proudly, "and only recognize as my superior the man who can glorify himself with one degree of folly more than me."

"It's a little impertinent," said the King, laughing, "to attack my prime minister! But why this accoutrement? You're clad almost as a dervish."[48]

"Alas, Great King, so many people in your court are usurping my employment that I can foresee the moment when it will be necessary to cede my position to them, and I'm trying on the garb of a solitary in order to ease me gently toward retirement."

"No matter! By the spirit of the prophets, while awaiting your replacement, you're always welcome. But do you not have some tale to tell us? I'm in a humor to listen to you today."

Kel-Anayet made a slight sign of the head to testify his consent, and immediately went to perch himself impudently on one of the corners of the royal sofa.

Abbas launched a glance fill of anger at him. "Slave! By what right to you award yourself the place of honor before me?"

"Slave or king," replied the buffoon, "the storyteller is always above the listener."

Abbas shrugged his shoulders. "It's necessary to show our wisdom in pardoning his extravagances," he said. "He's ill disposed, which is a pity, for he sometimes has common sense. Today the poor fellow is running after his reason."

"Why not?" replied Kel-Anayet. "Only the man who seeks wisdom can be reckoned wise; the man who believes that he has found it is a fool."

---

[48] Author's note: "In Persia, dervishes wear blue robes."

"You see, Bébut, I have my turn; he respects nothing. But let him begin his story, or, by my eyes, he'll soon be as wise as his ancestors."

Kel-Anayet commenced.

One day, Dalle-Mutaleha, the celebrated witch, her forehead crowned with carbuncles, launched forth from the mountains of Kaff, carried by the bird Simurgh, as rapid as the wind. She was heading toward Bagdad when she encountered the angel Tir-Aban over the isles of Ormus, mounted on Borak, the prophet's celestial charger.[49]

"Where are you going?" the witch asked the genius of the sciences.

"I'm going to console a scholar in his poverty," the other replied.

"I'm going to help a rich man who's succumbing to ennui in his ignorance. Which of the two is more to be pitied?"

"The rich man, undoubtedly."

"Perhaps; opulence has its consolations."

"The pleasures of the imagination are keener."

"Wealth is surrounded by honors and cheerful pleasures; a population of courtiers escorts it; it is for wealth that praise was invented, and praise is a sweet beverage."

"Which leads subsequently to satiety and disgust. The mortal I inspire is happy, even in his dreams; he possesses

---

[49] Author's note: "Dalle-Mutaleha is the Circe of the Orientals. The Persian poets report that the carbuncle, the imaginary gemstone nicknamed 'the torch of the night' because of the luminous glow they attribute to it, is formed in the head of a griffin or an immense eagle, doubtless the one that Saadi calls Simurgh and lives in the mountains of Kaff. Tir is the angel of the sciences, Aban that of the arts; we do not know why Jonathan combines them here in a single individual. On the third night after Mohammed's death the angel Gabriel brought him a winged horse named Borak, which he mounted in order to be transported to the heavens. (X.)"

everything of which he dreams; he lives incessantly surrounded by a fantastic world that he changes and destroys at whim; and when his mind is weary of engendering, he calls his precious books to his aid; and what gathering, even of sage and amiable men, can match those precious manuscripts, which enclose the purest intelligence of the noblest individuals of all time. Would he be happier if those who had composed them emerged from the earth to keep him company? I don't think so; few good authors are worth as much as their works."

"I could say a great deal about wealth, about the real advantages it procures, and show only the good side of things as well as you, but long arguments bore me and experiment is the surest way of arriving at the truth. Let us leave your scholar in his poverty and my rich man in his ignorance for a while, the former being easily able to support it be dreaming of opulence and the latter being habituated to it, and attempt a double proof on an individual for whom I will fray a path to fortune and you one to knowledge, on condition of then leaving him to his own devices, in order to make our observations in accordance with the ordinary progress of human life."

"I accept willingly," said Tir-Aban, "And I know just the person in Ormus that we need in order to put your plan into execution. He's a wretched fisherman named Ismael, poor and ignorant, but so weary of his fate that we'll only have to guide him a little to see him launch forth ardently on the double route that we'll open before him."

Ismael was then on the shore of the Persian Gulf, mending his nets.

"What!" he cried, dolorously. "Shall I spend my life in this frightful condition, only nourishing myself on watermelons, pilau and poorly-cooked beans, only having a wretched courdi of coarse cloth for a garment, which leaves my skin imprinted with its rude and harsh fibers, and only finding repose by lying on the ground or a mat—which I would bless, if the Euphrates had furnished its material, but no, knotty maize straw forms its tissue, and only effaces the imprint of my courdi with deeper and more painful furrows? And in order to enjoy those sad advantages it's necessary, at the peril of my life, to launch my terrada into the bosom of the sea, in order to catch the sturgeon and the destpich,[50] with such delicate flesh, with which I have been furnishing the tables of the rich for five years without ever tasting it myself. I don't know what the great quill has inscribed for me on high, but I'm unhappy, the gulf is deep and I might as well throw the fish one last bait that they aren't expecting."

It was at that moment that Mutaleha and her companion appeared before him.

"Ismael, said the witch to the fisherman, "your plaints have reached us. Would you like to become rich and powerful at a stroke? The opportunity is offered to you. The son of old Noserat, well-known for his opulence, has just died suddenly in his bed, and that fact is known to me alone. Your features and your voice offer such a conformity with his that it's impossible for anyone not to mistake you for him. Come with me; I'll give you the necessary instructions, remove the body and transport it far way, while you take his place."

Ismael nearly died himself from excitement and joy; he climbed up behind her on the bird Simurgh, and was soon introduced into the apartment of the dead man. One final instruction remained to be given to him: Noserat's son as afflicted by a slight blink of the eye, which it was easy, but important, to counterfeit, in order not to awaken suspicion. Ismael promised to be careful, and when his protectress had gone, after having promised to visit him secretly from time to time, he spent the night blinking in order to acquire the habit, and memorizing the advice of Mutaleha.

In the morning, slaves having presented themselves to help him dress, he allowed them to do it, blinking, and everything went well. He was covered with a superb zerbafe robe,

---

[50] The destpich, a kind of carp, is referenced in *The Travels of Marco Polo*, where Saintine presumably found it, but hardly anywhere else.

surmounted by a courdi of golden velvet; a belt of Termay wool embroidered with pearls further heightened his adornment, and his head was charged with a magnificent delbend ornamented with turquoises and rubies.

Poor Ismael no longer recognize himself; at every moment he was ready to dissolve in apologies to his slaves, borne almost to respect himself, and blinked his eyes more furiously than ever, to such an extent that the master of his wardrobe asked him whether he was indisposed. At that word, he shivered throughout his body, and was only reassured when he perceived the supervisor of his offices, who came to take his orders for his first meal. He ordered that he be served sturgeon and destpich, hoping perhaps to see again a part of his previous day's catch and finally to know other than by sight his old adversaries of the gulf.

Soon they were set before him, escorted by a multitude of delicious fruits, such as dates from Persepolis, pomegranates from Yezd, oranges from Hyrkania, quinces, and plums from Caramania, mingled with fine pâtés, dried and liquid preserves, slices of lemon, and powdered aromatic herbs to stimulate the appetite. Ismael could not conceive that anyone might need to have recourse to such means; he ate everything, gave himself an indigestion—the first of his life—and considered himself the happiest of men.

His predecessor's harem then received his visit. The young beauties of Georgia and Circassia made such an impression on him that, in his ecstasy, he forgot his fatal eyeblink; the congratulations he received on that subject chilled him with fear, and the dread of falling into a similar distraction preoccupied his mind so forcefully that he paid much more attention to it than the tender caresses of which he showed himself the insensible object.

Old Noserat saw the replacement for his son and suspected nothing. A fortnight went by for Ismael in the midst of the keenest enjoyments of luxury and opulence—during which, however, his borrowed infirmity put him to rude proofs. After that time the old man set forth on a journey in

161

order to visit the court, and left his pretended son the absolute master in his palace. It was then that the latter astonished the entire kingdom of Ormus by the sumptuousness of his carriages and the magnificence of his feasts.

In drawing rooms resplendent with gold, jasper and porphyry, the walls of which, clad in the transparent marble of Tauris, were encrusted internally with enameled squares and hung with rich curtains of silk and velvet embroidered with silver, and the most beautiful fabrics of Kerman, he summoned a host of traveling players, covered in tinsel and brocade, young, lively, nimble and charming dancing girls whose long tresses terminated in bouquets of precious stones, and who performed the most various diversions, by turns noble and burlesque, severe or voluptuous, before him and a few friends.

Then, everything that the mild climate of Persia produces of the most delicate fruits, fish and game was served, in golden vessels. The sideboard, which rose up in a pyramid, was crowned by a large quantity of bottles in Venetian crystal with diamond points, in which the vivid colors shone on wines of Shiraz and Georgia. Scented candles reflecting numerous gleams from their prismatic facets also threw off crimson sparks, while their perfumes of cinnamon and cloves were confused with the delightful perfumes escaping from the vermilion cassolettes suspended from the ceiling.

Then a troop of musicians...

"Spare us your descriptions," said Abbas, interrupting Kel-Anayet. "We know all that even better than you do. All you're doing at present is describing the last feast I gave."

"Why shouldn't I?" replied the storyteller. "Memory is the support of genius. While I speak under the influence of memory, the inventive spirit is in repose, and the chargers of narration are gathering new strength, in order to draw the chariot of the imagination with more rapidity than ever."

"Finish the story of your fisherman. I won't interrupt again; I prefer your descriptions to your explanation."

And Kel-Anayet continued.

Then a troop of musicians, carrying oboes, flutes and tambouras entered the banqueting hall, making the air reverberate with the sweetest chords. Ismael had golden cups of inestimable workmanship distributed to the guests, and after they had all intoxicated themselves with bhang and afioun,[51] he gave everyone a present, and the feast concluded with a general mascaré.[52]

Everyone was greatly diverted by Ismael's feast, but he had taken very little part in it, occupied as he was in activating or moderating the convulsive movements of his eyelids. Dalle-Mutaleha came to visit him during the night; he still made no complaint about his fate, but he found it awkward to be subjected to the inconvenient condition of blinking. She advised him to be patient, and promised to come back to see him soon.

The days went by and often found him in the same pleasures and the same annoyances. Old Noserat, on returning from his voyage, came to surprise him one morning in the middle of a great fishing expedition that he was undertaking on Lake Toranka. He seemed astonished by his son's skill in that exercise, and reproached him mildly for having given so

---

[51] Author's note: "The liquor named bhang, poueng or poust is, according to Chardin (vol. IV, p. 207) an infusion of poppy seeds, hemp-seeds and nux vomica. According to others it is a juice extracted from henbane mixed with opium. In any case, the abuse of that dangerous liquor, which Jonathan has already mentioned in his tale of Tam-Garai, causes dementia and leads to the most disastrous results. The Indians make use of it against criminal statesmen and pretenders to the crown, and, too humane to take away their lives, as the Turks, do or depriving them of sight in accordance with the Persian custom, they prefer to rob them of the use of reason, which is sufficient to have them declared unfit to reign. Afioun is the true name of liquid opium. (X.)"

[52] Author's note: "From which we get the word masquerade."

much care to an art that could not do him any honor. Ismael defended his former métier with such ardor that, while he was carried away, his eyes remained fixed and immobile; he thought he could see a thousand swords immediately turned toward him in order to punish him for his usurpation, and he was gripped by such fear that he turned crimson, stammered and fell silent.

Noserat mistook his anxiety and silence for submission, and took advantage of it, as a good father, to make him sense that it was more honorable to surround himself with sages and scholars and to deliver himself to the noble occupations of study than continually to seek the society of young debauchees, strolling players and dancers, acquiring no other sciences than those of the table or angling.

Our fisherman listened to the old man attentively and promised to take advantage of his advice. He found a double advantage in that. Science is a plant easily cultivated in solitude; there, he no longer had any fear of the gazes of the slaves who surrounded him incessantly, and whom he believed to be as many spies charged with inspecting the movement of his eyes. Furthermore, he could, without compromising his safety, frequent scholars who were incessantly plunged in their meditations, and astrologers whose sight was always turned toward the sky or fixed on a takium.[53]

That idea almost rendered him repose; he put it into execution, and soon, Ismael, who had sighed so deeply after the good things of the word, was only dreaming any longer of the riches of the mind, the treasures of science.

On retiring one evening to his apartments, he opened a manuscript at random and fell upon these words:

As many rungs of the ladder of fortune that you climb, it will be necessary to descend. The ladder of science has its

---

[53] Author's note: "A Persian almanack." A section of John Pinkerton's 1811 collection of voyages derived from Chardin calls a Persian almanack a *takumi*. Otherwise, like many of Saintine's exotic terms, it seems to be idiosyncratic.

support in the heavens, and time, which makes the palaces of opulence collapse upon their possessors, only adds to the glory of the scholar.

"That's advice that comes to me from the prophet!" Ismael exclaimed. "What do fragile goods matter to me: shiny vases that break in our hands, perfumes that evaporate, wines that intoxicate and succulent dishes that give indigestions? I've proved that too abundantly. The life of the rich is a continual drunkenness; the pleasure passes, the headache remains. And always trembling! Always blinking! No, that's not living. But slaking one's thirst on the water of science, hearing one's name repeated from mouth to mouth, casting durable and venerated works to the admiration of posterity, yes, that's happiness. Mostrazem dared to insult the scholar Coja-Nessir, and the insensate caliph was toppled from the throne of Bagdad. Sage Alfarabi, fecund Avicenna, Saadi, the nightingale of Iran, Cheket, the eagle of genius, gracious Hafiz, sublime Attar, oh, for the name of Ismael to pass like yours, luminously, to posterity, I would give half my life!"

"I accept the bargain," said Tir-Aban immediately, who entered, followed by Mutaleha.

Ismael was stupefied.

"What!" added the Egyptian. "My benefits are not sufficient for you?"

"Alas! That fatal condition, that insupportable hindrance..."

"Well, unfortunate man, can someone who wants to emerge from the condition in which destiny has placed him, in order to arrive at fortune and honors, get there without enduring crueler constraints and longer ennuis than yours? What you have experienced, many others have experienced before you; the slightest hindrance spoils the most perfect happiness; a pearl that goes astray in the adornment of a woman makes her forget the splendor of the diamonds with which she is laden. I confide you today to the cares of my companion, the only one capable of granting your new desires; I shall take away, from this moment, your importunate riches; the body of

165

Noserat's son, conserved by me, will resume its place, and the mourning of the household will only have been postponed by a few months."

"It's a matter of making a scholar of you," said Tir-Aban then.

"Of me!" Ismael repeated, in confusion. "Of me, previously a miserable fisherman? I can conceive that poor man might suddenly become a rich one, but an ignorant man..."

"The brute stone of Badakam becomes rubies when the sun's rays have purified it," the angel replied. "Come with me; science does not reside under gilded paneling; it's time to choose another shelter."

Ismael climbed on to Borak with him, and soon, Noserat's palace, the Persian Gulf and the kingdom of Ormus disappeared from sight.

Transported with the rapidity of an eagle into Irak Adjemy, Ismael found near the city of Tehran, on the edge of a stream, a small habitation, simple but comfortable, devoid of luxury but not without elegance.

"It belongs to you," Tir-Aban told him. You will find there by way of furniture, the most precious: books, and the instruments of mathematics and astronomy. Incense and myrrh will not burn for you in golden cassolettes, but turpentine and elcaya trees will lend you their shade and their sweet perfumes. Now, receive from me the gift of tongues; they are the avenues of the temple of science. But above all, if you want to enlighten reason, learn to doubt. Doubt is the door to knowledge; the man who doubts nothing, examines nothing; the man who examines nothing, discovers nothing; the man who discovers nothing might be a good student, but never a true scholar."

The angel touched him with his hand then, reminded him that it was at the expense of half his life that his name would be immortal, and launched himself forth on his celestial charger.

In a few years, Ismael rendered himself famous for his vast knowledge; the most famous doctors in Persia confessed themselves vanquished by him. His works on medicine, astronomy, theology, mathematics, natural history, poetry, etc., multiplied with such great rapidity, and were welcomed with such fervor, that the people did not take long to believe him the possessor of the seventy-two sciences necessary to be proclaimed Mouktehed,[54] and that fine title was conferred upon him, with the addition of the nickname of "the third master," Aristotle and Al-Farabi having long been considered as the first two.

The scientific prodigy of Irak no longer doubled his future immortality and enjoyed it in advance with delight. Princes sought him out and repeated his words as those of imams or prophets are repeated; the people threw themselves in his passage everywhere in order to obtain a glance from him, or touch the hem of his robe, and the greatest scholars of Asia traversed the seas in order to come and consult him.

In the midst of this universal praise, however, envy lay in wait, on the lookout for an opportunity to come to light. It soon arrived. Prolonged admiration is a burden for the multitude; its members welcomed with avidity the most contradictory rumors that circulated with regard to the leaned Ismael. He was accused of not being the sole author of his works, of having found them in old unknown manuscripts. Several questions smacked of heresy; he believed in the eternity of matter and was accused of atheism, even though each of his books commenced with a homage to God and his prophet.

That injustice revolted the scholar; it sickened his heart; in the chagrin that the bitter criticisms of which he was the object caused him, he would have liked to be able to extinguish the bright light that he had propagated among the ingrate

---

[54] Author's note: "The great scholars of Persia are named Mouktehed; the word designates a man who possesses all the sciences in perfection. The people alone are the dispensers of that noble recompense, which is ordinarily only granted two or three times in the space of a century. (X.)"

people. Almost discouraged, he retired to the edge of his stream, and let posterity the care of avenging his insult.

A young woman from Tehran, who had never read his works, but who was sufficiently generous not to speak any evil of him, pleased our philosopher, who married her. He had children by her, and his happiness increased with his family. In retreat, living without noise or ostentation, he only delivered himself to study in order to ornament his soul and charm his leisure.

His children grew up; he became their guide in the sciences; simultaneously cultivating his books and his garden, turning knowledge to the profit of virtue, he was astonished to feel happier than at the feasts in Ormus, at the courts of kings, or in the midst of popular praise.

One day, he was suddenly gripped by a sort of weakness. His wife and his children ran to him in alarm, with the exception of his eldest son, who was then in the city. They were surrounding him with the most tender cares when Ismael perceived that the terrace of his house was spontaneously illuminated, and that passers-by outside were murmuring prays for the dying.[55]

At the same time, Tir-Aban and Mutaleha appeared. The latter was holding a flower of the gulbad samour,[56] a fatal

---

[55] Author's note: "When a Persian reaches the final moments of life, torches are placed on the exterior terrace of his dwelling, in order to alert passers-by to pray for him."

[56] Author's note: "*Gulbad-samour* means 'flower that poisons the wind'; the Arabs call it *churk* and Thomas Moore, in his poem *Lalla Rookh*, designates it by the name of *Kerzereth*." Moore—a favorite English author of the French Romantics, who published *Lalla Rookh* in 1817—probably found the reference in Isaac d'Israeli's *Romances* (1799), where it is called *gulbad samour*, although that term and its definition are ultimately derived from Charles Owen's *A Essay Toward a Natural History of Serpents* (1742).

plant that has the property of rendering the breeze that passes over it poisonous.

"Ismael," said the witch, "You have made the sacrifice of half your life to glory; your immortality is commencing, and your final hour in this world has arrived."

Then, at the four corners of Ismael's bed, four funereal guests showed themselves; they were Monkir, Nekir, Mordad and Esrail, the angels of death.

"Divine prophet!" cried the philosopher. "To die! To die, when existence was so sweet! My wife, my children, it is necessary, then, to bid you my final adieux. Alas! May the renown of my name console you for my loss."

As Mutaleha presented him with the gulbad samour he cried: "Stop! One of my children is absent; may I not see him before dying? Tomorrow..."

"Any delay is impossible," Tir-Aban said to him, "unless you renounce the future honors of posterity. Even then, you could only prolong your life by three days."

"Three days!" sad the dying man. "And to sacrifice the great name that ought to survive me! Only three days! To put in the balance three days and centuries of glory! But I want to see my son again. Cruel genius of science, you have deceived me, like that of fortune. Take back your gifts; let me die unknown, but let three days still remain to me to spend in the bosom of my family, and press my absent son to my heart."

"The nobility of your sentiment disarms our rigor," said Tir-Aban. "Ismael, pursue your career tranquilly in the bosom of study and nature; you sacrificed fortune to a slight inconvenience; you are sacrificing glory for three days of existence; live now for our family and for happiness, and no longer think about obtaining in future ages a triumph that is illusory, since its conqueror is the only one who cannot witness it."

"Well," said the Egyptian, "which of the two of us has been defeated in the proof?"

"Both and neither," replied Tir-Aban. "Science and fortune are good for the man who is able to make noble use of them, but excess spoils everything; the base passions of a man cast themselves into the midst of prosperities to poison them. He only sees opulence as the means of satisfying his caprices and is avidity or enjoyment, and not of giving impetus to his generous penchants; he only sees in science a trestle for vanity. The example of the fisherman of Ormus ought to inform us that what is above wealth and glory..."

"Is repose," said Mutaleha.

"And virtue," said the angel.

At that point, Kel-Anayet, a veritable sage beneath the envelope of a fool, concluded his story. Abbas, who had been half-asleep for some time, woke up with a start on ceasing to hear his speech, like a miller when his mill suddenly stops.

"Well, fellow," he said, "it seems to me that your tale has a suffocating moral."

"He's forgetting his métier," added Bébut.

"No," retorted our pretended buffoon. "Are not casting good seed on ingrate earth, giving good advice to the deaf, and lessons in wisdom to the ambitious the actions of a fool?"

Bébut quivered with anger, and looked at Abbas, who, in order to avoid punishing the moralist, pretended to fall asleep again.

The Metaphysician

(France)

Remember, my son, that nature is covered by a bronze veil; that the combined efforts of all men and all the centuries have been unable to lift the corner of that envelope, that the science of philosophy consists of discerning the point at which mysteries commence, and wisdom in respecting them.

(Barthélemy, *Voyage du jeune Anacharsis*.)[57]

Callimachus, in Plato, says that the extremity of philosophy can be harmful, and advises not delving into it beyond the limits of profit.

(Montaigne, *Essays*, Book I, ch. xxxix.)

Toward the end of the century of Louis XIV, power, in its actions, seemed then only to be supported by religion, so theology and metaphysics soon became inexhaustible arsenals in which everyone sought weapons in order to attack it or defend it. The law of the Church having become that of the State, a large number of people, who had previously professed their religion without thinking of delving into it, had become skeptics in the matter of religion for political reasons, because proving the errors of Catholic priests was, according to them, to attack the actions of authority at their foundations and convict them of injustice and tyranny.

---

[57] Jean-Jacques Barthélemy's didactic romance *Voyage du jeune Anarcharsis en Grèce* was published in 1787 in four volumes; he had been working on it for thirty years.

But if the divine dogmas reveals by the words of Socrates, sustained by the pen of Plato and cemented by the blood of Jesus Christ, altered, stifled and deflected from their veritable meaning by the likes of Le Tellier and La Chaise,[58] served as texts for error and persecution, the adversaries of the Jesuits were scarcely able any more than they were to forbid themselves culpable excess, and religious intolerance only served to propagate atheism.

I was living in Paris then; the summer was pursuing its course; the sun, in the middle of its career, was projecting luminous radiance over the waves of the river, the tops of the trees and the domes of the palaces, giving them a vivifying brightness by which my sight was intoxicated. Alone and delivered to my meditations in a rich avenue in the Champs-Élysées, I was thinking about the power of the creator, and the countless reasons humans had for glorifying him, when I suddenly found myself accosted by one of my friends, a metaphysician.

All of his movements seemed to be impelled by a satisfaction that he could not conceal; his eyes were sparkling with joy, and as soon as I had turned to look at him, striking up a conversation like a man who, possessed by the impatience of passing on good news, has no time to waste in vain civilities, he said: "My friend, I've just been occupied in some very interesting work on the soul, and I can now prove that what is so called is nothing, in sum, but a word devoid of meaning. In sum, neither you nor I has ever had a soul."

"One moment," I said to him, recoiling three paces. "A word devoid of meaning is the one that you have just proffered; permit yourself to reduce yourself to the rank of the beasts; permit me to refuse such an honor!"

---

[58] The references are to the theologian Charles Maurice Le Tellier (1642-1710) and Louis XIV's Jesuit confessor, François de La Chaise (1624-1709), nowadays remembered for having given his name to Père Lachaise cemetery.

"Calm down," he said to me. "I knew in advance that you wouldn't yield without proofs, but, God be praised, I can furnish them. Let's reason coldly; I intend to combat the ideal existence of the soul not by means of vain declarations, all too common today, but by victorious arguments, drawn from the perpetual contradictions of the philosophers, and even saints, who have addressed the subject. Now, as Quintillian said, when men of sound mind, recognized as such, after entire centuries of impartial discussion, cannot agree on a cause and an effect, one must boldly deny the existence of both. It is thus that the thousand versions of ghosts, manes and phantoms have finally provoked the negation of sages, which negation is the only truth.

"I depart, therefore, from that principle, and hasten to pose my first question: what is the soul? 'A nature always in movement,' replies Thales; 'A number that moves of its own accord,' says Pythagoras; 'A subtle air,' replies Plutarch; 'It's rather an active fire,' adds Aristotle. 'You're mistaken,' retorts Hipponius, 'it's a very light water'; 'You mean a composite of earth and water,' says Anaximander. 'Silence! you're all right,' cries Empedocles; 'it's a mixture of all the elements.' With that, a thousand voices rise up together. 'It's a simple entity': Democritus; 'No, it's compound': Aristotle; 'It's a celestial fire': Zeno; 'It's a harmony': Aristoxenes; 'A mass of subtle and disconnected atoms'; Lucretius; 'A parcel of the divinity': Plato; 'A combat of the senses': Asclepiades.

"But where, at least, is its seat? Hippocrates places it in the ventricle of the brain; Epictetus in the stomach; Erasistratus makes it serve as an envelope for the head; while Strato contents himself with placing it in the eyebrows. 'It is in the blood,' say both Critias and Moses; 'yes, in the heart,' adds Empedocles; 'say rather in the diaphragm,' retorts Plutarch vehemently; 'get away, it's in the pineal gland,' replies Descartes.[59]

---

[59] At this point in the story later versions add the additional sentence: "'In the navel,' intone in chorus the venerable

173

"Must the soul come to an end, as Lucretius thinks? The Jews, who believe in God, don't believe in the immortality of the soul; the Chiriguans and the peoples of the Marianas islands, on the contrary, believe in the immortality of the soul but not in the existence of God.

Siméon, abbot of Xérocerque and the monks of Mount Athos, great partisans of the Omphalopsychites." A long footnote is appended by the author to that sentence: "It was toward the end of the fourteenth century that the sect of Omphalopsychites emerged. Those interested in the history of human follies will perhaps be curious to find here the method taught by Siméon, abbot of Xérocerque to those desirous of arriving at the state of quietude that the contemplation of the soul via the navel procures. This is the passage, faithfully translated: 'Being along in you cell, close the door and sit down in a corner. Raise your spirit above all vain and transitory things; then, extend your beard over your breast; turn your eyes, with all your thought, to the middle of your belly, which is to say, to the navel. Retain all your respiration, even through the nose; seek in the entrails for the place of the heart, where all the powers of the heart ordinarily reside. At first you will find the darkness thick and difficult to dissipate, but if you persevere, continuing that practice night and day, you will find—marvelous surprise!—an ineffable and uninterrupted joy; for, as soon as the mind has found the place of the heart, it knows what it has never known, it sees what it has never seen, and perceives itself luminous and full of discernment.' Thus the abbot of Xérocerque, with his beard on the breast and his eyes on the navel, saw himself luminous and full of discernment!"

This account of Simeon of Xérocerque and his advice originates from Claude Fleury's *Histoire ecclésiastique* (1721), but is copied in numerous later texts. The Quietist sect of Omphalsychites, otherwise known as Hesychasts, had, however, previously been mentioned in Louis Maimbourg's *Histoire du schisme des grecs* (1682).

"Is it material, as Tertullian, Averroes, Calderia, Poliziano, Pomponazzi, Bembo, Cardan, Cesalpino, Taurelli, Viviani, Hobbes, etc. sustain? Or immaterial, as the greater number of the fathers of the Church, Malebranche and all the Cartesians believe? Saint Jerome, Saint Augustine and Saint Gregory, taken for judges in the trial, declared themselves incompetent, and, in imitation of the areopagus, sent the parties away for a hundred years.

"Less timid than them, I do not seek to discover, like the ancients whether it is necessary to distinguish the soul from the mind, *anima* and *mens*; but, after so many evident contradictions and such prolonged doubts, I invoke the principle of Quintillian, I apply my negation, and declare loudly that the soul is a dream of our worthy ancestors, which it is necessary to relegate along with the philosopher's stone and stories of revenants. I hope that that will be the wherewithal to put the Jesuits in accord with the Calvinists!"

While he was speaking thus we had drawn away from the green pathways under which my metaphysician had found me meditating, and the Seine was now flowing at our feet in an uncovered space exposed to all the ardors of the sun.

"My friend," I said to the great exterminator of souls, gripping him firmly by the arm and constraining him to remain motionless before me in order to preserve me from the excessively immediate influences of the star; "I approve strongly of your manner of reasoning; in striking thus with annihilation every contested subject, you are smoothing out so many difficulties that you have almost convinced me, and you and Quintillian are great men."

"I don't deny it," he replied, "but permit me to take a slightly more comfortable position in order to receive your compliments; on my soul, I'm overwhelmed by the sun."

"What, the sun? You the enemy of prejudices, dare not liberate yourself from that one? You believe in the sun?"

"The sun a prejudice! I'm obliged to believe in it, damn it, since it's burning me!"

"Let's reason coldly," I said to him, fixing him with even more firmness in his present position. "I had believed until now in that admirable harmony of nature, the grandeur of man, the power of his thought, the marvel of creation delivered entirely to his industry, his superior reason imposed as a brake on his impetuous passions, indicting sufficiently the distance that separates him from other animals. Now that, by means of the law of contradictions, you have demonstrated to me that his thought is only material and that his existence is devoid of purpose, permit me in my turn, by means of the same arguments, to cure you of your errors regarding the sun.

"What is the sun? Is it a blazing cloud, a flamboyant rock, a fire that is extinguished and reignited, a mirror, a fifth element, a composite of several different fires, an intelligent flame, a globe that sends us rays of light, or which receives them, as was sustained in turn by Xenophanes, Metrodorus, Democritus, Philolaus, Aristotle, Plato, Antisthenes, Newton and Pythagoras? Heraclitus gives it a diameter of one foot, Anaxagoras the extent of the Peloponnese, while Eudoxus thinks it nine times and Thales sixty times larger than the moon, Lucretius supposes it to have the volume that it appears visibly to have, Anaximander reduces its circumference to that of a leaf, while Cassini proclaims it to be a thousand times larger than the earth."

"All right, all right! But it's burning me!"

"It can't burn you if it doesn't exist, and I have the wherewithal to convince you of that sophistically, so I shall conclude. Xenophanes wants every zone to have its own particular sun; Empedocles admits two of them, as Saint Thomas admits two souls—which you omitted to say, and which renders your argument even more irresistible—and finally, other physicists only recognize one. Thus, everywhere there is contradiction upon contradiction; I therefore invoke Quintilian's principle and yours, I apply my negation, and declare loudly that the sun is a dream of our worthy ancestors."

"Believe what you like," cried my metaphysician, disengaging himself from his burning position, "but your negation has damaged all the membranes of my brain."

"Go home and rest," I said to him, "And, metaphysician as you are, try to comprehend that the immortal soul is for the mental world what the sun is for the physical world: as a man, and king of creation, don't place your pride in trampling your crown underfoot and denying your immortality."

The Hermit of Lake Maggiore
(Italy)

How great virtue has to be, in order
to be able to shelter from events!
(Nicole, *Essais de morale*.)[60]

*O quantum calignis mentibus humanis
oblicit magna felicitas!*[61]
(Seneca)

Galeas III, of the illustrious Visconti family, after brilliant services rendered to the Emperor Wenceslas, was created
Duke of Milan.[62] Having returned victorious to his estates, he
relaxed from the fatigues of war in the midst of the pleasures
of a sumptuous court. Dances, concerts and carousels succeeded one another around him without interruption. One day,
he ordered a nautical feast on Lake Maggiore, and, followed
by a large number of richly-decked gondolas, containing the
most beautiful woman and the foremost Milanese lords, escorted by a host of boats charge with musicians, who made the
air resound with the sweetest chords, he gave his oarsmen the
order to head for an island, an uncultivated rock rising above
the lake, which has since, under the pleasant name of Isola
Bella, merited taking the first rank among the Borromean islands.

---

[60] The fourteen volumes of *Essais de morale*, by the Jansenist
Pierre Nicole, were published between 1671 and 1679.
[61] "Oh, what blindness great prosperity casts upon our minds!"
[62] The reference is to Gian Galeazzo Visconti (1351-1402)

The prince and his retinue, having disembarked on a gray-tinted terrain composed of schist and calcareous substances, were parading their saddened gazes over that solitude, of which all vegetation seemed to be limited to a few mosses and lichens scattered here and there, when they perceived, in a hollow, a grotto carved in a block of granite and covered with brambles and ivy. Gnarled and stunted chestnut-trees masked it on one side; on the other, an active and stubborn industry had deflected the waves of the lake in order to maintain a small field of rice.

"That can only be he dwelling of an outlaw or a hermit," said Galeas, and being, in spite of his brilliant qualities, vindictive and devoted, like all his family, he immediately presented himself, ready to punish or to pray.

A holy man, Anselme Giramo, had been the sole inhabitant of that desert for several years. The sight of the prince and his retinue astonished him without disconcerting him. Soon perceiving the ladies of the court, however, he blushed and lowered his eyes. A gesture from Galeas caused them all to move away, and the hermit recovered his modest assurance.

The prince talked to him for a long time, and was surprised by the accuracy of his responses and the variety of his knowledge.

"Why," he asked, "have you exiled yourself from the society to which you might be useful?"

"I have found happiness on this rock," Anselme replied, "and the fishermen of Lake Maggiore sometimes have recourse to my prayers or my advice."

"But how do you provide for your substance?"

"The produce of my fishing, the harvest of my rice-field, the fruits of my chestnut-trees, and even my brambles, suffice for my nourishment."

"But ennui must assail you in this place?"

"The man who has a pure heart and who can contemplate the waves and the sky has no fear of ennui. All the kinds of labor that I undertake here are pleasures for me, for they add to my wellbeing. Reverie and prayer seem to be sources of continual enjoyment; I am happy; what would I request of society?"

The ambitious Galeas quit him, astonished by the simplicity of his desires, and full of an elevated idea of his virtues. The good opinion that he had of Anselme was further increased by the various stories that the gondoliers and fishermen of the lake, interrogated by him, told of the sanctity and charity of the poor hermit. His intercession on their behalf with the saints never failed to procure them abundant catches or numerous passengers. His blessing was sufficient to drive away maladies and culpable thoughts.

The duke did not take long to visit him again, and this time, he appeared before the grotto alone. Anselme took advantage of the duke's good dispositions to make him hear the plaints of the people, which had reached as far as his desert. He reproached him mildly for his ever-increasing ambition, his prodigality toward his favorites, the excessive taxes with which his people were overburdened, and the blind confidence that he accorded to false sages whose astrological calculations served to rule his conduct.

The truth spoken in a soft voice and without witnesses is always better welcomed than the arrogant verity that slaps you in the face in the midst of the homages of the multitude. The duke was grateful to the hermit for having thought him worthy of understanding it.

"I sense that your advice might be useful to my glory and my subjects," he told him. "Until now, only our clowns and fools have had the right to make the truth heard in courts; may it make use henceforth of a nobler and more sacred organ."

At first, Anselme rebelled forcefully against the idea of living in a palace, but Galeas requested his assistance with so much unction, and it is so pleasant to exact a great man from his errors and to work for the happiness of a entire people, that in the end, weeping, he bade adieu to his grotto, his chestnut-trees and his rice-field, and left for Milan with the Duke.

In accordance with the remonstrations of the wise hermit, the prince distanced from his person the crowd of false astrol-

ogers, strolling players, buffoons and those grotesque and deformed dwarfs so common then among the Milanese, a deceitful and parasitic troop that was regarded at that time as an object of luxury in the sovereign courts of Italy.

Every day, Galeas visited Anselme in the modest apartment that he had chosen; he confided his hopes and projects to
him joyfully, submitted his entire future to the rigorous cen-
sure of the holy man, and quit him proud and content with
himself. Meanwhile, the severe frankness of the hermit did not
spare any of his defects.

It was then that a formidable league was formed against
the Milanese by the republics of Venice and Florence, which
only the genius and skill of Galeas could succeed in suppress-
ing. The Duke only departed to fight his enemies after having
received the blessings of Anselme, and ordered that everyone
in the palace should respect the will of is favorite sage.

In a matter of months he surprised Perugia, took possession of Pisa, Sienna and Bologna, concluded the ten-year truce
that consolidated his vast power forever,[63] and returned to his
capital, where he was welcomed by the felicitations of the
nobility, his people, and even Anselme Giramo, who, placed
in his passage, addressed to him a superb speech in Latin, of
which the text was taken from the words of Saint Luke: *Cum
redisset Jesus, excepit illum turba; erant enim omnes
expectantes eum.*[64]

The prince received Anselme's eulogies with even more
astonishment than pleasure, but nevertheless applauded himself for having merited the relaxation of his ordinary rigidity.
The next day, he was about to resume his former habits and go
to render his customary visit to the hermit, when the latter

---

[63] In fact, after successfully attacking those cities in 1402,
Galeazzo contracted a fever and died; his empire fell apart as
his would-be successors came into violent conflict.

[64] *Luke* 8:40; the A.V. has "And it came to pass, that, when
Jesus was returned, he people gladly received him; for they
were all waiting for him."

suddenly appeared in the hall where the duke was sitting, cleaved through the crowd of courtiers and bowed down before Galeas, crying with Jeremiah: *Constitui te super gentes et super regna, ut evellas, et destruas et aedifices!*[65]

"Saint Luke and Jeremiah are flatterers," the Duke replied, smiling, "and it's Anselme alone that I want to hear today." Everyone withdrew.

The conscience of the vanquisher of Florence and Venice was troubled by certain actions that equity seemed to reprove, but uses that the rights of war could scarcely authorize; in order to relieve his soul he confided his terrors and his uncertainties to his usual censor.

The hermit reassured him, calmed his dreads and said: *Domus Israel, et domus Juda...*[66]

"It's a matter of Florence and Venice," exclaimed the Duke. "Let's leave Israel and Judah, Jeremiah and Saint Luke aside for a moment!"

Anselme, after having proved to Galeas that his successes were entirely legitimate and his glory intact, added: "Nothing more remains today, great Prince, to convince Europe entire that your paternal affection extends indistinctly over all your subjects, but to compensate worthily those among them who during your absence, have maintained calm and prosperity in your estates; my frankness and my love for you make it a duty for me to enlighten your munificence by recommending to it above all the governor of the palace and the lord treasurer, whose zeal and activity have seemed to me to merit the most honorable distinctions."

"I'll think about it," said the prince.

---

[65] An abridged version of *Jeremiah* 1:10: "I have set thee [this day] over the nations and over kingdoms, to root up, [and to pull down, and to waste], and to destroy, and to build, [and to plant]."

[66] "The house of Israel and the house of Judah" from *Jeremiah* 11: 10.

When he was alone, he thought: *So my hermit is now a protector and a flatterer!* But then another important object came to distract him from those reflections. The Archbishop of Milan had died a short while ago; the cathedral of the city, then the most magnificent temple of Christianity, which had just been completed in accordance with the designs of Bramante, was awaiting a hand ornamented by the archiepiscopal ring to bless its new altars and proceed with its dedication.

Galeas decided to consult Anselme as to the choice to be made, and immediately went to the place where he lived. How surprised he was on seeing the hermit's apartments decorated with a taste and elegance difficult to conceive, and his antechambers obstructed by a crowd of parasites and solicitors. The room that he occupied was full of the prince's principal officers and the most distinguished artists in Milan, all of whom, in a humble and seductive manner, were surrounding the devout individual, who was nonchalantly lounging in a rich armchair, with homages and adulations.

Galeas suppressed his astonishment; at the sight of him, everyone stood aside respectfully, and the duke addressed Anselme. "I thought I would find you alone," he said, "and came to consult you about the choice that remains for us to make in order to replace the late Archbishop; but since I see my ordinary counselors here, they can aid us with their advice."

The governor of the palace and the lord treasurer approached the prince then. "Only one man," they said, "generally designated by the veneration of the people, supported by the Court of Rome, and above all by high virtues, seems called to fill that eminent position."

Anselme bowed his head modestly.

"I understand," said Galeas, and went on in a loud voice: "Anselme Giramo, I thought I had found in you a true friend, but I have only given myself one more flatterer; the poor and virtuous man is now no more than a protective and scheming prelate. A few months of residence in this place has sufficed to take away your virtues and perhaps your happiness. I should have foreseen it; a hermit at court is soon a courtier. Return to your rock in Lake Maggiore; my benefits will follow you there, since I am the sole cause of your fall. But today I need a man to enlighten me whose eyes are not dazzled by a worldly glare; you, who cite Saint Luke and Jeremiah so well, remember these words: 'Can a blind man can guide another blind man?' or 'Woe betide the man who uses the holy mission with which God has charged him to serve his ambition and is interest!'"[67]

"May your will be done," said Anselme then, in a contrite and repentant fashion, "but I still have one item of good advice to give you. Lord, if ever the desire grips you again to have a hermit with you, for his security and for yours, in the name of Heaven, change him every month..."

---

[67] Author's references: "*Luke* 6:39; *Jeremiah* 18:10."

The Twins

(England)

> Beware of politics.
> It is the rock 'gainst which are split
> The tenderest affections of the heart.
> (Stone)[68]

> Two in one, and one in two
> (Shakespeare)[69]

In one of the small towns of Devonshire, under the reign of James I, a woman brought into the world two children, twins of the male sex, who presented in their conformation a very singular phenomenon. Attached to one another by an external prolongation of the intercostal ligaments, they were condemned by nature to spend their lives in a mutual dependency. The physicians of the region declared unanimously that the poor innocents could not enjoy a month of existence; and already, affirms the scholar Dwisleyston, whose writings have not reached us, all the apothecaries in the county were disput-

---

[68] This quotation, given in English in the original, currently produces no hits via a search engine and no poet named Stone is included in the *Oxford Companion to English Literature*.

[69] Not Shakespeare, although it might be back-translated from a French version of *The Comedy of Errors*; the phrase occurs as given in Michel Drayton's *Mortimeriados* (1596), where it refers to lovers, not twins, and in a translation of Dante's *Inferno*, referring to a traitor condemned to carry his own head like a lantern.

ing the honor of ornamenting their shop-windows with them, in a superb bottle filled with alcohol.

However, the Devonshire twins deceived the predictions of the physicians and he hopes of the apothecaries; they lived.

As children, their mother enabled them draw together upon the double source of strength and health; as adolescents, the same masters lavished them with the nourishment of the heart and mind. They grew in age and knowledge; and they seemed even more united by their tastes, their travails and their pleasures than by the bonds that nature had imposed on their bodies.

When the time of passions commenced for them, amour came to put them to the proof, and found them simple and true in their sentiments, unshakable in their reciprocal confidence. The same woman had charmed them; their double rivalry only increased their fraternal tenderness, for neither of them could hope to be happy alone; the favored lover would always have been necessarily embarrassed by a third party.

Could the same thirst for honors and riches divide their hearts? They had to inhabit the same palace or the same cottage, and one of them, the possessor of a throne, would have been constrained to sit his brother upon it beside him.

They lived, therefore, in that pleasant intimacy, by virtue of the double existence that animates, embellishes and completes everything. Their arguments were devoid of fits of temper, their rivalry devoid of hatred. The passions, eternal torturers of other men, seemed to have lost their sting and their venom in regard to them. But a political idea came to occupy them momentarily, and the happiness of loving one another, understanding one another, and living with another self, were all destroyed forever.

Until then, John and William, the heroes of this true story, had loved their country without worrying about the fashion in which it was governed. But politics is a monster that invades everything: the right or the left side that one occupies, the flower whose perfume one respires, the garments that one wears, everything throws you on to its terrain and under its dependency, but the species of the right of mortmain that it has exercised for so many centuries.

On a certain day, therefore, John and William asked for a kind of hat to be brought to them, each desiring to choose one of similar form, in accordance with the custom that they had adopted of always dressing in the same fashion. The merchant presented them with two sorts, some with round tops and the others with inverted cones, then known as Jacobite hats. John, with no other motive than the caprice of his taste and the desire to follow a new fashion, chose a round-topped hat and asked his brother to do likewise. The latter, a very weak follower of new fashions, and somewhat attached to his old ideas, mores and costume, wanted to wear a Jacobite, as before.[70]

"A reasonable man," he said to John, waits for a fashion to become established before adopting it."

"I've seen similar hats," John replied, "worn by the most honest burgers, as well as a large number of baronets."

"My brother, the habits of our bodies are more closely connected than you might think to those of the mind; beware of contracting, without suspecting it, the need for change."

"Oh, my brother, a truce on rebukes and let's each only consult our taste. I'm taking one of these round felt hats."

"They're very popular at the moment," said the hatter, immediately, presenting John with one of the most elegant, which he had just brushed carefully. "All the partisans of parliament wear nothing else."

"Are you a parliamentarian, then my brother?"

"Why not, William? Parliament is a respectable body, which every true Englishman ought to honor."

William made no response and chose a Jacobite, which the merchant guaranteed to be in the best taste and much in usage at court.

"Are you a royalist, then, my brother?" said John.

---

[70] This is, of course, a satirical joke, based on the fact that parliamentarian soldiers were eventually dubbed "roundheads" because of the helmets they wore.

And that petty quarrel over attire led them insensibly, and without them suspecting it, on to the terrible and shifting ground of politics. Fencing for the first time in a language foreign to both of them, their argument took on a tone of bitterness and animosity all the greater because both sensing their weakness and inexperience, they could only sustain their new opinions with passion, and not with reasoning.

With each of their heads covered with the fatal subject of their discord, it was impossible for them to look at one another without finding a motive for putting forward a few more vigorous arguments forgotten in the heat of improvisation. They argued so much and so well that, by dint of talking about similar materials, William, without even shaking the nascent opinion of his brother, who was scarcely listening, ended up yielding to his own arguments. John was similarly captured by his own eloquence and, penetrated by the obligations that parliament ought have to him for such a sublime defense of its rights and principles, he attached himself to that celebrated body, like an advocate to his client or a benefactor to the person obliged to him.

Once the demon of politics is awoken, the entire inferno is shaken by it. Calumny and hatred did not take long to visit the two twins. Until then they had professed a sincere and tolerant religion; fanaticism took possession of their hearts. John became an ardent Presbyterian, and the golden candelabrum was illuminated, for him, like the torch of the Eumenides. William converted spontaneously to Catholicism out of hatred for the Whigs,[71] who all professed the reformed religion. A Roman priest came to see him frequently and gave him spiritual aid before the unfortunate John, who, even though he plugged

---

[71] This is anachronistic, as is the use of the term "Jacobite"; the Whigs emerged as a faction in opposition to James II in the 1680s, not in the build up to Cromwell's overthrow of the monarchy in the 1640s; nor were the English royalists Catholics, although they were not Puritans, as many of the Parliamentarian leaders were.

his ears and closed his eyes, was constrained by the effect of their bizarre conformation to watch, as an indignant witness, what he called Moabite impieties.

Like all weak and vulnerable souls, each of them thought that he was forced to adopt and defend the culpable excesses of his party. After having shivered with horror at the story of the massacre of English Protestants by Irish Catholics, William ended up approving of it loudly. John, in his turn, dared to give his praise to the infamous conduct of the Scots, who surrendered the unfortunate King Charles Stuart to the fury of the parliament.

Almost strangers to one another, they ceased to have any moral rapport. Their house became a club open to both sects. John no longer welcomed any but the "roundheads"—the Whigs, the parliamentarians, the Jacobites—while William's intimate society consisted of Catholics and Tories. Sometimes the two parties found themselves in one another's presence; insults resulted from that. One day, it even came to acts of violence; William, struck forcefully by John, fell to the floor, and necessarily dragged his brother down with him.

Both seized by the same inspiration, they immediately summoned a surgeon, not to bandage the slight contusions they had received in falling, but to operate, if possible, a scission between them. They preferred to submit to the risks of a painful and dangerous operation rather than be incessantly face to face and side by side with an enemy of their political and religious faith.

Several very experienced practitioners came to visit them and, after a long consultation, declared unanimously that the corporeal union had to be eternal. A very important artery, the ligature of which seemed impossible, was common to the two brothers. It was necessary to live, if only for hatred; they resigned themselves to it.

In the meantime, an unexpected event filled England with terror. An illustrious prisoner soon appeared before the judges of Westminster, and Cromwell triumphed.

William, in despair, fell into a profound sadness; the world had become odious to him. Eventually, possessed by the terrible malady that the islanders call "the blue devil," or spleen,[72] he resolved to put an end to his life. But he could not hang himself, nor drown himself, without the assent of his brother, so he poisoned himself.

No word had been exchanged between them for a long time when one day, after a meal of which William alone had partaken, John felt tormented by agonizing pains in his entrails. His Presbyterian physician came and said to him: "An alarm bell has just rung; doubtless some poisonous substance with be found among the aliments in the meal you've just had."

"I haven't had a meal," John replied, gripped by fear. "By order of the parliament and as a good citizen, I've been fasting for the profit of the State."[73]

The debris of William's dinner was still on the table. The physician cast an eye over it and cried: "Your brother has poisoned himself! That accursed common artery is doing you a bad turn by communicating the effects of the poison to you."

John looked at William, who, pale and scarcely breathing, was seeking to suppress his convulsive movements, in order not to be helped. He was, however. Love of life gradually resumed its rights over him, and, after a long illness, the two brothers, whom misfortune and suffering had not been able to reconcile, by order of their physicians, left London in order to breathe the pure air of the country in a small house they owned on the banks of the Severn near the walls of Worcester.

---

[72] Saintine might have obtained this mistaken impression from "Love," an 1823 poem by Ebeneezer Elliott, which includes the line "As spleen, blue devil'd when the moon is full."

[73] Author's note: "The English parliament, lacking money, had published a decree in 1644 to oblige every citizen to deprive himself of one meal every week and donate the money saved to the national case."

Never does nature appear so beautiful to us, and never does existence offer so many charms as during days of convalescence. One loves to throw oneself back into a new future; there are new projects; it is a new life that one recommences, so to speak, with all the illusions of the first youth. It was not absolutely thus for our Whig and our Tory, and yet, unknown to one another, they were seeing the sun again with a pleasure and tenderness that might perhaps have rendered them to nature and virtue, when unexpected events nearly plunged them back into excesses even greater than all the others.

While William is asleep, a Scotsman who supposes the two brothers to have the same political opinions penetrates into their apartment and tells John, the only one awake, that the Prince of Wales, the son of the deceased king, has just arrived in Scotland with a royalist army that has been formed in his favor. John, informed at the same time that the return in question is a vast conspiracy against the roundheads, and that the magistrates of Worcester themselves are supporting it in secret, immediately resolves to warn parliament.

For a long time, William had known the hopes and projects of the Tories; he soon discovered the intentions of his eternal companion. Frightened to the utmost degree by seeing the salvation of his party in such hands, and not doubting that his brother would employ all means to annihilate their last hope, he armed himself with what is called heroism in times of trouble and anarchy, but which merits the name of crime in vulgar epochs; he wrote to the magistrates of the city and denounced his brother.

The royal standard had just been raised in Worcester when the "advice of treason" signed "William" arrived in the grand council. It was decided to frighten the parliamentarians by means of a severe example, and the order was given to put John of Devonshire before a firing squad immediately.

William had not expected that abrupt denouement; he strove to make the officer understand that it was impossible to kill his brother without killing him, and that it would be inconvenient, and even impolitic, to cause a good Catholic Tory to perish in order to get rid of a Presbyterian Whig. He spoke for a full ten minutes about his opinions, his services, his artery and his heroism, but the officer had his orders, did not understand any of the explanations, and was in a hurry to finish with the matter.

Caught in his own net, William asked for a moment's delay, which he obtained, with great difficulty. Left alone, the two brothers talked for the first time in a long time. On hearing the voice of the companion and friend of his childhood, in contemplating the living image of his father, on the forehead of which the lead was about to break, William felt the full extent of his "heroism" and the evidence of his peril; he wept. John softened; they both looked at one another and extended their hands as a sign of mutual forgiveness.

Rallied by a common danger, and knowing every corner of their house, they slipped through a trap-door and reached immense subterranean tunnels that took them into open country. In the end, they escaped, avoiding by turns the soldiers of Charles II and those of Cromwell, and, having recovered from hateful passions, detesting equally parties that corrupt the heart, judges who condemn in confidence and officers who have people shot without listening to explanations, they finished their life as they had begun it, in the bosom of nature and amity.

Death struck them both with the same blow; they held one another in their arms, and, their eyes turned toward one another, they encouraged one another mutually in that terrible moment.

In the town in Devonshire where they were born I have seen the tomb in which they lie together. All around it, a multitude of mottoes have been engraved, which they had the custom of repeating in their old age. I have remembered the following:

Vengeance is only sweet in hope.

Political and religious hatred are siblings.

Superstition, with a miter on its head, always marches after civil wars; it comes to bless the daggers.

Once politics has passed somewhere, everything retains its livery and becomes suspect or sacred, an emblem of revolt or a rallying signal. Our wives manifest their opinion even in the manner in which they place their beauty spot on the Whig or the Tory side of the face—which is to say, to the left or right.

Almost all men, in their political opinions, consult their interest, and women their affections.

It is an admirable foresight of nature that puts the salvation of one's neighbor in self-love, and happiness in virtue.

Contradictions

(France)

Human actions are so strangely contradictory that it
seems impossible that they have emerged
from the same boutique.
(Montaigne. *Essais*, Book 2 ch. 1)

"Everything is contradictory in the world, I tell you: passions, morals, laws and honor, everything collides, everything
crosses, and the science of life is to be able, like a skillful pilot, to steer one's boat through the midst of so many contrary
currents. I've been a mariner for forty years; I've landed on
many coasts, islands and continents, and everywhere I've seen
the same thing; you're young and seem to be observant; you'll
see in your turn."

"But nature at least," said an interlocutor, "has its eternal
and invariably laws."

"I don't know. Some scholar or other said 'If habit is a
second nature, nature might well be nothing but a primary
habit,' and that scholar doesn't seem to me to be unreasonable.
Is it natural to sustain us with flesh similar to our own? There
are, however, cannibals. Is it natural for a man to have his
field tilled by his wife, and to prepare couscous and maize in
the meantime, or, to lie down at his ease and have himself
cared for as soon as the poor creature, standing up and still at
work, feels the pains of childbirth? I have, however, seen that
among my good friends the Kaffirs, who, except for their nasty mania for eating people and other primary habits, are the
best people I know, for they give us an ox for a nail and sell us
their children for a pint of eau-de-vie."

"Those are shocking things, but it's in the state of civilization that human beings, wiser and more enlightened, according to what I learned from my father, follow laws full of harmony, which imprint on nations a frank and regular progress, exempt from similar contradictions."

"It's possible that your father might know more about it than me; I haven't been able to study civilization, only having lived thus far with Turks, Japanese, Indians, Africans and sailors."

That conversation took place toward the end of 1815 between the young passenger Saint-Charles and Philippe Van Break, captain of the frigate *Amaranthe*, then traveling from the island of Ceylon to the coasts of France.

Saint-Charles had been born in Ceylon of French parents. His father, a man of merit, having emigrated during the disastrous epoch of the Revolution, had subsequently become one of the favorite counselors of the king of Kandy. Hoping that his son would succeed to his divinities, in the dread of seeing his heart float between the country that had seen him born and his original fatherland, he only talked rarely about the latter, and had had him educated in Buddhism, the religion of the Sinhalese. Mortally wounded in a battle against the English, however—who, not content with holding the king prisoner had also wanted to take possession of his estates—he had summoned his son, engaged him always to remain faithful to the laws of the strictest honor, advised him to depart for France in order to claim his title of citizen there, to live in accordance with the law and religion of that country, and had died embracing him.

Saint-Charles had immediately struck a bargain with Captain Van Break, an old friend of his father, who was setting sail for that destination. The captain was one of the mot singular men one could see, sometimes generous or selfish, sober or intemperate, his actions were rarely in accord with his principles. He could boast of having received a very good education, of which he had never made use; he was endowed with elevated ideas of justice and morality, which he had never put into practice. A pirate and a philosopher, he was found alternately worthy of those two titles in his speech. During the crossing, the worthy mariner became so fond of Saint-Charles that on his arrival, having resolved to quit the sea some time ago, he wanted to accompany the young man into the new world that presented so many reefs to his inexperience.

The southern regions of France appeared at first to augur very well; the richness of the soil and the vivacity of the inhabitants awoke in Saint-Charles' heart a sentiment of joy and intoxication that he took for love of the fatherland. He rapidly presented himself to the magistrates in order to obtain his diploma of French citizenship, as his father had prescribed for him. When he declared that he had thus far followed the religion of Buddhism, the municipal officer recoiled three paces, as if seized by horror, and then asked him who the Buddha in question was, who had a religion.

"Buddha is wisdom incarnate," replied the young man. "He is a God revered in China, Japan and Tartary; he visited the earth again not long ago, and his footprint is still found on the peak of Adam, one of the highest mountains in Ceylon."

"I know Adam very well, but I don't know Buddha, replied the municipal administrator, "and in spite of your papers, which seem to me to be in order, I have difficulty believing that one can make a Frenchman of a Buddhist. Go see Monseigneur the Archbishop."

Captain Van Break sustained that that response implied a contradiction, in view of the fact that the Pope can only give us a religion, and not a fatherland; that a certificate of confession was unnecessary in such a matter, and that a Buddhist could be French as easily as a Jew, etc.; and the great debate about contradictory things begun aboard the *Amaranthe* recommenced more ardently, for the captain was a man for whom, once having found a fecund text, a lifetime was not sufficient to continue to add glosses thereto.

Saint-Charles went to the home of the Archbishop, who, without seeing him, sent him to his chief almoner, who sent him to the curé, who sent him to the deacon, who received him very politely, and had him explain for the second time what a Buddhist was.

Understanding that it was a matter of a conversion, the good deacon did not believe himself worthy of such an honor and, out of humility, sent him back to the curé, who sent him to the chief almoner, who sent him to the Archbishop. This time the prelate was visible; he welcomed him benevolently, and told him that, in order to enter worthily into the bosom of France he had, like Saint Jerome, to shake off the dust of idolatry with which he was covered. It was advice, not an order.

"My dying father engaged me to do that himself," our Sinhalese replied, "but wouldn't your God disapprove of such a change?"

"That sacrifice can only be agreeable to the Lord when faith leads us to it."

Saint-Charles was instructed, found the religion of Jesus Christ preferable to the one he had professed thus far, and received the baptism that he was told would wash away his pollution and open the gates of heaven to his soul. Van Break was his godfather, and wept with joy in thinking that his friend would be named Philippe henceforth, like him. He thought he saw a son in the man who bore his name.

The next day, the new Christian appeared at Van Break's home followed by a superb mastiff, his faithful companion, which had saved his life in Ceylon and had accompanied him in his emigration. "I'm going back to see the Archbishop," he said, "to ask him to pour the holy water that will open the gates of heaven over my good Stanog."

"What are you doing?" replied the captain, uttering a long burst of laughter. "You're mixing up your Malabar ideas and your Christian sentiments. We're no longer in India; the beasts here have no souls to save, and it's committing a sacrilege to want to administer such a sacrament to anything other than a human being. In fact, the contradiction is in your mind, half-Indian and half-French—but that's what one exposes with these sudden conversions.

"This reminds me of a contradiction of that sort to which I was witness among my good friends the Kaffirs. The fathers of the Propaganda thought they had frayed the path to Christianity for a large number of them; like you, they had been baptized, and regarded one another as perfect neophytes, even though they bad conserved almost all of their 'primary habits.' Observing fasts and other austerities with sufficient exactitude, they believed themselves to be sanctified by that.

"One day, I went to visit them, not far from the coast, with a kind of philosopher, a very fine man, who also wanted to convert them in his own fashion. We found them eating nothing but potatoes and fish, because it was Saturday. My philosopher tried to indoctrinate them; he reproached them for their vices, their cruelties and their polygamy. They listened to him quite tranquilly, but he said to them imprudently that it is by virtues hat one pleases the Eternal, not by pretended abstinences, which only consist of a change of nourishment.

"On hearing such blasphemies, rising spontaneously to their feet, they cried, unanimously, in their baroque language: "Advising us to eat meat on a Saturday! The impious scoundrel! And, to avenge their outraged religion, their eyes scintillating with fury or fervor, however one cares to put it, they threw themselves upon him, chopped him up and ate him on the spot. I must, however, render them justice; they didn't take long to repent—not of having eaten him, for he was white and delicate, but of having eaten meat on a Saturday, which had become contrary to their principles.

"You see, just as you have remained Sinhalese, they remained Kaffirs in spite of the baptism. Fortunately, Philippe, my godson, you have a godfather who knows his religion; let's allow your Stanog to remain what he is, and not think any longer about his salvation."

Saint-Charles had a mind too elevated not to conceive the sublime goal of a doctrine that ennobled humans by placing a celestial barrier between them and other animals. He resigned himself to it, while regretting nevertheless that his faithful companion could not go to heaven with him.

As he headed toward the holy altars in order to offer God is actions of grace, he perceived that the church, surrounded by an immense crowd, was bedecked and decorated as on feast days, and the people surrounding it told him that they were about to proceed with the baptism of a bell.

He was amazed. "What!" he sad to Van Break. "That sacrament is administered to a bell? To brute and insensible matter? A bell can have a godfather and a godmother, but my faithful Stanog can't! Has a bell a soul to save, then?" That idea confounded him.

"It's a revolting contradiction," said the mariner. "You'll see that in France, the most civilized country in most civilized part of the world, we'll find as many of them as among the Kaffirs and the Sinhalese."

From then on, our young traveler began to observe what was happening around him with the sentiment of bitterness and criticism that one acquires as one feel oneself being abandoned by one's first illusions. He heard mention at that time of religious troubles that had burst forth in Nîmes and Montpellier. Astonished at first that a holy morality that commanded charity and the forgiveness of sins could drive men to such excesses, he enquired about the principles of the odious Protestants, whom he supposed to be Christians in the manner of Kaffirs.

A local bourgeois, who had not been a stranger to those horrors, told him tranquilly: "They're damned heretics, who refuse to recognize the Pope and the decrees of synods."

"It's the Pope, then, who has declared war on them?"

"No, for he receives and protects them in his estates."

"What are these decrees of synods?"

"I don't know and I don't care."

"Their beliefs are infamous, then?"

"Refrain from believing that, Philippe, my godson," Van Break interrupted, "for they follow strictly the precepts of the Gospel, the book that has converted you; but in sum, they're Protestants and we're Catholics; that's like saying English and French; a difference of denominations soon seems to make two nations out of one, and then both become excited, and heads become heated."

"That's true," replied the bourgeois persecutor. "You'll admit, however, that it's cruel to be exposed to finding oneself incessantly side by side with such heretics—but I'll leave you, because I'm dining today with two Turkish businessmen, friends who are arriving from Marseille. Adieu."

"Contradictions on top of contradictions!" exclaimed the captain. "In the interests of the Holy Father they torment those the Holy Father protects; Christians, the cut the throats of disciples of Jesus Christ, and dine with those of Mohammed!"

"What horror!" said Saint-Charles, red with fury and his eyes full of tears. "Are those the effects of civilization? If the dogmas of the two religions are the same, if both of them are based on the holy gospel, what does it matter that one passes from one to the other? I want to be a Protestant! It's more honorable to find oneself with the party of the oppressed than that of the oppressors!"

"Further folly, Philippe, my godson; you'd be regarded as a renegade, a lapsed individual, a heretic."

"Monseigneur the Archbishop told me that such a change was agreeable to the Lord when faith led us to it."

"He might have said what when it was a matter of quitting Buddhism for Catholicism, but he'd say the opposite today."

"He'd contradict himself, then?"

"Just like the others, Philippe, my godson; let's not catch fire so easily; you're on the right path, stay there. I once knew a man who, after having been a Catholic persecutor in Spain, embraced Protestantism and went to persecute the Papists in Ireland. Cruelty is in the man, not the religions; in the lands where Calvin is dominant, his disciples are intolerant in their turn; do you want to change religion incessantly in changing location?"

In order to get away from all those ideas, they quit the place where the sons of the ancient Gauls had raised the altars of Teutates again and were offering him human sacrifices.

Having arrived in Paris, a thousand new subjects of astonishment soon struck our two travelers. Saint-Charles saw idleness in honor there everywhere, and active industry almost scorned; people there became Academicians by virtue of political opinions and statesmen by virtue of religious sentiments; young people there seemed as prodigal with their fortunes as if they only had one day to live, and old men as miserly as if they expected to exist for another hundred years.

Everything seemed to a simple, naïve young man with no knowledge of the world to be as many contradictions. He eventually got to know it; admitted into a few salons, he studied its mores and usages. According to his observations, elegant vices and a few agreeable talents were sufficient to make a perfect cavalier. Virtues and piety were treated as affairs of speculation, only dupes ran the risk of scorn, and a cuckolded husband was stupid enough to believe that he was the one who was dishonored.

With his Sinhalese prejudices and his moral delicacy, Saint-Charles, placed in such a circle, soon became the butt of all the mockery and impertinence of the fops who paid their dues in society by lavishing epigrams and quips. Endowed with an easy-going character, he thought that petty war unimportant, until, grievously insulted, he found himself obliged to riposte, and did it so advantageously that his adversary, no longer in control of his anger, slapped him. Saint-Charles then recovered his sang-froid, reproached him for getting carried away, commiserated with him for yielding to shameful violence, and occupied himself with something else.

Charitable friends soon made him understand that he would lose honor if he did not demand a reckoning for such an outrage. The worthy young man could not imagine how, the wrong not being on his side, the shame was his.

"But the laws of honor!" people cried on all sides. "Wretch, you're doomed if you don't satisfy them!"

"Then I'll satisfy them," he said, "for my father recommended me always to remain faithful to them."

He went to find Van Break and asked him how one avenged an insult and how one terminated an affair of honor.

Our philosophical mariner assumed a portentous expression and replied: "Philippe, my godson, honor is a phantom that changes forms in changing places. In Pennsylvania I made the mistake of giving a rude slap to a worthy Quaker, who contented himself with offering his other cheek and was praised by everyone for doing so. A Corsican with whom I was in rivalry during my youth thought that he was honor bound to murder me, and died of shame because he was unable to do so. An Englishman offered one day to box in order to conclude a slightly heated discussion, and is doubtless still scornful of me today because I declined his proposal.

"Finding myself in Japan, I nudged a local nobleman with my elbow by accident, who, without saying a word, immediately drew his sword from its scabbard. I thought he was about to make use of it against me, but not at all; he incontinently opened his abdomen and fell at my feet, spilling all his entrails. Moved by pity, horror and astonishment, I tried to bring him help. 'Well, Monsieur,' he said, 'your turn.' I didn't understand him; I never wanted to understand him, and I was shamed by all the Japanese for not wanting to follow such a fine example.

"I went among the Tartars of Tangut, where another affair of honor awaited me. An honest husband of the region summoned me to a duel for having looked at his wife appreciatively; I was armed with a heavy hammer and he enjoined me to administer three blows to his back; he was to do the same to me thereafter, but I did it so effectively that he did not get up again, and I was taken away with a great deal of civility by his compatriots, delighted by my strength and my courtesy.

"Philippe, my godson, that is how the penal code of honor is interpreted variously everywhere. In France, one employs the épée or the pistol; but believe me, if you've been insulted, the man who has offered you the insult feels that he has the means to survive the reparation. You're not obliged to sacrifice yourself to conventions you scarcely know. Believe me,

Philippe, my godson, I have need of your life; let's abandon France and its eternal contradictions, and let's go to Pennsylvania."

That explanation did not satisfy young Philippe. Several times in society he had met a small black-clad man full of good advice and of respectable appearance; he went to find him and submitted to him the doubts that were tormenting him.

"Young man," the latter said, "your inexperience and air of candor have always interested me; I believe, therefore, that I can speak to you frankly and in your interest. The tribunal of honor is without appeal here; if you don't fight, you'll be dishonored forever, and I think—still in your interest—that it's better to run the dubious risks of combat than to be indubitably exposed for life to general scorn."

Saint-Charles understood those reasons, and while deploring the contradiction in the point of honor, which incessantly put the right side in the wrong; he called out the slapper and was, alas, sufficiently unfortunate and maladroit to kill him.

The innocent murderer was soon astonished to find himself summoned to appear before judges, but what astonished him even more was to recognize among them his little man clad in black, the giver of good advice, who, sitting on the right of the tribunal in the quality of the king's prosecutor, did his job and pronounced a vehement speech in which he summoned public vindication and the rigors of injustice against those who, scornful of all morality and humanity, tigers thirsty for blood, went to slake their thirst on their fellow citizens, on their brethren.

Why didn't he say that before? Saint-Charles wondered. *I certainly wouldn't have fought, and that poor young man who gave me a slap would still be inhabiting this world. What! The laws of justice aren't the same as those of honor? And the man who, in his own home, in my interest, advised me to have recourse to weapons, today, before this assembly, is seeking to have me punished for following his advice!*

The cry of his conscience already made him dread the judges' verdict, but the pronunciation of judgment was postponed for a week and no further mention was made of it.

"Well," Van Break said to him, when he saw him again, "how many contradictions are you bringing back to me from your session?"

"A great many."

He made him party to his previous reflections and the adventure of the little man in black.

"Does that astonish you?" said the captain. "At home, he spoke to you as a man of the world; in a frock-coat and hat he had the prejudices of his garments; clad in a robe and a square bonnet, he spoke as the king's prosecutor; that's the whole story."

Overwhelmed by remorse for having satisfied the pretended laws of honor, Saint-Charles promised himself no longer to observe any but those of the government and the Church, which he had violated in order to obey the others. But further doubts came to agitate him again. He thought he perceived that the ecclesiastical and political laws were no more in accord than the rest. The religion of the State often seemed to be in opposition to the laws of that State. The latter encouraged marriage and the theater, which the public treasury supported with its own funds; the former preached celibacy, prohibited spectacles and struck the king's actors with anathemas.

My father, I can see clearly, Saint-Charles said to himself, *demanded the impossible of me in recommending me to observe exactly the laws of the honor, the government and the religion of the country that I was going to inhabit. Can I not be a good citizen and a good Christian at the same time, then?*

His ideas were in ferment in his head; he sensed the need to expand them; but he resolved, in order not to collide with any authority, only to follow a single route and not to broach any subject foreign to the one with which he was dealing. The Charter, which he reread very attentively, gave him the right to publish his opinions; reading that sacred text convinced him that the regime under which he lived was entirely liberal and constitutional; he wrote in that sense, with moderation, and was put in Sainte-Pélagie for three months.

"Display the flag before which you want people to incline, then!" he cried, in exasperation. "Why abuse my credulity with false signals? Why punish me for marching toward the goal that you indicate to me? Is the law in contradiction with itself, then?"

"Yes," said Van Break, who came to visit him. "The law punishes the thief and the murderer, but does not prohibit the gambling houses, fencing schools and pistol ranges where theft and murder are formed. Philippe, my godson, will you never be wise? Why direct yourself against my advice? Thanks to the theory of contradictions that I have built, I'm sure now of no longer going astray. The method is simple: it is to act and believe in an inverse direction to what appearances counsel us to do. The contrary of what is done is almost always exactly what it is appropriate to do. You will see here people imprisoned for debt; as if they cannot only acquit themselves with regard to their creditors by increasing labor and activity, it is assumed that the result can be obtained by interrupting their commerce and their affairs, by forcing them to remain inactive for five years—which, more often than not, condemns them to poverty for the rest of their life."

A few prisoners had assembled in order to dine together; the godfather and the godson were among that number. The captain, full of his new theory, had soon brought the conversation round to the subject that occupied him incessantly; everyone made his contribution, everyone bought evidence to support it; heads were heated by the idea. Eventually, it was resolved, when the session ended, that they would collaborate in composing a dictionary of contradictions. At dessert, one of the guests, a poet, doubtless distinguished—for there is no shortage of men of letters in Saint-Pélagie—improvised, or appeared to improvise, a song in the form of a *complainte*:

Yes, everything follows the law of contraries;
Glory and honor are for the warrior

The man who, on the earth, however,
Only exercises the art of murder.
The merchant in the bosom of the town,
The cultivator in the bosom of the fields,
Are more useful to our wellbeing
And so are far less honored.

After having carried a sword,
And the terror of his land,
Sulla very quietly ended
His days in embellished calm;
Henri, the fourth of that name,
Crowned by victory,
Rendered a people who loved him happy,
And so he died assassinated.

Old Crates, a hunchbacked cynic
Seduced the heart of Hipparchia,
When, deprived of his tunic,
He laid his ugliness bare.
Singing in a lamentable voice,
The object of his heart was harmed.
Petrarch was much more likeable,
And so he was much less loved.

In the fine days of Melpomene
The great Racine was whistled.
Athalie was worth the trouble,
But the author was desolate.
That justice puts me at ease,
And ought to embolden me
Messieurs, my song is bad,
And so you are sure to applaud it.

In fact, it was applauded. Van Break did not run out of
eulogies, so delighted was he to see his theory already celebrated in song. The phrase "and so" was adopted or the dic-

tionary, the materials of which were already immense at the end of a week. In view of the number of its volumes, and as it will doubtless not appear before the Académie's, I believe I ought to give an idea of the work here by citing two examples. First I shall take the word:

EMPLOYEE. The simple employee is a man who works from eight o'clock in the morning until four o'clock in the afternoon; sometimes, his office even recalls him to work in the evening, and so his salary is very modest. The head of the office in subject to less exactitude; he is able to liberate himself from the chores of the evening and go about his affairs and is pleasures agreeably, and so that position is very well-paid. When he becomes a section head, he enjoys a considerable salary, and so he no longer does anything at all.

NOBILITY. A man performs a glorious deed, saves his country, sheds his blood for it, or becomes illustrious by his works; the right is conceded to him, on parchment, to procreate gentlemen. Is he one himself? No. He cannot become one; he is simply an intruder, a parvenu, a half-breed of the proletariat and the nobility. But his sons will be gentlemen; he will give them what he does not have; the acorn will produce a cedar; the river will be purified in drawing way from its source. All that is unclear, and so it is almost universally adopted.

Great deeds, however, are not always necessary to acquire letters of nobility. Finance buys them at a monetary price, poetry with sweet flatteries; and under the title of "services rendered to the State" a minister can gratify the husband of his mistress or his wife's lover, and so that institution has always been proclaimed the support of good morals and the rampart of the monarchy.

A wise old man appointed by virtue of his seniority as the president of the dictionary took charge of composing the introduction. It was read in general session. Not admitting effects without causes, he sought to unveil there the source of so many contradictions in the present state of society.

"Our civilization," he said, "is an old monument, whitened and patched up, the recently constructed parts of which are no longer on harmony with the old. On vast foundations laid down by our barbaric ancestors, the Romans built a few elegant porticos that are still standing. The feudal monster planted its towers and keeps there; centuries succeeded one another, erecting in the surroundings more uniform but less solid masses; they were overturned in order to rebuild with the same materials; externally, by means of plastering, the monument was given an appearance of regularity, but inside, it nonetheless presented an inextricable labyrinth, in which obscurity succeeded light, of tortuous paths and broad galleries.

"Our laws are a bizarre mixture of those of the Franks, the Romans and modern peoples; our moral code is a compound of chivalric rodomontades and philosophical reasoning; our religion a bundle of divine and eternal dogmas and ecclesiastical decrees, doubtless in rapport with the times in which they were promulgated, but often in opposition to ours. Infallibility being the dominant reason of our worship, the temporary decrees of the thirteenth century still afflict us today. For having forbidden the mysteries, impious and licentious parades, anathemas are still being launched against *Athalie* and *Polyeucte*. The proclamations and regulations of bishops have obscured and mutilated the Gospel, as our provisional laws have annihilated the spirit of the Charter.

"The thought of the legislator has never been understood. François I, in order to put the expression of the law within the range of the people, banished the Latin tongue for the tribunals, and our present legists still make use of the Marotic jargon of that century, almost as unintelligible for many people as the Latin itself. It is thus that institutions and usages always lag behind the ideas and needs of the moment. Such is the cause of so many contradictions, doubtless detestable; but let us compare the times that preceded us with the times in which we live, and, while awaiting better ones, let us be satisfied with our lot."

"Yes," said Van Break, interrupting the reading, "as I said to Philippe, my godson, aboard the *Amaranthe*, the science of life is being able to steer the boat through the midst of all those contrary currents."

Vengeance

(Africa: the Congo, the Cape of Good Hope, Senegal and the Barbary Coast)

It was from the height that human wisdom can attain
that Socrates cried to men: "It is never permissible
for you to render evil for evil."
(Plato, quoted by Barthelemy,
Anacharsis, vol VII, p. 72.)

At the end of the eighteenth century the kingdom of the Congo was governed by a prince who was the idol of his people; there was no talk of anything in the neighboring kingdoms but his prudence and his justice. Violence and cruelty formed the foundation of his character, but on succeeding to the throne, counseled by reason to take as a minister a man moderated in his passions, frank in his speech and incorruptible in his morals, his choice had fallen on the sage Maelo, with whom I had once traveled through a large part of the African continent, and no one was more worthy of the king's confidence than that Ethiopian philosopher.

Informed of his master's natural penchants, Maelo was incessantly constrained to use artistry with him even in his frankness. Sometimes he caressed him with merited praise, in order to excite him to conquer what he still lacked to complete the panegyric; sometimes, in telling him the story of some chief of a savage nation, he established between his hero and his royal listener comparisons that were oblique, but promptly grasped by the latter's consciousness, and such that he hastened to remove himself by generous actions from the shame of similarity. Suspended between good intentions and vicious instincts, between duty and caprice, the king nevertheless attempted sometimes to evade the virtuous tutelage of his minister, and the noble envelope under which he appeared to the eyes of his subjects was often on the part of tearing.

Indignant at an imprudent and unjust humiliation, his brother, the Mani, or governor of Bamba, a large province of the Congo, took up arms and declared its independence. Immediately, the king's fury no longer knew any bounds; he swore the death of the rebel and his accomplices, and a general levy of troops was ordered throughout his estates. At the time I happened to be in Banza-Sao-Salvador, and the singular spectacle that I witnessed seems to me to merit reporting.

In less than a fortnight, nearly a million men from all the parts of the Empire flooded toward the capital; the surrounding countryside was covered with them and the roads encumbered. Huts built in haste occupied ten leagues of terrain around the royal city, and, as that multitude, deprived of subsistence, trampling the crops underfoot, transported its nomadic villages everywhere that the last resources of cultivation remained, famine soon threatened to penetrate all the way to the monarch's palace.

Maelo was alert; his activity brought back abundance, but without being able to avoid disorder, and the king, sensing the necessity of disseminating that immense surplus of population, hastened the day of his great review.

Sao Salvador is situated on a mountain sheer on all sides; a path carved into the rock leads to the palace, not far from which is a vast square known as the Green Field, once an immense lake that Luqueni,[74] the first sovereign of the Congo, had filled in. It was there that the king appeared, surrounded by the Dukes of Batta and Sogno, the Marquis of Pemba and the Count of Sibeni—for since the Portuguese had brought Christianity to those lands, all the natives who professed that belief affected to adopt the titles, the usages and even some of the garments of that nation.

---

[74] Legend actually makes Luqueni Luasanze the wife of Nima a Nzima, the first ruler of the kingdom of Kongo.

The monarch, preceded by a numerous guard of Anzikis[75] armed with muskets and spears, emerged from the palace to the sound of trumpets, bagpipes and a kind of drum called an *ingombo*, made of a hollow tree trunk, and the sound of which, accompanied by that of *longa*, small bells like those attached in Europe to the necks of livestock, produces a very discordant ensemble. At his sides he had two young lords, one of whom carried his buckler and sword, sparkling with gem-stones, the other his commandant's baton. While two other officers, each armed with a horse's tail, refreshed the air around him, a third held a large silk parasol over his head to defend him against the ardor of the sun.

What astonished my gaze most of all, however, were the varied garments in which that bizarre cortege appeared. Those who honored themselves with the title of Christians showed themselves, in imitation of the ancient Portuguese, coiffed with light toques and ostrich plumes, or large hats with turned-up rims. Velvet, silk, and gold and silver brocade heightened their adornment. On the contrary, those who, still imbued with paternal superstitions, would have thought themselves half-guilty of the crime of apostasy if they had not dressed in the same ornaments as their ancestors, presented themselves proudly clad in a garment made from aliconde bark, and a light surplice that their wives had woven with loose fibers of the insanda or the mulemba laurel, and which was fastened at shoulder in the Greek manner, with the brilliant clasp replaced by a zebra tail, an ornament of honor in the Congo. A tiger skin accompanied that adornment worthily, entirely typical of

---

[75] Author's note: "The Anzikis are a savage people who live on the banks of the Bancaro near the northern frontier of the kingdom of Loango. Full of courage and skill in war, they sell their services to the African kings who can pay them; their fidelity is proof against anything. According to Davity, Dapper and Labat, they are cannibals, and in the markets of Montal, the capital of Anziko, human flesh is sold openly. (X.)"

the region. The costume was completed by sandals of palm-wood and a small brightly-colored bonnet, which bought out their black or coppery complexion fully.

The king stopped near the Green Field, in a place where a little pavilion had been erected for him, surmounted by a standard bearing, by way of a coat of arms, a silver cross enclosed by four escutcheons and accompanied by sable roundels arranged in a saltire—a present that had once been made by King Emmanuel of Portugal to his Congolese ally Alphonse I.

As soon as the monarch was seated, the entire inexperienced population, of which heroes were expected to be made, poured tumultuously out of the mountain path. Each of them was armed and clad in his own fashion; some carried a spear and a small buckler impenetrable to iron, made of the hide of an animal called a dante; others, almost naked, like the majority of their compatriots, advanced waving axes, sabers, or rusty rifles, many of which were deprived of their essential parts and only figured in the equipment as objects of luxury.

Several of those future warriors, desirous of putting on courtly airs, had also borrowed a part of their accoutrements from Europeans. Some were seen with heads covered with a kind of helmet formed from hippopotamus hide or the scaly skin of an enormous snake, but wore to accompany that terrible coiffure a Portuguese jerkin embroidered in gold, a silk mantle, or English uniform. I saw some who only veiled the condition of complete nudity commonplace in the region with a light plumed toque and a long sword, suspended from the waist. One of them had no garment from head to toe except for a false collar and cuffs.

They filed in front of the king, and their principal chiefs received from that prince insignia made of ostrich- and pea-cock-feathers pleasantly mingled together. Then cries of joy burst forth on all sides, resounding in the city that was vomiting forth the superfluity of that immense army, resounding in the surrounding plains, still covered with soldiers not yet inspected. The monarch declared himself content with the review and went back to his palace after having ordered that manioc, potatoes, tambas, and game should be distributed to the troops, along with a large number of gourds containing wine extracted from the mataba, a kind of palm tree that furnishes a very agreeable beverage.

However, Maelo made the observation to his master that the difficulty of nourishing such an accumulation of soldiers would necessarily lead to a desertion of which his brother, Duke Alvares, the master of the coast that provided the most abundant supply of zimbis—a small cowry shell that serves as money in the Congo and much of Africa—might take advantage. The king initially saw his vengeance more assured by surrounding the rebel with such an array of forces, and by virtue of an excess of pride, he thought he had an interest in marching at the head of an army as considerable as those that his predecessors had assembled, but when the prudent minister had cited, from their own history, a number of instances when the large number of warriors had harmed the enterprise, he gave in, and charged him with arranging everything in a fashion that would soon put his mortal enemy in his power.

Alvares had a hard and inflexible character. In open revolt against his mater and his brother, after having attempted in vain to have him murdered by an Anziki in is guard, he declared insolently that if he set foot in the territory of Bamba, he and all his army would be thrown to the pismires;[76] and,

---

[76] Author's note: "Pismires, or temites, called white ants, bugga-bugs or vague-vagues by various voyagers, are the scourge of India and a part of Africa because of the damage they cause not only to fruits, crops, cloth wooden utensils and even furniture, soon pierced and molded by their voracious jaws, but also to humans, whom they sometimes attack by night in myriads and devour, bones and all.

Considered in terms of their industry, those little insects might qualify as one of the marvels of creation. The structure and grandeur of their habitations, which sometimes rise up to twelve or fifteen feet in height, with such solidity that herds of buffalo and other wild animals and bound over them without shaking them, their prudent economy, their admirable foresight, and the symmetrical arrangement of their channels and subterranean roads, all place them far above wasps, ants, bees, crossbills and beavers for intelligence or instinct.

According to the observations of Henry Smeathman in his dissertation on termites, addressed to the Royal Society of London, if one compares their monuments with ours, calculating on a proportional scale the height of their workers and ours, their mounds are found to be four or five times taller than our highest monuments, and far more solid. Adamson, deceived by the regularity, the number of height of those singular constructions, thought at a distance that he was seeing a large village, and in that he was honoring the local inhabitants, whose huts are much smaller and less well disposed than those formicary palaces (*Voyage to Senegal* p. 153). Gaspard Mollien mistook them for columns symmetrically fashioned by human hands. (*Voyage dans l'intérieur de l'Afrique*.) Johnson, perhaps with exaggeration, gives them twenty feet in height and claims that one abandoned nest served as a retreat for him and a dozen of his companions to lie in ambush for game. (*History of Gambia*). Bosman only gives them a elevation of twice the height of an ordinary man (*Description of Guinea* p. 276) and Abbé de La Caille certifies that a heavily laden cart could not break them in passing over them.

In those burning climes nature has no agents more active than the pismires for preventing the pestilential vapors that the cadavers of elephants, elands, wild horses, etc. might produce, or entire populations of negroes slaughtered and abandoned by their enemies. Thanks to those insects, the African soil still experiences prodigious changes and mutations over its surface. In a matter of months, they clear the most impenetrable forests, destroying and carrying away gigantic trees that seem to have braved the centuries; but if the fields are cultivated, if human habitations are established in the place they have cleared, entire villages deserted by the natives for a more fa-

already commencing the execution of those impudent threats, he had subjected the king's ambassador, who had just summoned him to return to duty, to that horrible torture. The skeleton of that unfortunate man, devoured alive by those avid insects, had been sent by way of a response to the legitimate master of the Congo. It was before those frightful remains that the latter was intoxicated by his projects of vengeance. Tortures, iron and flames seemed to him too mild to punish such crimes; he accused his imagination of sterility in the matter of tortures, for it was necessary for him to see slowness in the death and despair in the suffering.

However, in less than two months, the duchy of Bamba was subjugated by a small army that Maelo had composed from men who had already made war. Soon, Alvares, abandoned by his soldiers, was imprisoned in a vast subterrain, with his immense family, for, having long renounced the Christian religion in order to follow the laws of fetishism, more favorable to pleasure, he had taken a large number of wives and had no fewer than two hundred children.

The king was ready to slake his taste for vengeance on the guilty party and all his relatives, but Maelo was not yet

---

vorable situation sometimes disappear under their iron mandibles; soon, no vestige of them remains; the mangrove and the baobab put down their roots again, and younger and brilliant vegetation returns as the legitimate queen, after a temporarily exile, to establish itself on the terrain from which it had been dispossessed.

The different species of termites or pismires, their mores, their transformations, their maneuvers, marches, war-cries and rallying cries, and the amours of the monarchical insects for their king or queen, all offer the greatest interest, and the most curious and animated tableau, and we engage the reader to refer, for more ample details, to the memoirs of the Baron de Géer or M. Smeathman's discourse, translated by Pierre Letourneur in *Le Voyage d'André Sparrman au Cap de Bonne-Espérance.* (X.)"

informed of his cruel projects. That idea tormented him; he had contracted the habit of not being able to act without his advice and approval. On the one hand, he feared that the sage minister, while recognizing the justice of the punishment, might criticize the terrible excesses; one the other hand, he hoped that the wise man, having visited almost all the countries of Africa in which vengeance is in honor, might serve his fury, by revealing to him some action in rapport with the present situation, some torture unknown in the Congo.

In order to get out of that uncertainty, using cleverness, he resolved only to ask him to recount adventures of that sort of which he had been witness or the auditor, without informing him of his secret thoughts, hoping that Maelo, by his speech, would give him examples to imitate, and legitimate the vengeances that he was meditating, not being able to criticize now what he had approved of himself in other circumstances.

"Your narrations please me, you know," he said to him one day. "Our Europeans have communicated the secrets of their beautiful language, and your speech is as sweet and nourishing as palm liquor. You have seen and observed so much in your long voyages that each of your words develops in my mind like a seed of millet in moist ground. Is it true, as it is said, that the majority of the peoples of this continent devote themselves with passion and without remorse to the most hateful passions, and that the memory of an insult remains very sharp in their hearts? I am unhappy; the misfortunes of others might be a relief to me. Tell me a story that will enlightenment as to the mores of those peoples, the firmness and the rudeness of their soul, their care in punishing an insult—in sum, their vengeances."

Maelo divined the king's thought. "Your desires are all-powerful for me," he replied. "I shall obey, and I shall cite you the facts of that genre that have struck me the most by their singularity or the terrible character with which they are imprinted."

And. perceiving that his master appeared to be listening with avidity to the orator, the Congolese poet gathered his ideas and commenced.

This is his first narrative.

The Hottentot-Boshi

Not far from the Cape colonies, on the banks of the Palamit, there is a fertile valley, the beauty of which is more remarkable by virtue of the aridity of the land that surrounds it. There, in bushy woods, where aloes flower in twenty different colors, where thousands of candle-trees and lataniers rise in columns and curve, united in vegetal porticos, where the African protea causes its silvery leaves to shine over the gold of gorse, which, surrounding its base, forms magical pyramids with it, where herds of agile buffaloes, blue spotted goats and errant gazelles roam. But sometimes, also, the roars of the lion and the panther are heard under the palaces of verdure; and packs of wild dogs, perhaps even more ferocious than them, similar to the mebbias[77] of this region, bring terror and carnage there.

Into that valley, a population of Hottentots, the powerful nation of the Hessaquas, transported its huts and its riches, under the conduct of its Captain Ruyter. The real name of that chief was Susoa, but having almost betrayed his companions solely out of love of European liquors, he had submitted to the protection of the Dutch, had been constrained to adopt the name of one of his patrons, and had received, as a distinctive mark of his power, a bamboo from India on which the arms of the Cape government were engraved.

An audacious and vigilant character, in a few years, Captain Ruyter had made his kraal, of village, one of the largest in Hottentot Holland. He had accustomed his subjects to activity,

---

[77] Author's note: "The mebbia of the Congo is a relentless destroyer of all other quadrupeds."

a rare thing among those peoples, who make sloth their sole divinity, and whose common maxim is that labor is suffering, and that thinking is labor. Among them were found smiths, potters, tanners, ivory-workers and rope-makers, so ease made itself felt everywhere.

Instead of the low, narrow and smoky huts in which entire families were heaped up in other kraals, they had spacious and comfortable ones, furnished with mats and provided with the utensils necessary to prepare their nourishment. Each of the inhabitants possessed a krosse to cover himself, leather boots in which to go hunting, a kirri, a rackum and an assegai with which to fight his enemies, and a flute and a gom-gom to dance after the victory.[78]

Three ivory rings round their arms served to suspend a bag of provisions and a small piece of wood burned at both ends known as a susa, which is regarded as a preservative against all magic spells. Finally, the poorest of them could still procure a pipe—the ultimate in wealth among other Hottentots—tobacco, knife and an ax.

Few among them, however, devoted themselves willingly to the pastoral life, which entailed more fatigues and dangers, for lions often visited their pastures. Bakeleyers, a species of bull trained for war and guarding the flocks, were able to bring back ewes that strayed into the plain, assembled the animals and defend them against the approach of strangers,

---

[78] Author's note: "A krosse is a sheepskin cloak, worn fleece inwards. The kirri and the rackum are sticks armed with iron or pointed bones; the former serves for attack, the latter for defense. The assegai is the African lance, as the rackum is the javelin. A gom-gom is an instrument in which the string traverses the hollow of a feather; the musician puts the pipe to his mouth and extracts agreeable sounds by blowing. There are large and small gom-goms. Kolbe thinks the instrument might be perfected in Europe. André Sparrman calls it a t'koi-t'koi."

but the terrible cry of the lion rendered them as tremulous as the lambs that they were charged with protecting.

Ruyter, or Susoa, whichever you want to call him, learned at one time that a troop of Hottentot-Boshis[79] had camped a few leagues from his kraal, in the thickness of a vast forest, and he resolved to take possession of the youngest of the band, in order to entrust them with the service that the bravest of his subjects seemed to refuse.

You are doubtless unaware, great king, that Hottentot-Boshis are enemies of all dependence, inhabiting woods and arid mountains. Hunting and pillage are their sole occupations; bloody flesh torn away and sliced by the large and trenchant fingernails, ants and locusts dried in the sun, provide their nourishment. Pointed ironwood sticks and reeds armed with a sharp stone are their assegais and arrows; a hollowed-out tree branch of which nothing often remain but the bark, sealed at the ends with snakeskin, serves as a quiver, and some crevice in the rock or the entrails of a ferocious beast becomes their sepulcher.

As soon as they are old enough to launch an arrow, they swear an oath on the heads of their elders never to torment the earth in order to constrain it to nourish them, not to debase their human dignity to the point of becoming guardians of animals, born free like them, and which can only belong to them by right of war.

In spite of that precarious and savage existence, those peoples are neither cruel nor deceitful. Vanquished and forced

---

[79] The reference is not, as might be imagined, to the Mbochi people of Central Africa but to the Kalahari "Bushmen" [from the Dutch Bosjesmans]. In the final version of the story, which he retitled "Tamus, the Saab," the author refers to the people in question as "Hottentot Saabs, ou Boschimans" [i.e., Saab Hottentots or Bushmen]. Saab is one of the words used the "Bushmen" to describe themselves. Later versions of the story are considerably revised, many of the esoteric terms being removed, as well as most of the footnotes.

into servitude, they try to recover their liberty without ever profiting from their flight to rob their master of the smallest object, even one necessary to their subsistence. A few, however, desirous of a more placid life, under the orders of a king who has no other rights over his people than that of always being the first to devote himself to the common good, go into the solitudes of Africa to shelter their little societies from the ferocity of Kaffirs or the tyranny of the Cape colonists.

It was on one of those latter populations that the captain, followed by a numerous and well-armed troop of his people, suddenly fell unexpectedly. The old men, and those who opposed the most resistance, were massacred pitilessly, as soon as Ruyter, seizing them forcefully by the hair, had uttered the war cry. The rest were tied up and led over the burning sands to the kraal, where their arrival was the signal for a general feast, during which the victor did not fail to drink copiously as a sign of rejoicing.

Amahote, the king of the poor Hottentot-Boshis, as well as his wife and a child the latter was nursing, were among the captives. In the division they fell to a smith who, by his harshness and the difficult labor in which he employed them, rendered their slavery even more unbearable and more humiliating than that of their miserable companions.

An escape attempt that Amahote made a short time thereafter, which was assisted by a large number of prisoners, was the result of that barbaric conduct. Captured near the Palamit, however, he was taken back to Ruyter, who, in order to frighten by his example those who might want to imitate him, after having ordered that he be attached to a stake in the middle of the circular space in the middle of the kraal, caused him to expire under the forceful blow of the samboc, a lacerating whip made of strips of the hide of a rhinoceros or a sea-cow.

The queen died of shock and dolor. The smith, whose cruelty was the primary cause of that double catastrophe, also felt the punishment, for he was deprived of his slaves, and moreover, they left their son still on the teat, who could only

221

cause him a great embarrassment. His character was not belied on that occasion; in order to get rid of him he invoked an ancient law of the land, which ordered that any child still requiring her milk should be thrown alive into his mother's grave. That demand being recognized as just, the following day was designated for the execution of that lugubrious ceremony.

The crowd, avid for such a spectacle, was already contemplating the feeble orphan, whose last sighs the earth was about to stifle, with a dolorous curiosity. A cruel arm had already seized him, when Susoa's only son, aged four years at the most, uttering lamentable cries at the sight of that odious marriage of life and death, threw himself on his father's bosom, gripped by terror, and by means of his tears, his pleas and his despair, obtained mercy for the innocent victim. Susoa offered the smith a black ram to make him renounce his property rights over the poor little creature, and not only took him under his protection, but took the place of the father of whom he had deprived him.

Pharaoh was the name of Susoa's son, Tamus the name of the son of Amahote. Tamus and Pharaoh were bought up together. Entrusted to the care of women, they learned over time the bizarre and difficult language that no human speech approaches and which, by its whistling, croaking and squeals, its inarticulate sounds, seems to be the natural link between human language and that of animals. Thanks to their teachers, they were soon able to sew, weave and even dye fabrics, talents common to all the Hottentots. Later the women instructed them in the usages and the traditions of the ancestors, the ceremonies and the laws of the nation, of which they were the depositaries.

Meanwhile both of them felt their strength developing. Tamus, younger than Pharaoh, found a guide and protector in him. Sometimes crossing the frontiers of the kraal, they roamed the banks of the Palamit in order to pick up a few little shells, of which they then made ornaments. Not daring to venture into the woods, they often visited the edge, surprised the edolio cuckoo in its nest, forced the retreat of a wild horse, or collected the delicious honey that the bees of the region deposited in fissures in the rocks.

It was thus that their almost fraternal amity was formed. Their character, however, was scarcely in accord. Pharaoh, indolent and weak, was, in the depths of his heart avid for pleasures and domination. Tamus, lively, ardent and generous, owing his life to his young companion, submitted to all his desires in order to prove his gratitude. The eventual result of that was that the captain's son, exaggerating in his own eyes the strength of the obligation that the Boshi orphan ought to have to him, became accustomed to seeing him as nothing but a devoted servant whom he honored with his protective amity.

Finally, the day came when they had to quit the society of the women in order to be admitted into that of the men. The inhabitants of the kraal sat in a circle in the middle of the central area; the Sury, simultaneously a physician and a priest, like the Ganga-Negombo of that immortal kingdom, proposed the admission of the postulants, and after having collected the voices of the assembly over them, went to fetch them ceremoniously, and declared them admitted to the rank of men, worthy of that name.

"Show now," he said to them, "the prudence of the chameleon, whose double gaze watches before and behind him at the same time; acquire the strength of the lion in order to combat your enemies, and the vigilance of the korhaan[80] in order to save your friends from peril. Above all, avoid the presence of women, like that of snakes."

Then, having made them crouch down on their heels, he watered their hair, coated with grease and soot, with his urine, and added: "Now get up; be happy, live long, grow, multiply, and may we soon see your beards appear!"

It was at that time that a new colony of the same Hessaqua nation came to settle not far away. Deputations were

---

[80] Author's note: "As soon as a korhaan [a species of bird] perceives a hunter it utters a cry to warn other birds to be on their guard."

sent on either side in order to establish relations of commerce and amity. One of those deputations was led by Amahote's son, who had scarcely arrived in the neighboring kraal when he was surprised by a violent amour for a young Hottentot woman who was easily capable of inspiring such a passion, for her physique and her costume would have obtained the suffrage of all his compatriots.

Her complexion, like that of all the inhabitants of the region, was dark olive, her eyes black and piercing, her lips full and brightly colored, her figure slim and shapely. Over her hair, powdered with buchu,[81] she wore the black-dyed stomach of a ferocious beast, by way of a bonnet, bordered with a double row of little shells and a strip of buffalo-hide whose brown hair protruded. A leather strap that surrounded her neck was charged with the same ornaments. A triple apron of greased hide gripped her waist,[82] and the large number of rings with which her arms and legs were surrounded enabled her to be

---

[81] Author's note: "Buchu is a yellow powder, which the Hottentots obtain by collecting leaves of *Spiraea africanus* when they begin to wither, reducing them to powder after having dried them in the sun."

[82] Author's note: "It is this triple apron that has given birth to all the tales told about Hottentot women and the cutaneous excrescences that serve them as a natural modest veil. The Jesuit Tachard who, out of respect for his robe, had doubtless examined the matter very lightly, was the first to spread that absurd rumor, subsequently repeated by a host of sedentary compilers who prefer to believe than go to see, or credulous and hurried travelers who only have time to pass through and report what they have heard. It is similar with the semi-castration of Hottentots, still attested by a few modern voyagers, which has not taken place among those peoples for some time." Guy Tachard only spent a short time in South Africa in 1686 when a ship carrying a Jesuit embassy to Siam was wrecked off the Cape of God Hope, stranding him temporarily.

recognized as belonging to one of the foremost families of the land, even though she had not marked her face with a black stripe, like all women of high rank.

Tamus asked her name.

"My name is Nealea," she relied, with a soft smile; for the young man had made almost as much of an impression on her as she had on him.

In order to link their acquaintance he presented her with a beautiful pipe made from the horn of an eland, very well sculpted, which he had received from one of the former subjects of his father, the other Hottentots only employing wood for the construction of theirs.

Nealea smiled again, accepted it, and presented him in her turn with a little vase filled with eau-de-vie. They both sat down on the ground then, and drank and smoked together. Their liaison was already far advanced when Tamus returned to his kraal.

His first concern on arrival was to tell his friend about the pleasant encounter he had had in the home of their allies. Pharaoh congratulated him and, surprised by the countless praises that he lavished on Nealea, asked to return with him, desiring, if possible, also to fall in love in the same place as Tamus.

For several days, however, Susoa's son went hunting so early in the morning that his childhood companion was unable to join him in order to make the desired journey together. Impatient with his lack of urgency and burning with the desire to see his mistress again, about whom he thought night and day, Tamus finally decided to go alone. He set forth immediately.

As he was going along a narrow path in the forest he saw the extremity intercepted by an enormous lion, which, sitting with its head high and its eye attentive, seemed to want to dispute his passage. Although he was armed, as usual, with a bow, a rackum and an assegai, he did not think it prudent to risk himself against such an adversary. Retracing his steps, he took another path, at the end of which the lion appeared again, immobile and in the same posture.

Incessantly directing his march toward his original goal, a new detour caused him to penetrate into the thickest part of the forest, from which he had difficulty getting out, for, although he was enveloped in his krosse and his legs were garnished with strips of leather, the brambles and spiny cacti had ripped his garments and lacerated his limbs. But he was going to see Nealea! One glance, one smile, would compensate him for his fatigue and his wounds.

Recovered from his terror, he was hastening to reach a nearby mountain at a rapid pace when, between two rocks that it was necessary to cross, the same lion, still sitting and still motionless, offered itself to his sight for the third time.

"Death or victory!" cried Tamus. "I won't retreat again. To you, fatal beast; I'll take your hide to Nealea, or your voracious cubs can share mine."

The first arrow he launched only skimmed the superb animal's flank; getting up slowly, it marched toward its attacker with a proud and disdainful stride. A second arrow struck it in the throat and pierced it through; then horrible roars caused the hundred voices of the mountain resound; with one bound it reached its enemy and, mouth agape and eyes blazing, it was launching itself in order to devour him when he pierced its heart with a thrust of his assegai and laid it at his feet.

Covered in the monster's skin, still warm and fuming, full of pride as a victor and full of hope as a lover, he advanced toward the habitation of the beautiful Hottentot. Suddenly, in the first man he saw, he recognized Pharaoh.

"Don't go any further," the latter said. "I've seen your Nealea; I love her; renounce her, or I'll die."

Tamus was stupefied. In the excess of his dolor, he broke the little piece of sacred wood suspended from his arm, and then he replied to his friend: "I've just killed a lion, which, like you, did not want me to reach her; but I owe you my life; I'll go away. Adieu."

Informed of his exploit on the mountain, Captain Ruyter, when he saw him return, wanted to award him the honors accorded to heroes who emerged triumphant from single combat with a ferocious beast.[83] Tamus refused everything, shut himself in his cabin and spent the night weeping.

Pharaoh married Nealea, who also wept. Pharaoh perceived that and said to her: "Are you like the edolio, which only announces good weather with a dolorous cry?" For several days, however, there was nothing but dancing and feasting in the two kraals, the men leaping two by two before the women, who, eyes lowered, followed the movements of the dancers without ever taking their hand or touching them.[84] Large vases filled with a mixture of milk and water, entire elands roasted and butchered, giromons, ostrich eggs and various fruits invited the inhabitants to appease their thirst and hunger.

In the evening, in honor of the moon, wine, eau-de-vie and arrack were drunk. The dancing redoubled its activity; heads became excited, the laugher noisy; cries and stamping feet were heard on all sides, always increasing, until it was perceived that Captain Ruyter, lying on the grass, gorged with meat and drink, was giving no sign of life. All his relatives immediately assembled round him, and after the Sury had lavished his cares on him in vain, they uttered horrible clamors, tore their hair, wrung their hands and all struck the patient's body forcefully in order to expel the evil spirit hat was tor-

---

[83] Author's note: "These honors involve the urinary aspersion common to almost all Hottentot ceremonies; the oldest inhabitant of the village then takes a lit pipe, draws a few draughts from it and passes it to another, who does the same; it make a circuit of those surrounding the victor, after which, the tobacco being consumed, the ashes are tipped over his head. Proclaimed a 'hero of the first order,' he obtains permission to wear in his hair the bladder of the animal over which he has triumphed."

[84] Author's note: "Not in accord with our author on this point, Kolbe claims that the Hottentots, even though loving music and dancing passionately, make no usage of these diversions in their marriages."

menting him. In spite of the benevolent cares of his family and friends, however, the captain expired.

The next day, neglecting the two spouses, no one thought was thinking any longer about anything but the funeral ceremony. The relatives of the deceased, wearing hanks of sheepskin covered in bushu around their necks, and the inhabitants, with furrows shaven in their hair, uttered cries of grief. After having deposited the body in a hole that they filled with earth from a termitary, and on which they built a mound of wood and stone, they repeated "Bo"—father—making contortions around the grave: "Bo! Bo! Bo! Susoa!"

When that final adieu was over, the men and the women, returned to their kraal, formed two circles, which received in turn the customary aspersion; after which, the Sury took a handful of ashes from the captain's hearth and sprinkled them over the prostrate individuals, and everyone went home.

Meanwhile, Tamus still regretted Nealea, whom he had ceded to his friend; the captain's death did not increase his dolor, for he knew that Susoa had been his father's murderer and the destroyer of his compatriots. He was thinking about those cruel events when he saw a few Boshi shaves approaching him, taking singular precautions in order not to be seen.

"Tamus," they said to him, "We have all resolved to take advantage of the confusion caused by Ruyter's death to recover the liberty that was stolen from us a long time ago. The forests and the mountains still have retreats to receive us. Come with us; you are the son of Amahote, you will be our king."

"I can't go with you," Tamus replied. "I owe my life to Pharaoh, and the Hessaquas have adopted me as one of them; but may the deserts protect you. Slavery is the worst of evils."

All their efforts to include him in their desertion were futile; they fled without him the following night, while the kraal, by the order of Pharaoh, instituted captain in his father's stead, was being transported to another location, still following the course of the Palamit.[85]

Several of the fugitives were recaptured and delivered to Pharaoh, who had just taken the name of Captain Riebeck. The latter advised their masters, in order to free themselves from any anxiety, to sell them to the Namaquois, who maintained a commerce in slaves with the inhabitants of Benguela. His advice having been followed, the former possessors of the Boshis acquired a large quantity of Guinea cloth, small barrels of eau-de-vie, glass beads and other European curiosities that purchased those slaves on our coasts.

The sight of those riches excited Pharaoh's envy and cupidity; he said that he wanted to see Nealea covered with those strange ornaments. Furthermore, in spite of the example of his father, the usage of strong liquor was his greatest pleasure, and was soon his most constant passion; for he was beginning to feel an envious jealousy against his former companion, whom be believed to be still loved by his wife and who, more robust and more skillful than him, the vanquisher of a lion, had all the virtues of a chief, while he only had the title.

Judging, on the other hand, that the captain of a kraal ought not to content himself with a single wife, he gave poor Nealea rivals within the space of a year. Tamus, still a faithful friend, thought he ought to make a few observations to him about the disdain with which he was beginning to heap the woman that they had both cherished so much. He then demonstrated to him that the state of prosperity that the kraal had had under Captain Ruyter was far from having increased under Captain Riebeck; the livestock, the principal wealth of the country, had been delivered to the voracity of ferocious beasts.

"By the flight of your fellows," Pharaoh replied to him, irritated by his just remonstrations. "But if we need slaves, war will give them to us." Calming down, he added: "Don't

---

[85] Author's note: "It is customary among Hottentots to do that after the death of their chief, and sometimes even that of one of the poorer inhabitants."

worry; there'll be no shortage of them, and we'll have enough to sell to the Namaquois. Before long, our women will be walking on the brilliant jewels of Europe and we'll be washing our hands in eau-de-vie. As for my livestock, let the tigers devour them tomorrow; I'll cede them today to the Sonquas,[86] who are furnishing me with a hundred men to aid me in my enterprise. Go prepare your weapons, Tamus, and cease occupying yourself with sheep and women."

The Sonquas did, indeed arrive. On the most frivolous pretext, Pharaoh declared war on a tribe of Kaffirs that had just settled in the vicinity of the Orange River. Uttering their war-cries, the Hottentots assailed them with a hail of arrows and rackums, wading off their enemies' arrows with the kirri when the latter, masters of a hill, descended upon them howling, armed with ironwood daggers and elephants' jawbones, with which they stunned those who dared to await their impact.

The victory was not decided, however; Pharaoh's inexperience harmed all the maneuvers of his little army. Tamus, seconded by the Sonquas, fell upon the strangers, assegais in hand, in vain. The latter dispersed immediately and rallied in order to attack in their turn.

It was finally decided to make use of the Bakeleyers, the bellicose bulls, which, well trained, fell upon the enemy furiously, knocking them down, disemboweling them and binging the most horrible disorder in their ranks. But those frightful auxiliaries of Pharaoh, poorly directed and only sparing the inhabitants of the country to whom they belonged, hurled themselves impetuously at the Sonquas, their masters' allies, knocked them over and rent them in pieces.

---

[86] Author's note: "A Hottentot people who sell their warrior services to other Hottentots, as the Anzikis do to the Congolese, as the Scythians once did to the Greeks, the Gauls to the Romans and the Scots to the French, and as the Swiss do to several sovereigns in Europe today."

Already, Pharaoh, surrounded by a troop of Kaffirs uttering howls of rage and vengeance, was about to fall under their blows when Tamus came to his aid and rescued him. Pursued, however, and reduced to a small number, the Hottentots fled, and a universal lamentation welcomed their return to the kraal.

"Was there any need for the Sonquas?" said some. "Could we not vanquish on our own?"

"Why didn't he let Tamus command?" said others. "A man who defeats lions would have been able to defeat Kaffirs."

Pharaoh heard these complaints and his pride was wounded by them. They stifled in his heart the gratitude he owed his liberator and reawakened all his sentiments of jealousy. To distract himself he spent the night getting drunk, and woke up the next day with new projects of war.

The elders having assembled on his order he said to them: "The crocodile only releases its prey when it does; nothing can make me renounce my designs. Our flocks are almost annihilated; well, let us take possession of those of our neighbors; let us seize the sheep and the shepherds together; we'll eat the former and sell the latter, and with the produce of our prisoners we'll have bracelets and adornments for our women, and fiery liquor or ourselves."

One of the elders stood up. "May the moon cease forever to illuminate you with its radiance if you act thus," he replied. "Our enemies were Kaffirs, who might have crossed the Orange River without hostile intentions, but they have defeated us; let us only think of repairing our disasters; we can think about vengeance later."

The indignant Pharaoh ran to gather the warriors who had fought with him the day before. "I am your chief! You owe me obedience. The inhabitants of the kraal of Nealea, my first wife, have insulted us by not lending us their assistance against the Kaffirs. Their cause was ours. Although weakened by our defeat, we are still superior to them in number; let us fall upon them, and let them compensate us for the losses that their cowardice caused us to suffer."

Already, a murmur of approval was rising among those avid men when Tamus interrupted: "What are you asking, Pharaoh? Undoubtedly you're our chief, but it's in order to protect us, as you swore to do when you received the right of command from the elders. Do you want to drag us into another unjust fight, whose result might be our complete destruction? Do you want to set fire to the hut in which you found a companion and sell her family to the Namaquois?"

"Why is a foreigner, a Boshi, involving himself in our affairs?" said Pharaoh, angrily.

"I'm not a foreigner here," his friend replied, "for you above all, and I've spoken with sincerity."

"Only a coward fears war."

"I've proved on the day that gave birth to this one that I'm not a coward."

"The ostrich sometimes imitates the cry of the lion."

"I've constrained the first of those animals to supply me with a mount,[87] and the skin of the other is still extended in my hut."

"Who do you think you are, to dare to contest my will?"

"My father was a king, and I have forgotten him, for I refused to reign over his subjects in order to remain by your side."

"Your father was a slave!" cried the son of Susoa, breathless with fury, "and mine was your master, for he exchanged you for a black ram. I have succeeded to his rights over you, and I shall soon be able to make use of them."

His heart swollen with rage, he went back to his dwelling, where he found Nealea in tears. Already informed of her husband's projects against her family's kraal, she tried to soften him, reminding him of the services and the devotion of his childhood friend; but he pushed her away rudely and struck her ferociously.

---

[87] Author's note: "A few inhabitants of Africa succeed in making use of ostriches as horses, and nothing matches the speed of those animals."

"I know your sentiments for the Boshi already," he said. "The smallest finger of your hand is still too long to be in accord with your desires.[88] My death would make your happiness by uniting you with him. Well, I'll unite you!"

Bribed by him, the Sury declared that he had caught Tamus and Nealea in adultery. The law condemned them to death. Pharaoh demanded that the so-called guilty parties be surrendered to his discretion. A few slaves, former herdsmen, still remained to him; their service having become unnecessary in consequence of his bargain with the Sonquas, he resolved to subject them to the same fate, and the following day, after having their arms bound in order to deprive them of any means of resistance, the monster set forth to march them personally to the land of the Namaquois in order to exchange, for glass beads and liquor faithful servants, an innocent wife and the most generous of friends.

When they quit the kraal the majority of the inhabitants followed them for a few leagues, uttering long moans. Finally, on the reiterated order of the captain, they withdrew, showing all the signs of the most profound dolor, and soon, no one remained with him except the men charged with accompanying the cortege.

By the end of the first day, Nealea could hardly stand; the terrible blaze of the sun had sapped her strength, and each of her plaints resounded in Tamus' heart and lacerated it. The latter had been marching with his head bowed, sad and silent; no sigh had escaped his breast, no tear had moistened his eyelid. He was thinking of means of revenge. And yet, when he saw the woman he had loved so much, and whom he still loved, suffering and weeping beside him, by his fault—for if he had not sacrificed his love to Ruyter's son, the latter would never have been Nealea's husband—convulsions of fury set his gaze ablaze and caused all the parts of his body to contract.

---

[88] Author's note: "A Hottentot widow who wants to remarry is obliged to have a phalanx of her little finger cut off."

He mastered the violence of his transports, however, in thinking that Pharaoh might enjoy his torment.

At other times, almost narcotized by the heaviness of the air and the effect of continuous and monotonous marching, his memory retraced for him almost involuntarily the happy hours he had spent with Pharaoh and under his fraternal protection; and, although the spectacle of his present woe then came to destroy those pleasant images, he could not expel that former amity from his heart entirely, which had been the source of all his actions for such a long time.

For his part, Pharaoh, a monster of pride and avarice, avid for vengeance and riches, in order to maintain his ferocity, recalled to his memory instances in which the skill and strength of Tamus had been causes of humiliation for him. He did not dissimulate Nealea's love for his former companion, and sought to persuade himself that the accusation he had caused to weigh upon her might have some foundation. Calculating then how many pleasures he would derive from the sale of his slaves, his imagination excited by the spirituous liquors of which he had made use along the route, he created in his ideas, in the future, an entire existence of pleasures, and did not think at all about his father's end.

Meanwhile, the caravan plunged into immense plains, sometimes sandy and sometimes rocky, or even covered with crystalline salts which alternately burned or lacerated the feet of the unfortunates conducted by the pitiless Pharaoh.

They are crossing a mountain covered with asperities and rocky spurs when Nealea, succumbing to the fatigue and the pain that the wounds in her swollen and bloody feet are causing her to endure, finally collapses, bruised and motionless, face down on the stones. Tamus, thinking that she is dead, utters a cry; a supernatural force suddenly explodes within him; his bonds break.

His eyes ablaze, he pursues Pharaoh, who, gripped by terror, flees with the rapidity of an arrow. Tamus reaches him, knocks him down with a muscular arm, and, relieving him of a large cutlass that is part of his armaments, before anyone can come to his aid, he says: "Pharaoh, I have abandoned subjects and a mistress for you; I have saved you from peril, and you have made me your slave in order to sell me. However, I also owe you my life, and I shall respect yours; but you shall live covered with my blood."

Then he leaned over Nealea's husband, holding him fixed beneath him, and plunged the cutlass into his own heart; and while Pharaoh struggled, howling, beneath that horrible aspersion, he enlaced him with his arms and rendered the last sigh on his breast.

Thus Tamus died and avenged himself. His vengeance was terrible, for fear and remorse troubled the mind of the unworthy Hottentot chief to such an extent that, possessed by a furious delirium, he fled far from his companions, rolling in the sands of the desert in order to efface the vestiges of the murder. In the attempt to annihilate those fatal traces, lacerating himself with his sharp fingernails, he believed that he could see his friend's blood running from his own wounds. The sight of that blood pursued him and redoubled his remorse; the force of his remorse caused him to tear himself with a new rage.

He only recovered his reason after falling into the hands of a party of Kaffirs, who treated him as a slave themselves, and sold him to the Great Namaquois.

"And what became of Nealea?" the king of the Congo asked his sage minister.

"Returned to the kraal with her companions, she was received there under the protection of a new captain, designated by the Dutch to succeed Pharaoh."

"In any case, your Boshi hero only seems bizarre to me. Why so much gratitude for a benefit whose author virtually ignored it himself? What is a vengeance that does not kill? He wasn't a true African. Believe me, he went mad before the other. Does a tiger tear its own entrails before the hyena that has stolen its cubs? The memory of an old amity does not forbid punishing recent insults. To avenge oneself is the act of a

235

noble heart, and only the death of an enemy constitutes venge-ance."

"Master," said Maelo, "the second example that I will cite you of the effects of that terrible passion will doubtless satisfy you. The story made me shiver."

And the king lent his ears again.

The Almamy of Bondou

Between the ocean, the Nigritie, the vast Sahara deserts and the Upper Guinea, there is a large expanse of land traversed by two famous rivers, the Senegal and the Gambia.[89] Three principal races occupy a considerable area in that territory; they are the Yolofs, the Mandingos and the Foulahs,[90] once known as the "red men." The last-named, confounded by marriages with neighboring peoples for a long time, have lost their original coloring. A class of men has resulted from that mixture with a mulatto tint, silky hair and flat lips, submissive to various princes or almamys.[91] In their numerous estates,

---

[89] Author's note: "The Gambia bears in that land the name of Ba-Diman, the Senegal that of Zanagha or Baleo, Ba-fing or Foura."

[90] Author's note: "The difficulty of African studies is greatly augmented by the multiplicity of that continent's languages and the dissimilar names given to each people by voyagers from different countries. Thus the Foulahs are called, by turns, Foulis, Pholeys, Poules and Foulahs by Cadamosto, Labat, Bruce, Moore, Barbot, Mungo Park and Mollien, who also designate the Yolofs variously under the denominations Jalofs, Jolliofs, Ghialofs, Gialofs and Yolofs." The "Foulahs" are generally known nowadays as the Fulani.

[91] Author's note: "The same observation as in the previous note; each of the petty kings of those countries bears a title that only belongs to his race and his nation. The Foulah have

which extend from Sierra Leone all the way to Timbuktu, separated from one another by foreign possessions, as coral beads on a chaplet are by ebony beads, the ancient religion of fetishes and that of Mohammed are equally professed.

Messlael had just been newly elected Almamy of the realm of Bondou, belonging to the Foulahs, when Boukari, the siratick of the realm of Bambouk suddenly invaded his estates at the head of a numerous army.

Still alarmed by a conspiracy of marabouts, Mohammedan priests, who had attempted to destroy the domination of his princely ancestors, although they had all been massacred in a single night as a punishment for their rebellion, Boukari, in order to prevent his subjects from allowing themselves to be seduced by the partisans of that religion, had resolved to destroy it in all the kingdoms surrounding his own. He was at the head of a numerous and warrior people possessed of great wealth, cunning, courage and weapons; it did not take him long to render himself master of the realm of Galam, which confined his estates to the north, soon traversing the River Faleme, which separated it from Bondou, to appear before Fatteconda, the almamy's capital, before the later could think about its defense.

To complete the disaster, the savage Djalonkes, former inhabitants of the land, to whom the Foulahs owed their own origins, were united by their beliefs with the subjects of the siratick. They descended from their inaccessible mountains, to which the followers of the prophet had forced them to withdraw, and supported Boukari's efforts against Messlael.

The latter, naturally mild of character and timid, not yet familiarized with power and command, and fearing to compromise the existence of his people, resigned himself, and retreated before his conqueror, only regretting that his mother, who was then living on the shady banks of the Nerico, could not accompany him to soften the pains of exile for him. He

---

siraticks, the Muslims almamys, the Mandingos mansas and farims, the Yolofs damels, boubs, tins, etc."

retreated toward the sun, reached the desert of Simbani, and only there, thinking about his misfortune, did he begin to weep. However, before crossing the Gambia, which formed the limit of Bondou in that direction, he dispatched one of his servants to the siratick to ask that he cede it to him in exchange for his kingdom.

The conqueror responded insolently to that message, and only sent a pair of iron annals to the almamy, declaring that, until he was far enough away to have worn them out completely, he would not be safe from Bambouk arrows.

Messlael, in despair, then crossed the river and sought refuge among the Mandingos of Geba, hoping in days still to come, and entrusting his destiny to a saphi,[92] in the form of a cross, which his mother had given him, and on which was traced a precept of the law of Mohammed.

Boukari took advantage cleverly of the flight of the vanquished almamy to consolidate his power in Bondou. He brought together the almamy's principal subjects and the leaders of his troops, as well as those of the Djalonkes, in a large public meeting, and said to them: "Let us become again what we were before; as you see, the ancient divinities of Africa have vanquished your Mohammed. If some of you still want to cling to that demon with the white face, well, we'll add his

---

[92] Author's note: "A kind of amulet, also known as a grisgris, dominis or teres. It is noticeable that many of the inhabitants of the country of which we are speaking wear ornaments in the form of a cross; some even trace that sign on the body by means of deep incisions. The idea of protection and good fortune that they attach to those objects seems to prove that in distant times the Christian religion had reached them. The Gospel, translated into Arabic and skillfully spread through those peoples, might have produced unexpected results there, which could only have turned to their advantage and given solidity and guarantees to the relations that the French of the coast maintained with them; but people today only think about the conversion of Christians."

turban and his book to the number of our fetishes. But the thing has happened before your eyes; you cowardly and trembling chief has run away. What can serve as an excuse for the flight of the feeble Messlael? Surprise? His youth? His inexperience? A lion is born with open eyes, so your almamy cannot claim descent from such a noble race. I have expelled him, as I should, for he was not the son of the brother of your former almamy.[93] One of the ferocious inhabitants of Maniana, who nourish themselves on human flesh, was his father; he is the fruit of crime; our gods will take care of justifying what I say. I put my hope in them. He has deceived you, and delivered you into my power. All of you who know the fathers of your fathers, will you consent to take for your governor the son of a koumi?[94] In continuing to obey him you risk becoming similar to those beings who were once like us but who, as a punishment for their sins, live today in the trees of forests, deprived of speech and covered with frightful hair. I have said enough; I leave you to reflect on it."

In order to support his speech, devoid of proofs, the Mumbo-Jumbo, a terrible divinity among those people, charged with watching over the fidelity of wives, did not take long to make his cries heard in the woods. Immediately, in accordance with custom, all the women of Fatteconda went in haste to Bentang—a vast clearing surrounded by trees—each of them affecting an air of joy and tranquility in order to set aside any suspicion that such a visit might be compromising.

Ornamented with care, those who belonged to kafirs, or pagans, were clad in brightly-colored loincloths, their bare arms and legs covered with rings and bracelets of tin or silver. The wives of buschreens—true believers—were distinguished by glass beads mingled with their hair and golden plaques shining on their foreheads.

---

[93] Author's note: "In almost all the parts of the continent, only a nephew can succeed to his uncle's power; the children of the sovereign revert to the common class."

[94] Author's note: "A cannibal."

Guefoulbe, the almamy's mother, a prisoner of the siratick, was conducted in their midst, by his order. After the customary dances and amusements, a great rumor announced the arrival of the Mumbo-Jumbo. He suddenly appeared, uttering terrible clamors, clad in a straw bonnet, a mask and a garment made of tree-bark. After a thousand bizarre contortions, he designated with his wand the unfortunate Guefoulbe, who, condemned as guilty by that sign alone, was attached to a stake and publicly whipped, after which she was declared to be a slave.

In the land of the Mandingos, Messlael learned about the insult to his mother, and no longer thought of anything but avenging her. He put on Boukari's present, the iron sandals, swearing to wear them away in the relentless pursuit of the execution of his project; and that man, who had been able to quit authority with so much insouciance, at the story of his new misfortune, became a hero whose soul was full of resolution, his mind of activity and his body of strength.

The inhabitants of Geba seemed to sympathize with his plight and had promised to take up arms in his favor. He took the case to the mansa, the sovereign of the country, and found him holding a broom in his hand, a sign of his power, but when he approached him to remind him of his engagements, the air suddenly darkened, and night interrupted the day. The frightened mansa cried: "Woe! Woe! The great cat has just put his paw between the earth and the moon."

Immediately, all the people assembled in order to drive away the catastrophe by which they were threatened, by dancing in honor of Mohammed to the sound of various instruments and the repeated clapping of hands.

The almamy waited impatiently for the end of that scene, but minds had changed in his regard, and the mansa said to him: "Your presence in this place has attracted the menaces of heaven upon us; be glad, however. Your mother has been declared guilty by the Mumbo-Jumbo, and that holy belief was born among us, where it is still held in honor; it would be to attract a thousand frightful misfortunes upon our heads to protect you; be glad, however. We welcomed you as a friend at first, and you would not want, like the elephant, to trouble the water that has slaked your thirst. Adieu, be glad."

A victim of the bizarre credulity of a people who conserved their ancient superstitions in the midst of their fervor for the new religion, the noble descendant of the sovereigns of Bondou resolved to seek help elsewhere. He crossed the Gambia again, near Pisania, penetrated into the realm of Alum, too weak to rise up alone in his favor, and after having made allies there he went into the vast country of Foutatorra, inhabited by Foulahs.

The powerful almamy of that realm received him as a sovereign and a brother. "I know your misfortunes," he said to him, and your mother will be avenged."

Immediately dispatching an envoy to Boukari, he made him a present of two keenly sharpened knives, declaring to him that if he rendered his kingdom of Bondou to Messlael and set his mother free, he, a bushreen would consent to let him shave his beard with one of those instruments, even though the siratick was kafir and descendant of the murder of marabouts; but if he refused to satisfy his proposal, he would make use of the other knife to cut off his head.

The envoy did not come back. In order to support his threats, an army was organized by the ruler of Foutatorra. The cavalry was numerous and almost all the foot soldiers possessed a rifle. Messlael, full of hope, put himself at their head. After a few days' march, however, it was necessary to cross an arid and sandy desert. The soldiers, exhausted by fatigue, began to murmur; inexpert or treacherous guides led them astray, and the discouragement was general when famine came to complete the horror of their situation in the midst of those solitudes. A large number died of thirst and lack of nourishment; the others dispersed in one direction or another, and Messlael, abandoned by everyone, needed to remember his mother and recall his projects of vengeance in order not to succumb himself.

Breathless and overwhelmed, with despair in his heart, he contrived to reach the bank of the Senegal, which then separated him from the Sahara, and after having quieted his hunger slightly with a few tomberongs,[95] he fell on the sand at the foot of a tree and went to sleep there.

If anything could have distracted him from his ideas and dolors, it was the scene that struck his eyes when he awoke. Beyond the immense river that was flowing before him, the great desert extended its white carpet to an indefinite horizon that was confounded with the sky. Siboa palms seemed to extend as far as the eye could see; gigantic baobabs a hundred feet in circumference, elevated their mountains of verdure into the sky, in which pelicans had built their vast nests, while numerous herds of elephants and giraffes were passing back and forth between their heavy branches, curved toward the ground. Further away, a giant among reptiles, a boa, was sliding its innumerable coils under the shiny leaves of calabash trees laden with enormous fruits, while, along the bank, long crocodiles were lying, soaking up the sun's rays, and the agitated waves were suddenly dominated by the monstrous head of a shark. In sum, the river, the desert, that prodigious vegetation and those colossal living things were all in proportion, and presented a spectacle unknown to the rest of the world, which human eyes can only witness in that part of Africa.

However, Messlael was scarcely touched by it; he was only thinking about his vengeance, his disappointed hopes, and the hope of realizing them soon. He picked up the little cross that was hanging from his belt and kissed it, while thinking about his mother, and disposed it in order to make a new charm to ward off his evil destiny. Having done that, he

---

[95] Author's note: "Small floury berries belonging to the plant that Linnaeus designates by the name *Rhamnus lotus*; it grown in arid terrain." *Ziziphus lotus*, as *Rhamnus lotus* is nowadays known, is native to the Mediterranean region, and is not the source of tomberong berries, as alleged by William Fordyce Mavor, from whom Saintine presumably derived this datum.

reached the village of Podor, where he hired an almadie, a boat made from a hollowed-out tree trunk, and, paddling it himself, followed the course of the Senegal until he arrived in the estates of the damel.

He was in the realm of Cayor, among the Yolofs, He had a great deal of difficulty reaching the damel, for that prince, having increased his wealth by commerce since making frequent contact with the French—a European nation that had founded a few establishments on the coast—was contemptuous of the simple and unostentatious life that still distinguished a few sovereigns of the interior of the continent. He even had in his service a troop of Moors, who defended the entrance to his topade, or enclosure, which enclosed nearly eighty huts.

Irritated by the obstacles that he encountered in trying to approach the king, his equal, Messlael, unable to be introduced into his kalde, or audience chamber, without submitting to a ceremonial and delays that his pride and his thirst for vengeance both reproved, resolved to accost the prince when he came out to respire the cool air of the evening.

The opportunity was offered to him sooner than he expected. Advancing proudly toward the damel, in spite of the menacing attitude of his bronzed cortege, he said: "Prince of Cayor, I am the almamy of Bondou. My father's brother once offered a refuge in his estates to unfortunate Yolofs; today a Foulah is requesting your assistance, not to recover his authority but to avenge his mother."

The damel, astonished by that abrupt apparition, contented himself initially with responding: "May Mohamed assist you, Brother." Recalling then the recent reverses of Guefoulde's son, thinking of the distance that separated his realm, from that of Bondou, he was hesitating to respond to his appeal, when suddenly, striking his drum loudly and agitating the silver bells suspended from his bonnet and the edges of his garments, a Griot mounted on a ostrich that he had been able to tame traversed the crowd surrounding the damel.

Placing himself in front of him, feigning one of the sudden inspirations by means of which those poets of Africa are so well able to impose respect and attention on the Yolofs, even their chiefs, the Griot said: "Damel, lend assistance to the bushreen against the kafir; Mohammed wished it. Might the fate of the almamy not await you? Might not every emperor, king, dey, tin, brack, siratick, tonka, damel, bourb, mansa and almamy experience a similar fate in his turn? The baobab yields easily to the ax and the hurricane; the ebony blunts the iron and braves the effort of the tempest. Remember that the Griot, like the chameleon, has a tongue as long as his body; if you want to be praised by him, commence by meriting the praise"

For his only response, the Prince of Cayor gave the order to his troops to get ready to march, and the Griot disappeared.

The preparations having concluded, the damel, clad in a red robe ornamented by the tails of elephants, with his head covered by a wicker bonnet surmounted by the tiny horns of a gazelle, came to pass his troops in review. Then he wished the almamy success, extended his hand to him three times and passed it over his forehead. Everyone did likewise, and the war was declared to have begun.

They traversed the land of Baol in order to embark on the sea and go up the Gambia as far as Pisania; but the demon had not yet fatigued Messael's constancy sufficiently. At the mouth of the river, a violent tempest dispersed the fleet and smashed its almadies against the rocks. He only escaped, along with a few Yolof soldiers, with the aid of the numerous pieces of debris with which the waves were covered.

His new hope was destroyed along with his new army; famine threatened him again. In his distress, the heavens seemed to come to his aid momentarily; the sea, as it withdrew, had narrowed the bed of the Gambia, and the mangroves that grew on its banks were curbed beneath the weight of oysters, which then, following the impulsion of the wind, swung in the air with a continuous clicking. The almamy and his companions who had escaped the shipwreck collected branches laden with that precious aliment, and headed toward the territory of Salum, where they were welcomed with cries of joy and marks of interest that made them forget their misfortune momentarily.

There, the friends that Messlael had made while going to Foutatorra told him that a Yolof Griot, traversing the country mounted on an ostrich, had roused it almost entirely in his favor by his persuasive eloquence and his threats in the name of Mohammed, and that that he had gone thereafter from Salum into Wouilli, whose inhabitants, neighbors of Bondou and already threatened by Boukari, seemed disposed to put an end to the crimes of that ambitious man.

At that fortunate news, the son of Guefoulbe felt his ardor redoubled and his hope reborn. He immediately set forth, blessing the Griot, and a few days later, at the head of an army of Mandingos from Wouilli, he reached the frontier of his former estates and found himself surrounded already by a large number of his faithful subjects, who had hastened to meet him in order to receive him in triumph.

His happiness was brief. The warriors on Bambouk, supported and guided by the Djalonkes through the mountain passes, surprised him in the midst of his joy, falling unexpectedly upon is army and dispersing it.

Fatality was thus attached to the fate of the unfortunate almamy of Bondou. Superstition, famine, tempest and war had all turned against his generous projects, but without being able to extract them from his heart. His desire for vengeance was even less eroded than his iron sandals. He could only count on himself henceforth, on his arm alone. A fugitive, plunging into the forests that separated Wouilli from the possessions of Bondou, he resolved to wait there for a propitious moment to conclude his vengeance and his mother's slavery with a dagger-thrust.

In fear of being recognized, he first abandoned and hid in the undergrowth the ornaments that might betray his rank or religion, and stained his face and body with liquor extracted from the tree known as komo,[96] in such a way as to resemble more closely a black Yolof than a coppery Foulah. Then he returned to the plain and skirted the paths that might lead him to Fatteconda, the present residence of the siratick, nourishing himself on the wild fruits of the dombock and the fig tree.

When he was a short distance from a village he saw a man emerge therefrom whose gestures and gait announced the greatest dolor. It was the same Griot that had aided him so powerfully with his speech in Cayor, Salum and Woulli, and whose valor had shone before his eyes during Boukari's unexpected attack.

Messlael traveled alongside him silently for some time and then, affecting an indifference that he was far from feeling, he asked: "Were you not with the almamy of Bondou In the recent battle in which he was defeated?"

Surprised, the Griot immediately looked around, recoiled a few paces, drew his box taut, and replied: "I was there."

"It's a friend who is speaking to you," said Messlael; I fought in the same ranks as you. But what motive led you to spring so ardently to the defense of a chief foreign to your nation?"

"I was born in Bondou," the damel's poet replied. "My father, banished from his homeland, received the hospitality of the former almamy there; my childhood was protected by that generous prince; I wanted to acquit my debt with his successor, but my gratitude is venomous and my kisses, like those of the boa, give death. In favoring Messlael's projects, I have caused the doom of that prince; his head is doubtless suspended today from the siratick's hut and making its most beautiful ornament."

"What? What do you mean?"

---

[96] Author's note: "*Pterocarpus draco*, from the black resin of which the medicine known as dragon's blood is extracted. (X.)" Again, *Dracaena cinnabari*, as *Pterocarpus draco* or dragon blood tree is now called, is not native to the area in which the story is set, but to the Yemen.

"Soldier of the almamy, do you not know, then, that after his victory, Boukari had Guefoulbe sacrificed to his gods?"

At this point a cry of dolor escaped Messlael's breast, and he was inundated by a cold sweat. He cracked his knuckles silently—a sign of profound despair among those peoples.

He remained mute, however, and the Griot continued: "The frontiers are guarded, and Boukari who is not unaware that his rival is in Bondou, has sworn by his fetishes not to emerge from his hut until he has nailed Messlael's head therein. A thousand emissaries distributed everywhere are lying in wait for such a noble prey; thirty slaves will be the recompense for the man who brings it, and it is doubtless already merited."

"And what is your design?" asked the unfortunate son of Guefoulbe of the Griot.

"I only have one arrow, but it is poisoned and my aim is sure; I'm reserving it for the siratick."

"Let's march together, then, for my dagger wants to reach the same target."

"Let's march," said the Griot. "Perhaps you were the guest or a relative of the almamy. Whether that is the case or not, I will second you; the jackal sometimes hunts with the lion."

After having carefully avoided a thousand encounters that might have been dangerous for them, they arrived in Fatteconda, and watched out ardently for a propitious moment to fit the arrow to the bowstring or to strike with the dagger. But Boukari, faithful to his oath, did not quit the enclosure of his dwelling—which proved to the Griot that the almamy was still alive.

Meanwhile, even though the city was inhabited by a numerous population, the presence of the two strangers nevertheless excited the suspicion of a few of Dambouk's chiefs. Messlael felt that it was time to act, and presented himself with his intrepid companion before the siratick's topade.

A troop of Djalonkes was guarding the entrance.

"We want to speak to the powerful siratick of Bambouk, Falam and Bondou,."

"What subject brings you to him?" asked the kafir's soldiers.

"We have rid him of his enemy and have come to claim the reward."

"I know the son of the infamous Guefoulbe," said a Djanke, "show me his head; it alone can give you access to the siratick's hut."

Messlael, hearing his mother insulted, was seized by an emotion so violent that it almost betrayed him and deprived him of the use of his reason. The Griot, perceiving his disturbance without divining the reason for it, and sensing the futile danger that there was in remaining any longer in the royal lair, declared that they had the body of the former almamy in the wood whether they had surprised and immolated the victim, that they would be able to find the place again and bring back the bloody proof of their devotion to the Boukari's orders.

Drawing away then, they went in haste to an isolated spot some distance from the city, where a fast-running stream flowed under gum trees. The sone, with its numerous leaves and its clusters of fruits, winding around the trees, would be able to hide them from all eyes.

They sat down to think about what remained for them to try.

The Griot was the first to break the silence. "Companion, if my features and the color of my skin were similar to those of the almamy, I would beg you to cut off my head and make it a means of passage for you to reach out enemy."

Messlael stood up, as if gripped by a sudden transport, and drew him urgently toward the edge of the stream.

"If that unfortunate prince, for whom you would sacrifice your life with as much abandon and devotion, were to appear here suddenly, would you obey him in everything?"

"What!" replied the Yolof. "Do you know where he is hiding?"

"Would you obey him? Answer."

"I swear it by Mohammed."

"Well, he is before you—look!"

And Messlael, plunging his hands into the water and wetting his face in order to make the traces of the komo liquor disappear, uncovered to Griot's eyes his familiar features and the color of his race.

"Now, friend," he said, "what you would have suffered, it is necessary to execute; cut off my head and take it to Boukari."

The Yolof recoiled, fearfully. "Almamy, I only want to strike your vanquisher in order to return your throne to you."

"For myself, I only wanted to strike him to avenge my mother! Assure my vengeance, even at the expense of my life; it does not matter."

"I cannot!"

"You swore to obey me; you swore it by Mohammed; companion, my only and faithful fried, if you betray my hope, I shall succumb nevertheless under my enemy's blows, and I shall die dishonored, and my mother will not be avenged, and I shall have failed in my oaths. Gather your courage, then, and execute my last will; I implore you in the name of your father, and I order you in the name of Mohammed."

The Griot then bowed before him. Messlael extended his hands to bless him, and soon fell, his heart pierced by a dagger-blow; his murderer, weeping, detached the head from the trunk.

At that moment, the sun was directly above the estates of Bondou; before it had plunged into the sands of the great desert, the siratick's life had ended and Guefoulbe was avenged.[97]

---

[97] This abrupt ending is expanded in later versions of the story to include a brief description of the Griot launching himself on Boukari "like a hyena on its prey, striking him with twenty dagger-thrusts"—after which he regales the latter's shocked soldiers with "cries of joy and songs of triumph." The earlier

There Maelo concluded his second story.

The king did not appear to be entirely satisfied.

"Your Foulah prince and your Yolof poet," he said, "are both worthy of admiration. This time, at least, the vengeance has killed, it's true, but the almamy was no longer there to enjoy it. If a panther had destroyed an entire herd of buffalo with a single exception, and the last one went to deliver itself to the voracity of its enemy in order to draw it into a trap where it perished, do you think that its example would engage other buffaloes to have themselves devoured by panthers in order to avenge it?"

"I have not been claiming, thus far, to give a example to follow," the minister replied, deliberately.

"The misfortunes of Messlael have touched me, but I believe that he ended up becoming almost as mad as your Hottentot Tamus. Have you never been witness to, or have you never heard the story of, an act of severity reasonable in its rigor?"

"My mind only conserves the memory of one. It was a striking vengeance, prodigious in its effects, which will remain in human memory for a long time."

"Let's come back here tomorrow before the sun is hot, then. I want to know it."

Delivered from the presence of his minister, the king gave secret orders for the punishment of Duke Alvares and his accomplices to take place the next day. His plan of vengeance was formed, the executioner chosen and the instruments of torture prepared.

Finally, the bloody day rose over the Congo. At the indicated hour Maelo presented himself before his master; he knew nothing of the latter's projects and terrible dispositions, but before struggling himself against that ever-violent will, he had this last story heard.

---

part of the story is, by contrast, severely abridged in later versions.

The Cherif of Maroc

Abdalla,[98] one of the sons of the famous Muley-Ismael, was occupying the throne of Maroc gloriously, when his nephew, young Muley-Bouffar suddenly excited the realms of Suz and Tafilet to revolt. He accused the emperor of failing the precepts of the Koran by not observing the fasts and austerities indicated by the Holy Book, and of nourishing himself on proscribed meats; of violating the laws of the State by overtly protecting foreigners, even Christians, to the determent of the natives of the land; and of crushing his subjects with taxes in order to heap rewards on his black phalanx, formed entirely of young slaves bought in Guinea and who, incessantly increasing in insolence and power, claimed sole disposition of the throne. To these imputations, true of false, which he was careful to accredit, he also added details regarding Abdalla's private life, on his debauchery and cruelties.

Although the people, who were accustomed to the sanguinary yoke of their masters, had seemingly added sins to the number of their rights long ago, those rumors, skillfully spread, sufficed to give malcontents an excuse to take up arms. An army was formed in favor of the young prince. Tafilet opened its gates to him. The santon, the founder of the holy city, had appeared, it was said in order to recognize and bless his authority. A host of Arabs and Berbers, avid for blood and pillage, quit the valleys of the Atlas and the oases of the Sahara to march under its ensigns.

The later, claiming to be the only veritable observers of the Koran, which they regarded as a sequel to the law of Christ, presented themselves before Bouffer and, after having congratulated him on his religious zeal, with their arms ex-

---

[98] Muley Abdalla, or Moulay Abdallah (1694-1757) was Sultan of Maroc several times between 1729 and his death.

tended toward the rising sun, they invoked for him the aid of Mohammed, Saint Augustine and Jesus Christ.[99]

The Arabs, in their turn, preceded by their Sheikh, arranged themselves around the prince, whom they saluted with the titles of Great Cherif, heir and descendant of the prophet, the glorious, very powerful and very noble Emperor of Africa, King of Fez, of Tafilet, of Suz, of Morocco, of Darha and of all the Alarbe—in sum, the pompous titles that Abdalla had adopted. They declared then that they had consulted their almanack and their astrological books on his behalf, and that God showed himself entirely favorable to his cause; they prognosticated that he would efface Solomon by his wisdom, Haroun by his magnificence, Jamshyd and Akemptas by his exploits and his generosity, and that under his reign the ancient treasures buried in the mountains of Miathir would be discovered.[100]

---

[99] Author's note: "The race of Berbers, distributed along the Atlas mountain chain, in the Great Desert and the Biledulgerid, claim to be aboriginal to those lands. A few authors make them descend from the Getules, Numidians or Garanangtes; others believe them to be the posterity of Saracens who invaded North Africa in the seventh century. In any case the two hypotheses explain the invisible aversion existing between them and the Moors and the Turks, present dominators of those lands. A large number of Berber tribes live independently, however, Traces of the ancient worship of Zoroaster are found in some, disfigured residues of Christian belief among others, but even the Mohammedans, who form the majority, have a religious respect for Saint Augustine, whom they call Sidi-Belibeck and whom they claim to have been born in Tagost, a considerable town in Suz. Jesus Christ—or Sidi-Nayssa—was, according to them, conceived in the womb of a virgin by Allah's breath."

[100] Author's note: "The Mountains of Miathir, dependents of one of the branches of the Atlas are celebrated among the people of Fez for the hundred wells hollowed out there, which

Intoxicated by such brilliant hopes, and prognostications of which he could be certain, the prince immediately had the parasol brought to him, an item of furniture necessary to all, but of which the sovereigns of Maroc retained the sole use, and he prepared to march on Meknes, where his uncle was then.

To the general surprise Abdalla seemed to remain inert, while his rival already dominated several provinces of the empire. Finally, he sent two messengers to his nephew charged with words of conciliation, but only received the heads of the ambassadors by way of response. Every day, however, officers were deserting his camp and going to swell Bouffer's. They all had injustices of the emperor to lament, and, surrounding the new sovereign with caresses and admiration, increasingly convinced him of the certainty of his triumph.

Perceiving that the time that was passing was adding to his forces, the young usurper waited tranquilly for them to be further increased by the desertion of the cherif's troops.

At first, hunting was his only relaxation, but he did not take long to bring his harem to Tafilet; he even augmented it with a considerable number of wives worthy of the bed of a sovereign by their beauty and their plumpness.[101] Being able to satisfy his slightest desires, almost assured of the future, he no longer listened to anything but his appetites and penchants, and, dispensing with the false austerity that he had adopted in order to achieve his ends, he summoned the host of his former companions, his vicious favorites, and spent the days and night foolishly dissipating the treasures levied from his new subjects in feasting and pleasures.

---

superstition believes to be inhabited by subterranean djinn, guardians of immense treasures. (X.)"

[101] Author's note: "In order to obtain the state of plumpness esteemed by those peoples, women mingled with their couscous a powder derived from the ellhouba seed; Moorish ladies have a complete confidence in that combination."

Holding a guitar in his hands, the only trophy that the Moors conserve today from their conquests in Spain, he took pleasure in exciting the joy of his guests personally, in getting drunk with them on wines and liqueurs forbidden by the prophet.

"But I'm a musician," he said, "and Mohammed permits men of that profession to infringe his laws against intoxication; drink, friends; the grapes of Zalag[102] ripen for us!"

Often, his head troubled by the vapors of that terrible drink, he yielded to all the excesses of his violent character. Mounted on one of his rapid horses, natives of the region, he directed it forcefully against isolated soldiers that he encountered in his path, and then stopped suddenly, on the point of colliding with them; and if one of them gave evidence of the slightest fear, slaying him with a thrust of his scimitar.

"I don't want cowards in my army!" he cried.

Soon, his excesses of every sort reached a peak. The Arabs and the Berbers, his allies, indignant at his conduct, the continual orgies and frequent murders that soiled is life, began to murmur. However, his ranks continued to swell with malcontents from the imperial camp.

Finally, he set forth for Meknes, where Abdalla was said to be still confined, retained by a dangerous illness.

A few leagues from Fez, a rather numerous army seemed to want to engage in battle, but as soon as the action began, it passed almost in its entirety to the other side. Nothing, therefore, any longer opposed his elevation; a few more days and the empire of Maroc would recognize him as its only sovereign. That hope was all the better founded because he had just learned from his new allies that his uncle Abdalla had hardly any forces in Meknes except his negro guards, whose general was very irritated with him, and who would already have abandoned him if he had not known the young prince's hostile dispositions towards him. Muley-Bouffer hastened his trium-

---

[102] Author's note: "A mountain situated not far from Maroc, in the province of Fez."

phant course, resolved to profit from that circumstance, and his army was soon camped on the banks of the Sabron.

Situated in a vast plain, provisioned with munitions of every sort and surrounded by high and solid walls, Meknes, the favorite abode of cherifs, might still have resisted the conqueror for a long time, but the latter was already contemplating its vast palace, built in the Moorish style, the sumptuous domes of which dominated the entire city.

Impatient to take possession of its wealth, the treasures accumulated in its seraglio, and to rid himself of a rival whom he detested all the more because, rendering him justice in the depths of his heart, he knew him to be more worthy of occupying the throne than himself, the imprudent Bouffer, without being astonished by the rapidity of his success; without reflecting on the facile and universal defection of the old bachas, once renowned for their fidelity, and the previously-devoted ministers who had now abandoned their master with unanimous accord to range themselves under the flag of a young hothead devoid of experience and virtues; without being alarmed by seeing them commanding in his camp and surrounding his person, resolved to employ the ways of seduction to attract into his interests the chief of the black militia, judging that to be easy, according to the reports that had been given to him.

With the aid of an Arab soldier, secretly introduced into the city, a pact was concluded between the prince and the old warrior; the latter promised to deliver the gates of Meknes and the person of the sovereign, on condition that the negro troops and their general conserved he prerogatives that had been accorded to them by Muley-Ismael and his successors. The condition having been accepted and guaranteed, the place was surrendered to the young cherif. He penetrated into it by night, at the head of a part of his army, almost entirely composed of former imperial troops, in order not to alarm the people, who scarcely perceived the new chief who was commanding them.

The prince soon learned that, in accordance with his orders, his uncle had been suddenly arrested and was being kept prisoner in the harem. Several chiefs requested insistently that he be allowed to live. An insolent smile welcomed their pleas, and his death was only deferred for one day.

In a vast hall draped in blue—the color of mourning among those peoples—Abdalla, stripped of his insignia of power, no longer even wearing the black ribbon on his turban that distinguishes all the members of the imperial family, appeared before the victor, his head bowed and his gaze imploring. A double escort of Moors and negroes surrounded him, sabers in hand, seemingly only waiting for a signal from Bouffer to spill his blood.

"You have triumphed," said Abdalla to the latter. "Beware of abusing your victory; is my throne not sufficient for you? Will the first act of your reign be the murder of your closest relative?"

"Vain speech!" replied the prince. "You must die. The repose of the people and my security demand it."

"Grant me life; I implore it in your own interest. By your example, inform your future subjects of the importance they ought to afford to the life of a sovereign. The faithful charger that has touched the sacred ground of Mecca cannot receive death at the hands of men; will the descendant and heir of the prophet be less respected?"

"Abdalla, the charger does not belie the nobility of his race; he is able to brave death; borrow his courage and resignation; for, as it is true that the moon gave birth to the stars, your last hour has sounded."

"My prayers do not bend your will?"

"Never!"

He was already getting ready to give the fatal order, when, from one of the minarets of the city, which rose to the height of the hall of judgment, he heard the talbe pronounced these words, while hoisting the blue flag: "People, pray for Prince Muley-Bouffer, who is about to die."

At these words, the pretended conqueror became troubled, and went pale, and, while a sudden thought revealed to him the trap into which he had fallen and the web in which he was enveloped, the soldiers whom he believed to be his accomplices threw themselves upon him, disarmed him and led him to the feet of Abdalla, who, ridding himself of the large mourning cloak in which he was clad, finally showed himself in all the splendor of his rank, with his hand on his dagger.

"Lower your pride, King of Suz and Talifet, powerful dominator of the Atlas and the Sahara, conqueror of the estates of Fez and Maroc," the son of Ismael said to him, with a disdainful gaze. "Have you enjoyed your omnipotence sufficiently? You have mistaken your vanquishers for submissive subjects, your guardians for courtiers and your captivity for triumph. You thought yourself worthy of disputing the empire with me, but, without leaving my palace, without risking the lives of my people, I have constrained you to come to deliver yourself into my power of your own accord.

"By what title, tell me, would so many brave men have enrolled under your standards? What were your projects? Do you know that yourself? What were your means of success? You foresaw nothing. What hope could your character and your virtues offer? A subject in revolt, the murderer of my ambassadors, you accused me of violating both the laws of the State and those of religion, but you spent your days in debauchery, and your debauchery cost your defenders their lives; it was wine and blood that was necessary for our pleasures. I have forced you to justify me, by your conduct of all the wrongs that your lying mouth imputed to me.

"You must foresee your fate, Bouffer, for you have condemned yourself to it. It is by your order that the execution has been prepared, that the slaves are awaiting a victim, scimitar in hand. 'You must die. The repose of the people and my security demand it.' When I asked you for mercy, you refused it. I pleaded, implored; your soul was insensible.

"Tortures and sufferings are not yet sufficient for my heart, calumniated, outraged and lacerated by you. You might scorn existence and dolor, but my vengeance will be heavier than you think. Charger of a noble race, arm yourself with courage, then, to hear your sentence. You wanted my throne, you wanted my life, and I forgive you, son of my brother. Live free, live happy, in the government of Talifet, of which I accord you the sovereignty. May that gift not be a punishment for the infidel inhabitants of that province! Now, Bouffer, let us see which of us is the more worthy to reign!"

Such was the memorable vengeance of Abdalla, whom the people of Maroc still place in the number of their greatest princes. The end of his reign was nonetheless soiled by shameful actions, but his generosity toward Muley-Bouffer protected his throne throughout his life, and his memory after his death.

That final tale of Maelo's had produced a great effect on the king's mind. He did not make any observation to his minister on what he had just heard, but he quit him pensive, with his eyes moist.

The previous day, by his order, the Great Council of Gangas had assembled, Those priests of fetishism had secretly favored Duke Alvares' rebellion in the hope of seeing the complete annihilation in the Congo of the Christian religion, which the king alone, by his example, still caused his subjects to respect. Refined in his vengeances, it was on them that he had relied for the condemnation of his brother, convinced that they would seek, by the rigor of their judgment, to drive away the suspicions that hung over their complicity. Moreover, summoning one of the Anziki of his guard, seduced and charged by his brother to assassinate him, he had accorded him mercy on the sole condition that he would be the executor of the sentence rendered against the Duke. Those barbaric dispositions were already made when the story of Abdalla was recounted to him by the philosopher with the black face.

He went immediately to the Green Field, where all the people, already assembled, were waiting in bleak silence for the result of that great act of justice.

The Gangas were present; the Anziki, his arms bare, surrounded by axes, mortars, braziers and cutlasses, was calmly making preparations to fulfill his terrible function. Next to him, in an iron cage, was an enormous lion that Alvares had

258

long made his fetish and his protective genius. Surrounded by his despairing family, his wives pale and chilled by terror, the enchained Duke soon appeared, testifying by his haughty smile and his assured step that he was about to brave the tortures.

His hair bristling in little tight tresses garnished with glass beads of all colors, the great Chalone, the principal pontiff of idolatry, got up then and pronounced the following verdict:

"I, Chalone,[103] assisted by the Ganga-Negombo, the Ganga-Negosei, the Ganga-Nepindi and other interpreters of the immortal gods, condemn Alvares, Duke of Bamba, for having wanted to attempt the life and power of the magnificent sovereign of the kingdoms of Cogno, Loango, Angola, Cacongo, Ambodos, the marvelous river Zaire, etc., to witness the bloody sacrifice to our gods of his wives and children; to have his eyes and teeth torn out, his feet crushed and burned, his hands chopped off and thrown to the lion, his mokisse, and the rest of his body delivered to the pismires."

On hearing that sentence the people shivered with horror. Maelo, bewildered, sought to read in his master's gaze, which seemed to be avoiding his own. Alvares, affecting an imperturbable composure, contended himself with replying to the

---

[103] Author's note: "Among the Gangas, the Chalone holds the primary place; he has the right to inflict the death penalty, by his own authority, on Congolese convicted of a crime against religion. According to the ideas of the adherents of fetishes, or mokisses, as the Chalone ought not to die a natural death, when he falls grievously ill, his successor has the right to kill him.

The Negombo, as we have already said, practices both sorcery and medicine. The office of Negosei is to enable to desires of worshipers regarding hatreds, jealousies, vengeances, etc., to reach the gods. The Nepindi is in charge of bringing fine weather or storms, desiccation or humidity."

great Chalone, in the most indifferent tone: "That can be endured."

Finally, the king got up in his turn and said: "Alvares, that is what the Gangas have decided, the majority of whom urged you to revolt; that is what the slave who promised to deliver you my head ought to execute; that is the offering that the lion, a divinized monster from which you expected glory and honor, ought to receive. But that perfidious soldier and these priestly impostors, prodigal with your blood, are only your accomplices, while I am your brother and a Christian. As a brother, I forgive you; as a Christian, I respond to your offences with benefits. Return to Bamba..."

The king could not finish, for the superb Alvares was already at his feet, bathing them with tears. "My king! My brother!" he cried, in the midst of sobs. "You have vanquished me, you have subjugated me. My courage resisted torture; it has fallen before your words. Make me your slave! My heart cannot suffer so much gratitude! Let me be glorious in serving you! How sweet it would be for me to die for you!"

The king lifted him up and hugged him. Then, turning to Maelo, he said: "You have taught me to avenge myself; I owe to you the best moment of my life."

The Story of an Antediluvian Civilization

Part One—Introduction

"If, being alone and having arrived by some accident among an unknown people, you see a monetary token, you can be sure of having arrived among civilized people," a French philosopher has said.

"We perceived a gallows on the shore; thank God, we're among a civilized people!" exclaimed an English philosopher.

The Englishman and the Frenchman are right. I confess, however, that there is another spectacle that grips me even more vividly in one of our great European cities; it is the sight of a genuine pauper killed by need.

What a fine discovery that is for a thinker! There is an entire world of ideas that, at that sight, agitates in my head. How much time, how much toil, how much trouble it has required sages, philosophers and legislators to produce such a sight for us; finally to decide that the honest citizen who cannot be a rentier, a property owner or an industrialist must die of hunger and poverty at door of a rich man or a dealer in comestibles! That, however, is seen every day; and such a death, let us agree, is sufficient for a country to give evidence of its high civilization.

But what is civilization? Where does it begin? What is its essence? Its origin? Where ought it to stop in its progressive march? The question is important.

I do not like arguments devoid of proofs and stories devoid of action. Enough theories and contradictory verities have blurred the question. In a few pages I will give the entire history of a civilization, from its birth to its death-throes.

A long time ago, a very long time ago, I found myself in Egypt, where I made the acquaintance of the Arab geographer Aly Abderrachyd el Bakouy, who died toward the end of the fourteenth century. He had in his possession a very precious book, printed before the Deluge on camel skin, in a large format.

Don't be frightened; don't open your eyes too wide. Do you think then, race of yesterday, that the old world in which you live waited for your coming in order to be enlightened by the sun of science? It had already been burned by it. Where would your most ancient and exact historian have found the sublime allegory of the tree of knowledge, then, except in the memory of times past?

Yes, printing existed before the deluge; before the deluge, cannon had resounded in the plains of India and Ethiopia, steamboats had gone up the rivers Nile and Ganges, and aerostats, fashioned as dragons, sphinxes and luminous columns, had struck the gaze of the people of Africa and the great peninsula of Asia when you were scarcely born.

Does that astonish you? But without going so far, has not what you invent today been invented before? The theory of Copernicus belonged to Nicolas of Cusa, who took it from Democritus; as for that of atoms, Gassendi was only the copyist of Epicurus, who was himself only the plagiarist of Leucippus; everything, including your religious and scholastic quarrels, can be found in the writings of Zeno, Pythagoras and Timaeus.[104] Your beautiful governmental and constitutional machine of the three powers, your jury and your thousand forms of judiciary, financial and political administration, which you believe to be new, had been tried in Sparta, in Rome, in Venice, and even in the forests of Germany. Even your telegraphs had already extended their long arms over the edges of the Persian Gulf, and since time immemorial your

---

[104] Timaeus of Locri is only known to history as the central character of Plato's dialogue bearing his name and its sequel, *Critias*.

modern invention of lithograph was known and put in usage in the cities of Teshu Lumpu and Lhasa.

You can still create, but you will always be later creatures, gods of the second or third dynasty. Civilization is older than you, your Greeks, and your Egyptians. All that can be proved; but that is only the detail of my subject, and I want to get to the objective.

The book that my friend Aly Abderrachyd had been found in a pyramid opened and searched in the year 225 of the Hegira—839 of the Christian Era—but no one had been able to decipher the strange characters in which it was written. Versed in the knowledge of ancient dead languages of the Orient, by dint of his care and application, I succeeded in comprehending the beginning, which revealed the importance of the work to me. It was thus conceived:

I began this work, the authenticity of which I guarantee, when, according to celestial observations, the sun was in the first minute of its entry into the court of the lion, coming from the head of the crayfish,[105] *all the other stars entering into that sign, the sun and the moon at the first minute of the ram.*

In accordance with those astronomical epochs, it was not permissible, as you can see to doubt the antediluvian date of the book and the pyramid. The book contained the annals of the old Ethiopian people, whose origin goes back long before our historic times, and in whom the torch of the science and the arts was perhaps illuminated for the first time.

I translated—or, rather, I first summarized in eight quarto volumes—that enormous collection. Then I eliminated, by turns, historical events devoid of importance, contradictory facts, and then the reigns and revolutions, which resemble all others. In sum, from summary to summary, I arrived at the one that followed, which includes, I think, everything that it is necessary to know about that great nation. It is, therefore, with

---

[105] I have translated *écrevisse* [crayfish] literally, rather than substituting "scorpion," although the more familiar name of the zodiacal sign in question is Scorpio.

brevity and concision that I shall relate its infancy, its youth, its virile age, its old age and its decrepitude.

There will only be question here of one individual people.

First Epoch: Infancy—Progressive State

The long valley of Egypt was still under water. Then, between the Gulf of Araby and the Hesperian Sea, a few scattered handfuls of human beings vegetated, devoid of religion and laws, delivered to their primitive instincts and their natural appetites.

Along the gulf were the Troglodytes, inhabiting caverns and nourishing themselves on fish or reptiles. On the banks of the Nile were the Blemmyes, who lived on vegetables that they owed to the fertilizing floods of the river, and perched in trees, leaping from branch to branch with a marvelous dexterity. Not far away, in an immense valley, the Garamantes had succeeded in assembling a few rare herds of cows, ewes and ostriches, from which they only took milk and eggs for their subsistence.[106]

All of them had initially lived, so to speak, one by one, only having recourse to force in their amorous encounters, lying in wait for a passing female, falling upon her unexpectedly if she did not seem disposed to receive their caresses; amour in those days often commenced with a combat, after which the victor sometimes left his lover pregnant and half-dead.

Around that mother, however, the family was established. There were only mobile families as yet. Their bonds broke by reason or by caprice. Children of an age to be self-sufficient were isolated. It happened, however, that sentiments

---

[106] All three of these hypothetical primitive human races can be found in Herodotus, although his reports are understandably garbled.

of affection, innate in human beings, finally developed. The mother surrounded her children with so much care that a pleasant habit kept them with her, Habitude created the first laws of society. The same bed brought together brother and sister, who easily became husband and wife. Those fraternal unions, decided by a hazard of position, later became a duty, and later still a crime.

Over time, each of those little societies entered into the path of ameliorations. The Troglodytes began to abandon their caves and built cabins on the river bank elevated with the bones and covered with the skins of large cetaceans that sometimes ran aground on the shore. That was their palace, while awaiting something better. They were no longer content with picking up the mollusks and fish that the sea cast up for them. When the waters of the gulf has gone down, they planted tree branches in the sand, close together, arranged in a semi-circle, and fish, conger eels and turtles that had advanced with the tide found themselves retained on their return by those barriers, the first products of nascent industry. Their abundance augmented their appetite, and instead of one repose per day they had two, which is already a progress in the manner of civilization.

The Blemmyes still conserved in the trees the aerial habitations that sheltered them from reptiles, ferocious beasts and the humid emanations of the earth, but, thanks to the disposition of branches and lianas, which they knew how to interlace there, they had succeeded in rendering them comfortable and spacious enough to contain a family. Experience had taught them to collect carefully and sow the seeds of different plants that satisfied their needs. Agriculture was born.

Among the Garamantes, the products of the herds had been multiplied, but without daring to touch their flesh; milk had taken on different forms, and had become a solid or liquid substance at the choice of the preparers. The skins of ewes and heifers that no longer produced served the pastors as cloaks or couches, and tents were already being erected to shelter them from the heat of the sun or nocturnal chills.

Let no one form too rosy a picture of that Golden Age born in Ethiopia, however. Thin black men whose bodies were covered in long hair, whose elbows and knees were armored with calcareous matter similar to scales, devoured by vermin, exposed to the intemperance of the seasons, the bites of snakes, attacks by lions and crocodiles, waterspouts and sand-storms, lodged pell-mell in narrow huts with their women and children, as wretched as them: such was the tableau that those favorites of nature then presented.

Far greater evils were in preparation for them, and those evils were to hasten their progress toward civilization; for if savage humans attain a supportable state too soon, the development of their ideas stops; they enclose themselves in the satisfaction of their primitive needs and remain stationary; their future in aborted. Fortunately for that future great people, rapine, war, pestilence, famine and conflagration came to their aid.

In order to plant tents or huts on some corner of that in-grate land, it was necessary for humans to dispute it with the ferocious animals that had possessed it before them. The instinct of defense soon led them to find weapons. With a reed, a pointed bone, the rib of an ox, and the sinew of a ram, the Garamantes had the bow and arrow. The Blemmyes invented the sling. The debris of the skeleton of a whale or a shark was the Troglodytes' first club.

A few of them, not content with putting a lion to flight, dared to pursue it to its lair. It happened that, exhausted by heat and fatigue, gone astray in a forest, hunger and thirst surprised them near the enemy they wanted to slay. They saw its blood flowing; they slaked their thirst on it; hunger drove them; they did more! Satisfied by that more substantial nourishment, more abundant that those to which they were accustomed, they settled in the woods and the mountains, where birds, goats, sheep, donkeys and horses offered them more facile prey and more delicate prey.

Thus was formed a fourth people, that of Hunters: a terrible race, whose sanguinary appetites soon knew no bounds.

The Garamantes had to be on their guard against them, as they sometimes descended into the valleys to slaughter the herds. It was necessary to fight. The Hunters were few in number; they were vanquished, but they took away a few prisoners of both sexes in their flight, for in those days everyone took up arms in their defense. (It is known that the closer a people is to nature, the nearer the women approach the physical qualities of the men.)

The Hunters kept the women for their usage; they killed the men, initially for vengeance and pleasure, and then ate them, by virtue of reflection and need. They got a taste for it, and they did not take long for them to render themselves redoubtable to the river-dwellers of the Nile and the Gulf, as well as the inhabitants of the valley. Woe betide the imprudent man who strayed too far from his brothers. Sometimes, in the bosom of a clump of palm trees, he saw two piercing eyes gleaming; then a hideous face launched forward, a tiger-man with his hair and beard red with blood. It was all over for him; the vigorous Hunter carried him away to his mountain, regained his lair and threw him, half-broken and stifled, still palpitating, to the voracity of his kin.

The people of the plain, in order to protect themselves more easily from the attacks of such cruel enemies, drew closer together. It was necessary to talk to one another, to understand one another. Those cries, sighs, whistles, exclamations, muffled and confused grunts, and noises in the throat, the language of imitation by which, with the aid of gestures, they sought to represent the sounds and forms of objects, soon took on a fixed value and became common to all. The objects to be designated multiplied with time, and that language of diphthongs and onomatopoeias was succeeded by monosyllabic articulations. Those primitive monosyllables still form the principal roots of Oriental dialects today.

Until then, humans had only been superior to other animals by virtue of the structure and mechanism of their hands, but it was in the voice that they were to find the greatest means of civilization. Then more intimate relationships

brought those savages closer together. Territorial encroach-
ments and reciprocal thefts must have afflicted the Blemmyes
as well as the Garamantes. From the created language there
resulted conventions that, for the first time, established a kind
of right of property; but that right of property was not individual. At first it only concerned the population; later, it had the
family for its object, and then, finally, the individual.

As soon as humans possessed the gift of speech, they
possessed that of lying. The imagination had awakened;
dreams were transformed into realities. The first man who was
able to captivate the attention of others by a story inclined to
the marvelous commanded the respect of the crowd and became the elect of the band. He was its legislator. Thus, among
the Blemmyes, one of those dreamers, doubtless abused himself regarding his vision, assembled his companions and recounted the prodigies of which he believed himself to have
been the witness.

"The sun had just set behind the mountain," he said to
them. "Cold and darkness were over the earth, and I was
asleep, when I was woken up by a flash of light. It was the sun
rising up again. With one bound it leapt from the summit of
the mountain into the middle of the sky and it started chasing
the moon, which fled its caresses and surrounded itself with
clouds in order to hide; but the sun parted the clouds and finally reached it, and all the stars ran toward them, and they
talked, and I heard them talking.

"They said that they had made the earth, the sea, the trees
and the stars; and he stars repeated: 'That's right.' And I remained astonished, listening to them; and they approached me
and they talked to me too. I asked them who had made human
beings, and they replied to me that it was the earth, so that it
could nurture and nourish them, as a mother does her children.
Then I asked them by what means one could force it to give
them that nourishment, so that there would be no lack of it,
and they indicated to me all those means.

"Then there was a loud noise up above. The stars spread
out over the surface of the sky; the moon disappeared; the sun

went back to the mountain, and went back to sleep—and when I woke up again, it had resumed its customary place, on the side opposite the one where I had seen it fall, and it was daytime."

After that vision, Sabaism[107] was established among those cultivators in all its purity. The sun and the moon, the regulators of the seasons, saw the people salute their rise with cries of joy, and strike their foreheads on the ground when they disappeared from the horizon.

Already the instinctive sentiment that inclines us to proclaim a superior and supernatural power was manifest among the other peoples, but in various ways. The Troglodytes worshiped the sea; among the Garamantes, the king of the herds, the ox, whose horns were the most elevated, the neck most muscular and the coat most brilliant, was revered as the source of all prosperity. Soon, that ox spoke and dictated the law. Even the ferocious Hunters had their dreamers, and saw reappearing in their midst the bravest of their companions, dead under the teeth of lions.

The ox Apis of Egypt, Osiris with the ram's head, the Sabaism of the Arabs, and the Greek Hercules all obtained their origins there.

However, numerous scourges seemed bound to annihilate the nascent society. A pestilential air caused by the stagnation of waters had struck the Garamantes' herds with mortality and sterility, and, pressed by lack of nourishment, following the example of the Hunters and by the order of the sacred ox itself, they finally decided to drink the blood and eat the flesh of oxen and sheep. Swarms of locusts had ravaged the fields of the Blemmyes; the Blemmyes threw themselves on the locusts and fed on them. In order to attenuate the disas-

---

[107] Sabaism is the worship of the sun and other celestial bodies; Saba was allegedly an ancient kingdom located in what is now south Yemen, the existence of which is dubious, in spite of its endorsement by the Old Testament (English versions render it as Sheba) and the Quran.

ters caused by tempests, which overturned the feeble barriers of branches erected on the edges of the gulf, the Troglodytes fabricated nets with a species of rush,[108] and their fishing, more abundant, even provided them with a surplus of fish to dry in the sun. It was doubtless then that the quotidian three meals became customary for them.

The conflict between people and the elements conspiring against them had, therefore, only brought them closer together and caused them to multiply their means of subsistence. Another benefit became the immediate consequence of that. During days of privation, famished populations attacked neighboring colonies; they were pillaged, beaten and devoured, but the thefts added to their notions of wellbeing; they had seen, and imitation did the rest. The Blemmyes, in their turn, had nets to cast into the Nile; the Garamantes imposed on their fertile soil, free of production, the vegetables that it was to bear. Possessors of herds, they did not take long to discover the usage of fertilizers. Abundance softened their mores, inspired the idea of exchanges, and commerce was invented.

Until then, barbarian customs born of necessity had constrained old people to put a term to their useless days. The Troglodytes made an exception of old women first, as the root-stocks of the family. The richer Garamantes renounced the sacrifices entirely.

One day—an immortal day in the annals of ancient Ethiopia!—a storm fell upon the fields of the Blemmyes, set fire to a few trees and consumed them; they were the ones in which the cultivators had their lodgings and stored their provisions. That terrible phenomenon struck their eyes for the first time. At the sight of the flames devouring their habitations, they first armed themselves with bows and slings to repel the new enemy, and the boldest even launched themselves forward to fight it hand-to-hand; they soon came back to their companions uttering frightful screams of pain and rage. When the fire

---

[108] Author's note: "The dys, still found today in Egypt and Abyssinia, whose fibers serve to make cords."

was extinguished, weary of consuming—for no one among them had thought that the water of the Nile could do anything—they found vitrified matter under the ash, fragments of hardened clay and a few particles of mineral substances that had melted. The vegetables that the fire had approached had acquired tastes and savors much preferable to those they had had before, and later, they began to adore what they had cursed.

All that was doubtless the effect of an initial experiment; a few volcanic eruptions also facilitated the knowledge of the making of metals, but for those who like long details I refer them to my eight quarto volumes or, better still, my large one printed in camel-skin.

The sea and the stars had only wakened in the hearts of those savages admiration and respect; fire alone had a cult. The necessity of that powerful agent had been sensed, and the necessity of maintaining it in order to conserve it. Designated people were committed to that care; every family had to furnish its share of wood and reeds; to protect it from the rain that might have extinguished it, they imagined constructing a vast shelter. Such were the first priests, the first temple and the first offerings.

Second Epoch: Youth—Progressive State

All the seeds of civilization had been found. Let us allow the centuries to go by, and cast a further glance over adolescent Ethiopia.

Vegetal soil, in extending, has enabled resources to increase and contained the sands. Destructive animals have disappeared. Look, on the river banks, at the wind agitating the ears of barley and maize, or causing thousands of pirogues and almadies to sway over the gulf. The sound of the ax resounds; cedars and sycamores are sliced up under the hands of laborers; the bark of palm trees and mulberry bushes has furnished cords and garments; a white and finished cloth has emerged from the fruits of the cotton-bush. Modesty has been born, and amour with it; and thanks to them, the weaker sex is beginning to play its part in domination. Everywhere, in the plain, on the mountain slopes, in the depths of valleys, through the broad leaves of fig-trees, the eye glimpses the villages of cultivators or pastoral tents. There, at intervals, confused cries rise up, the bleating of flocks, the distant sound of the horn or the reed flute; words are no longer sufficient for the human voice, and monotonous and cadenced songs are audible.

Each village, each tribe, contains a family—only one, for, in accordance with their system of alliance, in multiplying, each family has remained distinct. The patriarchal epoch has arrived in households; utensils of stoneware and terracotta, vases of every form, have replaced the Blemmyes' calabashes, the Garamantes' ox-horns and the Troglodytes' turtle shells. Only the Hunters still drink out of the skulls of their enemies; divided today into numerous peoples, always at war, they still fight over the mountain or forest that has the most game, while in the plains, peace reigns almost incessantly.

What has maintained it? What bond unites all those hordes of fishermen, shepherds, cultivators that are not brought together by any family alliance? The same belief! The guardians of the sacred fire have become the priests of the sun, the god Rem (Ram, Rama, Brama); they speak, threaten and act in his name. Henceforth, all woes and all scourges have their first cause in the wrath of God, and it is only by virtue of the powerful intervention of the priests that it can be deflected. It is by virtue of the dread they inspire, in declaring themselves depositaries of the lightning and masters of the elements, that they have subjugated humans to laws and society has been set upon broad and solid foundations.

All superstitious terrors came to request their assistance, and they welcomed them all. Their Olympus was opened to ruminant gods, to scaly gods and to gods of stone and metal; but all of them required offerings; one god demanded barley and fruits, another the first-born of the flocks or the first fish of the catch. The gills, the bile and the intestines were for the gods, the rest for the sacrificer. At that price they took care of maintaining order, rendering justice and regulating differences between families. Perhaps they had no other goal than increasing a prosperity that was brought to them, but what does it matter, if their individual interest engendered general wellbeing?

The common center at which everything came to end, they alone could also assemble and coordinate the first elements of the sciences, although, as has been said, astronomical, meteorological and mathematical observations were initially due to cultivators, not to herdsmen. They were able to develop and verify the calculations of astronomical science, but they did not invent them. One does not learn to know something merely because one has time to examine it, but because on has an interest in doing so. The signs of the demarcation of terrain, effaced by the Nile floods, the cause of rains or droughts, and the prognostication of winds and storms: that was what attracted the gaze of the Blemmyes and enabled them to discover the innate rules of geometry and astronomy.

The pastors, living in the midst of flocks, forced to provide for their nourishment and keep them away from harmful vegetation, to watch over their maladies, often changing location, were the creators of the natural sciences. The magi of Ethiopia collected the observations of both parties, and, the only ones gratified with leisure, in the midst of that society rendered active by need, marched with long strides along the road of discovery.

Their power came from their knowledge. The increase in the population soon forced some families to emigrate. Some descended the Nile and established themselves in the oases of Egypt, scarcely emerged from the waters, or in the verdant valleys that extended between Egypt and Arabia.[109] Others

---

[109] Author's note: "Our author doubtless wants to designate here the place that has since served as the bed of the Red Sea, when the waters of the Gulf, elevated by the Deluge, broke through the strait of Bab-el-Mandeb, thus separating Egypt

headed toward the interior of the land, seeking fertile terrains on the shores of lakes or rivers.

At that time the first shoes were invented. The emigrants, obliged to undertake long journeys over burning or stony ground, enveloped their feet in cloth or animal hides; beneath the hides, some—doubtless women or children—by a refinement of delicacy, attached fragments of tree-bark by way of soles. Those who made use of oak bark for that purpose did not take long to perceive that it gave the skins of sheep or oxen, by virtue of friction, a solidity and a softness they had not had before. The art of tanning had been discovered.

It was thus that a great deal of knowledge was born of necessity and hazard. But if I said everything I would lose myself in the details, and my reader with me. Let us return to the emigrants.

Understanding that the dispersal in question might harm their power, the priests thought of stopping its flow. Ethiopia was encircled by infernal divinities. There were typhoons, monstrous serpents, men with the heads of lions or crocodiles, who were on the lookout for travelers and wandering tribes, men with only one leg and men with four, and men without heads—tales repeated centuries later by the French voyager Jacques Cartier, who was only repeating the Latin naturalist Pliny, who was himself repeating the Greek philosopher Aristotle.

In order to disarm those terrible gods, new altars were raised, before which blood flowed. A cult of terror entered more profoundly into the human heart than a cult of love. The priests saw their power increase. They resolved then to divide

---

from Arabia, as, by virtue of a similar effect, that great cataclysm separated France from England, Spain from Africa, Sicily from the lands of Naples, etc., but the straits of the Channel, Gibraltar and Messina. The land of Atlantis, which was only an Ethiopian colony, and the route from Africa to America, which then extended over land from Guinea to Brazil, disappeared in the same epoch."

the family, in order that a single will—their own—could act on the masses without competition. It was a matter of destroying the paternal sovereignty of the chiefs of the hordes, and only forming a single bundle of all those federated peoples.

The heavens did not take long to explain themselves by scourges; they rejected fraternal unions. Until the seventh degree of consanguinity, marriages were declared incestuous and impious. But the empire of habit was not easily destroyed; it was necessary to employ the great sacerdotal phantasmagoria.

Already the study of the stars had given the priests of Ethiopia a means of irresistible terror. Via their voice, the god Rem, the father of all the gods, announced that in so many days, at such an hour, if the fishermen, cultivators and pastors had not renounced their infamous practices, with one breath, he would extinguish the light of the sky, dry up the waters of the Nile and the Gulf, and make the earth nothing but a desert of sand.

That day arrived! At the predicted moment, when the recalcitrant saw a sudden obscurity interrupt the light of the sun and the sea agitating noisily, when they felt a glacial chill fall upon their heads, gripped by fear, it was with their faces to the ground that they swore to submit to the order of the gods.

When the eclipse ended, all were resigned, and the primary bond of the primitive family had been broken.

Thus, science in human hands was at first nothing but an instrument of deception—but that deception was to give society the unity that made its strength. Previously, individuals had formed into families; now, from the mingling of families, a people was finally about to emerge.

It was only with the aid of time that theocratic power succeeded in fashioning that nascent nationality. Instead of the advice and orders of the chief of the tribe and the laws of habitude, general laws were required. They came from the heavens, all of them, even those of simple policing. The ablutions that maintained cleanliness, so necessary in large assemblies of human beings; the fasts, means of hygiene and public economy; the abstinence from certain kinds of nourishment, which, at certain times, gave the flocks, the fields, the fish and the game time to repair their losses; usages of propriety, duties and pleasures: everything was prescribed and regulated by the imperious voice coming from on high.

A new powerful means of civilization, writing, also aided the priests in the extinction of patriarchal forms. Until then, the elders, the sole depositaries of the ancestors' experience and traditional stories had owed part of the respect by which they were surrounded to the need that people had for them. A few primitive paintings served at first to represent events of which people wanted to conserve the memory. But those paintings only served to aid the memory of the heads of families, who were their natural explainers. Hieroglyphs, which succeeded those dubious representations, only offered a symbolic meaning as yet, but when writing arrived, the ultimate perfection of the hieroglyphic system, the wisdom of the ancients, the theories of arts and crafts, and historical traditions could all be conserved and explained without the help of old men, who then saw their influence becoming progressively weaker, and the breakage of the paternal scepter under which the great family had bowed down for so long.

From the new state of things, new needs were born. In order to satisfy them, it was necessary to have recourse to labor. The community was no longer there to protect each of its members; wealth was individual; it required effort to attain it. From that came a general competition, which the priests were able to direct cleverly. The mountains of Ethiopia and the banks of the Nile contained immense quarries of precious minerals; the earth was opened up to withdraw calcareous stone and alabaster, which yielded more easily to the chisel. Mechanics and its instruments improved. It did not take long for granite, porphyry and the most precious breccias to be exploited in their turn, and temples rose up in the middle of cities to offer sanctuaries to the divinity and vast and comfortable lodgings to his priests.

It seemed that civilization, having arrived at that state of development, was no longer able to regress, when a great event occurred that nearly stopped the human mind in its progress.

Having withdrawn for a long time into the mountains that formed the Y on the shores of the Hesperian Sea, the Hunters finally emerged and headed for the Nile, as numerous as the trees of their forests, as impetuous and terrible as the wind that torments the desert sands for forty days.

At first they had fought among themselves; then a stronger population, more valiant or more adroit than the others, had succeeded in subjugating them all. Force had done for them what cunning had done for others. They too now only formed a single people, but their government was far from being similar to that of their former brethren. In war, as in the hunt, one single thought was required that directed everything; a king therefore marched at the head of that nation of soldiers. Sober, indefatigable, practiced in the handling of weapons, mounted on elephants, on ardent horses, as active, submissive, bridled and civilized as them, they had little to fear from the adversaries they sought. After a few months, all were vanquished, one fraction massacred, one drowned, the rest on their knees, sweating with fear and begging for mercy.

The newcomers showed themselves to be clement. They did not take long to adapt to the peaceful and abundant life of the cities. While oppressing the vanquished, they gradually adopted their mores and their usages, as the Tartars were later to do with regard to the Chinese and the Franks to the Gauls, circumstances shaping events. There were then two distinct people in Ethiopia: one condemned to labor and hindrance; the other in complete leisure, living on triumph. Idleness, the right of the strong, the privilege of the master, then commenced to be in honor, and turned to the profit of intelligence. Not all the thinking heads of the nation were any longer to be found in the colleges of priests. The liberal arts, medicine and architecture were born or developed in the bosom of that bodily repose. By that means, the victors only added to the force of the progressive movement of the common society. Some of their usages were also found good and convenient, and the horses did not remain as idle as the cavaliers.

But the king of the Hunters, habituated to command alone, soon thought about repressing sacerdotal power. Twenty uprisings had taken place in the name of the fatherland and the gods. After bloody executions without results, a rapprochement was necessary. Physical force and moral force made a pact. The victors united their gods with those of the vanquished; they were, as I have said, the bravest among their warriors; simulacra were made of them in stone and marble; sculpture and the arts were born. The priests promised their support to the throne. In response to their voice, the people prostrated themselves before their new master, proclaimed the Son of the Sun. There was in the State both a civil power and a religious power. Commerce and laws were in vigor. Money was struck, there were hangings; society was complete.

Third Epoch: Virile Age—Stationary State

Let us leave centuries behind again during which an infallible struggle was established between the two heads of the state.

By giving entry to their temples to the idols of the victors, the priests had acquired a sure means of dominating the matters of the nation and turning the conquest to their own advantage. The education of the kings was confided to them. In order to hold them more narrowly in dependence, they brutalized them. Some of them wanted to shake off that insupportable yoke; those they divinized.

Enclosed in the sanctuary, invisible, surrounded by homages and respects that isolated them from the people, they only appeared before them on solemn days. Then a pomp was deployed of which it did not seem that the descendants of the Troglodytes, the Blemmyes and the Garamantes ought to be the witnesses.

Early in the morning, drums, trumpets and cymbals resounded in the streets of the city to announce the presence of the god-king. The cavaliers put on their brilliant armor, the officers and governors their gold-braided robes and their plumed hats. All of them went to their designated posts, and when the sun seemed to stop, suspended and dazzling, over the summit of the temple, the doors opened to the sound of harmonious instruments and choirs of young acolytes; the king emerged, silent and motionless, overladen with silk, brocade and garments fringed with gold, covered in topazes and emeralds. He was lying on a magnificent carriage pulled by giraffes. A crowd of priests surrounded him and unrolled rich carpets over his route; a double hedge of initiates, mounted on elephants, caused perfumes and flowers to rain down on his head. Acclamations and shouts rent the air, the sound of drums and trumpets redoubled; the people prostrated themselves, the priests sang, the king plugged his ears, and, when the ceremony was over, everyone returned to his affairs and the God to his prison.

There is little more than the splendor of that cortege to give an idea of the development of the arts and civilization of that ancient country. The time of perfection had come. The first Auxuma,[110] the city of marble and porphyry, rose up, with its gigantic monuments; the Isle of Meroe, consecrated to the sciences and religion, was covered with temples and obelisks. A college of priests resided there, charged with putting in order the history of the gods of Ethiopia. Exclusively occupied with astronomy, it was in the revolution of the stars that they found that exceedingly difficult and complicated history, the obscurity of which still caused the vulgar to marvel. Rem reappeared there in a thousand allegorical forms, as the Brahma of the Indians did later, or the Jupiter of the Greeks, of whom

---

[110] Auxuma is an alternative term for the city of Axum or Aksum.

Lilio Giraldi[111] has assembled two hundred and fifty denominations.

The eternal abuse of allegory contributed more than a little to the subsequent overturning of the mythological system. Science could not always remain foreign to penetrating minds, and as soon as they had found the key to the edifice, it threatened ruination.

Already, in order to shore up that religion, which was only any longer suitable for the masses, they had recourse to initiations. In order to conserve its dupes, they provided themselves with accomplices. In those initiations, where everything became simple and natural again, where the knowledge of the true, unique God was revealed, the priest allowed a glimpse of the prodigious discoveries they had made in the physical sciences. The laws of attraction and repulsion, the causes of winds and tides, the revolutions of the celestial bodies, the parabolic movement of comets—nothing was unknown to them. They had predicted the sinking of Atlantis, and even announced a second, more general Deluge produced by a comet, which, in its course, disturbed the planet Venus.

It was in accordance with those predictions that the first pyramids were built, which subsequently served as a model for those of Egypt, and that the people of the Nile deposited their dead in the vast hypogea hollowed out under mountains. According to their beliefs, which passed on to their successors, the conservation of bodies was the indispensable condition of their resurrection; it was not enough to embalm them; it was also necessary to place them in security from the invasion of the waters.

The science of the priests rendered Ethiopia proud; their power was seen therein to be cemented by gratitude as much as superstition; but their number seemed to increase with that of their gods; their temples began to weigh upon the soil. The people, whom the spectacle of luxury and facile enjoyments rendered more demanding, murmured against the charges, the

---

[111] The Italian scholar Giglio Gregorio Giraldi (1479-1552).

privations and the fastidious duties that religion imposed on them. The laws, born of religion, were no longer in accord with mores, but the priesthood, infallibly, refused to take a step backwards.

Personal interest then struggled against beliefs; the first philosophers appeared. Prudent, perhaps timid, they only attempted at first to improve the laws of the priesthood, but that was to touch them, and they were persecuted. The irritation that they felt in consequence inspired audacity. They dared to distinguish civil laws from religious laws, preparing the former as a scaffolding that would sustain the social body when the others collapsed, ruined by the weakening of beliefs. The kings surreptitiously favored the innovators and conspired against the altars to which they were enchained.

The priests triumphed again, for their voice was omnipotent over the people. To weaken them, it was necessary to use against them the weapon that was their strength. Their adversaries spoke in their turn in the name of religion. Sects were established; even the priests were divided, and revealed the secrets of the sanctuary. There was enlightenment in the struggle; sage reforms occurred, and the spirit of examination slowly prepared another order of things.

Science, therefore, was being done at Meroe, there was discussion in Auxuma, there was thinking in the colleges of priests, and there was controversy in the assemblies of philosophers when suddenly, the colonial populations of Egypt and Arabia, having become numerous and powerful, rushed toward the source from which they had emerged. It was necessary to take up arms to fight them; formidable fleets covered the Gulf; the love of the fatherland worked miracles and, after long wars, Egypt was entirely subjugated and the Arabs were pushed back beyond the Yemen.

In order to keep its conquests, however, and impose upon its enemies, it was necessary to conserve a permanent army, and as soon as the physical strength of the nation was represented, royalty took refuge in its camps and reclaimed its rights.

The way had been prepared by philosophy and by schisms; the priests resigned themselves to allowing the leaders of the nation to reside in a palace and no longer in a temple, but they took their revenge by ceasing to divinize them. The sun was no longer the father of the monarch, who easily consoled himself for that; the country, governed until then by the gods, was now governed by men, and did not complain about that, for the new king took in hand the interests of the masses who lent him their support and, in order to complete the devaluation of the clergy, propagated enlightenment into the lowest orders of the nation.

It was in that epoch that the Ethiopian Arabs, emigrating toward the Persian Gulf, encountered a few individuals of the white race for the first time. On either side, terror equaled surprise. When the news reached Auxuma, there was general doubt regarding it. Only the old women of the people believed it right away, for ignorance is not astonished by anything, and, if necessary, explains everything: they were demons engendered in the sand by the light of the sun, some of those the ancient religious legends identified as forming a ring around Ethiopia.

For the learned, that explanation was insufficient. A long discussion of the subject began among them. The most subtle among them succeeded easily in demonstrating, by means of thousands of convincing reasons, the falsity and impossibility of the fact: it was a traveler's tale, a vision, a chimera, a marvelous story that the priests had invented in order to occupy once again the credulity of good men. In the interests of philosophy, a refutation was required; that was easy to do; it was done. But it had only just been published when one of those individuals, so extraordinary by virtue of their white and pink skin, their silky hair, their flat lips, their aquiline noses, etc., was taken by surprise, captured and sent to the king, who sent him to the philosophers, and the arguments recommenced.

We render justice to our scholars, few of whom, before the living and material proof, persisted in denying his existence; his presence appeared to them to be a sufficient demonstration. But another question remained to be debated: was he really a man?

Yes, said some, for he has the form of one, he articulates words, he laughs when he looks at us, he knows how to weave mats and he stands upright.

No, replied the others, because he does not have black skin, has no wool on his head, does not seem wonderstruck by the beauty of our women and does not appear to understand what we are saying.

The argument went on for a long time. While waiting for the singular being finally to take his place marked in the nomenclature and classification of natural history, the president of the assembly, a great philosopher who had a daughter almost as philosophical as him, took him into his home in order to observe his instincts and habits more comfortably. The father studied him from his direction and the daughter from hers. After a laborious examination and profound research, the father said: "He isn't a man!" and the daughter repeated: "He isn't a man!" By dint of talking about it, however, they ended up no longer agreeing. The daughter doubted.

In order to convince her, the father went to seek, in the conversation of his learned colleagues and the texts of the authors most in credit, a host of irresistible arguments. Without being disconcerted, tranquilly, in silence, the daughter prepared one no less conclusive. In order to solve the great problem, she did more, and she alone out of the entire assembly of doctors devoted herself in the interests of science, and the debate was still going on when a little mulatto was born and cut through the question.

They still quarreled a little more, but in sum, the proof was there, visible, alive and palpable: the skin an intermediate shade between black and white, the head garnished with a silky wool or a wooly silk, the semi-aquiline, semi-flattered nose, of an Ethiopico-Persian nature. The productive collusion of the two species proved their complete analogy. For scientists and philosophers that had to be sufficient; but in deciding too hastily, it was necessary to fear colliding with the religious prejudices of the nation and infringing the rights of the priesthood. It was therefore decided to submit a detailed report to the high priest in order to request from him the admission of the new individual to human society.

There was first a matter of explaining the origin of the white race. This time, the argumentation of the doctors of Ethiopia was consequent and conscientious. The accounts they received of the populations of Asia announced that they were rare, disseminated, ignorant and devoid of religion. They concluded in consequence that the race was new on the earth. Without arguing differences of climate, the Persian and Arabian Gulfs being almost on the same latitude, without discussing the existence or non-existence of a colored or colorant dermis, subordinating the religious question to the purely physical actuality, they recognized two creations of humans, at a centuries-long interval. In the former, God had been pleased to compose the Ethiopian negro, the eternal type of true beauty; in the second, the power of the workman or the quality of the material being in default, he had only been able to produce white humans

There was discussion, and dispute, and almost as much argument in Meroe as in Auxuma; finally, by a decree emanating from the sacred college, the equivocal being with the flat lips and the aquiline nose was promoted to the rank of human being. (If that promotion appears ridiculous to you, remember that a few thousand years later, it required a papal bull for the Americans to obtain the same honor.)

Priests and scholars assembled then. The new initiate had had the time, thanks to the cares of his philosophical negress, to learn the Ethiopian language, a primitive language, the clearest and most beautiful of all languages. He was summoned to appear before then and was interrogated regarding the people from which he had emerged, their beliefs and original traditions. This is what they gathered:

In the beginning, the country they inhabited had been entirely covered with cold, dead and deep water; no plant grew there, no animate creature populated it, except for a marvelous fish with a human face which roamed that immense sea alone. It was named Oannes (Oën, Oüs, Zéons, Zeus, Deus).[112] Weary of his solitude, one day he warmed the icy water with his breath, and marine beings of all species were born Oannes remained in their midst for some time in order to teach them the means to employ for their subsistence and their reproduction; then, with a second breath, he warmed the waters again, a part of which rose up in vapors, forming clouds, from the bosom of which Oannes reemerged in a new form.

The diminution of the waters had left a large area of land uncovered. A third breath from on high fecundated it, after having created the birds during its traversal of the air. Then Oannes formed the first man, Adam, and gave him two companions, Eve and Lilith. Eve was the more beautiful; she was the mother of the white race; Lilith, devoid of reason, mute and as hairy as a wild beast, gave birth to hairy men devoid of speech, the apes.

That was what the young savage declared.

His discourse astonished the philosophers and the priests greatly. The hairy man excited their surprise especially, but, having had the fact of his existence verified and having acquired the certainty, they wasted no time in discussions of this occasion and, after a short session, and with a unanimity of votes, the ape was declared to be part of the human species, from then on divided into three genres: black men, white men and hairy men.

If I have digressed momentarily from my story, at least that small diversion will have served to prove the great antiquity of African civilization, and how advanced the science

---

[112] Oannes was the name given in some ancient Babylonian writings to a mythical being, part fish and part human, who allegedly taught humankind wisdom. The entity acquired a new lease of life in French literature because of its significant symbolic employment in the visions of St. Anthony featured in the various versions of Gustave Flaubert's *La Tentation de Saint Antoine* (final version 1874)

were in that epoch, since even recently, thanks to the fortunate investigations of our scientists in the field of physical varieties, the ape (the orang) had finally reconquered the place of which he was so long dispossessed; he is the brother of us all, and if a debate has begun that subject between our modern doctors, let us render them the justice that it is simply to decide whether the ape is part of the human genre or the human part of the ape genre.

As for the preexistence of the black race, do not the traditions of the most ancient peoples inform us that the color black was then the emblem of strength and beauty everywhere? The black stone of the aboriginal Arabs is still honored today among the Muslims and deposited by them in Mecca; under the same form, the sun was worshiped among the Phoenicians as Heliogabalus, and the Krishna of the Indians is, those peoples say, the most handsome because he is the blackest. If that genre of beauty is still subject today to the eternal controversy of science, science furnishes us itself with new arguments in favor of our preadamites, for if nature in her productions always proceeds from the small to the large, and the imperfect to the perfect, it is evident that the black man, endowed with less strength, beauty and intelligence than the white man, must have preceded him in the long procession of created beings, since the different variations of animal, and even vegetable, forms were only the trials of nature, in learning to make humans—a philosophical axiom that I have borrowed from Jean-Baptiste Robinet, who borrowed it from Pliny.[113]

---

[113] Author's note: "Pliny says that convolvulus was the apprenticeship of nature learning to make a lily. *Convolvulus tyrocinium naturae lilium formare discentis.*" The French naturalist Jean-Baptiste Robinet (1735-1820) published the five-volume *De la nature* [On Nature] in 1761-68; his proto-evolutionist philosophy appears to have been a considerable influence on the present essay; he too waxed lyrical about the relationship of the orang-utan to humans.

If necessary, the Hebrew texts and their commentators will come to lend us their support. Ancient rabbis, seeking to explain the words of Scripture that testify that after the murder of Abel, Cain withdrew into cities, admit that human existed before Adam, which finally renders comprehensible the double denomination of sons of God and sons of men repeated several times in Genesis. "There were giants on earth in those days," the sacred historian tells us of the second creation. Without denying the existence of giants, something too well proven, as everyone knows, can it not be supposed that the family of Adam designated by that name the ancient inhabitants of the colossal cities and prodigious monuments that struck their gaze when they commenced their migrations toward Ethiopia, then deserted, and the height of whose constructors they judged by a calculation of probability based on the height of the edifices? Having clearly posed, sagely discussed and sophistically proven that, let us return to the subject that we left behind.

The kings of Ethiopia, then, had just freed themselves from the intellectual tyranny of the priests. Thanks to them, thrown out of the temple, the sciences were rid of their mysterious allure and their enigmatic jargon, and became vulgar. Crafts and arts all progressed toward an unexpected perfection. Printing came to lend its powerful aid to enlighten the idle populations of the cities. Speech, writing and printing are the three steps by which that society was to arrive at the highest degree of civilization; when that third element of force was found, a third power showed itself in the state, that of the people.

Abuses were introduced into the palaces, as before in the temples. Habituated previously to seeing themselves surrounded by religious pomp, the kings had replaced it with a military pomp that served them as both an ornament and a rampart. Imprisoned in the midst of their court, however, deceived and led astray by the very people on whom they lavished the treasures of the nation. They isolated themselves from their subjects voluntarily, as they had initially been obliged to do. Appropriating and dispensing for themselves alone the liberty, glory and wellbeing of all, they fell asleep in the midst of feasts and orgies. The people woke them up with a cry of revolt.

Alarmed by the energy of that action, royalty and the priesthood came together in order to fight it, so those two great powers, former enemies, were in league against the one to which, in turn, they owed their strength. After a long and terrible struggle, it was necessary for them to come to concessions; a new organization, nobler and greater, was acquired by society. Philosophy and religion moderated one another, seeming to march toward the same goal; the throne was lowered, it touched the ground, but it was consolidated by the security of its base.

The time came, following the course of things of this world, to consecrate that new form: religion, laws, mores, customs, everything was moving in harmony. Public reason was in progress; the exaggeration was effaced day by day, there was an advent of eclecticism in everything. The distinctions and excessively profound divisions that separated people rather than regulating their classification, had disappeared. There were no longer vanquished or victors, but a single people; it was the great epoch of Ethiopia.

A few movements of revolt, a few changes in the royal family, came from time to time to break the monotony of that state of propriety, but that did not change anything in the demeanor of the nation, and only had a slight influence on the civilization of the country.

My annalist counts for that period twelve dynasties of kings, as there had previously been twenty-four reigns of gods, who had died more or less advanced in age.

Having arrived at that degree of splendor, Ethiopia could only decline.

Fourth Epoch: Old Age. State of Decrease.

Not according to my own opinions and opinions, but in accordance with the incontestable facts collected by my Ethiopian annalist, with which I have only mingled brief reflections, by virtue of a habit of loquacity for which I reproach myself, I have already made known the three ascendant, progressive epochs of my individual people. It only remains for me to talk about its old age and decrepitude.

The primitive family, the patriarchal family and the national family as forms of population; the priests, the kings and the people as political powers; fire, the founding of metals and mechanics as industrial means; speech, writing and printing as intellectual means: such were the principal motors that signaled the road of civilization, the infancy, the youth and adulthood of our great African people.

The division of property, the division of labor and the discoveries of the arts had permitted repose to a large fraction of the population. Even the people had obtained their ration of leisure; there were holidays recognized by law, and further rest days indicated and consecrated by habit. As for the rich, with the exception of moments that nature reclaimed from them for sleep, their life was at their free and voluntary disposal. The route was traced before them, flat, green, cheerful, shady and free of obstacles; they could walk and run there, according to their reason or their caprice. They were the recognized privileged heirs of extinct generations, and, protected by the written law, the sweat and fatigues of the ancestors were credited to them, and exempted them from labor. A part of their time was given to pleasure, another to idleness. Amour also had taken on an immense development. It was no longer merely an instinct, a need; it was an occupation, a necessity, a habit of luxury. The influence and power of women was dominant, and made itself felt everywhere.

But amour is not a full-time pleasure. In idleness, an ardent avidity for new emotions is born and grows increasingly. The sciences had furnished an aliment to those new desires to begin with; after them, and born from them, mental labor had been popularized. Literature ornamented, fecundated, soothed, extended and multiplied philosophical discussions and even scholastic quarrels, which aided in killing time as well as other things. Literature had found science ready-made and exploited it, recycling it for its own benefit after having put it within the range of all by means of embellishments and circumlocutions; for if the scientists come first, it is to sniff, dig and shift the soil that hides the treasure. With their heavy and ponderous gait, their patience and their instinct, they dig up the truffle, and the litterateur, after having cleaned it, eats it, to general satisfaction.

Thanks to both of them, enlightenment penetrated everywhere; mores were polished, varnished and shone, along with the language, with beautiful semblances and deceitful spangles. Literature became a power in its turn. People divided into two camps, as always, over a literary question, as they had once done for a political question, and for a point of science as for a point of law. But today the people were the judge; they formed a circle around the athletes, applauding the best speakers, not the best thinkers.

Paradox came to lend its aid to talent, which, impatient to test its strength, only demanded a new route in which it could develop at its ease, caring little as to whether it was straight or tortuous. Everyone, in order to shine in turn, caught the bold maxims on the wing, and were impregnated by that innovative genius, donning the fine clothing of rhetoric without examining its solidity. The reign of intelligence was proclaimed; people wanted to shine therein, and they shone; they displayed their luxury without fear of sumptuary laws; they showed off their loquacity, their knowledge and their fine speech as if in a luxury garment elaborately embroidered on the outside.

Thus, dangerous and menacing doctrines were welcomed and fêted, thanks to their rich envelope! Prizes were only any longer awarded to seductive appearances.

The activity of the social body quit the center for the extremities; its vital strength was exhausted in surfaces. By virtue of too much friction the passions were worn away, and people believed that they could do without them. Character traits were effaced by imitation, as distinctive facial features were by the mixture of races; but no one wanted to see that as anything but an amelioration.

In fact, society gained by it in the short term; but great actions ceased. Politeness, amenity, complaisance and gallantry, mechanical and elastic virtues acquired in the greenhouse, a banal mask on which all faces and all minds were modeled, replaced good faith, frankness and honesty, slightly vulgar but more reliable companions. A general wellbeing made itself felt; but that wellbeing could only decrease henceforth, like a balloon inflated with air that a puncture was sufficient to flatten.

Bodies were enervated, and minds seemed to be reinforced at their expense, by dint of an irritation and active fever that chilled the limbs and lavished its heat in the brain. People had immoderate desires, but lacked the constancy to realize them; they projected vast schemes without worrying about the implements and materials; in sum, they enlarged the horizons before them, but only had little legs with which to reach them.

Meanwhile, industry came to the aid of indolence, and multiplied the enjoyments in the midst of which the nation seemed to be asleep.

At the aspect of a prolonged calm, the priests and kings no longer thought about storms, and only remembered their former power in order to regret it. They engaged imprudently in difficult routes; partial and ill-timed attacks to place. The people took stock, and quickly came to aggression without excitement. They had numbers in their favor; they kept in reserve the residue of collective energy; and the love of innovations, the need for new emotions had to give them auxiliaries in the enemy camps. Their tranquility was mistaken for lack of interest; the attempts were redoubled; finally, they rose up; there was an upheaval. Priests and kings, altars and throes

291

were all smashed. The nation itself, dragged by the movement with which it was imprinted, like a ship devoid of sails and a pilot, could not rally, and twenty republics were established.

An initial surge of excitement had multiplied the strength of the people a hundredfold, but that moment passed; it was necessary to fall back into the embarrassments of a new reorganization.

Revolutions can renew and reinforce the vital principle of a people, but when that people is worn away by civilization, that political moxa becomes a periodic necessity for it. Its curative effect is of short duration. The present can only be judged by the hindrance that is felt; the future is only seen in terms of what is hoped therefrom. One change summons another; every revolution incubates its counter-revolution.

On the one hand, the habitude of a soft bed in a well-sealed or well-ventilated room, a table well served at a fixed hour, the demands of an amorous passion (and we know that amour is a product of civilization, a creation of a complicated society that does not enter into nature, as Cabanis[114] said after Hobbes, who was only repeating his master Bacon, who was repeating Socrates, Antisthenes, Diogenes, etc. etc.); offended commercial interests; an unhealthy temperament to protect; and the needs of luxury and ease, result in a lack of strength, tenacity and perseverance, and the principle for which one has fought, by virtue of which one has triumphed, never receives its entire application, and cannot arrive at all its consequences.

On the other hand, minds rendered blasé by too great an exercise of thought, fashioned to paradox by amour and controversy, stimulated by the arts, by poetry, by the usage of strong liquors (a powerful cause of irritation that ruins both the constitution of the individual and that of the country, as

---

[114] The materialist philosopher Pierre-Jean-Georges Cabanis (1757-1808), a physician and educationalist, was apparently a considerable influence on Saintine's thinking in his youth, but by 1832 the latter had abandoned materialism and reconverted to a kind of deism.

Delisle de Sales[115] fortunately discovered after Montaigne, after Bacon, after Avicenna, after Galen and after Hippocrates) soon cease to see the end that they had wanted to attain, in order to occupy themselves with a more distant, more dubious goal, but which, by virtue of that fact, opens a broader quarry to the imagination. People speak in the name of the better, of perfectibility; no one any longer understand, and arrives and nothing but new divisions, new collisions and new revolutions; that is what Puffendorf[116] has proven before me, and Bacon before Puffendorf, for Bacon has said everything , fathomed everything, which ensures that he is cited everywhere, although he is scarcely read.

To get back to our improvised republics, let us first recall, in the interests of their defense, that the experience of history was then nonexistent for human beings. Every new theory of government infatuated them without being examined, for no point of comparison was discoverable.

A federative link was lacking those new States, which, far from seeking union, tended to divide further. Every city wanted to be a center; every village, an indocile satellite, only gravitated in an irregular fashion around its municipal planet, and the movement of repulsion increasingly dominating that of attraction, the village found its tangent in order to become a planet in its turn. People were returning, without a doubt, to the system of the patriarchal family, except that the paternal scepter was fragmented and disputed.

---

[115] The philosopher and utopian writer Jean-Baptiste de Lisle, known as Delisle de Sales (1741-1816), author of the mammoth *De la philosophie de la Nature* (1777), the evolutionist philosophy of which led to his imprisonment, seems to have been another of Saintine's youthful heroes, abandoned for the same reason as Cabanis.

[116] The German jurist and political philosopher Samuel von Pufendorf (1632-1694), another important contributor to the development of the materialistic ideas that Saintine is attacking with the zeal of a convert.

At length, each of the new States broke, caught up in the general machine, took its rank, and found its equilibrium, which sometimes came to disturb that of an envious and ambition neighbor, ill at ease. War did not neglect to trouble those pigmy democracies. Conquest traced new divisions on the map of Ethiopia, but, whether they lived under a municipal system or a dictatorial power, the masses remained impregnated by a evolutionary principle, against which governments dared not struggle.

Everywhere, anything that might recall the memory of sacerdocy or royalty was rigorously proscribed, which imposed an obligation to change everything in a country whose legal basis had been theocratic and despotic for such a long time.

That went ahead. People deranged, demolished and destroyed without knowing what to put in place of what was being removed. Emptiness was everywhere; the tablet was wiped clean, but in order to reconstruct upon it, systems succeeded one another, and a general doubt seized minds. Everyone vacillated in the midst of disrupted habits, seeking, for support, to cling on to an idea, a power or a belief, but remaining uncertain, dazzled, seized by vertigo, in the bosom of the surrounding skepticism, before an object that vanished under the hand.

Ceasing to hear a voice resonating in the sanctuary, the people thought themselves deserted, no longer raising their eyes to the heavens to ask for assistance, and gently, without shocks, in the midst of unprecedented progress in the sciences and arts, the civilization sensed the seed of its death germinating within it.

The kings had gone, the gods would not take long to follow them.

Fifth Epoch: Decrepitude. State of Decomposition

It is with suspicion that I am concluding the story of this singular people. Can one add faith to the story that remains for me to tell? For myself, I confess, conviction is almost lacking, and, but for the great antiquity of my manuscript and its unassailable authenticity, I might have thought that a profane hand had given a fantastic tale drawn from a modern source as a complement to the exact and faithful annals of the old Ethiopians.

In hatred of priests, religion was rejected; even the dogmas on which common morality was founded were disdained and forgotten. Sophists arrived who, by means of irony, destroyed even the intimate sentiment of the divinity; it was extinguished. The action of tribunals had to replace religious action, and the suppression of Hell only profited the executioner. Soon, atheism had its century of fervor and delirium; it had its missionaries, its enthusiasts and its martyrs.[117]

Suddenly smitten by a phantom that they had created, and which they called "the Truth," these people analyzed and dissected error in order to purify it of all ferment. After the laws of religion, the laws of propriety were attacked. The etiquette of cities, the elegant policing of salons, which maintained harmony in large meetings, which served as a barrier against audacity and disorder; those solemnities of marked

---

[117] Author's note: "Incredulity submitting to torture in honor of nothingness! The fact might appear to be beyond all plausibility, but the reader knows and will recall—for a reader knows everything and remembers everything—that a sect of atheists has existed for a long time in Turkey under the denomination of Muserrins, which has a rather well-furnished martyrology. Only a few years ago one of its adherents, the savant Mahomet Effendi, preferred to die under torture rather than pronounce the words: *God exists*." Mahomet Effendi was the name—or rather the title—by which an ill-fated Ottoman ambassador to the French Restoration court was known there.

days, which often aided in the retying of bonds of family and amity; puerilities when they are envisaged from a distance, occult institutions, the hidden wisdom of legislators, which, at close range, are easily revealed to the philosophical observer, were all attacked, lampooned, mocked and destroyed.

Only adopting for a guide physical and positive reasoning, re-edifying society in accordance with exact and material ideas, everything needed a mathematical or physiological basis; its duties were sought in organic nature and its principles in calculation.

They came to explain vices and virtues by temperament, temperament by climate and nutrition, a new system then and resuscitated since by Locke, who borrowed it from Gassendi, who had borrowed it from many others. But our Ethiopian sages did not stop at the theory; the application took place in its full development.

In some cities, the principal magistrates only obtained their employment by submitting to a hygienic regime prescribe by law, from which they could not deviate without suffering the most rigorous penalties. They had to abstain from any aliment that might, by bringing vapors to the brain, altering the economy of their ideas. They dined in public, in order that everyone could appreciate both their sobriety and their respect for the law. When a verdict was rendered, if the party found guilty and sentenced could prove that in the twenty-four hours preceding the judgment, the judge had failed in his duties by some excess at table or secret debauchery, the judge and the judgment were set aside.

It was very little to have a sound head; having a sound stomach became the indispensable condition to succeed in employment, for if the vase is impure it pollutes the healthiest liquid. Indigestion was only permitted to proprietors and rentiers; among the rest, gross appetites became suspect. The stomach had its accounts to render. Anyone who experienced a malaise had to justify it; anyone afflicted with chronic gastritis had to hand in his resignation and renounce an administrative career. Thus, during strolls, on meeting in the street, people only accosted one another or saluted one another by saying: "How is your digestion?"

In other cities a kind of senate was established, which had to discuss the interest and needs of the public. All temperaments were represented there in cleverly calculated proportions, in accordance with the digestive habits of the population. There, it did not matter that the carnivorous orator was succeeded by the ichthyophagic orator; the herbivorous or graminivorous orator responded to both of them. One demanded a law that maintained the integrity of forests or pastureland, ad protected the reproduction of game or livestock; the other rose up in forceful protest against the draining of ponds and the obstacles raised to marine fishing. Another deplored bitterly that troubles that were agitating the country, the numerous crimes that afflicted it every day; he could only see one remedy, which was to order, for the poor class, the general usage of barley bread, much more favorable to mores than more substantial nourishment. He extended himself then on the advantages of vegetable cuisine for bringing populations to order and repose, an incontestable verity that did not prove that the juice of meat was poisonous to modesty and probity.

The Carnivore relied, that it was not when war was imminent that one ought to think of putting the nation on a mollifying diet. "We need courage and patriotic enthusiasm," he cried, "so multiply game and livestock; raise an army that will only be nourished on partly-cooked, bloody flesh; let it be sated, let it drink blood, as our ancestors the hunters did, and I'll answer for the victory!"

The Ichthyophage had his turn. He pronounced against excesses in nourishment; he did not want either debilitants or irritants, but a *juste milieu* between the two systems, which was fish, neither flesh not vegetable, but which contained half the principles of each. He generously abandoned its preparation to the choice of the consumer. The herbivores could eat it with fine herbs, the carnivores with meat sauce, which ought to rally all opinions to his. Then he returned to the necessity of establishing watercourses and ponds, digging canals and favoring marine fishing. "You all know," he added, "the certain effect of ichthyophagy on the increase of the population; if you fear war, only the general usage of fish will increase your forces, repair your losses and assure you of success!"

Then everyone debated, became excited, got carried away, until the omnivorous delegates of the republic, who composed the majority of the assembly, arrange everything by concluding the session.

Physiological legislation, being the order of the day, necessarily passed from the senate to the tribunals. Violence was punished by bleeding and a debilitating diet that brought the aggressor back to a normal state of moderation. All vices were punished by bleeding and purgation, and a brake was put on all the passions even amour. Then a remarkable work appeared *On the Application of Leeches as a Curative Means in the Tender Affections, taken to Overexcitement.* The book was a great success, which did not prevent the majority of the amorous having recourse to the ordinary means of possession and satiation. Vesicants were also employed in certain cases to enfeeble cerebral energy and deflect importunate and harmful desires, in accordance with the well-known axiom *ubi stimulus ibi fluxus,*[118] which Hippocrates translated from Ethiopian into Greek, the school of Salerno from Greek into Latin, and which the savant Monsieur Broussais has just formulated anew from Latin into French.

Bleeding, however, conserved its rights to preeminence, inscribed in the codes; bleeding was still the great protector of mores, people and property, and executioners and philosophers marched with lancet in hand.

In accordance with the same exact ideas, marriage had been made to a contract, a bargain no longer heightened by the pomp of temples and the assistance of God. There were fixed-

---

[118] Literally "where there is a thorn in the flow," repopularized in the era of bleeding—a therapy whose vocal enthusiasts in France included the physician Francois-Joseph-Broussais (1772-1838), a passionate advocate of leeches.

term marriages, lease marriages and trial marriages, according to the more or less mobile penchants of the individuals, the presumed duration of the action of amour or the need one had for a companion or an associate.

A rich and free woman ready to undertake a long voyage married in order to provide herself with a support, a surety and a protector during the journey, but on her return she dismissed her horses and her spouse.

A businessman, in need of funds, united himself with someone who could procure them for him as a warranty or a mortgage; she entered his bed in order to supervise the employment of her capital, and when the enterprise was complete, the head of the company and the household made his inventory and rendered his accounts; the matrimonial and commercial association was dissolved and the profits and the children were shared out.

Polygamy, permitted to the rich provided that the conjuncts did not live under the same roof, authorized them to take as many town wives and country wives as they could nourish and lodge.

In some trial marriages, encouraged by the government, the procreation was attempted, by skillfully combined mixtures of capacities, of future administrators or philosophers. The procedure was mathematical and rational. Thus, a geometer father with a calculative and pensive brain, and an artistic, sentimental mother with a vivid imagination made...a simpleton! But what human combination is not subject to failure by virtue of lack of foresight and unfortunate hazard? It was just a matter of starting again with new elements. With patience, one always gets there in the end.

By reasoning, the barriers of the first legislators had been overturned; by reasoning there was soon a return to fraternal, incestuous unions; and, in fact, for people free of prejudices, who did not feel those repugnances of nature common to semi-civilized peoples, who were not afraid of eclipses, a mother and a sister were women who like any others, perhaps more than the others, had the right to aspire to all the homages of the heart and the senses.

Thus, the primitive family reappeared; on that double ladder of civilization, the steps had been climbed on one side and descended again on the other; and, deceived by the false lures of a mendacious wisdom, a fallacious improvement, they believed that they were still advancing, and found themselves face to face with their first forebears, their savage ancestors.

Already, the horror that humans experience in nourishing themselves on the flesh of their fellows had almost entirely ceded to reflection. "Why deprive ourselves of resources?" the carnivorous philosophers said. "Are humans composed of other elements than animals? Is their blood poisonous? Alone among all the beings of creation should they be condemned to rot, useless to everyone?" And soon, in public markets, human meat was sold, in slices, joints and quarters, by weight. People even ended up ambitious to have the stomachs of one's friends of fellow citizens for the honor of a sepulcher. It is an idea like any other, which proves that the wife of Mausolus did not have the honor of the invention.[119]

Then, cooks and aged maidservants were seen in markets and butchers' shops, choosing the most delicate morsels with discernment, indicating it with a finger, sniffing it, haggling and carrying it away to regale the family. The culinary art gained by it, for in the beginning it was only by dint of seasonings and preparations that the habit could be acquired; later, it was eaten roasted or boiled—no matter!

Thanks to that usage, which became almost general, knowledge of human anatomy and comparative anatomy spread to all classes; anthropophagy led to immense scientific progress, but a few inconveniences also resulted from it. Indi-

---

[119] Artemisia, the sister and husband of the Carian king Mausolus, became famous for the extravagant expressions of her grief after his death, which allegedly included consuming his ashes mixed with wine—a popular subject for historical painters, including Rembrandt.

vidual security was imperiled. Every individual, even if he only wore dilapidated garments, still represented a positive, negotiable value in cash. Beggars, vagabonds and the unemployed undertook in the evenings, on the highways as well as open country, a regular hunt for human game, which did not fail to alarm belated travelers and hamper circulation. Even the poor ceased to have a safe-conduct signed by misery.

Other singular usages resulted from that mode of alimentation and the improvement of physiological science, which I cannot pass over in silence in spite of my desire to be brief.

In one celebrated city there was an illustrious literary society, the glory of the empire. It was from its ranks that the officers were chosen charged with appeasing or repressing the quarrels that arose between citizens, for it had been understood that the majority of disputes were only engendered for want of agreement as to the import of a word, and that policing ought to be entrusted to peaceful, considered men capable of appreciating all nuances and rectifying all linguistic arguments, who, more often than not, brought the parties into accord by means of a grammar lesson.

Thus, the literary men enjoyed universal esteem. But their number was fixed. When one of them died, the one who was elected as his successor had to pronounce his eulogy in full assembly. In order to enable the competitors to appreciate his most secret qualities, it was the custom to deliver the body of the deceased to them; for, according to their theory, virtues and talents being only the fortuitous results of the development and disposition of organs, complete justice could only be rendered to the great man after his cadaveric autopsy. The corpse was therefore brought in great pomp into the midst of his former colleagues, and aspirants for his place, who would be his judges. The ceremony was beautiful and imposing.

To begin with, each one emitted modestly his ideas and opinions regarding the ex-member of the society insofar as he could appreciate his merit by solely by his actions and works. In this, criticism used all its rights nobly, for it was about to be justified or annihilated, without appeal, by the anatomical inspection.

One man believed in the genius of the dead man and sought to support his verdict by some citation from his writings, scintillating, in his opinion, with beauties of the first order (that was already the expression). Another saw nothing but stylistic pretentions, false warmth, common ideas newly dressed, and flatly refused to recognize the genius of the predecessor, only granting him a facile intelligence, more bizarre than original, more obscure than profound. That debate regarding intelligence and genius was prolonged in the following centuries, and still endures.

Another speaker rendered homage to his character, cited the features of his life, imprinted with grandeur and nobility of soul (although no one believed in a soul then, the word had remained in the language by force of habit); he thought that the source of his virtues was generosity. Yet another drew a very different conclusion from the same actions, and did not see anything for their primary motive but vanity. Who was right? That was what they were about to find out. Armed with speech, the advocates had debated the pros and cons. Armed with a scalpel, the judges were about to pronounce.

The body was, therefore, delivered to the competitors, who, after having examined it fiber by fiber, measured, compared and weighed the lobes of the brain, judged its intellectual capacity in the bony capacity of the skull, decided the case in favor of one or other party, awarded or withdrew the crown, and conferred, at the end of the session, a diploma of glory that even posterity could not refuse to ratify without injustice, for it would lack the vital piece of evidence. The dead were no longer embalmed.

It sometimes happened that our physiologists discovered, to their surprise, that the great man they had admired as a poet while alive had only been organized by nature to make an architect or a musician. The disappointment was great, but the scientists do not allow themselves to be beaten so easily. A new examination of his works, thanks to their commentaries, revealed the fictitious means by which he had succeeded in usurping his poetic crown; but if the composition and charm of his verses were attacked, at least he was rendered full justice with regard to the beauty of the monuments he might have been able to construct, or the suavity of the songs he might have composed.

That grave competition concluded with a meal, for which the dead man paid all the expenses, for he was eaten as the final means of verification. When the deceased was young and fresh, the competition was necessarily great; old and dry, he found even more aspirants for his place ready to meet the required conditions, so many people, in that epoch, wanted to figure in an academy.

So much for the philosophical and governmental sciences; with regard to the industrial sciences those people, rid of hindrances and freed from brakes, but always feeling spurred, and running, bridle down, along the road of indefinite ameliorations, presented a picture no less curious.

The energy that they had drawn forth in their political upheavals was exercised in destroying or improving the work of their predecessors. On the ruins of temples and palaces, monuments useless henceforth, solid and comfortable habitations were built, in which luxury, brought within the range of the majority, summoned everyone to enjoy its delights.

But increasing industry could not stop there; arts and crafts were soon signaled by a movement of ascension that no longer seemed stoppable. Chemical and mechanical discoveries, gases, steam and powder, came to lend their support to inventors, to improvers as well as destroyers; for everything has its downside. They marched upon the enemy with tubes that launched iron, lead and pebbles without interruption, merely by means of simple air pressure. They went further; a highly ingenious machine was invented for siege warfare that could blow up a city at a single stroke, bastions, ramparts and inhabitants included.

Soon, vessels without sails and oars seemed to be skimming in running over the surface of the seas; horseless carriages driven by a powerful and secret force furrowed all the high roads and by-roads. Mountains were transplanted and valleys filled in; the beds of rivers were displaced and their sources dried up, others being made to spring forth from the ground. There were fountains of iced water, warm water and hot water, at will. By the direction of subterranean gases they even obtained incessantly-animated reservoirs of flame.

Everything was submissive to human genius, to humans who forced the earth to produce in accordance with their wishes, to be transformed in accordance with their will: who, by means of dykes, had tamed the gulf and constructed cool and secure habitations even beneath its impetuous waves; who saw numerous aerostats, aerial fleets submissive to their powers and directed by them, balanced in the air like animated luminous globes, like multicolored stars! It was magical!

A rich man needed to multiply his senses then in order to empty the cup of ambrosia that civilization filled for him to the brim. Along with his town house and his country house he also had his submarine house, in order to enjoy freshness and shade when the devouring heat of summer weighed heavily upon the earth, his yacht to cradle him on the waves, and his balloon in order to launch forth into the clouds and travel through the air; and in each of his habitations, where the arts and sciences competed fervently to satisfy his most frenzied desires, he had a charming woman whom he could replace at intervals.

If he desired solitude, all the enjoyments of luxury and the senses could follow him there. He dismissed his wife and his numerous domestics. Retired to an apartment constructed expressly, mobile and mechanized, he flicked a switch and harmonious music was heard; he pushed a button, and succulent dishes covered his table. He dined three times if that was agreeable to him, for he digested as he dined by means of certain digestive essences due to chemistry.

Another pressure, and the floors sank down, the ceilings and walls opened and transported him into verdant arenas edged with odorant bushes, marvelous plants that flourished and blossomed at will thanks to the employment of electricity.

Yet another pressure and, without quitting the mobile seat on which he was stationed, he traveled through bathrooms in the midst of jetting water; galleries of paintings in which the most attractive and exciting forms ignited his desires and awakened his imagination. Then he caused certain perfumes to evaporate from his cassolettes, the skillful mixture of which procured him tender vertigoes of gaiety and folly, and put him to sleep gently thereafter, in the midst of seductive and voluptuous images that came to enchant his dreams.

(After long research into the nature of those perfumes, I have reason to believe that nitrogenous gas, brought to the state of nitrous oxide by the removal of a part of its oxygen, enters into their composition, and became the principal cause of that sensual and transitory asphyxia.)[120]

Whatever it might be for the rich aristocrat of Ethiopia—the cares of his friends, his family, his servants, the caresses of his mistresses—art substituted for everything around him. If necessary, art would have substituted for and imitated him, for human automata had been successfully constructed, which walked, opened and closed their eyes, caused mechanisms to operate, ate, digested and talked—the only thing they did not do was think, and that was perhaps not an indispensable condition to meet in order for the copy to resemble the model in all points.

Life wore away quickly in that game. More often than not, in the magical solitude, the rich man only savored fully the joy of being alone; and in the midst of masterpieces of art, verdant arenas and jets of water, he only paraded his ennui. But the people, who believed him to be happy, cried out against the rich, as they had cried out against the priests and

---

[120] Humphry Davy, a Romantic poet before he became a famous chemist, notoriously supplied nitrous oxide to Robert Southey and Samuel Taylor Coleridge as a potential source of inspiration.

the kings; the people cursed the progress of the sciences, which did not turn to their profit, and especially the general employment of mechanics, which forced them to warm themselves in the sunlight, with folded arms and empty stomachs.

In fact, in vast workshops, numerous workers had initially been occupied in the preparation and confection of textiles, utensils and objects of art; but new discoveries arrived and a part of the workforce was replaced by machines. A machine wove wool and linen; a machine sawed and polished stones; a machine shaped, melted and sculpted metals; a few men sufficed for surveillance and to set everything in motion. Soon, thanks to the incredible perfection of mechanics, with the aid of water, air and steam, only a single individual, who started a mechanism, was necessary for a workshop. It did not take long for him to become dispensable. A dog, turning in a mobile iron cage, replaced him; but the dog ate, grew tired and required care; it was killed, and was replaced in its turn by a mechanism

Discovery was applauded. The glory of the inventor excited envy and caused all heads to turn. He was surpassed. Industry had its miracles!

In one of the squares of the city a monument was constructed, surrounded by boutiques whose foundations communicated with the interior of the monument, which was occupied by a machine of extreme complexity. An ox was introduced into that interior; then, without the intervention of the human hand, the machine operated. The animal was killed, bled and butchered; its skin, prepared, tanned and cut into pieces, was transformed into shoes in various forms, leather bags and bindings for books; its bones became cups, flutes, buttons and toys of every sort; its hooves and horns furnish trumpets, combs and a thousand other small objects of marquetry; its flesh, passed through fire, divided, mixed and seasoned, presented various meat dishes. Its intestines had become the strings of musical instruments, its hair a solidly-woven stuffing; its sinews and its blood, everything had its employment, everything was subjected to a special preparation; and after a few hours the machine, ceasing its movement, threw out into the various boutiques each of the products destined for it.

Economists acclaimed the marvel, and a population of beggars agitated in the streets; public benevolence had to help them and shelters were opened for them; but the economists wanted the benevolence to be suppressed and the hospitals closed—which, they said, maintained idleness and prevented useless people from dying. Finally, the economists were no longer dreaming of anything but workshops without workers and cities without inhabitants.

Death was, therefore, in the bosom of the social body. In the midst of its refinement of luxury, its excess of civilization, a victim of indefinite amelioration, of limitless improvement, Ethiopia was dying, slowly being extinguished on its rich camp-bed, afflicted by an indigestion of the fruits of the tree of science.

Until then the laws had favored the increase of the population; they took a contrary direction. What was the point in multiplying arms when there was no more need for them? Why compromise the face of opulent and tranquil idleness by allowing the forces of poor and turbulent idleness to increase? The gaze of the hungry man always seems to cast a menace into the midst of the orgies of the earth's fortunate; the plaintive plea of the beggar sometimes reaches them, as the importunate demand of a usurped right. The footsteps of the man who possesses nothing seem, in gliding over the fecund earth, to want to divide it up and share it out in equal proportions. All of that troubles the mind, diminishes the appetite and agitates slumber; it is necessary to terminate such a state of embarrassment.

To the profit of the public treasury, a tax was imposed on marriage so excessive that it was no longer within the range of the poor. Celibacy was compulsory for those who could not expect any other enjoyments from society but those of the family. Possessors of large fortunes believed that they were coming to the aid of a State that was tottering by virtue of a

307

superabundance of useless existences by surrounding themselves with a cortege of servants, lodged, nourished and paid; there was a people in livery and a people in rags, but of citizens, none.

Numerous emigrations took place; the springs of government relaxed and weakened. Egypt rebelled. In order to suppress it, workers were enlisted; as soon as they were armed, they threw themselves upon the looms and smashed them, on the economists and killed them. The servants were enlisted; they made common cause with the workers, and all of them threw themselves on the rich and pillaged them.

Disorder was everywhere. Driven by white populations, which had become numerous and powerful, the black Arabs quit their oases and verdant valleys and spread out in floods over the banks of the Nile, attempting to establish themselves there by force. Love of the fatherland was invoked against them, but political egotism had destroyed it a long time ago. For a long time, imagination had been extinct in brains desiccated by calculation, along with the arts and poetry, which alone maintain the sacred warmth in the soul of a people.

Enthusiasm, that *divinus instinctus*, had had its wings broken between an algebraic equation and a philosophical argument. Struck in the heart by a blow from a pair of compasses, it was dead, while people discussed the theory of utility since brought to light by Jeremy Bentham, who had found it in the writings of Hume, who got it from the ancient Romans, who got it from the ancient Greeks, who got it from the ancient Egyptians, who doubtless got it from our ancient Ethiopians. Without enthusiasm, there is none of the electric courage that determines success.

Unable to hope for victory, they negotiated a peace, with gold in hand. Such a denouement encouraged new aggressors; war, becoming a productive speculation for the enemy, was reproduced in all its forms and at all points. A soil that could not be defended was no longer cultivated. The laborious arms, with which it had been thought possible to do without, were lacking for the maintenance of canals, roads and machines.

Grass corroded the land, rust corroded the iron; gangrene was in the limbs and the entrails of that bald, enfeebled, worn out society. The treasures buried to hide them from the rapacity of the Arabs no longer infiltrated the veins of commerce, which was weakened by paralysis. All the springs of government stopped.

Decrepit Ethiopia no longer colonized its civilization; it no longer expanded outwardly; barbaric people came to attack it in its bosom and each of them carried away some of its debris. The sea invaded its shore; sands reappeared everywhere. Typhon triumphed over Osiris; Osiris and civilization had already passed into Egypt.

Conclusion

What, then, is civilization? Where is its first seed found? And what will be its culminating point?

We have seen barbaric peoples, scarcely emerged from their swaddling-clothes, cruel without malevolence, brave without honor, avid without avarice, living without laws, without mores, without beliefs, without any other guide than their instinct and their appetites; they submitted then to the verity of their nature, a naked and miry verity, which seemed to emerge from a quagmire rather than a well, and which, if it had a mirror in hand, would have been frightened by its own image.

Their first legislator is merely a dreamer who transformed his dreams into reality, acting on their imagination, the primary faculty of infant peoples, by means of absurd tales. At his voice, people come running, and their capricious amours are submitted to the laws of marriage; their pleasures to conventions; their life rights and liberty to rules and limits. The circle of his auditors has traced the placement of the first city, and civilization in its entirety has emerged from a lie.

Yes, a lie! Why hesitate to proclaim it? The time has finally come to dare to dig into the question to lay everything bare. Is it today, is it in our epoch of frankness and sincerity that it is necessary to allow ourselves to be frightened by a word? Let the partisans of the lie raise their heads, then, let them cease to do battle against the banner of their adversaries. Their cause is as fine, their army as numerous and rich enough in illustrious men of all times. Legislators, philosophers, poets and prophets, respond! Orpheus, Homer, Hesiod, Moses, Zoroaster, Numa, is it not by deceiving them that you opened a future of force and glory to your fellow citizens? You, Lycurgus, was it not by supporting yourself on the lies of the Pythia that you founded the cult of virtue in Sparta? Is truth alone good? Can truth alone can suffice for everything? Let us finally understand the word of Fontenelle; it was that of a sage, not a courtier.

The lie thus came to be established as the primary base of human society, and from its birth, civilization dates. The truth only came later, feeble, vacillating and sterile, lending itself first to all forms, changing its name and face from one latitude to another, a slave of laws and mores, more mobile even than the lie; it was misunderstood, disdained. It was grafted on to that vigorous wild stock; both of them, united, lent one another strength mutually, and peoples were able to sleep in peace beneath their intertwined branches.

But, error bringing profits, everyone wanted to sell it. The best things are subject to abuses; quantity discredited the merchandise, that the first movement of civilization stopped there.

It was sage, it was prudent and it was indispensable to lie to humans in order to submit them to the political and religious yoke of society; but perhaps it would also have been wise, prudent and indispensable to create civil duties for them that were closer to the line of nature, not to extinguish their instinct and penchants so much, to demand of them mores rather than virtues, not to stifle their passions but to direct them toward the common interest. I admit that, in that circumstance, it is necessary to lie to humans as little as possible.

Everyone admits a necessity in the political order. One cannot think, and never will be able to think, of opposing the will of an entire people. If they want liberty, and are worthy of it, it is necessary to give it to them with all the precautions that can render that liberty profitable. Well, in that case, are the will of nature and the demands of the passions to be less disdained? If you try to bridle them too forcefully, they will explode; mores will overturn the laws and disturb and agitate your social order, which will not take long to crumble, for it will no longer be anything but a scorned lie, and the lie itself, in order to be good for something, needs to be respected.

Legislators, it is necessary to ender virtue facile, in order that it should be within everyone's reach and that the virtuous man should not be an exception to the general rule—which is scarcely reassuring for him and very humiliating for the others.

The second movement was one of reaction, like everything in this base world. War was declared against the prejudices that had founded the society, but which, by virtue of their multiplicity, were impeding the march of the human mind. To begin with, there was a prelude of choice and restraint. The parasitic branches were pruned; those which bore good fruit were respected, and the tree only bore better ones.

Unfortunately, the descendants of the Troglodytes and the Garamantes did not know the art of stopping at the appropriate point. After them came the improvers who formed squadrons and mobs. A general hunt was ordered. The most inoffensive error, and the mildest illusion, could not escape them. Without thinking that the truth is not easy to digest for all brains, they deployed their pikes against everything that had the appearance of falsehood. Everyone wanted to demonstrate his penetration and cleverness; they thought they were erecting a new monument, but they only destroyed the one that had been founded with great difficulty. After unprecedented labor, after having dug up the ground and dispersed the earth turned over, they found themselves in the midst of debris, sitting on bare, sterile subsoil, with an empty sky overhead.

311

Then the excess of civilization recreated barbarity, then, in the heart of societies without worship and unions without bonds, the Epicurean and the Kaffir, one crowned with roses and the other decorating his ears with the jawbones of his enemy, shook hands while mocking human reason, which one of them had not attained and the other had surpassed.

Where, then, is it necessary to place the boundary-marker on the road of civilization? On what day ought further innovation no longer to present itself to the great council of the nation without a noose around its neck?

I don't know.

But what I do know is that the only two peoples who have resisted the action of centuries are those of India and China, because they were able to stop in time on the route of improvement, and surround the lie of their civilization with powerful barriers.

Those are the conclusions that I thought I was able to draw from the knowledge acquired from the Ethiopian annals. Was it really worth the trouble of reading, translating, summarizing and commenting on that enormous volume, printed before the deluge, on camel-hide, in a large format?

Jonathan's Soirées

Prologue

[The Prologue, the first section of which is given the title "Encounter in Calabria" and the second "My Friend Jonathan," is only slightly revised in its early pages from the version contained in Jonathan the Visionary, *so I shall not reproduce those pages. It begins to deviate sharply at the point in the second section when Jonathan tells the narrator that he lived in Paris during the reign of Louis XV under the name of the Comte de Saint-Germain, and the narrator asks him: "What do you think of that time, compared with ours?" and Jonathan answers:]*

"You have exchanged pleasure against reason, or rather against reasoning. Today you are more serious madmen, and in consequence sicker. Then I saw philosophy, a new religion, on the defensive, rally its partisans around it, promising them triumph in the future, and people had faith in its promises, because, in spite of the mockeries of the great skeptic,[121] there were still beliefs in the depths of hearts in those days.

"Today, you possess liberty and tolerance—those dreams of your forebears, those precious goods, which were their pride and joy, although they only possessed them in hope—but you do not believe in them! In their place, you want to substitute an ungraspable chimera; you enjoy them by denying them, and you will lose them for not wanting to recognize their identity and call them by their name!

---

[121] Voltaire.

"Like the dog in the fable you let go of the reality in order to set forth in quest of a shadow that abuses you, and the day is perhaps not far off when that treasure, which you have coveted for so long and conquered at the price of so much suffering, you will trample underfoot and leave behind, broken and mutilated, in order to undertake its vain pursuit again.

"Blinded in your false path, incapable of stopping on the steep slope, you are describing once again the fatal circle of anguish and misery, during which several disenchanted generations, weary of the earth and cursing heaven, will be extinguished on your route. Then, having returned to the point of departure, you will believe that you have moved forward; you will rebuild part of the debris you have made and proclaim yourselves its founders!

"You will warm up with your breath the liberty half-dead beneath your feet and you will proclaim yourselves its saviors! You will cry victory, and you will inscribe on your flags: Progress and Civilization! Vanity, I tell you, all is vanity!"

"You're severe, my friend."

"I have the right to be," he replied. "Among so many peoples and during so many centuries, I have seen, in the name of a pretended improvement and a chimerical perfectibility, men marching to their ruin and breaking in their hands the instruments that Providence had placed there to render them happy and sage, as far as sagacity and happiness can extend down here, with their incomplete nature."

And every day, in support of what he advanced, Jonathan cited me a thousand examples drawn from different epochs and different countries; and he specified the dates so clearly, described the events so well, retraced with such a lucid sagacity the causes that had engendered them, describing the principal actors in the dramas with such a true and evident physiognomy as he went, that to refuse to believe that he had witnessed all those grave catastrophes would have been impossible—because, of the majority of them, history says not a word. Where, then had he learned all that? Invented things are not created so easily, and are always recognizable in passing.

Oh, if only I had been able to retain in my memory and transcribe immediately all the stories that I heard then! How the annals of peoples would have been augmented and rectified! What services would have been rendered to our scientific and other academies! I only have for proof the beautiful history of an antediluvian civilization, of which he also recounted the principal phases at that time, but which I had the good fortune to find later in his papers, when my memory no longer preserved any trace of it. What new light has it not cast on the veritable state of things in ancient Ethiopia before our historic ages!

For myself—should I admit it?—of my old friend's stories, it was not those that charmed me the most. But when he recounted to me those piquant events, from which his mild philosophy stood out so clearly, those anecdotes, sometimes imprinted with the marvelous, by turns ancient and modern, Oriental and Occidental, which transported me as if by the stroke of a magic wand from one end of the world to the other, from Siberia to Africa, from India to France, and the century of Pericles to that of Louis XV, I felt drawn to listen to him by an irresistible attraction. Those mores and usages, so different, those costumes and ornaments, so varied, all seemed to play before me and shine in passing before my eyes. I drank by turns from the waters of the Ganges, the Nile or the Ilissus; I was intoxicated by the perfumes of the turpentine tree or the elcaya; I allowed myself to be transported with the narration to the heights of the Cordilleras or the cool valleys of Persia; with joy, my feet left prints in the sands of deserts or the enchanted shores of Lake Maggiore, and I believed that I felt successively on my brow the burning embraces of the Simoom and the caresses of the Etesian breezes.

O sensuality of the listener, so well-known to the Arabs when, sitting on their heels in the evening, eyes half-closed, heads swaying, placed in a circle around their chief, they let themselves drift to the recitations of the poet! Plunged into a species of somnolence by the monotony of the human voice, by the warm vapors escaping the earth, but the aromatic smoke of the narghile, only hearing alert among their senses and substituting for all the others, it was through the ears that a new life, all illusions, penetrated into their minds. What was described to them they saw, they smelled, they touched; what was recounted to them, they dreamed. I too understood your delights, I spent entire and successive evenings absorbed in my role of listener. And what poet of Araby could ever have matched Jonathan? What other narrator would have been able to call to his aid the knowledge of all times, all places and centuries of experience?

Both leaning on a table, or with our foreheads resting on the chimney-breast, we abandoned ourselves to our expansions of intimacy, illuminated solely by the light of the hearth. Suddenly, in the middle of a philosophical discussion, the need to shore up a theory with a fact made itself felt in my old friend; immediately, I saw him stand up, interrupt the argument commenced, remain for a few seconds in profound silence, integrating the numerous pigeon-holes of his powerful memory, shake his head vigorously, as if to reanimate by stirring it a memory that might have lain dormant there for centuries.

As soon as he had found it, he marched around the room with long strides, rapidly meditating his subject. Like the painter who first takes care to prepare and charge his palette, he put a certain elegant art into disposing his colors in advance, in order to add to the verity of the picture that he was about to trace. That was his pride as a narrator. He often set out to prove that no detail had escaped him. The names of men and things, the costume worn by some person at the moment when he came on stage, the tree on which he was leaning, the dog asleep at his feet, the bird passing overhead: nothing was forgotten, and if a slight languor in the story sometimes resulted from that, I was far from complaining of it! For the man, the dog, the tree and the bird each had its distinct physiognomy, animating one another, designing a group, forming an image with the sandy or verdant, arid or florid soil that unfurled beneath them, with the bright or cloudy sky that covered them, and completed for me a picture in all its harmony and its wholeness.

In order to enjoy those conversations, so substantial and so varied, more frequently and more at ease, I had transplanted my tent next to Jonathan's—which is to say that I had quit my lodgings in the Saint-Germain quarter in order to live near him at the height of the Faubourg Saint-Honoré, where he fixed his winter residence in Paris. In the same way, when the return of the swallows announced that of the fine season, when the arm and perfumed air of beautiful April mornings came to dilate our longs and make our spirits rejoice, my old friend, suddenly losing his taste for the great city and its inhabitants, its pleasures and its fashions, quickly ridding himself of his bizarre accoutrements, his fake elegance and his borrowed attitudes, seemed to be reborn to nature and simplicity. Then his liking for voyages, that eternal need to change location and travel the world, returned to him, and if his ardor did not impel him to cross the frontiers of France, but only to roam our provinces, to the north or south, east or west, forgetting my reluctance to haunt the highways, equipped with my light luggage, with my tread firm and my ears alert, I followed him.

O my beautiful evenings in Provence, Touraine and Burgundy, what memories you recall to me! For on the banks of the Loire, the Yonne or the shores of the Mediterranean, as in the heights of the Faubourg Saint-Honoré, it was almost in the midst of near-total darkness that Jonathan's narrative faculties awoke. How many stories full of marvels, and often imprinted with naivety and bonhomie, I heard during those peregrinations from the inexhaustible storyteller! Why did I not mistrust my ingrate memory and collect preciously every day the pearls that fell from the lips of that incomparable man? But how could I foresee the catastrophe by which I was menaced? How could I know that the spring in question, the sources of which were alimented by the largest glaciers of the Alps, was about to dry up? Alas, thus it was to be—apparently, at least.

The moment has now come to relate an event that I was far from thinking possible: the most unexpected, most extraor-

dinary and most improbable event of all those making up Jonathan's life.

III. On the Sea Shore

We had just traveled through a large part of Normandy.
As we went along the delightful banks of the Seine, from
Rouen to Le Havre, my old friend had told me the extraordinary story of Guy d'Albrot, which I shall soon retell for you,
and when he showed me with his extended finger on the
moonlit waves the place where the unfortunate Burgundian
archer found the end of his troubles, I would have sworn that I
saw, unfurling along the watercourse and its surface, the silver
thread of the inexplicable and inextricable white hair, at which
the river-dwellers on the left and right of the Seine have marveled for such a long time, without being able to comprehend
it.

Jonathan had never seemed to me to be in such a cheerful
humor by day, and so enthusiastic for narration in the evening.
Since the early morning there had been joyful words and
pleasant expansions; after nightfall there were stories more
numerous, more compact and even more varied than usual,
stories to make one forget hunger and sleep.

We visited Le Havre, in the vicinity of which he seemed
to have lived in different epochs. He only showed himself
more expansive and more interesting in his confidences in
consequence. I had great difficulty in recognizing in him, I
confess, my Calabrian sorcerer or my Parisian fop, so much
joyful humor and bonhomie did he show in speaking, instead
of the somewhat emphatic and declamatory tone that he had
sometimes affected previously.

For each of our stations there was a curious anecdote. At
the extremity of the sad suburban district of Perrey, near the
four roads, in the place known as "the Goblins," on the heights
of Ingouville as in the village of Sanvic, where he found the
residue of the Saxon race that he had once seen covering those

same banks and whose mores, language and costumes still live today in the marshlands of the Croisic; in the delightful valley of Sainte-Adresse, which owes the consecration of its name to an impiety, as in Bléville, whose church, entirely made of black stones, seems to have been built by the hands of demons; in Graville, whose renowned subterrains were once the theater of so many frightful events, as in Orcher, where the celebrated Guy d'Albrot sleeps under a layer of petrified moss—everywhere, in sum—his memory evoked a thousand memories that tradition has not even conserved among the oldest inhabitants of the region.

And according to those stories, sometimes terrible, sometimes imprinted with a mocking philosophy, Jonathan became once again as good-natured as before, and abandoned himself, with all the hectic imagination and sensory freshness of a child, to the pleasure of enjoying the air and the sun, analyzing a flower or an insect, picking up a seashell or a starfish, listening to the sound of the waves on the shingle, and watching the last surges of the rising tide covering our feet with white foam.

One might truly have thought that the voyage had rejuvenated him, renewing his body and his soul, so much had his features recovered serenity and so naturally did smiles come to his lips.

Except—and this is something that it took me some time to perceive—that when, on the jetty at Le Havre or from the high cliffs that rose up near the town, his gaze was directed at the other side of the Seine estuary, at its right bank, his eye suddenly immobilized, contemplating a point on the opposite shore; his brow darkened again, and he seemed to be preoccupied by grave thoughts.

He sat down then, and, with his elbows on his knees and his face in his hands, his eyes still fixed on that same place, I heard him murmur words to which I could not attach a meaning, such as "I'll never turn back!" and "We shall see!"

The point on the other shore on which his attention was thus fixed was the town of Honfleur.

One evening, we were both on the sea shore; the sky was somber, the wind fresh; and after one of Jonathan's stories, which had interested me greatly, when the clouds opened a passage for the moon's rays, I was prolonging my pleasure watching the flocculation of the waves, the dancing of porpoises and the rapid flight of gulls when I saw in the distance a long blue flame, which, running over the waves, seemed to be dancing like the porpoises and flying like the gulls.

"What's that?" I said, utterly nonplussed.

"That," he said, after a moment of silence, during which he seemed to be studying the progress and the bounding of the flame, "is the accomplishment of what must be!"

That response was not sufficiently explanatory for me to be content with it.

"How can it propagate itself over the sea like that?"

"It's not on the sea, but on the shore."

"What shore?"

"That of Honfleur."

"It's a conflagration, then?"

"No."

"What is it, then?" I asked him again, with a sort of urgency.

This time, he made no reply.

"You have no intention to visit Honfleur?" I said.

"No later than tomorrow, we'll go," he said, in a solemn and gravely articulated voice. And he repeated: "I won't turn back!"

"Will we stay there for a time?"

"I don't know, but it isn't my intention. I only want to go through Honfleur in order to go to Caen."

"So we're only going to stay in Caen?"

"No, it's four leagues further on, on soil that was once sanctified, and is still holy today—in sum, toward the village of Lantheuil—that we're heading. There, yes there, the mystery will be accomplished. But before anything else, it will be necessary to get out of Honfleur. We shall see!"

Without understanding him, I nevertheless divined that in Honfleur, he anticipated an obstacle capable of interrupting his voyage.

"Isn't there another means of reaching Caen or Lantheuil?"

"There's more than one, but won't have recourse to them. Once again, I don't want to turn back! Tomorrow, we'll embark on the ferry from Le Havre that will take both of us to Honfleur. There, it might perhaps be necessary for us to separate."

"What!" I exclaimed. "A separation! With what end? Are Caen and Lantheuil no longer the points at which you want to aim? Have you changed your mind and will the port of Honfleur see you embark for some distant country?"

"Fate will decide!" he said, taking my hand and shaking it, as if to give his words a more penetrating meaning.

But I was still a thousand leagues from perceiving his thoughts clearly, and, responding to him with an expression that spoke more in favor of my heart than my intelligence, pressing is hand in mine, I said: "No! No separation! If you leave, I'll leave with you! I, too, want to travel in my turn. I want to see the countries about which you have talked to me so frequently. Go on, decide, shall we embark for Senegal, Turkey or India? I'm ready!"

"You cannot follow me where I shall doubtless go; your time has not come," he replied, without showing the slightest emotion at the fine impulse by which I had just signaled my devotion to his person. "No matter—you're still young, and you can wait for me. We'll agree a place of rendezvous...or rather, it's already agreed. There is only one; it's in Lantheuil in sixteen years...sixteen years! That's a long time, isn't it? But I'll furnish you with the means of being patient."

"Sixteen years...that's very little for you," I replied, "but not for me! Or rather, my friend, it's impossible, you're toying with my affection. Me, quit you! You won't demand that! No, never! You can't have allowed me to contract the pleasant, imperious habit of seeing you and listening to you every day, at all hours, only to interrupt it suddenly, to break it pitilessly, and for sixteen years! In sixteen years, I'll be old! You don't know what it is to grow old, but will time, which has always respected you, respect me?"

"We'll be able to force it to do so!" he said.

"Oh I sense that, away from you, I'll grow old rapidly, for you've become so necessary to me!"

"I said other things just as touching, and while I spoke to him I had tears in my voice and in my eyes, and I kissed his hand, which I was still holding, with respect and tenderness. I ought to say, however, that he did not appear to be any more touched by my despair that he had been a few moments before by my proposal to leave everything, family and fatherland alike, in order to go with him. From that moment on, I began to perceive that my friend Jonathan did not have a heart endowed with a very exalted sensibility—or, at least, that time had chilled it considerably.

When I had stopped speaking, he spoke in his turn, but his thoughts showed themselves from the outset of his speech so well-swathed in mysterious cloth that, in spite of myself, I ceased to pay him a sustained attention. Involuntarily, I recalled my first encounter with him in Calabria, when, in order to evade indiscreet questions, he had replied to each one in a foreign language. Only this time, he seemed to have taken care to make my mother tongue into a completely unintelligible language for me.

As he went on, however, his voice increasingly contracted an emphasis so solemn and profound that it chilled me with I know not what inexplicable fear. When that voice no longer made its monotonous and shrill tone heard, I turned toward my companion. The moon had then triumphed completely over the clouds and its light was falling directly upon him. I found him in the same habitual posture, crouching, with his hands under his chin, his elbows to his knees and his gaze fixed, constantly attached to the opposite shore. I cannot say what strange pallor extended over his features. Whether it was a reflection of the moonlight or the result of a painful emotion, it had a character by which I was frightened, and from that moment on, I did not doubt that I would soon be the witness of some great supernatural event.

The following day, early in the morning, we were at sea, heading for Honfleur. During the crossing, Jonathan, in a charming and talkative humor, appeared to have completely forgotten his somber apprehensions of the previous evening. He did not even change his manner when, in accordance with an old custom, the pilot of the ferry, uncovering his head, after having made the sign of the cross devoutly, cried in a lugubrious voice, at the sight of the mountain against which Honfleur is situated: "Behold Notre-Dame-de-Grâce! Commend your soul to God!"

IV. The Four Elements

Remarkable by virtue of its position at the mouth of the Seine, dominated to the east by the promontory of La Roque, which advances there like a subaltern Adamastor, charged with inspecting the tributes delivered by the river to the sea or counting the vessels that, sunk with all hands and cargo in stormy weather in the dangerous waters of Quilleboeuf, the ancient little town of Honfleur, framed between the pictur-esque coasts of Vassal and Grâce, initially shows its whitened strand, its harbors no longer sheltering anything today but fishing-boats, but its curious and noisy population suddenly covers the narrow jetties as soon as the watchman signals the great event of the day, the arrival of the ferry.

In the lower part of the town, the steep streets seem to be transformed into a vast fish-market, and what awakened my attention most vividly, I must confess, was seeing a host of shrimp and little crabs fluttering in the streams, swollen by the deluge that the rising tide had just brought, the bright colors and dubious march of which rested my gaze involuntarily. I am very easily distracted, and all of that leaping, colliding and struggling, following the course of the stream, as if to get back

323

to the sea, had preoccupied me strongly enough to make me forget momentarily the sinister idea in the midst of which we were making our entry to Honfleur, when Jonathan's voice rang vibrantly in my ear and drew me out of my abstraction. Crabs, shrimp and everything else then disappeared from my eyes.

"Let's go! Horses! Horses! A carriage!" he said, in clipped and breathless speech. "Let's not waste a moment! It's necessary to get out of Honfleur as quickly as possible, if fate leaves us the faculty! Daring to traverse it is already audacity; to stay here, to eat here, to sleep here, even to rest here, if only for a few seconds, and lean a shoulder against one of its walls, is to deliver oneself! Let's go! Move! Move!"

The moment and the circumstance did not appear favorable to me as yet for explanations, so, as soon as the carriage and the horses were ready, we set forth, following the rude and long rise that form the outskirts of Honfleur beyond the Caen Gate. Our rig, composed of two poor nags, traveled slowly, at a walk, and as we climbed higher, if anything had been capable of giving me new distractions, having only received demi-confidences regarding the great mystery, of which I still did not understand anything, it would have been the spectacle that our horizon enclosed.

Behind us, Honfleur fled, with its low red roofs, its ports, where sailing ships were already swaying in the last undulations of the outgoing tide, its shores, laid bare, gradually enlarging, uncovering their fine white sand, on which hundreds of gulls, fulmars and curlews were coming to settle, while ships illuminated by the setting sun glided over the sea in the distance.

That was what I saw on looking backwards, while our carriage advanced painfully over the steep road.

In another direction, Notre-Dame-de Grâce suddenly appeared, and its mountain, with its spiral paths, with the fresh habitations suspended on its flanks like eagles' nests; with its long cross, which inclines over the sea and seems to dominate it like a sign of hope and salvation; with its chapel, from which a long procession of mariners was then emerging, bare-headed and barefoot, after having doubtless deposited on the Virgin's altar, as ex-votos, a picture representing the terrible storm that they had just escaped by virtue of the evident protection of Notre-Dame-de-Grâce.

That was what I saw to my right, while the poor horses, already half out of breath, only continued their route stimulated by the vehement insults and the whip of our driver.

On the other side of the road, there were wooded hills; in the distance, clumps of osiers and hemp-fields, rectangles of rye in the midst of trees of all dimensions and all kinds of foliage; various long iridescent grasses in fallow fields; and when a last ray of sunlight cast a golden reflection over all that verdure, when the evening breeze agitated it, mingling all those plants and all those branches, it was a spectacle to cause ecstasy. Then, closer to us, valleys snaked along the curves of the mountain, suddenly plunging with their apple-trees in flower, and during the commencing twilight, when the sea mists came to veil the florid, blooming valley, one might have believed that ne was looking at an inferior sky, a magical sky, strewn with innumerable white stars; and when gusts of wind lifted the mist and shook the trees, swirls of snow launched forth from those marvelous depths, rising in columns and falling back in white rain; the wooded hills, the buttresses of the mountain and the edges of the road were braided by them, as if thousands of daisies had suddenly blossomed there.

That was what I saw to my left, while advancing, still slowly, up the slope—for, in spite of the stimulations of our honest conductor, his paltry nags seemed to be threatening to stop on the road.

Personally, I did not complain of their slowness, which permitted me to examine and detail at my ease the beautiful works of nature by which I was surrounded. I have always taken great pleasure in that kind of contemplation, and never, I believe, had I abandoned myself to it in a more entire fashion; so I had completely forgotten therein my dear companion and his ambiguous predictions regarding our passage through

Honfleur when a long sigh uttered beside me suddenly brought my ideas back to my friend Jonathan.

That prolonged sigh, which had just escaped his breast, was of satisfaction; that was indubitable, given the air of well-being and delight that his physiognomy expressed. "My God! My God!" he murmured thereafter. "How weak I am! I, who have always boated to superbly that I fear nothing, who deceives myself so thoroughly in that regard, rejoice in seeing it draw away again! But at least," he added, "I didn't turn back!"

I confess with all the simplicity of my soul that I believed frankly that the exclamation regarded nothing but the redoubtable, predestined and ensorcelled little town of Honfleur. In fact, it seemed to be drawing away from us; nothing could any longer be seen of it but its outlying district and the eastern tip of its port. We were about to reach the ridge of the road, a few more rotations of the wheel, a few more steps of our horses, a few more oaths and cracks of the whip, and the old town of Honfleur would disappear from view, and only the fertile plans of Calvados and the lush valley of the Auge would strike our gaze.

At that moment, our horses baulked and collapsed; the shafts, harness and reins all broke at the same time; the carriage, left to itself on the slope of the mountain, rolled backwards with an ever-increasing velocity, dragging in tow the debris of the swingle-bars and harness.

If we had lost time making the climb, it was not the same in the descent. One might have thought that invisible horses, vigorous this time, having harnessed themselves to the rear of the carriage, were drawing us backwards. One might have thought that everything was collaborating to make us reach, with the greatest possible promptitude, the new goal that fatal destiny had mapped out for us. The wheels did not deviate for a single moment on the stonework of the causeway, and, the speed still increasing in proportion to the square of the distance, we went on and on, rolling faster and faster.

Jonathan, plunged back into silence and immobility, kept his back obstinately turned to his new destination, like a criminal being led to execution, not deigning to move his head to look at the town of Honfleur, which had already reappeared before us, further magnified by every bound we made toward it. He did not utter a cry or make a gesture to invoke the protection of God or human assistance, but allowed himself to be led where fate was taking him.

As for me, panicking, agitating, clinging on to the edges of the carriage as if to stop its fight, my hair in disorder, my eyes fearful, my arms taut, I frightened myself with the idea of the danger that was menacing us. Believing that at any moment we might be broken against the calcareous masses to the left or hurled into the depths to the right, I saw with terror the fresh and gracious scenes that had been displayed to my gaze with so many charms a short while before—for it was no longer anything but abysms, rocks and precipices, causes of death and destruction.

It was thus that, still moving, still rolling, we made our reentry to Honfleur, where we finally came to a halt in the middle of the public square, to the general amazement of the inhabitants. There, our good fortune determined that the carriage was shattered by its impact with a solidly built wall; otherwise, we would have been thrown into the sea.

After a somewhat perilous leap, I found myself on the ground again, on my feet, slightly stunned but basically safe and sound. When I recovered my senses my first concern was to look for the other. He was nearby, still in his meditative position, his hand under his chin, his head inclined and his eyes staring. He did not seem to have suffered any accident during our rapid descent and our terrible halt, and yet, at that moment, I rediscovered in his complexion the singular pallor that had already struck me during our mysterious conversation on the shore of Le Havre. That pallor was not to quit him again.

"Let's go! Forward! Let's go, let's get out of the town!" Jonathan said to me, taking my arm. "In the name of Heaven, let's get out of his accursed town!"

He drew me away, and I followed him.

"All this," he repeated, on the way, "is perhaps only a matter of chance, one of those accidents that might happen to anyone! In any case, I'm ready."

We found a shelter outside the outlying districts, in the direction of Vassal. Once installed in our little inn, Jonathan gave multiple orders in order that we could go on to our destination immediately.

This time, it was agreed that we would climb the mountain on foot, and that the carriage would join us on the road to Caen. But whatever he said and did, black night had fallen, and neither the carriage not the driver was ready to depart. It was necessary to wait for the following morning, and we were obliged to go to bed in order that the time would pass more rapidly.

I was harassed by fatigue. Jonathan and I wished one another good night.

Scarcely were we in bed than a frightful tumult filled the whole house. People were running up and downstairs, knocking on travelers' doors repeating: "Get up! Get up!" Then the cry "Fire!" was heard. We hastened to get dressed.

I was struck by amazement. All the noise had surprised me in my sleep, and in my confusion, further augmented by the obscurity, I had difficulty reassembling my garments. A beam of light came to my aid, but that beam of light came from the fire, which was already menacing us at close range, and if it dissipated the obscurity, it was far from calming my fear. So, almost paralyzed mentally, my gaze confused, I touched my clothes one after another without knowing where to begin. I became irritated, got impatient, came and went, and got no further forward.

As for Jonathan, costumed from head to toe, with every appearance of calm, sitting in a corner, he was waiting for me. I have to admit that I was profoundly touched by that mark of interest, but, the moment not being favorable to an expansive scene, I retained my gratitude internally. Eventually, with God's help, and Jonathan's, I succeeded in dressing myself almost decently.

In the meantime, time had pursued its march and the blaze its course. When we opened the door of the room, a column of flame rose up before us and forced us to recoil. Only one means of getting out remained to us. It was not me who found it, however; I was annihilated. Without wasting time, my philosopher suspended our sheets from the window, solidly knotted together, and by the protection of I know not what celestial power, we found ourselves on the ground yet again without any mishap.

"Let's go! Let's go! And be careful not to take the route to the town if you don't want to be separated from me," Jonathan said to me.

We therefore took the route that he had indicated, but a blazing hedge soon barred our passage; were obliged to make a turn to the right, and then to the left, and then a detour, and then another, and we had already ceased to be able to orientate ourselves when the fire alone, more rapid than us, our only illumination, traced the route that we had to follow. It was necessary to march before it, for it surrounded us and drove us. Then we found ourselves in the middle of a road bordered by houses. Were we going toward the coast or toward the town? We did not know, and it was important to know.

However, through the smoke by which we were surrounded, my companion distinguished a few unfortunate inhabitants, and approached them. He found them occupied in the hasty salvation of their livestock, their treasure and their families. Some were precipitately loading their effects, already partly burned, on to carts, to which they quickly harnessed themselves; others were emptying their houses through the windows; furniture silverware, crockery, everything, was rebounding, splintering and breaking as it fell on to the pavement. Some were carrying their aged relatives on their shoulders, others were breaking down the doors of the rooms in which their children were sleeping. And on all sides there were the terrified screams of children, the desperate sobs of women and the imprecations of men. All of that was combined with the whinnying of horses and the bellowing of cattle attained by the fire in stables and byres, the roar of the flames and the wind, the crackle of splitting wood, crumbling beams and collapsing roofs. How, in the midst of all that, could we ask for directions?

Jonathan did not dare. The conflagration was getting rapidly closer and closer. Pursued by it, drawn away by the fugitives, whether we liked it or not, it was necessary for us to take the route that was offered to us as a unique path of salvation, and it was thus that, at the behest of our bodies, almost unwittingly, we found ourselves for the second time in the middle of the public square of the cursed town of Honfleur.

"Again!" said Jonathan, with a convulsive movement of chagrin. "Am I doomed not to escape then? No matter! It is in my human nature to oppose resistance until the end.

"Let's go! Let's go!" he cried again, dragging me away, pulling me along by fore, although I was not opposing any resistance, for my confidence in Jonathan was so great, I had such a high opinion of his intelligence and his strength, that, in spite of the fate that only seemed to be tormenting me by repercussion and only attaining me by aiming at him, it was only with him that I sought my refuge and regarded myself as almost secure. He dragged me away, therefore, and made me descend rapidly toward the port.

There he stopped in front of the principal harbor, and shouted at a coastal mariner who had just returned and was standing in his boat, his arms folded and his mouth agape, surprised by the great glow rising over the town, which was reddening his face.

"Ahoy, friend! Is that boat yours?" Jonathan cried.

"Yes, Master, and the last payment will have been made on it two years ago come Saint Peter's Day."

"Well, would you like to earn some gold?"

"You could offer me silver and I wouldn't refuse, but what do I have to do?" said the owner of the boat."

"Take us by water, and immediately, without respite, without you and your men quitting the oars, and by forcing the sails, from here to Caen."

"Is that all? Where's your luggage?"

"Burning over there!" said Jonathan, extending his arm toward the district we had just quit.

"That's all right," the boatman replied. "It's to the profit of the angels, for it's said that they dress in clothes that fire has purified. But is your purse burning out there too? For it's good to hear mention of gold, but even better to see it."

With a gesture of impatience, Jonathan took a long, full purse from his pocket and made it clink. "Here is it," he said, "And let's make haste!"

"Yes let's make haste to settle our accounts, that's just," said the boat-owner. "It's good to see gold but it's even better to touch it; let's calculate. You seem to be in a hurry to leave and I'm in a hurry to go to bed. Furthermore, the night's cold and the sea's choppy; there are currents between Honfleur and Caen; it'll take three hours to take the boat. How much for each?"

"A hundred francs!"

"And for me?"

"Double! And all paid in advance."

The man in the boat took two steps back, in evident surprise, swiftly took off his cap as a mark of consideration, gave a thrust to the tiller, and in a blink of an eye was beside us where we stood on the dock.

Jonathan counted out the sum, and when he held it in his hands, weighing it and recounting it, the mariner said: "If you're honest men, it's God who's sent you to me; but even if it's the devil, be welcome! And even if you set fire to the town with your own hands—which is quite possible—as I don't possess anything there but a poor net, a poor bed and two poor first cousins, the whole lot can go up in flames and I'll still be gaining more than I'm losing."

"Let's go!" said Jonathan.

"Let's go!" repeated the captain. He then made a kind of loud-hailer with his hands disposed as a funnel, but, either because the tumult reigning in the street prevented the mariners he counted on accompanying him from hearing him, or because they had gone to the theater of the fire in order to render assistance, no matter how he shouted, turning toward all the taverns in the town, no one appeared.

"A curse on coastal mariners and the rabble of Honfleur!" he muttered between his teeth. Then, perceiving by the signs of impatience given by Jonathan that it was necessary to finish with it one way or another, he turned toward us and exclaimed: "Damn! A bit of resolution, my lads! Let's not count any longer on those accursed water-rats. They're amphibious, you see; as soon as those gulls touch land they turn into pigeons, and while I'm talking they're probably making love three leagues away. But when it's only a matter of rowing, one man's as good as another. There are three of us, counting you and me. That's enough! The sea's going down and in a quarter of an hour the *Belle Julie* will have her keel in the mud, so there's not a moment to lose. Is that all right with you?"

Jonathan's only response was to leap into the boat immediately. I followed him, not without murmuring inwardly about the bizarre necessity that was putting an oar in my hand, given that I was already harassed and half-asleep, and have always had weak arms and delicate hands.

Finally, we emerged from the port, and the gentle swaying of the waves, the freshness of the night and the pleasure we experienced in sensing for the third time that we were outside the walls of the accursed town, the double movement of force and abandonment that constrains a rower to look alternately at the sky and the sea—the sky strewn with stars, the sea scarcely wrinkled, scarcely quivering, and which, in reflecting the stars, divided them, broke them and unraveled them in order to form networks of gold and light in its bosom—all, to begin with, made us forget our fatigue and the terrible annoyances of the day.

We shaved the coast. Nothing impeded our progress, neither currents nor reefs. Jonathan, nailed to his bench, was causing the oar to move as if that had been his lifelong occupation; my eyes were going mechanically to the coast of

Grâce, which we were then turning in reverse, and the captain, with one hand on the tiller and the other in his pocket—doubtless seeking and palpating his gold therein, which he had contrived not to share with anyone—was humming in a good-humored tone one of those little creole airs, which, in the mouth of a coastal mariner means *I haven't always kept in sight of the shore!* when, spontaneously, all three of us looked at one another in amazement. The sail had just collapsed and stuck, shivering, around the mast; the tiller deviated under the master's hand, and the extremity of the oars stiffened in ours.

"The wind's changing," said the coaster, leaping to his sail. "Ho! Have no fear, you two, but keep rowing. There's no danger."

"There's danger so long as I can see that before me," murmured Jonathan, darting a long and sorrowful glance toward the town of Honfleur, which was no longer illuminated by a sinister glow, but enveloped by black smoke, though which shone, at intervals, the lights of a few outlying houses or the lanterns of the jetties.

At the same moment, a nocturnal wind, damp, cold and glacial, rose violently, and in spite of our combined efforts, seemed determined to push us toward the coast. Half-risen from his bench, Jonathan paraded a searching gaze around us in order to take exact cognizance of the situation; the boatman had stopped humming his creole air, and I, examining them both with terror, believed that I could see visibly written in their faces by the movement of their lips and the furrowing of their brows, the frightful future by which I was menaced.

"Out to sea," said our mariner, "and let's tack, or else my boat will be torn by those rocks at surface level, or broken against the cliff!"

We started rowing again, tacking back and forth, redoubling our efforts. I do not know what judgment Jonathan then made of our situation, but I began to criticize the folly of my blind devotion to his person. My hands were bloody, my body streaming with sweat, and my face marbled by cold. Suddenly, the wind redoubled in strength and the boat, driven in a direction contrary to the one we wanted to imprint upon it, seemed to burst in all its rigging and creak in all its length.

"Furl the sail!" cried the owner.

Jonathan seized the sail, and the sail ripped

"Let me do it, damn it! Just hold the bar for a minute in my stead."

Jonathan set himself at the tiller, and the tiller snapped.

"To the devil with Jonahs and improvised sailors!" howled our captain then. "Take the oar again, and believe me, if your conscience is heavy, say your prayers."

Jonathan took the oar again, and the oar broke in his hands; the debris of the oar and the tiller struck the timbers of the boat several times, with a dull and monotonous rattle; the tatters of the sail, after having floated in the wind, curled and swelled and twisted before us on the surface of the water, offering frightful simulacra of a drowning man; and the boat touched bottom, as if on a sandbank, and the sky, entirely darkened, made all the magical reflections vanish: all the lovely mirages, the gold and silver enameling of the moon and stars.

Suddenly, as a vulture from the depths of the clouds falls upon a poor pigeon and carries it away, palpitating, into the air, a horrible whirlwind fell upon our vessel, so frail and dislocated, plunged it into the depths of the gulf, hoisted it all the way to the summit of a wave, spun it around, and finally launched it through all the waves, all the hazards and al the perils of the ocean.

I do not know what countenance my friend Jonathan conserved at that critical moment; as for me, as if were suddenly clad in armor of ice, I felt an indescribable chill penetrate all the way to the marrow of my bones, as the Psalmist puts it; I only had time to elevate my thoughts toward God, and remained soon afterwards entirely deprived of consciousness.

I only emerged from that state of stupor on experiencing a forceful impact. I opened my eyes. Divine mercy! We were in the middle of the town of Honfleur for the fourth time, skidding over the paving stones in our wretched boat, which the furious waves had hurled far beyond the jetties!

V. The Three Secrets

All three of us set foot on the ground. Our boat-owner, as soon as he had recovered from the astonishment caused by the disasters of the night and his terrestrial navigation, fled without saying a word, taking us, in all probability, for sorcerers, if ever there were any.

Jonathan, paler than ever, nevertheless held his head high; his gait did not seem to be suffering any effect of recent events, and in his features, over which a defiant smile sometimes seemed to be issuing a challenge, the imprint of fatality mingled with that of resignation.

That was what I remembered later having observed in him, for at the time, stunned by so many various emotions, I thought that I was still in the boat at the moment of the hurricane, still in my bed at the moment of the conflagration and still in the carriage at the moment of the fall, and I felt the angular paving stones of Honfleur vacillating under my feet, as turbulent as waves, and I thought that I suddenly saw them rise up to form a steep slope over which I was dragged, and then flames sprang forth; they burned me feet, and the sea-wind froze my face; I was walking in my sleep, dreaming as I walked; I was bewildered and brutalized, and of my entire ordinary provision of sane ideas, one alone remained to me, which was that I had to follow Jonathan…and I followed him.

"Let's go! Let's go!" I repeated in my turn, by virtue of a sort of mania of imitation.

"No," said Jonathan. "This time, it's necessary not to attempt again to escape from here. It would be weakness, it would be cowardice. We'll stay. Destiny has pronounced. Water brought us to this place, the earth brought us back when we wanted to get away the first time; fire drove us back a second time, and the air has just thrown us back again violently. The four elements of Empedocles are in conspiracy against me. The predicted day will not take long to dawn; I'll wait for it!"

While he was saying that, in the public square of Honfleur, where we had just arrived, I was shivering as I listened; my eyes were closed, my teeth were chattering and a nervous tremor was agitating all my limbs. It's true that I had a fever. He deigned to perceive it, and as morning was already announced, we went into the Cheval Blanc inn, where he asked for a bed for each of us and a physician for me.

I had slept for twelve hours when the doctor arrived. My fever had departed with my fatigue and all my troublesome impressions of the day before, and the doctor was about to leave when, at a plaintive sigh uttered by my poor friend Jonathan, he suddenly turned toward him, and seemed struck by the sickly appearance of his face. He came back the following day, not for me but for my companion.

Jonathan received his cares without believing in their efficacy, and spent the time of his visits discussing with him the various theories of medicine that had succeeded one another for three centuries, like simple maters of fashion. He departed from that in order to try to demonstrate to him the vanity of medical science. The doctor appeared to marvel at his patient's vast knowledge, but combated his heresies against science ardently. Their argument became heated. The patient held firm, the doctor got carried away, and that little controversy seeming to reanimate Jonathan, I thought he might owe his cure more to the doctor's fits of temper than to his prescriptions. As for thinking that the malady might have a disastrous denouement, I carefully refrained from that.

One day, however, as I showed the doctor out, I said to him, in a rather detached manner: "Well, is his indisposition never going to end? When will he finally be rid of it?"

"Soon," he replied, with a gesture of the shoulders and the eyelids which gave him a sufficiently pitying expression.

"What! You think he's in danger?"

"Certainly."

"You're joking!"

"Within three days," the terrible doctor said, then, in a sepulchral voice, "your friend Jonathan will be dead."

Him, die! One can see that you don't know him! I was about to reply, as the old soldier did later in talking about Napoléon—but he had already gone.

When I went back into the invalid's room, I still had a smile on my lips. Jonathan asked me why; I hesitated at first over telling him, but he insisted, and as I was unable to resist him, I said: "I'm laughing at your doctor. He only believes that you can die of your malady!"

"If he believes that, he's right; if he's said so, he's told the truth," said Jonathan, raising himself up on the bed and looking at me with a sharp expression of force and conviction. "I can die of it, and I will die of it."

"You!" I cried, amazed.

"Yes, yes. Sit down, listen to me, and don't interrupt, for time is pressing and I have a great many things to tell you." He resumed his air of benevolence and continued: "Yes, my friend, the time has finally come to tell you the truth. For a long time, certain signs, infallible presentiments and the revelations of an omnipotent art have allowed me to glimpse that on the edge of the ocean, in the small town of Honfleur, my long and miserable existence would finish—or rather, that the action must be accomplished here that I call the great Spagyry, which only prepares the Entelechy."

My heart was too broken at the time to understand the Greek. I did not ask him for any explanation, and he continued:

"I did not fear corporeal annihilation sufficiently for that condition to close the bounds of the city where we are to me entirely. Then too, what can I tell you? I experienced I know not what violent desire to verify, even at the expense of my life, whether destiny would keep its word and whether my science had lied to me. You have seen the persistence with which I have struggled against destiny in order to constrain it to retract its decree. My efforts have been vain, and ought it not to have been thus? So much the better," he said, with a

337

smile of satisfaction, as if talking to himself. "My calculations were therefore exact!"

For a few moments he remained plunged in a profound meditation, his hand on his forehead, his eyes half-closed, and his lips muttering, as if preoccupied with mysterious computations.

Finally, he turned toward me again.

"That was the secret that I owed you first of all, for having shared my perils and my fatigues in recent days. Now, there is another that I want to grant you as the salary of the amity and devotion that you have never ceased to testify to me, and most of all for the confidence that you have had in me, you, my faithful companion, my guest, my listener, the shadow of my body, the echo of my voice, the mirror of my thought!"

Until then, in accordance with his order, sitting at the foot of his bed, suffocated by the shock that the news of his imminent demise had caused me, and by the grief that I felt in consequence, I had remained in a state of stupid dejection, my head slumped over my breast, not retaining either my tears or my sighs. At the announcement of that second and important secret, however, I confess with humility that curiosity suddenly extinguished grief within me; my tears ceased to flow; I raised my head and my fixed, widened eyes stopped, avidly interrogative, on Jonathan.

"What is it, then?" I asked.

"That secret is the art of prolonging life, doubling its duration, and even going beyond that. I can communicate it to you; I have promised it to you; I owe you the knowledge of it—but might it be a fatal present that I am going to give you? Think about it, hard!"

"Why fatal?" I replied, with vivacity. "Life, in being prolonged, permits a more certain practice of science and virtue! No, no! Have no fear for me. Living for a long time is the means of living better and living happily, for it requires time to learn wisdom, and even happiness."

"Would you like to try it? So be it!" the philosopher went on, with a bitter smile, presenting me with a little booklet of yellow and stained paper with greasy and worm-eaten binding: an old and dilapidated volume that was only sustained on one side thanks to reinforcement of parchment, and on the other by clasps of oxidized copper.

"Open that book, which for more than a century your modern scholars have trampled underfoot; it contains the treasure we covet."

I opened the book. It was the treatise *On Renovation and Restoration* by Paracelsus.[122] Jonathan explained to me how, by collecting certain flowers, at the time of day that Paracelsus calls *balsamaticum tempus*, which is shortly before sunrise, putting them in a bath of sand and a bath of sea-water, in the Athanor, for the duration of an entire philosophical month, which is forty days, following the numerous preparations indicated in the book, once can easily succeed in renewing in the human body the humid radical, the natural heat, and the mercury of life, the principal constituents of our existence.

When Jonathan had finished speaking, I put the book in my pocket preciously, and was about to testify my gratitude to my benefactor, as was appropriate, when he continued:

"There is a third secret even more important than the other two, the arcanum of my entire life, the key to my treasures of science, the torch what will entirely dissipate from your eyes the doubt and darkness in the midst of which I have appeared to you. The first two I have confided to you, I have made you a gift of them, but that one it is necessary to buy."

"Speak. What do you demand?" I said, impatient to hear that new revelation, which, like an intellectual star, would enlighten my reason, transform my blind faith into logical

---

[122] *The Book Concerning Renovation and Restoration* exists in English as a pamphlet extracted from volume two of the omnibus *Hermetic and Alchemical Writings of Paracelsus*, edited by A. E. Waite. Its authenticity is dubious, the efficacy of its prescriptions even more so.

conviction and make me a philosopher and not a believer. At least, that was how I judged the matter then.

"It is necessary to buy it with a oath," he said, "by a terrible oath that you must renew over my grave. It is necessary to swear to me to carry out my final instructions faithfully; then, the secret that you desire to know, I will tell you, but later…yes…*later!* For a sufficiently long time must go by before that confidence."

"Oh, blessed by God!" I exclaimed. "That consoling word proves to me that if the moment of your death is marked in advance, at least it is still distant."

"As distant as one day is from the next!" he replied.

"What! Is tomorrow the fatal day, the day of our separation?" I asked him, with the sharpest anxiety.

"Yes, it's tomorrow."

"But the secret, when shall I know it, then?"

"*Later! Later!*" he articulated, slowly.

The terror with which that word chilled me, ringing twice like a death knell, is unimaginable. What! Tomorrow he was going to die, but it was to a later time that he as postponing the revelation of his secret! It seemed to me that there was about to be a mystery between me and the tomb. By blood surged forcefully in my arteries; my heart was beating violently in my breast.

"Master," I said, tremulously, "don't abuse the weakness of my senses and my reason; in what place and at what time shall I see you again?"

"Have I not already told you? In Lantheuil and in sixteen years. Do you fear, then, not living from now until then? Do you not possess now the hermetic means that prolongs existence?"

"Yes," I replied, "but you, if I can believe your affirmation, will then have ceased to be for a long time!"

"Incredulous!" he murmured.

"And I making this terrible oath, which might compromise my salvation before God, at least deign to explain to me…"

"Silence!" he interrupted, sharply. Then, resuming his vibrant and solemn voice: "Once again, listen to me without interrupting me, for the moments are flowing rapidly, and the final hour we are to send together has already begun."

I made a movement as if to mark my surprise, but he put a finger over my mouth.

"Yes, the last, for during the night of this day, and during the morning of the day that follows, neither you nor anyone else is to penetrate my room and approach my person until the second hour of the afternoon. I require solitude in order to collect and assemble my soul. Will you respect that order, or at least have it respected?"

I nodded my head as a sign of engagement.

He went on: "Now, since faith is weakening in your heart, I am no longer demanding an oath and I shall limit myself to begging my companion insistently to carry out my last instructions. He shall know them." He added, offering me his hand, and suddenly softening the inflection of his voice: "Will you, the man that I have loved most in recent times, reject my plea and refuse even to hear me?"

"Oh!" I cried, sobbing, falling to my knees and extending my hands toward him. "Speak! Command! Those instructions, the last will of my master, whatever they are, I will execute, even at the expense of my life and the salvation of my soul—I swear it!"

A triumphant smile appeared on Jonathan's face. I cannot explain the ascendancy that the man had acquired over me. It only required a word from him to silence my scruples and reawaken all my belief and my attachment to his person.

"Come on, calm down," he said to me, benevolently. "Did you think, then, that the oath might be harmful to you? I only wanted to enchain your devotion, to force you to survive me, not to tyrannize your conscience."

And I assured him that the tears I was shedding were solely caused by his imminent demise.

"To what part of my being are you addressing so many regrets?" he replied. "Is it to my soul, *hospes comesque corporis?*[123] But it cannot die, as you know. Is it my body? Has it ever lived—the true life, at least, that of thought? The great philosopher whose science you will soon put to the proof yourself has said: *Domus eat emer mortue, sed eam inhabitans vivit.* What does it matter that the house falls in ruins, if the guest is immortal?" Then he muttered between his teeth: "On a long road, is there only a single inn that opens before the traveler?"

I paid no attention to those words then, which I recalled *later*.

Then he communicated his instructions. They consisted principally of the care I was to take to transport his body to the village of Lantheuil, observing in that regard a ceremonial that there is no need to report here.

Then, doubtless touched by my cares, and my apparent resignation, he drew me toward him and said to me in a low voice: "That secret, my great arcanum, which you desire to keenly to know, I ought not to reveal to you yet, but perhaps I can tell you in advance of what it consists. Come alone at the appointed hour, and if all is not finished, you shall know."

Then he embraced me silently, made me a sign to leave his room, and fell into a profound meditation.

I spent the night with my ear to his door, but I heard nothing. In the morning, the doctor arrived and the servants of the inn presented themselves; I sent them away, with the best reasons I could find.

Finally, the second hour of the afternoon chimed on the town clock, and I took it upon myself to go into Jonathan's room.

Even paler than usual, his eyelids lowered, he had his hands outside the bedclothes, and they were cold. At first I thought it was all over, but a sigh escaping his breast made me believe that he was only asleep.

He was not asleep; he was meditating. No quietist had ever plunged more profoundly into the abysm of reverie; the

---

[123] "My body's guest"—from a poem by the Emperor Hadrian.

body seemed to have been divorced from the soul already; the senses were to longer serving as intermediaries between them. I appealed to him in a loud voice; he did not hear me. I shook him forcefully; he remained insensible.

With the keenest ardor, however, with all the force and power of my desire and my will, I aspired, not to the perfect knowledge of the great arcanum, but, if I could not put my hand in the bag, at least I wanted to read the label. Had he not permitted me to hope? A vain hope, doubtless, for there he was, deprived of all sentiment. He had no more than a minute to live...and I was desolate.

After a few seconds of almost complete annihilation, at the moment when I was least expecting it, Jonathan was suddenly reanimated. He raised himself up on his elbow and, with his eyes wide open, he cried: "Fo, Pythagoras, Hermes Trismegistus! Confucius, Socrates, Jesus Christ! Genghis Khan, Alexander, Napoléon! Cubic root of the sacred number! Nine bodies, three souls! Triplicity in unity, triplicity in triplicity! Three heads, three hearts, three arms employed by God to instruct, to moralize, to mingle the peoples! Science by fire, morality by blood, legislation by the saber!"

And he spoke thus for a few more minutes, without it being possible for me to give a meaning to his words.

"My friend," I said to him, then, taking his hand and fixing my eyes on his in order to constrain him to bring his thoughts back to me. "You promised me..."

"I have seen it," he said, interrupting me. "The Omphalopsychites could not have seen it more lucidly; I have seen it in its purity; it is reposing now, but its wings are quivering, it is going to depart!"

Alas, I thought, immediately, *his faculties are going away, delirium is taking possession of him and I can no longer hope for anything from the poor moribund.* "Jonathan! Jonathan! Come round!" I cried, nevertheless. "Come round! Drive away these vain thoughts and think of me; I am here, awaiting the execution of your promise."

He looked at me, made no reply, let his head fall back on the pillow, closed his eyes and seemed to lose his breath. I plunged toward him, lifted his head, massaged his temples, made him respire salts, and put my hands over his heart in order to recall life to it; and in his pressing and multiple cares that I rendered him, a sort of savage fury was dominant that I could not define. My curiosity, in full exaltation, had become pitiless.

Finally, I shook him so rudely that he opened his eyes.

"It's you," he murmured. "You, my faithful disciple? Here…this box…it contains some of my veridical stories…I gave it to you."

"It's the arcanum I need!" I cried.

"I can't…adieu!"

"No! No adieu yet!" I said, violently, and in an imperative voice, as if my will ought to have been sufficient to render strength and reason to him. "No adieu until your engagements are fulfilled! I need my salary!"

"Have I not given it to you already?"

"Yes, the means of prolonging my life by a few miserable years—and what guarantee do I have of its success?"

"Incredulous! Incredulous!" Jonathan repeated, in an almost extinct voice.

"No, I'm not incredulous," I went on, becoming increasingly animated, "and the proof is that the arcanum, of which I'm not asking to know the essence but the nature, it is only by virtue of my faith in you that I can understand its sublimity."

"A sublime arcanum, indeed!" said the dying philosopher, whose voice resumed a grave and articulate clarity momentarily. "Perhaps I am its sole possessor on earth today."

"I believe it!" I said, agitated by a sort of frenzy. "But in my turn, it's me who ought to have possession of it."

"Later!" he repeated.

That last word completed my exasperation.

"But once again, are you forgetting that death has you in its grip and is about to carry you away?"

"Yes," he murmured, in a desperate tone of voice. "Annihilation might come for me if you trouble thus the peace and silence of my passage!"

"My salary!" I cried. "I need it! I want it!"

"Mercy!" he sighed, with an effort, in a suppliant voice.

"No, no mercy! By failing in your last promise, you're relieving me of my oath! Let whoever wishes take care of your remains! Give someone else your instructions! Adieu!"

"Mercy! Mercy!" he repeated again, and in a tone even more suppliant, but which was not sufficient to soften me, for, normally so timid and so sympathetic, I know not what ferocious need to know rendered me cruel and implacable. I went out. He called me back.

"Well, then, come closer," he said, "and listen carefully."

I leaned over the bed, my heart palpitating, my eyes and ears attentive; but already Jonathan seemed to be struggling again against dolor or delirium. He remained mute and immobile for a few seconds, and during that time, incapable of pity, my imperious voice resonated in his ear, my interrogative eye was on the lookout for his last gaze, and my convulsive hand shook his, already cold, as if to force him to consecrate to me the instant of life that remained to him.

Finally, wiping away the sweat streaming over his forehead, raising himself up and leaning on his elbow, he turned his head toward me, opened his eyes, now immeasurably wide, in which the disk of the pupil seemed to disappear beneath an obscure and vitreous veil, and in a hoarse voice that gradually faded away, he said:

"That secret…the great secret…is the means of never dying."

And he expired.

VI. Lantheuil

For three days I walked, accompanying the body, weeping and meditating along the route; weeping over my harshness at my master's death-bed and meditating on the inexplicable causes that might have transformed the submissive disciple into a pitiless torturer. In any case, what result had I obtained from that vain revolt?

The cart that was carrying Jonathan's remains went on ahead and I followed it. This time, nothing supernatural raised any obstacle to our journey. We went through Caen and headed toward the earth of Lantheuil, so hospitable and so holy, according to my friend's ideas. After having traversed, in broad daylight, the fields of Calvados, fertile but with little shade, breathless with heat, exhausted by lassitude, and the village of Pierre-Pont-Tourné, I finally perceived the verdure of trees, masses of foliage that rose above me and refreshed my sight. Then, in a hollow, sheltered from the sea winds and those from the north by a double rise in the terrain, there was the beautiful Château de Lantheuil: the terminus of our journey.

I had not passed through the gate of the large courtyard when two men came to meet me. One was the illustrious castellan, an excellent man whom one knew fundamentally on seeing him, and of whom one could have believed that one had loved him for ten years after having known him for ten days. The other was the local curé, an amiable fellow, although perhaps slightly lacking in tolerance on certain points, for he prohibited his parishioners from dancing, but gave them an example of all the virtues, which could, strictly speaking, pass for a compensation. He had loved Jonathan because of his religious sentiments.

Both had just that moment received a letter in which Jonathan had instructed them in advance of the precise hour of his death and the day of his arrival at Lantheuil. Thanks to the excellent organization of the post in the region, the letter had taken the same time to reach them as the deceased himself.

The three of us lifted up the body to transport it to the upper floor of the château and hide it from the gaze of the curious and the profane, for the inhumation had to be secret.

Jonathan could not be buried in holy ground; the curé opposed that because of the regulations, but he consented to bless the place of his sepulcher, wherever it might be.

Beyond the long and magnificent avenue of beeches that formed the verdant girdle of the terrain of Lantheuil, in an area full of hedges, brushwood and bushes, we dug a ditch, orientated from east to west, and in the evening, at the hour when narration came to easily to Jonathans lips, we went to look for him where he was in order to carry him to his last refuge.

Since that time, the upper floor of the Château of Lantheuil, which the dead Jonathan had inhabited, has remained closed and sealed permanently.

In humid and somber weather, under a gray sky, which the moon illuminated faintly through rare gaps in the cloud, the funeral procession set forth. The castellan and the curé, in the lead, sustained the head and I, in the rear, the feet—always following, until the end.

The three of us alone formed the cortege; further away, however, at a distance, three women—three sisters—aided us with their prayers and followed us with their gaze from the terraces of the château. One of them, tall, proud and imposing, was standing between the other two, and drew them closer when they were distracted by meditation, one gazing at the ground and the other contemplating the sky.

When everything was said for Jonathan and I had covered him with earth, the castellan gave him a tear and the curé a benediction, and they drew away. I stayed, remaining with my old friend in order to execute a few of his last instructions.

First, after having dug lightly in the soil, I sowed seeds that he had given me. During the day I had collected two tree branches; I planted one, garnished with its foliage, at the head of the grave, toward the east, and the other, stripped of its foliage and burned at its two extremities, like the magical susa of the Hottentots, I embedded at the dead man's feet; and there, on my knees with my arms extended, I renewed to Jonathan the oath to come back and see him in sixteen years.

My engagements were fulfilled. Thirty-six hours later, rested, refreshed and almost consoled—I do not know how—no longer experiencing, so to speak, any other chagrin than that of quitting my hosts. I took my leave of the curé, the castellan, the three sisters, in the most amiable fashion in the world, and returned to Paris,

VII. The Young Woman

In the middle of the last century, an illustrious voyager—not a voyager *per urbem*, but *per orbem*—traveled the polar seas for the advancement of science or fishing for whale. He encountered on the way, traveling alongside him, not on a ship but on an ice-floe, a young and handsome Samoyed, with a fat nose, a yellow complexion and particularly distinguished, like a bat, by his little eyes and long ears.

Our voyager, after having attracted the handsome Samoyed by throwing him a piece of raw fish, which he devoured instantly, gave him a large glass of bear's blood and a small glass of whale oil to drink, and the young man, tempted and enticed by all those good things, consented to go with him to France, where everyone was able to see him, like a curious beast, in exchange for a small remuneration.

Thanks to the illustrious voyager, the handsome Samoyed was presented to the king, immediately after the members of parliament, who had come to make a remonstration; he saw the court on a gala day; he saw Versailles on a day of great fountains. Then, after a sojourn of a year in the capital, he was politely returned to the seventieth degree of northern latitude.

Having arrived in the polar sea, he leapt on to the first ice-floe that came along, bid adieu to those who had brought him, and returned home, promising himself to enjoy the astonishment and admiration of his compatriots when he recounted to them the marvels he had witnessed.

Scarcely had he been recognized than the entire population, clad in their finest seal-skins and fish-scale headgear, ran toward him. They surrounded him and interrogated him, with the most ardent demonstrations of joy and curiosity. Then he talked about Paris and the Parisians. They laughed in his face. He told them about Louis XV and his court. They thought he was mad and turned their backs on him. He talked about Versailles and the great fountains. They declared him bewitched and beat him.

The man with long ears held firm at first, determined to make his compatriots hear reason, but the argument concluded by turning against him entirely. Far from persuading the others that he had seen Paris, Versailles, the king and the great waters, it was, on the contrary, the others who persuaded him that he had seen nothing, that he had gone astray on his ice-floe, that he had fallen asleep and had a dream—and, by dint of hearing it repeated, he ended up being perfect convinced of it.

Then, believing that he had recovered his sanity, he made honorable amends, declaring that he had never contemplated women as beautiful than the Samoyed ladies, never admired adornments as sumptuous as those of seal-skin and fish-scales, and never seen any great fountains except those launched through the blowholes of whales. To reward him for his retraction, he was regaled with bear-meat and walrus-oil, and he swore that he had never had such a tasty meal.

Well, it was the same for me when I returned to Paris.

I described my encounter in Calabria; I recounted the miraculous incidents of my journey in Normandy with Jonathan, his predictions, the conspiracy of the elements against him, and if people did not laugh in my face, turn their backs on me and beat me, it is only because civilization is more advanced in Paris than on the fringes of the Glacial Sea.

As supportive proofs, I published a few of Jonathan's stories; they were treated as works of fiction and I was congratulated for them. Perhaps my vanity helped to shake my convictions, and in my turn, I also ended up believing that I had slept and dreamed.

Time went by, and, in the same way that it wears away projections of marble, it partly effaced the reliefs of my most vivid impressions of youth. I married, I had children; my ideas changed course; my memories, like my affections, were concentrated on my family—but I lost my wife, and the grief that I felt in consequence, and the embarrassments of paternity that were augmented thereby, had three-quarters driven Jonathan from my memory when, recently, family affairs, the matter of an inheritance to be regulated, summoned me to the city of Caen.

Could I sense that I was so close to Lantheuil without seeking to dissipate the cloud by which my reason was still obscured?

I would like to believe, I thought, *that the flame wandering over the shores of Honfleur, the descent of the roadway, the conflagration of the suburb of Vassal, and the whirlwind falling upon our boat and hurling it over the jetties, were all visions. I would also like to believe that Jonathan, with his Calabrian brigands, his prophetic words, his science, is magic and his secrets, was making fun of me—but in sum, sorcerer or not, he died in my arms in Honfleur, and I buried him with my own hands at Lantheuil. Why should I not visit his grave? Yes, I'll go; I owe that homage to the man who offered so much recreation to my ears, the friend whose last sigh I received!*

And I went on with greater vivacity: *Yes, damn it, I'll go! I'll go, if only as a distraction, as a satisfaction, and, in sum, to determine whether there is a grave at Lantheuil, whether Jonathan ever existed, whether I had a dream, whether I was afflicted by madness, and whether all those fine marvels, to which I was the only witness, happened in Italy, in Normandy or in Charenton!*

So I went to Lantheuil, and my heart beat faster on seeing the château again, the gate, and the two ponds at the entrance, for I recognized all that. So, I had been to Lantheuil before. In what circumstances? My memory did not trace any others than those following Jonathan's death.

I encountered the curé. "What news is there?" I asked him.

"Nothing good," he replied. "Mores have declined, the villagers dance. How could it be otherwise? We have a peasant woman among us who plays the violin."

And he drew away.

I encountered the castellan. "What news is there?" I asked him.

"Everything is going well," he replied. "Agriculture has improved, and education too. We have a peasant woman among us who speaks Latin."

And he drew away.

I did not see the three sisters again.

Going around the château to the left I found myself in the magnificent avenue of beeches. I was gripped by a frisson, for it seemed to me that in approaching those places I was about to be subject once again to a supernatural power. I searched with my eyes through the trees for the place where the grave ought to be for a long time, but in vain. Instead of a wilderness, an uncultivated terrain strewn with brushwood, I saw unfurling a green lawn encircled by steams, traversed by a diagonal path, at one extremity of which there was a small stone bench set against a willow.

I searched elsewhere, believing that I had orientated myself poorly, and when I found myself back on the edge of the lawn, I perceived a beautiful young woman on the little bench, leaning against the tree.

In order to get back to the path I passed close to her; she looked at me with great attention, and a vivid redness colored her forehead and cheeks. I had too many reasons to be modest not to attribute that sudden coloration to a simple impulse of modesty and timidity, so, after having saluted the beautiful young woman, I was about to go away as quickly as possible when she stopped me with a gesture of the head, and made me a sign with her hand to come and sit beside her.

I am no longer young, but the presence and the proximity of a young and lovely woman has always acted upon me in a sensible manner. The nervous tremor that I experience then contracts my heart and makes my blood flow to my face; so, in that circumstance, when I found myself near the young woman, sitting on the same bench, I am certain that my blush could rival hers.

Each of us, doubtless in order to recover from our emotion, seemed at first to be waiting for the other to speak.

Finally, after a rather prolonged silence, she said: "You're very late."

Astonished, I turned toward her abruptly in order to demand an explanation, and our eyes met. I cannot say that what I experienced then was shock and surprise; it was an indefinable sentiment, for I was unable at first to explain its cause. It was no longer the presence of the woman that was acting upon me, but my emotion, and my blush had just been renewed, under a different influence.

Have you ever, at the most unexpected moment, seen through the windows of a strange house, a beloved figure suddenly appear, making signs of intelligence to you? Well, I too, in the eyes of the beautiful young woman that I did not know, had just seen a gaze of recognition shine, a gaze that time had been unable to make me forget, and which changed my entire being in posing upon me—but that gaze demanded a response from me.

"In what respect am I late?" I stammered.

"What about the sixteen years?" my interlocutor replied. "Should you not have been here, on this spot, on the very day that marked the expiration of sixteen years? You had sworn! And for a month, I've come to wait for you here, in vain."

I was astounded. The memories that she recalled to me, memories that I thought buried forever in Jonathan's grave, how did she have the power to evoke them? Who, then, had rendered her the depository of that secret, on which I had always been able to remain silent? I reflected, and calculated mentally the epoch in which I had bid a final adieu to Jonathan. The young woman was correct, and, thanks to hazard, I was only a month late.

"As you see, I've come," I said, with a little more assurance. "But I've searched in vain for the place where he lies."

"You've searched for it, and it's hiding beneath your shadow!" she told me. "This bench on which we're sitting is your friend's tumulary stone, and the tree on which we're both leaning is the tree you planted yourself on his tomb."

"Is it possible?" I exclaimed, already on my feet and examining, by turns, the bench, the tree and the young woman. "What, this willow..."

"Is the leafy branch turned toward the Orient."

"This bench...?"

"Is the barrier placed before a cadaver to defend it from the voracity of wolves!"

"But you," I said, "who know all these things revealed to me alone, who know the words addressed to me alone, by a mouth that the finger of death closed forever as soon as they were articulated, whose birth scarcely goes back to a time of which you speak as if you had seen it, who are you?"

She stood up in her turn, made a movement toward me, smiled at me while addressing to me one of those gazes so full of things of the past, and held out her hand with an air of familiarity and old acquaintance.

"I'm the one who told you to come; I'm the one who has been waiting for you." And, as I testified by my disturbance and agitation that I still did not understand, she added: "I'm the person who promised you a salary, and I'm the one who has come to pay you!"

"A salary?" I asked utterly astonished. "And of what kind is that salary?"

"It's a matter of acquitting a debt, by revealing to you the third secret that remains due you by Jonathan."

"Mercy!" I cried, opening amazed eyes. "Am I, then, after sixteen years, going to reenter the world of magic from which I have already emerged mad? Jonathan! It's in the name of Jonathan that you're introducing yourself? But that inestimable arcanum, the precious secret with which he was to repay my devotion and my cares, was the means of not dying, and Jonathan is dead!"

"You can see that he is not," she replied, "since here I am!"

I recoiled, seized by right; my head was reeling; I was dazzled and dizzy. Full of irresolution, torn between my reason in revolt and my curious credulity, reawakening within me, not knowing which of my senses I ought to accuse of lying, whether it was my sight that was abusing me or whether the words I had just heard were a vain noise produced by the excitement of my own thought coming to my brain from my ear without having struck the external air, I put my hand to my forehead and, tottering, leaned against the willow. There, prey to a nervous tremor, I could no longer tear my eyes away from those of the incomprehensible young woman.

Like a snake that forces a wren to come toward it of its own accord, she exercised her fascinating power upon me—for her gaze was Jonathan's! Yes, that gaze, it had struck me immediately at the first sight of the young woman, but how much more it troubled me at that moment, after the words she had just pronounced, and when I found it again in her, with a certain tone of voice and certain mystical forms of language that reminded me entirely of my old companion!

Without recovering from my disturbance, after a long silence employed in examining one another. I said: "Are you Jonathan, then?"

"Understand me more clearly," she replied, smiling. "No, I am not, or rather, I am no longer, the person you have just named, and yet he lives again in me."

"In you! But by what marvel…?"

"That's the secret that it will be necessary to tell you; but I've been here too long to tell you today, and time is pressing, for my mother is waiting for me. So, why are you so late? Until tomorrow, then!"

"Until tomorrow," I replied, without adding another word, and without making a gesture to retain her—but God knows with what strange anguish I saw her going away so abruptly. Was she not taking with her the key to the strange enigma that was commencing for me? And, I swear, I did not expect to see her again, so much did our conversation seem to me to resemble an apparition rather than a reality.

The next day, however, she returned; she returned with modesty in her cheeks, candor on her forehead, her eyes lowered, and seemed intimidated by seeing me again. This time, she seemed to belong to her sex entirely, and I found her charming thus. Her adornment, more careful than the day before, and a church book that she was holding, allowed me easily to divine the dominical day, and I was greatly astonished, I must admit, to see that singular young woman conforming, like her companions in the village, to the laws of coquetry and the vulgar rules of family and religion.

The impression that her presence made me experience then was such that, without thinking about our interrupted conversation of the previous day, I spoke to her at first about my satisfaction in seeing her again, the good grace with which she seemed to me to be provided by that new attire, and I finally came to enquire about her age, her place of origin and her family.

She was fifteen—she appeared to be at least eighteen!—her father, named Jean-Baptiste Renard, was one of the Comte de T***'s farmers.[124] Born in Lantheuil and raised in the city, her life was not evidently distinguished from that of her companions in play and school, except by virtue of the singular facility with which she learned everything that she was taught.

That was what the lovely young woman told me briefly, her eyelids modestly lowered; and while I was taking pleasure in hearing her naïve account, smiling at her, I drew closer to her on the stone bench, and by virtue of a privilege that she had authorized the day before, I had taken one of her hands in mine—pressing it rather tenderly, I confess—when the narrator suddenly stopped, raised her head, smiled, and the mock-

---

[124] The Château de Manneville in the commune of Lantheuil was long associated with the Turgot family, ancestors of the economist Jacques Turgot, Baron d'Aulne, considered to be one of the key popularizers of the philosophy of progress.

ing gaze of Jonathan, escaping from her pupils for a second time, suddenly changed the course of my ideas and brought me back to serious matters.

Shrewdly, she perceive that and, responding to my thought before I had even taken the trouble to formulate it, she said: "Yes, let's get back to more serious occupations, for it remains for me to instruct you in what you have desired so much to know. Once, even violence seemed to you to be legitimate, in order to arrive at knowledge of that great secret; today, very little suffices to distract you."

"I'm listening," I replied, red with shame.

"Oh, such a confidence requires a few preparations," she continued, smiling. "As before, then, be an attentive and not a distracted listener. I'm going to initiate you into the great arcanum, and must enable you before anything else to understand it."

She placed herself more comfortably on the bench, adjusted her dress, and adopted an attitude of calculated importance. These were very nearly her exact words, which a hind of solemnity rendered trenchant as they emerged from her mouth.

"You admit in human beings—do you not?—two distinct parts: the body, an inert, material envelope, a temporary vestment, of which the earth furnishes the fabric and the tissues, and the debris of which it reclaims; and the imperishable soul, which sets the machine in motion, pours heat into the blood and sensibility into the nerves and causes thought to arise in the brain."

I did not know where she wanted to go, but I was still listening.

She continued: "According to your modern beliefs, in shedding its initial vestment of flesh, the soul launches forth toward the heavens. Wrong! That cannot be the case; a single proof down here is not sufficient for the justice of God! Virtue has more than one contest to go through; vice has a right to more than one redress before appearing before the tribunal on high; and often, during its pilgrimage on earth, a single soul utilizes many human envelopes; many vases are broken before the divine essence that perfumes them by turns finally evaporates."

"But that's the theory of metempsychosis that you're professing!" I said, interrupting her.

"Exactly! For it's the only true theory. In order to be convinced of that, many people only need to appeal to their own consciousness. The soul always transports with it a few confused traces of the past, and if anyone interrogates his memories of another life with perseverance, more than one distant echo will awake in response. Have you not yourself, in your rapid excursions through France, or when you once traveled in Italy and Calabria"—that young woman raised in Lantheuil, who had never left her village, knew about my voyage to Italy!—"arrived at the sight of a picturesque location or a ruin till standing and conserving its original character, and thinking that it is not the first time that those objects had struck your gaze? Has not a vague memory, awakening in your mind, said to you in a whisper: 'You have already visited these places in another time!'"

"In fact, that's true!" I exclaimed, already disposed to listen favorably to my pretty professor. "Such is the intimate sensation I experienced, I admit, when I saw the road from Milan to Florence, and the Capitoline hill in Rome. I even recall having felt something similar in France...yes, near Auxerre...a farm...a watercourse...barns shaded by elms... I could have sworn that I had lived there, and, on seeing those things for the first time, I searched instinctively for the windmill that did indeed rise up to my left and the manor house, of which my eyes had not yet distinguished the roof, but which I designed before me on the other side of the hill! The manor house had become a factory, but I seemed to remember it as it had been before, and I described its heavy perron, massive and turning, its low and gilded balustrade, its large arched doorway and its peristyle, which expanded in the arc of a circle as it advanced toward the main courtyard, as if to welcome those arriving to its hospitality. All that had been succeeded by a narrow and steep stairway, and a little door. Replastering and resurfacing had changed the face of the old monument outrageously, but, whether by virtue of memory or illusion, I saw once again the cracked and blackened walls, carpeted with snapdragons, celandines and toadflax, its turrets, its high widows, and its balconies, and I could even have seen again, I believe, the former inhabitants of the old manor. if the mockery of my companions had not arrived at that point like a cold shower to calm my brain and put a brake on the deviations of my imagination."

"Well," said my interlocutor, "in Italy as in France, those were as many interrupted memories of your former existences."

O marvel! I had been by turns Italian and French! Perhaps one of the great citizens of ancient Rome, perhaps also a Burgundian farmer! The latter estate appeared to me to be more probable; I don't know why.

"Is it possible, in that case," I said then, as if talking to myself, "that metempsychosis has some reality?"

"Am I not the living proof of it?" my village girl of Lantheuil replied, folding her arms and posing on me once again her gaze of another epoch.

"Everything is unveiled to me!" I exclaimed. "Jonathan is within you; it's his soul that is animating you!"

"It has taken you a long time to comprehend that."

I was astounded, flabbergasted; I seemed to be entering another world.

She explained to me then, with a few details how souls sometimes received great modifications from the bodies in which they fixed their lodgment, citing as a primary example herself and Jonathan."

"One adapts to one's prison," she said. "Thought hides more or less narrowly in the lobes of the brain; it moves there is a different sphere, establishing other relationships with what surrounds it. Thus, in my new nature as a young woman, the senses incline toward the objects that proceed from my age and my sex, and I often find myself in complete discord with my previous existence. In many respects I have adopted frankly the vulgarity of my new station. The soul has need of those times of calm. The peasant woman rests from philosophy; then too, we can admit between the two of us that Jonathan, in pushing to excess his research in vain sciences, did not always conserve a very healthy understanding. He was a trifle fanatical, something of a charlatan, was he not? Can we agree on that?"

My first impulse was to spring to the defense of my old friend, but, reflecting that it was against him that I was debating, I remained silent, and my professor in a skirt returned to her lesson, for she had not yet told me everything.

"Nothing was ever more clearly demonstrated," she continued, "than the beautiful doctrine of the transmigration of souls, a primitive doctrine, an eternal verity, a celestial revelation, which, via the golden chain of philosophy, passed from the Orient into Greece, from Fo, the son of In-Sang-Vao, to Pythagoras, the son of Mnesarchus. In Crotona, from the height of his beautiful terraces shaded by plane trees, Pythagoras allowed it to spread through the Occident, via the filiation of his disciples; and do you know" he added, suddenly challenging me, "what became of the soul of Pythagoras?"

"I have absolutely no idea," I replied, without reflecting overmuch on the naivety of my words.

And the pretty lecturer recounted to me all the metamorphoses of the philosopher's soul, or at least the principal stations that it had made in bodies of different sexes and various estates, going back as far as the siege of Troy. That story interested me to the highest degree, and I count on publishing it when its turn comes. I gazed with admiration and surprise at that young and lovely child, in whom knowledge, eloquence ad everything were innate, explaining to me without difficulty the immense system of Pythagorean philosophy, and giving me proof of it by unfurling, act by act, the great complex existence of the philosopher.

I confess that, in admiring her and listening to her, by virtue of an involuntary movement, which it is doubtless necessary to attribute to the sustained attention that I was lending to her, I drew closer to her person again. My eyes had cased to avoid hers, and my arm, passed behind her and set against the willow, was serving her as something on which to lean, when suddenly, concluding her story, she revealed to me as the final station of the soul of the soul of Pythagoras, the body...of whom? Of Jonathan!

So the pretty girl that I had before my eyes, the pretty girl with the vermilion tint of youth and candor, the pretty girl whose waist I was clutching, was both Jonathan and Pythagoras! I withdrew my hand and recoiled with the same movement, utterly nonplussed by the role I seemed to be playing with regard to the soul of two great philosophers.

Having recovered from my disturbance, I heard Pythagoras, Jonathan and the young village girl from Lantheuil say to me: "Do you understand now how, sixteen years ago, your traveling companion seemed so well informed regarding the past, and could even, by going back through the centuries, exclaim: 'I have seen it!' Well, will you add your faith to metempsychosis now?

"Oh, believe me," my charming teacher continued, "metempsychosis exists, even for many people who have no suspicion of it. How many men, unwittingly, know something solely by virtue of reminiscence! Hence the phenomenon of precocity, of which I am an example in this locale, although I take great care to conceal more knowledge than I show; hence, in the arts, those Pica della Mirandolas of every species, that host of sublime children who are sent to Paris to enter into competition with albinos and two-headed calves; hence the revelations of facts that were believed never to have been known, the unexpected discoveries that are modestly attributed to genius but are only owed to memory, the aptitude of certain men for manual labor for which their aristocratic education could not have fashioned then, and the flight of certain others toward knowledge from which their wretched and precarious situation seemed to distance them forever; hence, too, the tastes that from one sex seems to pass to another; the love of clothes, perfumes and frivolities among men occupying serious employments. Was I not told once in Paris that all your young men are pomaded and primped liked old courtesans? That proves clearly that the previous station of those souls was a feminine body—and so on, for I would have too many examples to give you."

Interrupting herself again, she added: "But in sum, what conclusions do you draw from all that?"

"I drew the conclusion," I replied, "that those awful women who ride horses, play the violin, talk politics and know Latin have recently been men."

She started to laugh. I was not fortunate in the replies I made to her.

"The conclusion that it's necessary to draw from it," she went on, in a graver tone, "is that forgetting or remembering is all the difference there is between life and death, and pay attention!" Then, raising her voice and placing her index finger in front of her mouth: "For the man whose soul remembers, what is death down here? A change of costume, a simple formality to fulfill. But the forgetful soul allows the thread to break by which its successive existences are linked to one another; it loses its individuality, or rather, it remakes a new one at each spagyry, and its various phases, strangers without any identity between them, no longer compose any but isolated lives, tenebrous in their past as in their future, and no longer the great Pythagorean existence that is about to commence for you. For the secret of not dying is remembering! That secret, Jonathan promised to enable you to put to your own profit, and I am now ready to accomplish his promise."

I stood up, gripped my emotion. *The moment has come, then*, I said to myself; *the* later *has arrived!* And my knees trembled, my eyes misted over and I sensed a perfume of ambrosia reaching me.

Suddenly, the bells of the parish started ringing at full tilt.

"The mass, already!" exclaimed my pretty Pythagorean. "I can't miss it without revealing our mysteries. And then," she went on, lowering her eyes with an expression full of modesty, "it's a duty. Adieu, then—until tomorrow!"

And after a few words exchanged in haste, hardly giving herself the time to turn her head toward me, light, nimble and agile, she raced across the lawn, leapt the stream, went around a thicket and ran along the broad avenue of beeches. I saw her blonde head reappear, momentarily, along an elder hedge; then she disappeared completely, and I remained there, dazed, for a full quarter of an hour, scarcely able to get over what I had just heard, and still waiting for my secret!

In accord with the pretty Norman, our subsequent meetings were no longer to take place by day, but under the protection of darkness, in order that her absences should be less noticeable. I therefore saw her again that evening, by moonlight, and whether because that time of day had an influence upon her as it once had on my old friend Jonathan, or because familiarity, rapidly established between us, rendered her more confident, as soon as our first evening there were stories after stories, which made me forget the great affair of the arcanum.

What can I say? As before, perhaps more than before, I found a charm full of pleasure in that. They spilled from a mouth so fresh and so red! I became a passionate listener again. At first they clashed in their forms with those of Jonathan; they had more suavity, more simplicity; and yet, the same moral thought animated them; they had departed from the same soul.

It seems to me to be important to say that, in order to clarify certain contrasts of style existing between the different stories that I propose to publish following this introduction; for, under the appearance of a story divided into chapters, it really is an introduction that you have just read, an introduction indispensable for anyone who wants to appreciate the events and the morality of his work fully; an introduction full of incontestable verities and which will not only give the reader the knowledge of a host of things fallen into forgetfulness but also, if he wishes, to put him on the way to perpetuating his existence Pythagorically.

For eight evenings, my pretty story-teller was punctual at our rendezvous; then an evening passed without her, and then another. I already believed that I would not see her again, and I was all the more desolate because, until then, the little time that she had been able to give me at the end of the day had always gone by rapidly in the midst of the intoxication of storytelling. As for the arcanum, I was still waiting for it.

Finally, one evening, I saw her coming toward me, out of breath, for she had hastened her pace in order to arrive in time. That evening she appeared anxious and agitated, and without giving me time to say a word, she said: "My debt is not yet acquitted. Now or never is the moment to allow you know the arcanum. There isn't a moment to lose."

I allowed her to speak then without interrupting her, and when she had said everything, she went away even more rapidly than she had come.

That great, the inestimable secret, the means of never dying by connecting one life to another by memory, I finally possessed! Yes, it was owed to me and it was revealed to me. Bountiful God, I render you thanks. In spite of all the declarations of a tearful philosophy, life is good, and it is always agreeable to think that one owes to oneself the power of immortalizing oneself other than by the benefit of posterity.

In an impulse of irreflection and generosity, I initially conceived the idea of making that secret public to the profit of my contemporaries, in order that the experience so dearly acquired during this century would not be entirely lost; but I was soon deflected from that project for fear of abuse.

If such a privilege became general, would it not render hatreds and rancors eternal? Death itself would no longer suffice to efface certain insults and silence certain passions. And how many people would be discontented with their lot in thinking about what it was in another form!

Once metempsychosis was proven and universally practiced, would it not also be necessary to arrive at recognizing the rights of souls? And see what a perturbation in our Codes, our usages and our property that would entail! For if the soul is an individual, for having passed from one body to another, for having changed vestment, as we Pythagoreans say, am I to be deprived at the same time of everything that belonged to me before on earth? Is not some house, some wood or some farm nonetheless mine?

"Yes," you might cry, "everything would be finished at each spagyry," as we Pythagoreans also say.

"But what about debts? Who would pay them? What guarantee would there be for creditors? In the present order of things, there are still people who prefer to strive to repay than to blow their brains out, but in the other, would it not be simpler to die than spend five years in prison? You could close the doors of Sainte-Pélagie, the Palais de Clichy and all the branches."

"Well, the soul would be responsible, then," you might say, "and whatever its lodgment, the guest would inherit or pay, according to the circumstance."

"Good! You've changed your mind. But have you reflected? By virtue of our transmigration into another body, most of the time we have changed family, if not, we have at least changed rank; from elder brother we have become a younger brother, etc., etc., etc. Imagine the upheaval in the lands where the laws of privilege and the rights of primogeniture still exist! What new and ruinous laws of indemnity would become necessary again! And then, for placements in the State, pension rights... A child, by proving that he had within him the soul of an old soldier, might claim his pension for forty years of campaigns on land or sea, for dying for one's country would no longer be a sufficient reason or losing one's pension rights. The country would be forced no longer to be ingrate! That is impossible! How could many demands be satisfied?

I shall be frank. Alongside these grave considerations of general wellbeing, what prevents me from rendering my secret public is, above all, my own particular interest. *Instead of giving it to everyone*, I said to myself, *why not only sell it to a few? That would certainly lead to far less inconvenience and might bring me much more profit.*

My decision is thus irrevocably made. Immortality, in the Pythagorean manner, is not such a despicable thing that it cannot tempt a large number of honest people. From this day forward, I shall put it within range of the rich—under the seal of secrecy, of course.

Before concluding, I can understand at this point the curiosity of certain readers, impatient to know what became of my pretty Norman, Mademoiselle Renard.

The same evening when she confided the arcanum to me, she disappeared from the locale, in spite of her fine semblance of love for the pastoral life. I was not very anxious about her fate. She knew enough to succeed easily, and could, as she chose, make herself a couturier or a fencing-master. I ought to add that I have recently glimpsed her on the boulevards of Paris in a magnificent caleche. She had flowers and all manner of plumes on her head, and was even more charming thus. After she had made me a rapid sign by way of an amicable salute, her fan dropped from her hand and fell outside the vehicle. I picked it up and I kept it preciously, for today, nothing any longer remains of my old friend Jonathan but his traveler's staff and his fan. They can be seen in my home, between noon and two p.m., as supporting proofs.

N.B. I forgot to inform the public that for persons whose fortune does not permit them to afford Pythagorean immortality, I have at their service the means of prolonging life in accordance with the principles of Paracelsian "renovation," which have succeeded perfectly thus far. For the latter article there are different prices, according to the degree of longevity to which one aspires.

In conclusion, I perceive with regret that, thanks to the general impulsion given by our epoch, which is even more industrial than literary, the story of my friend Jonathan, first degenerating into an introduction, has finally passed into the state of a Prospectus. I could not do anything about that, and it only remains for me to give you my address, in case Pythagoras, or even Paracelsus, tempts you.

P****

Saint-Nicolas de Courson (Forest of Compiègne)

On the evening of the day when Monsieur P**** wrote those last lines—which is to say, 13 June 1837—the terrible storm occurred of which the Forest of Compiègne will long retain the sulfurous traces and in which so many multicentenarian oaks, old witnesses to the hunts of Henri IV, Louis XIV, Napoléon and Charles X, were struck by lightning and felled. Sheltering under one of them, Monsieur P****, who hoped to surpass them in age thanks to Paracelsus, before recommencing, thanks to Pythagoras, was hit by the lightning and died instantly, a deplorable accident not foreseen by the two great philosophers.

Asked by Monsieur P****'s family to cast an eye over his literary papers, I found there the stories, alternately light and grave, naïve or philosophical, appended here, the majority of which had already been told, but he had taken care to revise them and improve them for a new edition. If one finds that some of them have a family resemblance to recent productions, it will be recalled that *Jonathan the Visionary* dates, literarily speaking, from 1823. A date responds to many things today!

As for the singular story of the two Jonathans, cast in the guise of an introduction and until now completely unpublished, I had at first seen it only as a sort of allegorical fiction destined to serve as a preparation for that which is to follow, and I already held, or thought I held, the key to Jonathan, the castellan, the curé and the three sisters. Jonathan was the experience of life, the old knowledge with its importance, with all the consoling credulities of one epoch and the elevated reason of another. Jonathan was the mixed being who had to go to the grave placed between the philosopher castellan and the slightly fanatical priest. The three sisters, I took at first for the three theological virtues in order to make something of them; then I discovered that they expressed clearly, albeit symbolically, reason between over-stimulated imagination and excessively positivistic science, or true belief between fanaticism and incredulity. As for the modern Mademoiselle Renard, her veil did not seem to me to be easy to lift, and I was piling supposition upon supposition in her regard when Monsieur P****'s elder son certified to me that the symbolic form was entirely antipathetic to his father's habits.

The latter really had materially seen, known, frequented, loved and followed Jonathan. For twenty years he had talked to his family incessantly about the philosopher who was no more, and whom he mourned, and about Mademoiselle Renard, who had succeeded him and who was then running around the streets of Paris with feathers on her head. Monsieur P**** believed in Jonathan and the efficacy of the arcana that he wanted to sell for his profit.

That of Paracelsus is known; on the subject of the other, the elder son, an honest and disinterested man if ever there was one, was kind enough to reveal to me gratis that it simply consists of "assembling one's soul." as Jonathan did a few hours before dying. Assembling one's soul is a matter of reflecting, rallying one's most important memories in order to dissolve the, mix them, filter them and concrete them into a single intellectual action, reduced to its simplest abstraction. When one has thus quintessentialized one's gross baggage into a small package, one reduces that small package further, one condenses it, one accumulates it in a smaller portion, and when that small portion, all thought and intelligence, has been subjected to the last degree of compression of which it is susceptible, thanks to the elasticity of fluid and gaseous bodies, like cerebral spirits, it passes with us, and in the new life that the soul recommences, one remembers. That is all there is to it. Anyone who wishes may try it!

The elder son cited a thousand other proofs in support of his father's good faith; among other positive facts, he had known Jonathan's cane since childhood, and he had seen his father red, trembling and stammering with emotion, coming back from his walk along the boulevards with Mademoiselle Renard's fan.

It was therefore impossible for me to doubt the good faith of Jonathan's friend. I ought, however, in order to acquit my conscience entirely, to declare here that, although ordinary enjoying all his reason, Monsieur P**** had had attacks of madness in two epochs of his life. The double cause does too much honor to his sensibility for me to think of omitting it here. The first occurred after the rupture of his first amour and his voyage to the kingdom of Naples; the second after the death of his wife and his voyage to Lantheuil.

As editor, one word remains or me to say; it is the last.

Jonathan's narratives, which might be called fictions, tales, stories or novelettes, as the reader pleases, although varied in form and tone, all tend to the same goal, they are all the expansion of the same great thought, and in their ensemble complete a system of moral philosophy that might be summarized by the old axiom of ancient wisdom: *In media stat virtus.*[125]

Paris, August 1837.

---

[125] "Virtue stands in the middle" (Aristotle)

The Prophecy of Jean de Milan

(Mexico)

> Ambition is just only in this: that it suffices
> for its own penalty, and puts itself to the torment...
> So powerful is vanity that it disguises and snatches from
> our hands the verity, solidity and substance of things,
> in order to cast us to the wind and oblivion.
> (Pierre Charron, *De la sagesse*, Vol 4, chs 3 & 22)

Toward the middle of November 1518, Fernand Cortez, with a little fleet composed of ten ships, departed from Santiago, the capital of Cuba, turned north, then east, then called at the port of Trinité, reached the island of Cozumel, and finally, between the Gulf of Mexico and that of Honduras, discovered the coast of Yucatan, the object of his search.

It does not enter into my plan or my tastes to follow him during the course of his conquest. Great men are the legitimate prey of historians. Let the latter disfigure them as they wish, in accordance with their passions, their country or their beliefs— it does not matter to me. What I like to take for the subject of my stories, as you know, my friend, is not the man whose name has remained in all memories and whose true features are hidden behind the heroic mask, but the unknown, isolated man whose actions have only made a noise around him. Oh, but sometimes, with those forgotten existences, great lessons have passed unperceived.

Cortez' fleet carried to the shores of Yucatan a young Mexican who, for some months, had been living as a companion in the midst of Spanish bands. Zacatl was about to see his homeland again, from which he had been abducted when Hernandez de Cordoba had come to explore that edge of the

American continent for the first time. Taken to the island of Cuba, presented to Governor Velasquez and treated with benevolence, being timid and mild in character, he had easily allowed himself to be seduced by the novelty of the spectacle that had struck his gaze at the military and mercantile court of Santiago.

For a first good treatment they had begun by making him a Christian, under the patronage of Saint Melchior. They then thought of teaching him usages and the Castilian language. Francisquillo, Velasquez' jester, and Jean de Milan, his astrologer,[126] charged with the education of the new convert, enabled him in a very short time to respond to the governor's views by serving as an interpreter in the expedition that was in preparation.

Zacatl was content with his lot. The gaiety of Francisquillo and the profound knowledge of Jean de Milan, although he was not in a condition to appreciate it, gave him an idea of Spaniards that was both very elevated and very agreeable. The thinkers of today, incredulous and superficial, would smile ironically in imagining the nature of the disciple of a jester and a charlatan, for it is thus that grave and studious men who devoted their lives to the search for absolute truth have been labeled in recent centuries. It is necessary to agree that the hermetic discoveries were then already lost to the world, but the luminous furrow that they had left behind them still attracted the gaze of science and genius, and fortunate efforts sometimes resuscitated a few debris of Ptolemy's *Almagest*. People had not ceased to be credulous in the sixteenth century; they were happier for that; were they less sage?

At any rate, in the company of the astrologer Zacatl lived tranquilly without worrying about the future; and if he

---

[126] I have left the name Jean de Milan, like "Fernand Cortez" as Saintine renders it; converting it to Giovanni da Milano would risk confusion with the painter of that name. According to the historian Bartholomé de las Casas (1484-1566), Diego Velasquez really did have a jester named Francisquillo

memory of Yucatan sometimes came to mind, he immediately recalled the fatiguing concerns in which he had spent his youth, and he hastened to forget it.

In the midst of his new friends, it was not necessary for him to brave the ardors of the sun, to dig the earth in order to multiply cuttings of agave and seeds of roucou there or, to water cacaoyer flats for long hours of the day. How he now preferred to those laborious occupations those of furnishing his memory with strange words and kneeling before the altar of Saint James; for the Catholic Melchior thought that the Spanish language and the mass were the labors by which he was paying for the hospitality one received.

Cortez hastened the departure of his fleet. At the moment of embarkation, Zacatl, appointed as interpreter for the little army, the future conquerors of Mexico, presented himself to Jean de Milan. The latter, taking him in his arms affectionately, said to him:

"Melchior, I like your mildness and your docility, and in quitting you I experience all the regrets of an eternal separation. Yes, my son, I consulted the stars for you last night; they are favorable to you, I think, but I will not see you again, for, if my science has not abused me, you will live in your own country, you will die there surrounded by honors and your name will remain in veneration among your people. Go, my son..."

At that moment Francisquillo arrived, laughing in bursts. He had heard the astrologer's last assertion. "By the soul of the Genoese Columbus," he exclaimed, "I believe that it will be necessary for me to cede the fool's bauble to our faithful Melchior, for it's more often than not for an act of folly that one leaves one's name in human memory!"

Jean de Milan's last words had made a considerable impact on the mind of the young Mexican. They seemed to open a world before him; like Cortez, he also had his conquest to make!

During the crossing, all his ideas were concentrated on one alone: the great honors that awaited him in his homeland.

While had had lived among his brothers, no dream of opulence or ambitious desire had ever come to brush his naïve soul. Transported into the midst of a foreign race, all of whose movements were regulated by avidity, hearing around him nothing but talk of riches and power, he had understood the need to elevate oneself and aggrandize oneself that existed in the human heart, but he had not felt it. Now, he felt it, and every moment that brought him closer to his homeland redoubled its force and its exigency.

But what were those honors? Under what aspect would fortune appear to him in that land, where he had vegetated, poor and unknown, for a long time?

Soon, another sentiment, a consequence of the first, developed within him: the country that he had left without regret, he loved for the benefit that awaited him there. The Spaniards, whose active and enterprising genius had initially caused him to marvel, then appeared to him for what they really were: valorous brigands.

The fleet had doubled the point of Catoche. Its landfall was near the Tabasco River, and the inhabitants of the region, who tried at first to oppose Cortez's disembarkation, frightened by the noise of the canon, dispersed in disorder. Zacatl thought that the moment had come when his brilliant destiny was about to be accomplished. Could he not, reanimating the courage of his compatriots, disabuse them regarding those terrible machines of war, which they mistook for thunderbolts, and regarding the Spaniards, whom they believed to be gods, thus meriting, as the liberator of his homeland, the fortune that awaited him there and the honors reserved for him, in accordance with the prophecies of Jean de Milan?

There was no more doubt: the opportunity was before him, it was necessary for him to seize it! He avoided the vigilance of his former hosts, hung from the spines of a nopal the European garments provided by the munificence of Velasquez, arrived in Tabasco, presented himself to the chiefs, rallied the fugitives and marched with them to battle.

Defeated for the second time, the inhabitants of Yucatan hastened to conclude a treaty with Cortez, and only turned their fury against the man who, by his advice, had caused their disaster. But Zacatl was in flight again.

The target of the hatred of his own people and the vengeance of the Spaniards, he wandered through the woods and the grasslands for an entire month, heading toward Oxaca, only asking for hospitality at the door of isolated habitations, and cursing the astrologer's prophecies.

Finally, he reached the limits of the province and thought that he was safe. The name Melchior resounded in his ears. He turned round. It was one of his companions of the crossing, a Castilian soldier who was part of the forces that Cortez had directed toward Tlascala. Zacalt was frightened.

Running nimbly, without looking behind, he launches himself in the direction where uneven and tormented ground give him the hope of escaping gazes more easily. Without moderating his speed, he continues crossing terrain that was incessantly rising for a long time. Exhausted by fatigue and heat, he stops and listens, putting his ear to the ground. No sound is audible. Is it prudent, though, to return to the plain? No.

After having rested for a while, he resumes his route. The daylight disappears, hunger torments him, a cold wind chills him. He lies down under a kind of oak, the bitter fruit of which becomes his only nourishment.

The next day, several profound gorges appear in front of him. He penetrates at random between two ranges of basaltic rocks and marches all day, no longer finding around him any other vegetation but fir trees that show their black and tangled crowns here and there.

He is in a branch of the mountains that have since received the name of the Cordilleras.

The wind continues to blow violently. Desperate to find subsistence in the midst of those savage rocks, and fearing that it might be necessary for him to walk for a long time yet before reaching one of the slopes of the mountain, he finally decides to go back down.

Scarcely is his resolution made, however, when a confused noise alarms him. He thinks he can hear, vaguely, rising toward him, the barking of a dog, mingling with the articulations of the human voice. In Santiago he had been impressed by stories told about the terrible packs that Jean Ponce trained to discover and devour the islanders of Puerto Rico. He no longer doubts that the Spaniards are on his trail, and that hounds thirsty for blood are serving as their auxiliaries to discover his retreat. Redoubling his celerity, he gathers what remains of his strength, goes through the ravines and over the rocks, and arrives at a place where the rocky gorge ends by flattening out.

It is only there, however, that he glimpses the imminence of the peril that threatens him. The summit of the mountain is divided into two parts, which are only connected by a long and narrow crest, which seems to join them together like a wall constructed between two towers. Zacatl advances to the edge of the first plateau. To his left, over an immense distance that the simultaneous disruption of the Cordilleras allowed him to discover, he glimpses the immeasurable, mute, motionless sea; to his right, he perceives nothing but precipices, of which his eyes cannot fathom the depth, in the midst of which surge rocky points. Above his head, the higher mountains launch their prodigious peaks, covered in eternal snows, into the clouds, seemingly placing him in the center of the abyss.

His sight is troubled, vertigo makes him totter; everything appears to be spinning around him. He crouches down, his hands seeking the ground, which he thinks he can feel trembling under the efforts of the wind. But that wind also brings him cries, more distinct sounds of voices.

It is necessary to cross that bridge, to reach the great plateau. It is the only means of salvation that remains to the poor fugitive. What insensate would dare to cross it after him, if his life did not depend on the success of that temerity? Zacatl arms himself with resolution; he invokes all the gods of

374

Mexico—for the moment of peril brings him back to his first, his veritable belief—and he draws himself along face down, on his hands and knees to reach the narrow path suspended in the air; he crawls; he goes forward.

He is about to reach the second plateau when, on that ribbon of earth whose breadth is three feet at the most, in front of him, under his breath, an enormous snake appears. Its yellow-spotted body bars the causeway, over the flanks of which its extremities are dangling. Merely at the right of it, Zacatl thinks that he can already feel the grip of its coils and the swellings of its poison. He makes a backward movement. The barking resonates in his ear more clearly, coming closer. Guided by its ferocious instinct, the dog has discovered its prey; it has crossed the first plateau. Zacatl hears it all the way to the end of its course.

Before him and behind him, death! To either sides, the abyss! It is as if he were framed before four tortures.

His thoughts become troubled, and die away. A feeble glimmer of hope reanimates him. He gets up in order to step over the reptile...

Dizziness seizes him, a gust of wind tips him over; he falls...

And only the tatters of his body would have reached the bottom of the gulf if, in his fall, by virtue of a mechanical movement, his hand had not grasped a strong root projecting from the rock. It was from there, suspended in mid-air, that he heard the Castilian dog panting and ferreting along the crest. Awakened by him, the snake slid over the steep slope of the precipice and took refuge in a fissure in the mountain situated beneath Zacatl's feet.

Pale, with his hair bristling and his limbs stiff, he felt his arms stretching and his strength weakening.

The noise above him had ceased. He tried to find a point of support and, aided himself with the inequalities of the wall, clinging on to brushwood and corners of rock, he succeeded in getting back to the causeway, and finally found himself on the second plateau.

Penetrated by a religious sentiment after having escaped such a great peril, with what unction he thanked the gods of Mexico for the protection they had accorded him! He swore to forget henceforth the deceitful hopes to which the vain knowledge of the men of Europe had given birth in his heart. In his eyes, Jean de Milan was no longer anything but an impostor. Thus judge the vulgar, who attempt to interpret words of wisdom with false ideas.

Zacatl no longer had anything to do but follow the slope of the route. He appeased the thirst that was burning him with waster contained in the densely-packed and tapering leaves of the Cordillera pine. He walked all night, always following the slope of the paths, and when day dawned, his heart beat joyfully one perceiving in the distance the brought and shiny verdure of the avocado[127] and the sapodilla, and the festoons of the climbing grenadilla.

His hunger, which had ceded until then to violent emotions, suddenly awakened at the sight of those soft and flavorsome fruits, and the further forward he went the more the landscape before him developed the richness of its vegetation and the variety of its locations. Beneath him there were plains covered with maize, and then a beautiful lake whose jagged edges extended between the ridges of the mountain; then, at the other extremity, there were forests of cedrelas and liquidambars. He heard and saw around him a multicolored host of chattering parrots, tigrillas, whose songs are so sweet, and tiny hummingbirds with dazzling plumage that live in flowers and seem to be flowers that can fly themselves.

Fatigue, suffering, dangers and ambitious desires were all effaced from Zacatl's mind. Having become once again he insouciant child of Mexico, he walked freely and joyfully, respiring the perfumes of the morning, smiling at the trees, the rocks and the birds that were singing as he passed. How he loved his country then, and how he preferred it to all the marvels of Santiago!

---

[127] Author's note: "The *Laurus persea* of Linaeus."

376

As he approached he fruits he had covered, he saw an old man sitting in the shade, whom he recognized by the rich golden ornaments and precious stones encrusted in his ears as one of the opulent inhabitants of the region. A light cotton fabric covered his shoulders, and varied plumes retained by a network of fish-scales composed the rest of his adornment. Two slaves were stationed nearby in order to drive away importunate insects and assist him in walking.

The old man's name was Rhaomazi. He was of noble blood, and had lived for a long time at the court of Montezuma's predecessor. For ten years, having retired to the rich domains that he had obtained from is ancestors and the generosity of the sovereigns of Mexico, having no family and no children, he spent his days in pleasant repose and the practices of religion. As soon as he perceived the young traveler he sent one of the servants who accompanied him to meet him.

"What brings you to our valley?" he said to Zacatl. "Are you the son of one of my vassals, and have you come from making war in our distant provinces? The names of fathers have remained in my memory, but even the features of children escape it incessantly. You may reply."

"I was born in Yucatan; misfortunes took me away; I've been walking for a long time; it has taken me three days to cross the arid heights, and I'm hungry."

"My house is ahead of you," the old man replied, "on the edge of the lake. Open the door, naming Rhaomazi; you'll be welcomed. I don't refuse three days of hospitality to travelers; may the gods take account of them, for my children will never go to knock on your door."

A young woman did the honors of the old man's habitation; she supervised the domestics, received strangers, maintained order and neatness everywhere, and fulfilled next to her master the functions that Abishag of Shunem exercised with respect to the holy King David. Axa was pretty, according to the idea that her compatriots had of beauty. Her eyes were large, her nose broad and flat, her forehead low and her hair black. She conducted Zacatl to the room he was to occupy. He found a mat there on which to repose and bags full of palm leaves in order to sit down. She came back later to set before him maize dough, birds cooked over embers and the fruits of the sapodilla and grenadilla that had seduced him so much in the beginning—but once again, his hunger seemed to have calmed down. He gazed at the young woman and found the country in which she lived even more agreeable.

The first two days went by rapidly. Toward the middle of the third, the old man summoned him. Pipes were placed before him, and a liquor composed of cacao, vanilla and roucou; for tobacco and chocolate had been in usage among the Mexicans long before the arrival of Cortez, and believe me, of all their conquests, those were the ones that the Spaniards conserved the longest.

"What do you intend you do now?" Rhaomazi asked Zacatl. "Toward what town will your steps direct you?"

"I don't know," he young man replied. "Hazard alone brought me to your door; I'll allow myself to be guided by hazard again. May it give me another host as respectable as you!"

"Listen; I believe your soul to be pure, your arm vigorous and your eye vigilant. I've seen you, in order to help my servants in their labors, imploring orders from Axa. A man who seeks to pay for his hospitality by means of his good offices pleases me, and if such is your desire, you can stay with me."

Zacatl bowed.

"You'll be charged with the guard and maintenance of the chinampas."

Chinampas were floating islands of a sort, which the Mexicans had the art of making by extending a strong layer of rushes, reeds and maize stems over large rafts of light cedrela wood, covered in clay. Care and time consolidated the edifice, on which bushes of all dimensions soon sprouted, and pavilions surrounded by freshness and shade.

It was to the maintenance of one such raft that Zacatl's occupations were limited; his life was easy and his leisures numerous. A month passed, and then another. Every day, his master, accompanied by Axa, came to visit the chinampas, and sometimes, two pirogues harnessed to the floating garden caused it to travel all the sinuosities of the lake, the breezes of which the old man loved to respire. He also took pleasure in Zacatl's conversation.

Cortez was then marching toward the capital of the empire; the obstacles were smoothed in his path; he only encountered before him populations of cultivators, for, like the bees of their homeland, the Mexicans only knew how to produce, and had no stings with which to defend themselves.

Rumor of the armed visit of Cortez to Montezuma had reached as far as the peaceful valley, and Rhaomazi listened with surprise to the details that the son of Yucatan gave him regarding the mores of the Castilians, their vessels, their iron armor, their cannons and their horses. Gradually, the old man grew so accustomed to seeing and hearing him that the latest addition to the number of his servants became the one of whom he was fondest. He could not do without his presence, and when fatigue or the humidity of the air did not permit him to go to the chinampas, the young man received the order to go to the habitation.

Incessantly spending his days in the presence of the young woman, Zacatl increasingly felt the sentiment that had been born within him when he first saw Axa. He loved her. But there is another passion that, once lodged in a man's heart, can become dormant there, but not extinct: ambition, a devouring fire, which reignites in all the hearths of the soul; a frantic desire that lends its force to the energy of other desires. The pupil of Jean de Milan had known it; he believed himself to be liberated from it, but he sensed it reviving when he thought of his amour.

Could he hope to be happy while he coveted his master's favorite slave? No word had ever escaped his lips that might have explained his thought to the person who was its object. No benevolent glance on Axa's part had told him to speak or to dare. Ought he to compromise by a word the placid fate that he enjoyed in the company of his powerful rival? But that rival was weighed down by age. Day by day, life seemed to be abandoning him, and his tomb could not be far away.

Well, when he is dead, will I be any more loved? Do I have, like him, fields that grow green in the sun, slaves who obey me, adornments and treasures to offer?

A sudden idea seized him. At first, he did not dare to weigh the promises of that idea, for fear of seeing them vanish. Eventually, he returned to it, examined it, and became attached to it. His future was there in its entirety. Rhaomazi had no children, no son and no nephews; in accordance with the laws of Mexico, he could leave his heritage to one of his vassals or his servants. That preferred servant would be Zacatl!

The old man already had a paternal amity for him. The route was open to him; no obstacles would stand in his way. All the cares, patience and resignation that were required, he would have. One day, the domain would be his. He believed that, he wanted it, and he swore it!

Doubtless, his benefactor would not leave Axa in abandonment; he would place her under the protection of his heir, of his adoptive son. Perhaps he would even order their marriage!

So many simultaneous dreams of happiness melted poor Zacatl's heart that he seemed to have lost his reason therein. He cast a dominating gaze over the entire valley, cracked his knuckles, and broke a few feeble saplings with his foot as if to carry out a act of possession; then, suddenly, like an insensate, he plunged into the middle of a clump of nopals, whose spines traces multiple bloody furrows on his skin. In accordance with his beliefs, he thought that those slight wounds would disarm the gods and ensure his future prosperity.

Scarcely two months had gone by when Zacatl's hopes seemed close to realization. His master fell ill.

Immediately, Rhaomazi's servants made the house resound with cries and lamentations, but Zacatl's lamentations and cries rose up far above those of others.

The old man was surrounded by cares and assistance, but Zacatl's cares were more assiduous, just as his dolor appeared more profound. One might have thought that, by virtue of a special gift, he was suddenly liberated from the need to eat and sleep. Night and day, incessantly by the old man's side, he was occupied with nothing but him, with him alone, and he rejected the aliments that were offered to him. He made sure that his master's mat was soft and her covers light, he maintained a pure and fresh air in the room, and chased away inconvenient flies and dangerous mosquitoes, prepared soothing beverages personally and made him take them, pronouncing powerful words that he had learned, he said, from the men of Europe.

The invalid thought that he obtained relief therefrom, and, touched by the devotion of such a faithful friend, no longer wanted to have anyone but him for a physician and a companion. Even Axa only appeared in his room rarely. The other servants, irritated by such a preference, went away cursing the intruder who had come to steal the affection of their master from them, and when Zacatl happened to pass through their midst, he no longer encountered anything but menacing gestures and indignant gazes.

What did those marks of hatred and scorn matter to him? The day was perhaps not far off when all those malcontents would be forced to bow down in his presence.

Meanwhile, Rhaomazi's illness grew worse; his limbs swelled and were covered with ulcers; his body emitted a noxious and cadaverous odor. Zacatl was no less urgent and no less assiduous beside his bed. The eternal thought that dominated him enabled him to triumph over disgust and fatigue. Certain of the inefficacy of his remedies, he continued to soothe the invalid by covering his wounds with herbs chosen and blessed by a priest; around his head he placed jalap flowers, the virtue of which ought to drive away the evil spirits of the air.

But the pestilential atmosphere in the midst of which he lived, the scant nourishment that he took had finally weakened him. The benevolent old man, who had perceived his thinness and the pallor of his face, demanded that he take some rest and more substantial nourishment, and ordered him to quit him for several hours every day. Zacatl was constrained to obey.

In moving through the habitation he expected his presence once again to excite the murmurs and the malevolent words of the other servants, but it did not. Since they had learned about the desperate state of their master, unable to explain the perseverance of the difficult and dangerous services that Zacatl rendered him, they had come to believe in their turn in his devotion; and that devotion they supposed to be even greater and more heroic that Zacatl had wanted it to appear.

Custom had long dictated in Mexico that on the death of a noble and rich lord, a slave or vassal was sacrificed on the tomb of the deceased, in order to serve him in the other world. Time had softened that cruel law, and for some years, it was voluntarily that the victim sometimes offered to keep the dead man company. Well, that voluntary victim they saw in the stranger who owed everything to Rhaomazi's benevolence.

It was thus that those simple and grateful people had believed that they ought to interpret the conduct of Axa's ambitious lover. So, when they saw him again, he no longer found in their features and in their welcome anything but evidence of interest and veneration. Everyone hastened around him; some brought him vases full of perfumed water with which to wash him, others invited him to take more care of such a precious life, and placed succulent and sought-after dishes in front of him.

Zacatl was proud and charmed by the change that had overtaken the hearts of his former companions in toil and trouble, but he was far from penetrating its cause. At first he attributed it to the high idea that must have been conceived of his piety toward the worthy old man, and then to the presentiment that enlightened everyone to his future good fortune; and he enjoyed in advance the happiness thus far unknown to him of seeing himself surrounded by homages, imposing respect on his peers. He enjoyed that with delight and intoxication.

Ambition rarely shows itself without an admixture of grandeur. If the esteem of men is not always the prize that it obtains, it is almost always the primary target that it proposes to itself, for is there a greater joy than commanding those who have the right to be scornful of us? Zacatl thought, in fact, of the effect that the veneration of which he had become the object on the heart of Axa, and he enveloped himself with his false virtue with increasing care.

One morning, taking advantage of a moment when the invalid was sleeping, he was walking along the edge of the lake and gazing with a scornful expression at the chinampas attracted to the bank, as he tried to decide to whom to confide its guard when his master's property had become his, when his name was pronounced, and he saw, occupied in cutting rushes, the two slaves who had accompanied Rhaomazi under the clumps of sapodillas when he arrived in the valley.

Their conversation seemed animated. Zacatl placed himself behind a bush. One of the two workers was applauding himself for having been the first to discover the stranger coming down the hill, and he said: "Rhaomazi has nothing to repent in the good welcome he gave him; no house ever received a more grateful guest. Our country will glory in it."

"Has virtue become so rare on the edge of the lake?" replied the other, with a hint of bitterness.

"Virtue wants first of all that one should admire virtuous people, and it's for that reason that I pronounce Zacatl's name with admiration. Yes, I admire him, for I confess that I would not have had his courage."

"I would have had," said the second slave, whose name was Guazinn. "I would have had it if the master had loved me. Is the sacrifice so great, then?"

"You think that now, but one judges the warrior on the day of the battle," his companion went on. "Perhaps you would have weakened at the decisive moment."

"It's the accursed stranger who will weaken," Guazinn put in, with a movement of violent chagrin. "Well, if his virtue weighs upon him, let him cede his place to me, and to his shame, I will still accept!"

They fell silent. Slowly, Zacatl took the path back to the habitation, and on the way he reflected on what he had heard, and began to be astonished that the cares he had given to the old man excited so much surprise. However, he thought the man who had refused him his esteem unjust, and thought himself worthy of rivaling him in devotion. He wanted to force his admiration, and, seeking to deceive himself, he attempted to persuade himself that, in the role he was playing in regard to the old man, interest and ambition were only secondary. He recalled the generosity of his master, the amity with which he honored him, and strove to become emotional in thinking about his imminent death—but that word brought him back to reality, and anxiety took hold of him in thinking that the dying man had not yet manifested his last will and designated his successor.

So it was with a keen emotion that, on reentering the invalid's room he saw all the servants of the house assembled there, and perceived that as he approached they were all murmuring as if with joy and respect. The faces had an expression of solemnity that further consolidated his belief. The old man had doubtless spoken, the heir of so much wealth was known.

What did he not experience when Rhaomazi, indicating him with a gesture, said in a halting but still distinct voice: "There he is! May his virtue attract the protection of all the gods to us!" And everyone bowed, and he went on: "I thank those gods for having given me at the end of my career a friend so faithful and devoted; I sense that life is about to leave my body; come forward my son!"

Zacatl advanced in a humble and modest attitude, but his heart was swollen with pride and his rapid thoughts caused to pass before his eyes all the verdant fields of maize, the rich habitations, the numerous slaves, the woods, the meadows, the valleys, and the mines of gold and silver that he would soon possess.

Rhaomazi went on: "Zacatl, I have no children, and our laws permit me to choose my heir among my servants, in my adoptive family. Who could merit that preference better than you? Who is more worthy than you to succeed to my power and wealth? My first thought was to repay you thus for your services and ensure the happiness of my vassals. All the wealth that I possess, say one word, and it is yours..."

In the heart of the ambitious pupil of the Spaniards, unknown transports of joy and voluptuous anticipation rose up, which he had great difficulty containing. While he was believed to be overwhelmed by grief, it was Axa, amour, avidity and ambition that made his heart palpitate and moistened his gaze beside the bed of his dying benefactor.

Eventually, however, he was getting ready to reply, searching within himself for the expressions with which to express his gratitude to the old man, when the latter, having recovered the respiration that his lungs were beginning to lack, continued, almost without interruption: "Yes say one word—there is still time. But I have just learned that, driven to the end by your sublime devotion, you do not want to quit your father and that...if I die...you will die with me! If it is thus, I consent to it; it will be a joy for me not to be separated from the man who loves me so much. I have seen two of the sovereigns of Mexico, taken to the mountain of Chapultepec, accompanied to the land of souls by a great number of servants and faithful warriors, but I doubt that in that host they encountered down there a soul worthy of comparison with you. Now speak, and let your will alone decide your fate."

Zacatl remained astounded. When in hope, already rich and powerful, he was within reach of the goal of his ambition, that singular recompense offered to his zeal, to his cares, his sufferings and his privations seemed to him to be a frightful irony. He raised his head. All gazes were fixed upon him, filled with pity and admiration. He sensed a kind of confusion suddenly destroying the noble prestige through which he was seen. It was necessary to speak, however, since one word would revive his fortune.

Constrained and embarrassed, he turns his eyes to those of the old man, searching for that response, less difficult to find than to articulate, and he perceives Axa by his side, her arms extended toward him, seemingly in ecstasy before his courage and his virtue. He sees the extent to which the devotion credited to him aggrandizes him in the young woman's eyes. His heart is troubled; he hesitates…an indefinable sentiment confounds all his ideas.

What! Is it necessary for him, before Axa, to blush and show his weakness, to extinguish the last hope of a dying man who was his benefactor and believed him to be his friend? Love of life is, however, still combating, with all the strength of youth and desire…

A face appears at the entrance of the room; it is that of Guazinn, the slave who, that very morning, had displayed such a lofty courage, had seemed to predict his weakness and showed himself desirous of taking his place! On that face, Zacatl believes that he glimpses an expression of mockery and challenge. Everything is revealed to him! He knows now the source of the admiration he inspired in advance and the devotion of which everyone believed him capable. Is that slave, then, going to steal from him the respect and the homage that still surrounds him? Will that disdained servant die with his master, then, while he is heaped with his gifts?

He no longer hesitates! His soul rises to the height of sacrifice; he suddenly strips himself of the base passions that a vulgar amour and a cowardly ambition have thrown into his heart; his features take on a sublime character of enthusiasm; he marches toward he old man and falls to his knees before him.

"My father," he cries, "I shall die!" Then, in a stronger voice: "I shall die…if you die."

The same evening, Rhaomazi had ceased to live. The priests, the sacrificers, took possession of Zacatl, first having intoxicated him with praises, and when they day of the funeral arrived, he was crowned with flowers and dressed in rich garments; and as he emerged from the temple to be taken to the place of sacrifice, in the crowd that was gathered around his passage, he recognized Axa. He beckoned to her; she came running and knelt before him,

"Are you coming to see me die then?" he said to her.

"No," the young woman replied, "I would not have the strength; but one last time, I have come to honor you, for if I am to know happy days again, it is to you that I will owe them."

"To me?"

"We have both shared the master's favor; duty required one of us to follow him; perhaps he would have demanded it of me, and I fear death so much!"

Axa went back into the crowd, and the cortege continued its march.

A few paces further on, Zacatl thought he recognized a voice dominating all the others, celebrating his praises with loud cries. It was Guazinn's. Zacatl stopped again and wanted to talk to Guazinn for a moment, perhaps in order to delay the critical moment.

"Well, do you still detest the accursed stranger, and are you jealous of him, as before, and are you still disposed, as before, to take his place?"

"No," said Guazinn. "I admire you in my turn, and I honor you like the others, more than the others. When I pronounced he words of which you are reminding me, life was odious to me, for I loved Axa, and did not believe that I was loved. But today I obtained a confession and a promise from her; soon, she will be my wife, and I no longer want to die."

Zacatl felt his legs become unsteady, and had difficulty holding himself firm, as was appropriate, in the middle of the procession, which set forth again, still accompanied by a numerous population and increasing acclamations.

Rhaomazi's body, carried by slaves, headed toward one of the mountains forming the base of the Cordilleras, where his tomb had been prepared. Zacatl followed him, surrounded by priests, one of whom was carrying a sword of hard wood, edged with trenchant stones. It was necessary for him to traverse the rich fields, the fertile plains of which he ought to have been the possessor.

Finally, to the sound of reed pipes and seashells, the beating of drums and the benedictions of the people, who kissed his hands and his garments; in the midst of the pomp of the procession and a thousand cries extolling his virtues, his throat was cut.

Under the knife, the prophecy of Jean de Milan came back to his mind: "You will live in your own country, you will die there surrounded by honors and your name will remain in veneration among your people."

Perhaps he also recalled the words of Francisquillo: "It's more often than not for an act of folly that one leaves one's name in human memory!"

The Island of the Coconut Palm

(The East Indies)

Why do you tell lies ungratefully about the earth, as if it did not nourish us?

Why do you sin irreligiously against Ceres, the inventor of holy laws and shame the gentle and gracious Bacchus, as if those two deities did not give you the wherewithal to live?

(Plutarch, *Moral Works*,
"Whether it is moral to eat flesh.")

Virtue has its mildness in the midst of the dolors that surround it.

(Confucius, Maxim IX.)

Toward the end of the last century I found myself in the East Indies, where, driven by my continual need for activity, I had gone to observe the progress of the company of English merchants, which, so humble in its beginnings, had made a commodity of justice and good faith in order to take mild possession of the benevolence of the sovereigns of the land, and which, after having raised armies in order to dispute with the Dutch the commerce in pepper and cinnamon, nowadays sells people and thrones into the bargain.

In Madras, on the coast of Coromandel, I made the acquaintance of young Edward Seyton, from an old Scottish family, and the grandson of the famous Child whose name figures so sadly in the early enterprises of the company.[128]

---

[128] The reference is to Josiah Child (1630-1699), governor of the East India Company until his removal following a policy dispute.

Seyton, brought up in London in the midst of noise and brilliance, only saw happiness in the pleasures that great opulence produces. After his father's death, he had sold what he called the modest patrimony of his family, realized twenty thousand pounds sterling—half a million Tournois livres—and had come to India, he said, to make his fortune. He had mild manners and a lively mind; we often debated together, and although rarely in agreement, intimacy did not take long to be established between us.

In the two years since he had quit the pleasures of London, his capital was far from having increased with the rapidity on which he had counted in his dreams of opulence.

"Will it be necessary, then, for me to grow old far from my homeland and my friends," I heard him cry one day, "and only to possess treasures when I can no longer make use of them?"

"What prevents you from enjoying your fortune immediately?"

"Can it satisfy my needs? How unfortunate man is," he added. "This life is nothing but a disappointed desire, a deceived hope. Heaven only seems to have endowed him with thought in order to make him feel the poverty of nature more keenly; he is born covetous and can obtain nothing; his young and ardent imagination creates before him a world full of sensuality, the reality of which incessantly arrives to dissipate the charm; his eye embraces an immense extent but his hand is impotent to seize it. The corner of the earth in which he is born does not produce enough for him. The aliments that ought to nourish him, the liquors that ought to calm his thirst and maintain his strength, and the garments that ought to defend him against the intemperance of the seasons, are all placed far away from him, dispersed, and it is only at the cost of punishing travails and certain perils that he can render himself possessor of them."

"But you're only speaking here about the small number of men whose social position or wealth has led them to savor everything and exhaust everything, and in whom the fatigued senses have created new needs."

"Do the others exist?" the young man replied. "The only man who can believe in happiness is the one who exercises his faculties of sensation is their full plentitude, and who enjoys his strength by virtue of the abuse that he does to it. Unfortunately, you're right," Seyton went on, in a calmer tone, "it's a small number. How many existences have to be sacrificed to those! It requires the efforts of an entire people for the happiness of a king! Do you think that these unfortunate Indians who surround us don't curse life? Are they happy?"

"Perhaps they would be, if your compatriots didn't have the same idea of happiness as you."

At that moment we were joined by an officer of the company, who had just received news from London. After the initial information, and when the newcomer had given Seyton a few details of his friends in the metropolis, he said: "Have you heard mention of Henry Middleton?"

"Undoubtedly. There's a fortunate man!" Seyton exclaimed, turning to me with a triumphant expression. "A distinguished rank, a considerable fortune, magnificent town houses in London and Edinburgh, a house of pleasure on the continent, a hunting pack reputed throughout the north of England, the finest carriages, a sumptuous table, a box at Covent Garden and one in Drury Lane, friends and mistresses everywhere! Oh, at least he's rich, he's able to enjoy himself, and give his revenues a well-calculated circulation."

"There might well be a congestion in his finances," replied the officer, laughing, "for Middleton is dead."

"Dead!"

"He killed himself."

"What! Did he experience disastrous losses?"

"No, he certainly had enough to live, and the most agile horse couldn't have made a tour of his estates in twenty-four hours."

"He was betrayed by his friends or his mistresses, then?"

"That's improbable. His friends were well-nourished, his mistresses well-paid. He killed himself because he'd had enough of life."

"How old was he?" I asked.

"Thirty-six."

"So, a fine fortune!"

"What does the number of his houses, his servants and his mistresses matter?" I cried in my turn, turning to Seyton. "Even the richest man only has five senses to exercise; if they're used up, he's old! He seeks in vain to reignite the fire of imagination that animates him, that divinizes everything; his heart beats less ardently, desire no longer has any empire over his impoverished and fatigued blood; then he sees with bitterness that Heaven has only delivered to each individual a certain quantity of emotions to spend; that in order to enjoy his happiness for longer, it's necessary to be sparing with it, to put oneself on a diet of reason. When he has dissipated it foolishly, and he no longer sees any future for himself—for the future is everything for a man whose intelligence and imagination are over-developed—life has lost its goal. Rich, honored, but blind in the soul, he is like a fine carriage that has no horses, a vessel laden with goal but which has no sails, no compass and no pilot."

The death of Henry Middleton gave impetus to Edward's reflections. He ended up agreeing with me that too great a fortune, like too much power, was often a misfortune. One day, he was even tempted to sell the shares he had acquired in the Indian enterprises and try out a peaceful and facile existence, but in that epoch the company was in the midst of the embarrassment of a long and stubborn war; it was necessary for it to hire numerous armies, by friends and disarm enemies; the expenses exceeded profits for the moment; the shares would have been sold at a loss, and Seyton's new projects were postponed.

"Perhaps," he said, "my patrimony might have been sufficient for me, but if I sell today I'll only have an income of fifteen or twenty thousand at the most. That's not enough to live happily.

In vain I repeated: "The Company is in a difficult situation; the French seem to want to fray a path to India through Egypt. Beware of compromising everything by trying to conserve everything!" He only saw the misfortune of being reduced to an income of twenty thousand pounds. He was no longer thinking of anything but the loss he had made of his youth, which he had dissipated without profit, for pleasure. Melancholy took possession of him, and he ended up believing himself to be the poorest among the most unfortunate of men.

However, the Company did not spend its treasures without glory. Haider Aly and the brave Bailiff of Suffren were no longer there to contain English ambition. Tippoo Sahib saw the empire founded by his father near to crumbling under British cannon. That entire great movement of peoples and armies, all those grave interests in competition at the extremity of the peninsula, seemed to reawaken Edward Seyton's attention.

We were both witness to the ruin of Mysore and the death of Tippoo. That great fall made him cast an ironic glance over his own misfortunes, like the nervous and tearful wincing of a fop falling silent at the sight of a mother's grief. But the rich spoils of Seringapatam, laid out before his eyes, soon returned him to his ideas of opulence, his regrets, his sadness, and his eternal refrain on the impossibility of being happy without a large fortune.

He was, therefore, again in those dispositions when an important mission summoned him to Male, the capital of the Maldives. It was a journey of several days; I decided to accompany him, and we embarked at Banian on the Malabar coast in the most favorable weather. The wind soon changed, however, and after having tacked vainly in the Gulf of Sind, we were forced off course.

On the third day, however, we perceived numerous groups of islands. The wind calmed down; nightfall was not far off, and, fearing to collide with one of the thousand reefs of the Maldives, we dropped anchor before a kind of sandbank that showed a few hundred paces ahead of us.

The captain of our brig, an old mariner who had sent his life traveling those waters, told us then, to occupy the time, the history of the sandy ridge that we had in view.

After describing to us at length the coast, the capes and the inlets, indicated the direction of the currents and the position of the reefs, in order to enable us to appreciate his nautical knowledge, he said:

"Once, that island was cultivated and several families lived there at ease, for there was a spring of good water, not too salty, and the soil was fertile. One day, though…a long time ago…a frightful tempest, such as had never been seen in human memory, devastated the entire gulf. The waters rose, seething, to a prodigious height. A great number of islands suffered in consequence, especially that one. It disappeared entirely for the several days that the torment lasted.

"Finally, the sea calmed down, and it was seen to return to the surface of the waves, but stripped bare, no longer anything but a hideous skeleton. The sea had devoured everything: the inhabitants, the dykes, even the soil. Only one man and one tree escaped the disaster. You can still distinguish, through the mist, near a little white cliff, a tuft of verdure, reminiscent of a light cloud fixed over the island. It's a coconut palm, which, it's said, was maintained upright by the debris accumulated around it. As the waters retreated they took away that support, but the roots of the coconut palm were secure in the sand; it remained in place. As for the islander, absent from the region during the hurricane, he now represents the entire population."

"What!" exclaimed Seyton. "A man lives on that rock?"

"So it's said."

"But how can he survive there?"

"I don't know."

That story had piqued our curiosity, and it was decided that the following day, at daybreak, we would go to visit the island.

Having disembarked in the shore, we saw nothing at first that could make us suppose that there was a human being in that arid solitude. There was no trace of vegetal earth; everywhere, there was a crude chalk, covered here and there by mounds of sand. We did not take long, however, to see the summit of the palm tree again, of which we had lost sight as our boat approached the island. The further forward we went, the more the palm tree grew in front of us, but we searched in vain for some clue that might indicate the presence of the islander. Eventually, our excitement was great on discovering a hut at the foot of the tree constructed by human hands.

So a man lived, or had lived, in that desert! Undoubtedly, it was an unfortunate who, weary of his fellows and of life, had come here to bury his regrets. He had died there of dolor and misery, or perhaps, from the height of one of the promontories he had gone to rejoin voluntarily the beloved population he had survived.

Such were our thoughts, when, from the depths of a grotto hollowed out in a rock even more arid and deprived than the others, we saw an Indian advancing toward us: the inhabitant, the proprietor, of the island! He was an old man with an olive complexion, and very thin, but whose stride still testified to strength and health. As soon as he perceived us, instead of seeming intimidated, he came to meet us at a rapid pace, and an expression of satisfaction was painted on his face.

After he had, in accordance with custom, wished us good health and prayers for the poor, he went into his hut and bought out a few coconuts, some sun-dried fish and a bowl full of palm wine, and crouched down with us, after having laid a mat on the fine sand that carpeted the terrain around the coconut palm.

That hospitality, so confident and so modest, the location of the scene, the simple and grandiose tableau that surrounded us—a rock, the sky and the sea!—and the mental disturbance that grips a civilized man when he feels that he is in such an isolated spot, so unknown to the world, all concurred to strike the mind of the proud Englishman with astonishment.

And yet the spectacle was not without charm for me! A light breeze was rippling the gulf; the sun, which was rising behind it, illuminated the crown of the palm tree, whose gigantic leaves cased long strips of light and shadow to agitate before us. The light expanded and tinted everything with varied hues. One might have thought that a movement of life and pleasure was manifest in the isle, which had appeared so deserted and desolate.

Seyton, who initially turned his gaze incessantly toward our ship, of which only the topsails appeared to us above a stony massif, was soon no longer thinking about anything but interrogating our host. The later spoke Arabic, the language in use among the Muslims of the Maldives. We were able to understand him, and a familiar conversation was established between us.

"What can have made you decide," Seyton asked him, "to live alone in this abandoned place?"

"Destiny," replied the Indian, folding his arms over his breast and looking up toward the heavens. "After the disaster, when I came back here to see whether the waves had spared the tombs of my father and the woman who had been my companion, I found nothing, for the sea had taken away the living and the dead. The palm trees that I had planted in the two epochs when God blessed my family, had disappeared with my two sons. Only one tree remained on the island, and it was the one by which my father had signaled the day of my birth. The will of Providence ordered me to stay here. I am here, and I thank it for that; it knows better than we do the place where we ought to live happily."

"But it must always be necessary for you to have recourse to your compatriots on the neighboring atolls?"

"Oh," said the Indian smiling, "for twenty years I alone have been sufficient for my needs."

"What! But your garments, your nourishment..."

"Everything is here," he said, pointing to the tree." Is not the coconut palm born from the blood of a god?[129] Everything is here," he repeated, gently hugging the tree in his arms. "Are its broad leaves not sufficient to over my cabin and protect me from the ardor of the sun? I weave my mats from the most slender of its fibers. In its fruit I find the milk that slakes my thirst and gives me health, the kernel that nourishes me, and the oil that makes my limbs supple and reanimates my taste. The first bark furnishes me with the precious fiber with which I weave my loincloths and the nets that provide me with fish—for the human appetite is demanding, and the same nourishment is not always appropriate. Do I not also owe the bowls and my household utensils to it? What have I to desire?"

"Man is not born for isolation. Have you never envied the fate of other islanders, your neighbors?"

"I admit that it is pleasant for me to see a human face! But I sometimes receive visits from fishermen, and their rarity renders the enjoyment more vivid. My memories are here; what would I do elsewhere? And what about my tree? Can it be transplanted, like me? Is it not my brother by birth, my benefactor, my sustenance, the interpreter for me of the decrees of Providence, the book in which I find written all the sweetest emotions of my youth? My father planted it, and my mother surrounded it with cares when both of us were young and still weak. It was the witness to the happy epochs of my life; each of my years elapsed is inscribed in its stem by a new circle. Leave it? No! Count its knots; it will tell you my age, and tell me whether it is today that it is necessary to commence a new existence? And what about my wife's tomb? Who would take care of it? Her body is no longer there, but it has been; it's there that I like to remember, that I like to pray.

---

[129] Author's note: "The Indians of Malabar think that the god Iaeora or Ishuren, jealous of his son Ceuxi, cut off his head, which fell on Mount Calaga and was changed into a coconut palm."

It is the first action of my day, and I had just accomplished it when the sound of your voices reached me."

"But what about ennui?" I said to him. "Does it not sometimes come to surprise you and render your life a burden?"

"Ennui? I cannot know it; all my moments are occupied. The three harvests of my fruits, their preparation, my fabrics to weave, my accommodation to enrich, my cabin, my nets to repair, and the fishing, so pleasant in good weather! And then, I'm not alone on the island. Numerous families of seabirds have fixed their residences behind those rocks, nearby. Look, you can see them skimming the strand and the sea with their wings and climbing again close to us with the approaching wave. Well, none of them is a stranger to me. They're my neighbors, my companions, and my friends. They know me, and don't fear my presence."

In fact, several of those birds, with long beaks and blue and white wings, were soon fluttering around us, and settled, grouped on a small eminence situated to the Indian's right. He threw them a few remains of fish; then they disappeared, to go to circle again over the edges of the gulf.

"That's one more resource that heaven puts within your reach," I said to him.

"Me, seek to destroy them! Without necessity? What society would remain to me? On the contrary; far from harming them, when my fishing is abundant, they have their share of it. They come in response to my voice, and I enjoy the pleasant spectacle of their games and their amours."

"Those are your pleasures?"

"They're not the only ones. The morning sun, the sight of the sea and the sky, the ships that pass, the green flies that warm by night, shining luminously like little stars; from time to time, the wine of my tree..."

"So your happiness lacks nothing?"

"Alas, yes!" replied the old man, whom that last question seemed to cause to reflect momentarily. "I would have liked it if betel still grew on the island. Once, its branches enlaced with the branches of the agoti-tree; they multiplied, brilliant and perfumed, alongside that wood of date-palms." As he spoke he pointed at a patch of denuded ground strewn with blackened mosses and gray lichens, on which date-palms might have existed at one time, but where no trace of them remained. "However, I procure some in exchange for a few coconut shells that I sculpt carefully, and sheets and ropes woven with the fibrous tissues of my coconuts."

"What, you even carry out commerce?"

The Prophet has blessed the labor of men and the products of the tree. He has accorded me superfluity. But sometimes, during the season of winds, the visits are rare and betel is lacking. What man is perfectly happy? It appears that you, strangers, are experiencing an even greater privation, for your teeth do not have the red color common to those who make use of the plant."

"It does not grow in our homeland," said Seyton.

"Unfortunate land! But doubtless God compensates you with other favors, for his bounty is inexhaustible."

A simple man, who, in the midst of great privations, still praised the prodigality of Providence! We quit him, marveling at a philosophy so naïve and so sublime. Beyond the gulf, an empire had just fallen under the blows of insatiable opulence, but I do not know whether the spectacle that the poor islander had given us did not make an even greater impression on us than the profound fall of the Sultans of Mysore.

For some time, Edward Seyton no longer dared complain loudly about fate and calumniate destiny; before such a memory, his ambitious desires fell silent without being extinguished, for all men understand a great lesson, but few of them are able to profit from it.

After having stayed in Male for some time, ready to quit the Maldives, we wanted to visit our host and his palm tree again. We took him some betel. But the sage Indian was not to receive the price of his hospitality. When we arrived at the island we no longer saw the crown of the coconut palm rising up like a light parasol of foliage. A hurricane had destroyed everything. The tree had been uprooted and the man was dead. They were lying next to one another.

We hollowed out the trunk of the palm tree; the body was deposited therein, and the sand of the shore covered them both.

The island is still called the Island of the Coconut Palm today.

The White Hair

(Ancient France, Normandy)

Vanitas vanitatum...![130]
(Solomon)

About half a century ago, after having stayed in Le Havre for some time, I had just set forth in order to go to Rouen by water, in a large boat with sails and oars, which served in those days to maintain a correspondence between the two cities.

No incident had varied the beginning of our journey. The weather was favorable, the wind fresh, and we were sailing, pushed from behind, when, above Caudebec, in a place where the river did not appear to have any currents or reefs, the boat seemed to encounter an invincible object, which caused it to recoil three times.

The oars were put in the water, the direction of the tiller was changed, and again, in spite of the oars and the wind, the boat was abruptly turned back.

The passengers were beginning to get anxious. The captain, calm and motionless, stopped steering the boat momentarily, ordered by oarsmen to suspend their efforts, and said, tranquilly: "Let's stop and wait. It's nothing...it's the White Hair."[131]

---

[130] Vanity of vanities—the first words of the book of *Ecclesiastes*.

[131] The original, of course, has *Cheveu Blanc* [White Hair], which becomes the basis for an etymological flight of fancy of marginal relevance to the story that cannot be translated

Everyone, or nearly everyone, was content with that explanation, and everyone remained silent, with the exception of a worthy bourgeois from Picardy, with whom I had linked acquaintance in Le Havre, and whose curiosity was keenly excited by the captain's precise declaration.

Not wanting to be the only one ignorant of a matter of which everyone seemed so well informed, he advanced timidly toward a passenger who was standing apart and whistling while watching the wake of the boat—for the boat was already continuing its route—and said to him: "Monsieur, I'm not from these parts; could you explain to me the nature of the obstacle that held us back just now?"

"Hasn't the captain just told you?" the other replied. "It was the White Hair."

"But what is meant by the White Hair?"

Then the passenger turned toward him, looked at him with an expression of astonishment, and, after seeming to reflect for a moment, he said: "I don't know," and resumed whistling.

Two individuals sitting on bales of merchandise, sheltered from the air and he sun, were playing cards in the storage-space fitted under the rear quarterdeck of the vessel. Their open faces and friendly manner inspired confidence in my Picard. After having watched them play for a little while, appearing to take an interest in the various chances of the game, he repeated his question.

"The White Hair?" said one of them. "A thousand heads of hanged men! One can't travel along the river for a day without having one's ears deafened by it. For ten years now, I've been making the trip from Quilleboeuf to Bouille and from Bouille to Quilleboeuf twice a month, coming and going—which is to say that, four times a month, for ten years, in consequence, four hundred and eighty times, if I can count, whatever boat has transported me and my bales, I've always experienced the same shock at the same place, and heard the captain repeat the same phrase: 'It's nothing; it's the White

Hair.' But I confess that I've never thought of asking for an explanation, which probably wouldn't interest me very much."

"It's an old tale of the region," his comrade added, "some old devilry; we don't understand anything of all that."

And they resumed playing.

The Picard became bolder in his interrogation, and, instead of addressing himself to isolated individuals, he threw his question boldly into the middle of a group of passengers who were standing near the oarsmen's bench. A stiff black-clad man with a bald and bulbous forehead turned to him.

"It's easy to explain the Cheveu Blanc by etymology," he said. "The word *cheveu*, in this case, is a corrupt word and signifies absolutely nothing, in spite of what people say. Fortunately, etymological science can rectify the errors of tradition. *Cheveu* is here for *gébennes*, a Celtic word, of which the French have made *cévennes* and the Low Bretons *céveuns*, and which signifies hill, or eminence. You will understand that between *céveuns* and *cheveu* the difference is hardly detectable. The *cheveu blanc*, or rather the *céveun blanc*, is therefore nothing but a marl or chalk hill, which opposes an obstacle to the passage of the boat."

"That's stupid," replied a rustic cattle merchant.

"Thank you for the compliment," said the scholar.

"It wasn't one," replied the cattleman, removing from his mouth the pipe from which he was drawing abundant puffs. "But know, my good man, that there are no more any hills of marl or chalk on the bed of the Seine than there are Low Bretons. If those hills existed, the water would be tinted white, and it isn't. That's what I say!"

"The word *blanc* has no value," replied the polyglot, without being disconcerted. It's a disfigured word, and *black* in the Teutonic languages signifies *noir*, so the *cheveu blanc* is perhaps a black hill."

"To the devil with black and white!" said the man with the pipe. "Truthful and clear-sighed people have affirmed that they have seen distinctly, with their bodily eyes, the White

Hair that blocks the river from one bank to the other. It's a white hair, and nothing else! Do you understand, my lad?"

The scholar smiled. "One can find another explanation," he added. "*Kivos* signifies sandbank..."

"There have never been sandbanks at that location," said an oarsman, half-rising from his bench.

"We have many more," the inexhaustible etymologist went on. "*Gaveu*, which, in the Norman language, signifies *vine-branch*..."

Everyone burst out laughing; the rower picked up his oar and the cattleman his pipe, and the scholar shut up. But after that luminous discussion, my bourgeois Picard was no further forward. I made him a sign; he came over to me

"Why not ask me?" I said.

"You're not from the province."

"No matter."

"What! You know this tradition, which even the memory of the local inhabitants hasn't preserved?"

"Oh, the fishermen of Dieppe and the woodcutters in the forest of Brotonne can tell you a thousand disfigured versions in which God and the Devil play a leading role. Today, I'm perhaps the only man who can tell you the original and veritable story of the White Hair. But do you believe in magic?"

"I'll believe in anything you like, but tell me the story of the White Hair!" cried my interlocutor.

We made ourselves comfortable, trying to compose a sofa out of the packages of merchandise surrounding us, and I began my story.

*

Guy d'Albrot was the seventh son, and the natural son, of the noble Comte d'Oudales, who, toward the end of the fourteenth century, possessed the richest fiefs in Normandy from Lillebonne to Montivilliers. What was singular in the birth of Guy d'Albrot is that, on the maternal side, he was descended from Duc Richard Sans-Peur[132] by a series of illegitimate, sometimes incestuous, unions that covered an interval of four centuries, without a single marriage consecrated by the church interrupting the long chain of bastardy during all those successive generations.

Guy, scorned by his brothers, a child fashioned to thought by misfortune, fled his father's château, from which he had been repelled by humiliation. Wandering over the rich hills of Gonfreville and Saint-Vigor, he paraded his gaze ecstatically over the wooded valleys that snaked beneath his feet, or the vast sheet of water that the mouth of the Seine extended before him.

There, he was free, his head proudly raised, and it was always with a profound regret, when the shadows of evening suddenly mingled with the mists of the river, that he returned to the paternal manor.

He found his six brothers there, in the great hall carpeted with mats of rush and straw, comfortably seated before the hearth on a rich bench with a back, the center of which was occupied by the Comte d'Oudales. With their greyhounds lying at their feet, they were occupied in discussing hunting and tourneys, talking about venery and falconry, jousts and quarrels, for the instruction and entertainment of the servants.

Thinking himself protected by the attention that these noble speeches were exciting and the smoke that obscured the hall, Guy tried timidly, and without being perceived, to make his way back to his accustomed place on the pages' and grooms' stools. When he arrived, however, the falcons, suddenly waking up on their perches, agitated their bells and flapped heir wings; or, signaled by the muffled growling of the dogs, the newcomer was greeted with a paternal admonition regarding the negligence that he brought to listening to those noble conversations, and petrified by the scornful gazes

---

[132] Richard I of Normandy (933-996), who consolidated the feudal system in Normandy, had numerous illegitimate children, whose precise number is unknown.

launched at him simultaneously by six pairs of eyes, which seemed to say: *Is he made to understand such noble things?*

In fact, Guy d'Albrot, contrary to the custom of sons of good families, did not know either how to handle an ash-wood lance, with his sword and his escutcheon, nor how, when tipped on to his back, to seize his dagger dexterously in order to search for the joint of a collar, nor, in a game of quintain, how to smash the old rusty helmet coiffing a stake in the middle of the courtyard with a blow from a mace while his horse was galloping, nor any other aristocratic maneuvers. He did not know how to armor a horse or train a dog, nor how to direct a hooded merlin by whistling.

What did he know, then, the poor child? He knew how to read! And that alone, in the eyes of his six brothers, was sufficient to testify to his shameful origin.

Yes, Guy d'Albrot knew how to read, thanks to the château's chaplain, a man whom profane studies had tempted him to emerge from theology, and who hid beneath his robe and his air of humility a mind sufficiently enlightened to merit the honors of the pyre.

Having served Monseigneur d'Oudales with a brief and worthy hunting mass, the chaplain, in order to awaken the imagination of his pupil, taught him to read the works of the Brabantine Cordelier Guillaume de Ruysbroeck, alias Rubruquis,[133] and the more recent but no less marvelous voyages of the English knight Mandeville, of Norman origin.

---

[133] The traveler known in English as William of Rubruck (c.1220-c.1290), who accompanied Louis IX on the seventh crusade, and then set forth in 1253 on a failed mission to convert the Tartars to Christianity. After spending some time at the court of Mongke Khan he returned to France, where he gave the king a elaborate account of his travels, in Latin, signing himself Willelmi Rubruquis, which became an important source of geographical and anthropological information. Its publication was rapidly followed by a volume claiming to relate the travels in the Far East of a fictitious English knight

Guy found an infinite charm in that reading. One day, however, after having read the chapter in which Mandeville talks about the serpents of Sicily that devour children born of illegitimate unions, Guy suddenly became alarmed on his own account.

"Is that true, Father?" he asked, in an anxious voice.

"It might be true," replied his instructor, who saw a route open to arrive at his objectives, "but there are means of warding off those malevolent beings. That's one of the least difficult effects of the occult art that certain favorites of science possess, perhaps excessively calumniated in our day; for, while persecuting them, people profit from their discoveries. What else but a magician was Roger Bacon, who rediscovered ardent mirrors in the last century and indicated the composition of gunpowder, which is used in battles nowadays, and will one day change the face of the world. My son, if the power of God has no limits, that of human beings is also great."

The first step was taken. The pupil interrogated further, and the master then explained to him how, by means of the calculated combination of metals, the mixture of the juices of plants, the force of the gaze and the will, and even certain gestures, accomplished in the atmosphere of life that envelops each individual, humans possessed a power that error and ignorance dared to curse, but by which God was not offended, for his prophets, his elect and even his son had acquired or received the gift of them.

Guy took up his books avidly and marveled again—and this time the astonishment painted on his face was mingled with joy and not dread—at the passage in which Rubriquis says that there exists, beyond Cathay, a country favored by Heaven, whose inhabitants, exempt from infirmities of age,

---

called Sir John Mandeville, which is highly fanciful but became far more successful, probably for that reason; although far more popular in its English translation, it was almost certainly written in French, possibly by the Fleming writer Jan de Langhe.

live for many years and die without having known old age. That idea of a long life, and especially an eternal youth, threw into Guy d'Albrot's imagination a sensation of pleasure, vague as yet, but as sweet as hope.

"Father," he said, "is that possible?"

"I don't know, my child," the priest replied, "but my ignorance on the point does not authorize me to deny it."

The young man listened ecstatically. The marvelous stories of Mandeville and Rubriquis, and the revelations of the chaplain, filled his heart with ardent desires for sciences and voyages. One the latter point, his father's will had to master his own, but science was within his reach. That evening, when everyone in the château was asleep, enclosed with his master in the little room that served the chaplain as a refuge, he received his first lesson

So, there is Guy d'Albrot in the process of scaling the tree of the knowledge of good and evil, already darting a possessive gaze at the fruits of science, which often become poisonous in our hands. I ought now to make known to you other matters which it is no less essential to reveal to you for the sake of the clarity of my story—after which I promise to hasten the narration, for I can easily see the impatience you are in finally to arrive at the White Hair.

("That's true," replied my Picard.)

Guy d'Albrot was handsome, and proud of that beauty, a distinctive type with which nature had endowed all his illegitimate ancestors. In that matter, at least, he did not excite the scorn, but rather the envy of his brothers, living portraits of Monseigneur d'Oudales, who had a true face of a knight, good for hiding under a visor, which the saber and broadsword could hack and slash without regret. Guy thought of only loving his beauty in a spirit of vengeance, but his vanity found so much reward therein that there was no means he would not employ to make it stand out advantageously, to the detriment of his six brothers, who could not compete with him in that genre of superiority.

Although, like the varlets and the pages, he only wore serge chemises, while his brothers wore fine cloth; although he only girded his waist with a broad strap of Irish leather, from which hung a single velvet purse, while his brothers wore belts with silver studs and golden clasps and chains; although his cap was less conical and less elevated than theirs and the tips of his shoes not as long and curled, the chambermaids of the château and the wives of the burgers and vassals of the estate, saluted him with a murmur of admiration when he went past, so well was all of that gallantly adjusted. And I cannot guarantee that the flattering murmur in question did not occupy his mind just as much as his projects of knowledge and travel, when he was dreaming on the heights of Saint Vigor.

What seems to prove that is that the further his progress in the occult sciences went and increased, the more his thoughts turned toward the goal that the reading of Rubriquis had caused him to glimpse: the conservation of his youth and beauty. But chiromancy, necromancy, magical mirrors, formulae and rings, sympathetic metals, constellated stones, phylacteries, talismans, gamaheus and all the other products of science, to which too great an importance might then have been attached, employed in all their forms, with all their influences, did not promise the result that the young adept wanted. Importuned by his demands, the chaplain admitted to him, with sincerity and naivety in his heart, that he felt incapable of guiding him as far as he wanted to go. He told him that all he knew was that Arab philosophers had occupied themselves successfully with that genre of research.

Guy no longer dreamed of anything but a voyage to the Orient, and fate did not take long to open the route to him in a singular fashion.

At that time, a sort of crusade was undertaken against the Turks, who, under the command of their Emperor Bazajet, had made an irruption into Hungary. A host of French knights, headed by the Duc de Nevers, the eldest son of the Duc de Bourgogne, marched to the aid of the Hungarians. Monseigneur le Comte d'Oudales could not fail to use such a noble expedition for his sons' first enterprise in warfare. He proclaimed within his domains "a gathering of armed men for all those, noblemen or serfs, wishing to carry away the halloo and the chaplet of bravery and rectitude," as your compatriot Jean Froissart puts it. After having levied for that purpose a tax on his vassals in honor of Christ, his coffers full of denier lambs and écu sheep, all genuine golden coin, he assembled around him cavalry and infantry, machines of war of all sorts—ancient Norman catapults, new French cannons and bombards—and one morning, at sunrise, after mass and drinking, he quit his domains of Oudales and Lillebonne, never to return.

Yes, never to return! For, although he arrived in combat armored in iron and chain mail, plated with fine Milan steel, he and his six legitimate sons were cruelly unhorsed and slain in the plains of Nicopolis in Bulgaria, where the Turks carried out such a great massacre of foot-soldiers and knights.[134] May God preserve them! Let us say no more about it and return to the sole individual who remained of that noble lineage,

Guy d'Albrot found himself in his father's retinue, but not in the quality of combat, because Messire d'Oudales had judged long before that the last of his sons, given to reading and scholastic studies, was only good for making a monk or a cleric, and had only brought him with him to serve as a witness to his feats and those of his other sons, so that he might one day relate them on good vellum, enlivened by pretty pictures and portraits, in order to enrich the chronicles of Normandy.

In fact, in accordance with paternal good will, Guy found himself close to the melee not on a good warhorse like his six brothers but on a mare—a mount that a mere squire would have disdained in those days—with his head and body unprotected by a helmet, hauberk and coat of mail, but in a simple

---

[134] The Battle of Nicopolis, in which the Ottoman Turks won a resounding victory over Christian forces, was fought on 25 September 1396.

toque; for in accordance with Norman custom, only knights had the right to wear a hauberk. So, when the Orientals had contained the Christians in the middle of a circle of iron, in the great confusion of animals and men, if the Turk who raised his curved Damascus steel over Guy d'Albrot did not cleave him in two as dexterously as a woodcutter splitting the trunk of a fir tree, it was because the chaplain's pupil summoned his magical science to his aid—or perhaps the infidel was touched by his youth and his handsome face.

"All right!" cried the interlocutor, "but my dear monsieur, can't you abridge your preparations, for I haven't yet heard mention of the White Hair. No one today, in fact, could arrive at that subject! Perhaps I ought to have settled for the etymologist's explanation. Here are the heights of Montigny, and I fear that our journey will end before your story."

"Don't worry," I replied. "Are we not comfortably seated, gently cradled on the water, in the fresh air, beneath a veiled but cheerful sky? My story is following the movement of the boat; I shall slow it down or accelerate it in accordance with the waves and the wind, and I still hope to arrive at the end before the captain. I shall continue.

"Guy d'Albrot accompanied his vanquisher to Asia, and no more mention of him was heard for forty years..."

"Forty years!"

"Neither more nor less. So close your eyes upon the epoch about which I have just been telling you, only to open them again forty years later."

It was one evening, in 1435 or 1436. The English were then masters of Normandy and a large part of the realm. Charles VII in Reims and Henri IV in Paris had both been sacred kings of France, with equal satisfaction on the part of the people, and the war between them was continuing fiercely, at the expense of the same people. So, one evening, in a hostelry in Rouen, situated in the main square, where Jeanne d'Orléans had been burned a few years earlier, English soldiers were at table amid pots of cider and ale, emptying them in honor in the Dukes of Bedford and Talbot and to the shame of the Duc de Bourgogne, who had just broken with his former allies.

The young leader of those men-at-arms, fatigued by a day of debauchery, extended in a corner of the room on a long leather armchair, was asleep and dreaming about his amours in the midst of the clinking of glasses and goblets. That young man, Sire André de Mauny, French by birth, had remained English at heart, and the Duke of Bedford had put a company of archers under his command.

Scarcely had the soldiers' last toast resonated under the vaults of the smoke-filled room than the young captain suddenly rose to his feet, alert and wide-eyed, and threw a gold écu into the midst of a group of drinkers, whose faces, brightened by the ruddy reflection of lamplight, seemed to be illuminated by the wine of the find land whose master they had just been cursing

"Well said!" he cried to them. "Shame upon that Burgundian hart! Glory to the English!" Then, lowering his voice: "that's enough gorging on ale and cider; empty a pot of brandywine in honor of the Norman beauties, but let the service not suffer. Drink and keep watch!"

The soldiers responded to those words with a joyous acclamation, during which he went back to sleep, for noise was soporific to him.

"Oh!" cried my listener. "You're telling me another story now! I've heard it said that we'll arrive at Bouille before long, and the White Hair hasn't appeared. Let's leave your Captain de Mauny aside..."

"The Sire de Mauny," I replied, "is to play the principal role in the mystery that has excited your curiosity so much; pay attention, then, and don't interrupt me again if you want me to finish."

He shut up. I went on.

The soldiers carried out the first part of their young leader's orders, but when they got ready to carry out the second—which is to say, to patrol the town in order to maintain repose there, if necessary—as they turned their eyes toward the main square, then illuminated by magnificent moonlight (for I believe I've told you that the hostelry that served them as a guard-room was situated on the main square) they perceived a man dressed in a singular costume, doubtless a foreigner, who seemed to be motionless, in great contemplation, on the same spot where the poor young witch of Orléans had rendered her pure soul to God in the midst of the frightful anguish of the pyre.

It was a windfall for the archers, who could attempt an important capture without having to go very far.

"By Saint Martin," they said, "who can that rogue be who is keeping quiet and paying where the witch was roasted, as her soul is roasting in Hell? An old Armagnac, a royalist from Bourges, some accursed sorcerer or leprous Jew! He isn't even dressed as befits a Christian. Let's go!"

They all launched themselves toward the contemplator and brought him back to their captain, whom they found awake, for the momentary silence in the room had sufficed to extract him from his pleasant slumber.

The prisoner presented himself clad in a long furry kaftan, retained by a rich belt. His noble and handsome face, and his keen and penetrating gaze, undoubtedly might have partly disguised his age if his long white hair had not borne evident testimony of sixty years.

(Here, at the words "white hair," my bourgeois Picard stifled a murmur of satisfaction, but without interrupting me.)

The Sire de Mauny got ready to interrogate him, examining his bizarre adornment curiously: his toque circled by a silver ribbon and ornamented with a cluster of sapphires, but devoid of a feather; his red boots, decorated with gilt but devoid of spurs; his robe, lined with thin fur but presenting no trace of a blazon; and his thick and silky belt from which no weapon or chaplet was suspended.

413

It's some circumcised Saracen, he said to himself, *but I'll force him to kiss the crucifix, to swear by Mohammed, or confess what he is.*

His eyes then encountered the stranger's, and he was seized by a sudden frisson that ran through his entire body and froze his words in his mouth. In his turn, the stranger appeared to feel a painful emotion on examining him, so many secret influences and antipathies were manifest between them, without their being able to account for them.

"On my father's soul," Mauny said, later, "the sight of that man threw me into trouble and disarray, as it's said that the fays of Burgundy, the *vouivres*,[135] do when they look at you with their eyes of diamond."

The interrogation was postponed until the following day, and the stranger was locked in a cellar, securely bolted and barred.

"He'll need to use his purse if he wants to get out," the archers guarding the door said to one another, and for the rest of the night they sang aloud the ancient refrain of men-at-arms:

The prisoner
Who has no money
Is in danger
Of finding himself
Hanged or drowned,
The prisoner
Who has no money.

The following day, however, when the Sire de Mauny said to his men: "Open the door!" the captive had disappeared.

There is no need to tell you, I think, who that captive was. You've guessed it. (My interlocutor nodded his head.)

---

[135] *Vouivre*, or *guivre* in a heraldic context, is sometimes translated as "wyvern," being able to take the form of a snake or dragon as well as that of a human woman.

But it must seem singular to you to see reappearing in this world with his head whitened, a man who had only cultivated the magical art with so much constancy in order to free himself from the insults of old age. (A second affirmative nod of the head.) Alas, old age had come—but his, it is true, did not resemble any other.

After the terrible misadventure of Nicopolis, Guy d'Albrot, retained for some time by his clement captor in courteous imprisonment, found a means of paying his ransom, and, free, he traveled the Orient in search of the depositaries of science. Science beguiled him all the more as it incessantly enabled him to glimpse the goal, the object of his ardent desire. He had even encountered in an isolated canton of the Yemen an Arab family whose members, initiated into the mysteries of magic, possessed the secret he was pursuing. Among them, the grandfather and the grandsons appeared to be brothers. But they had put too high a price on the revelation of their arcanum. Guy preferred only to owe the knowledge to himself, and his multiplied attempts promised him success.

One more day, he said to himself, *just one day, and I'll no longer grow old!*

One more day, he said, the following day. *If the first glimmers were not the true ones, at least they have put me on the road, and shall I retreat when I only have to march straight ahead?*

He marched, and from trial to trial, experiment to experiment, his youth went by, and then his maturity. He was no longer pursuing the secret of remaining young, but the secret of rejuvenation.

However, like the miner who, while digging in the earth in order to extract copper ore, discovers a seam of gold, d'Albrot had encountered something better than what he sought: true knowledge, preferable by far to his futile beauty. But of that vast knowledge, which could have raised him above all the men of his time, the immense but dangerous power that magic confers on its elect, did he always make worthy usage? That is what you shall judge.

("We've passed Bouille and are skirting the forest of Roumares," said the listener. I pretended not to hear him and continued.)

"On his return to Normandy, Guy d'Albrot traversed Rouen, where he was subjected to the brief imprisonment inflicted on him by Sire André de Mauny. He wanted to see again the places where he had been young and handsome. He was convinced that youth and beauty would return to him there, where they had germinated and flourished for him.

His father's fiefs had reverted to the crown of France, which had been able to dispose of them as it wished. The greater part belonged to a noble lady, the widow of a noble and powerful knight.

The bastard of Messire d'Oudales only thought faintly of appealing against the decree that had deprived him of his heritage, for he had bought back great wealth from the Orient. To tread underfoot again the grass of the valleys of the Seine, to dream again on the hills of Saint-Vigor and Gonfreville, that was all he required for the moment.

One day, he saw a troop of young women coming toward him, all dressed in mourning. He had no doubt that the one marching at the head, who wore the veil and the girdles of a widow, was the present mistress of the Château d'Oudales, and the others the ladies her retinue. He hid behind a hedge in order to watch them pass by—a movement of modesty and timidity that doubtless stemmed from his habituation to Oriental customs. But the ladies sat down at that place in order to rest, and conversed in order to distract themselves.

He had plenty of time to admire the pretty face of the chatelaine and her logical and subtle mind. That was to his misfortune, for his sixty years and his great discoveries in the physical sciences did not protect him from a foolish and frenzied passion. He fell in love as one does at twenty, when one has an ardent heart and an excited head. It was his first amour; it was a transport, a delirium.

I believe I have mentioned that his old age did not resemble any other. In fact, either because his attempts at durable youth had had a commencement of effect, or because his simple and studious life had sheltered him from vulgar passions, his features were less marked, his wrinkles less pronounced, than would have been expected at his age. A virgin heart was beating in the old man's breast, and a young man's imagination was struggling beneath his white hair.

In accordance with the custom followed almost generally in France at that time, a widow possessing the king's fiefs, when her mourning was complete, had to remarry, under penalty of forfeit. Guy d'Albrot got it into his head to reenter his father's possessions by that door. Wanting to please and make an attempt on the damsel, he quit his kaftan and had himself dressed by the most renowned tailors. He had a tight-fitting garment of fife cloth, with a swollen breast, velvet bands and sleeves of every sort, lined, furred, pendant and changeable—in sum, thirty-six pairs of sleeves, as one said in those days; he had clasps and ribbons to retain his breeches, also beribboned, and a plumed hat garnished with Siberian marten. He was adorned, titivated, aromatized, and searched anew and with more ardor than ever for a means of rejuvenation, and, after having interrogated the occult at again at length and cabalistically, he found nothing better than covering his white hair with a blond powder that had been much in use in the previous century, and which a few young lords in the two courts were trying to bring back into fashion. (Calvardines, or perruques, were not invented until the following reign.)

In that equipment, he presented himself. The lady was pleased to begin with by his instructive and varied conversation, and like him for his company. He knew so much! He had seen so much! Then too, she admired his handsome features and the noble expression of his face, which she believed only to have been altered by the sun of Turkey and the fatigue of traveling. Without believing him to be in his first youth, she was far from suspecting his veritable age—there was so much amour in his eyes! For the dozen years that she supposed him to have more than her, would she reject the homage of a rich, gallant man abundantly endowed with fine acquired

417

knowledge, a man who only employed his treasures and his knowledge to soothe and console everyone who approached him? For Guy d'Albrot was good and benevolent, and more than one of the beautiful widow's ladies-in-waiting remarked that he had slender and very pale hands.

Finally, I don't know whether any philter was involved, but she appeared politely disposed to put away her mourning dress in his favor, when a great misadventure occurred.

The Normans of the Roumois and the region of Caux began to weary of the English yoke, to which they were no longer accustomed. The garrisons of Quilleboeuf and Caudebec were reinforced, and troops were posted all along the two banks of the Seine. The Sire de Mauny, with his archers, came all the way to take up a post in the town of Saint-Vigor.

Having heard mention of the beauty of the Dame d'Oudales, he recalled having known her late husband, the knight, and thought that propriety demanded that he visit the château.

There he found the happy couple together in a large room decorated with finely-woven tapestries and paintings on enamel, which represented the conquest of England by Duc Guillaume, such as one sees in the design of the famous Bayeux tapestry. English at heart, he initially attributed to the sight of those pictures the kind of frisson by which he was seized as he approached the beautiful lady. He could not accuse the temperature, for the room was well-sealed and provided with a shutter and a draught-excluder. But when he fixed a more attentive gaze on the chatelaine's companion, in spite of his fine clothes and yellow powder, he believed he recognized in him the aged Saracen, his escaped captive, and he remembered the first impression that the man's gaze had caused him to experience.

Great was his surprise on rediscovering him there! He pulled himself together, however, and as the hour of vespers arrived, the beautiful widow had candles of Le Mans wax brought; then the pages served conserves of berberis, preserves, fine Caudebec pâtés, spiced, honeyed and herbed

418

wines, and claret on a small table. The principal lady-in-waiting arrived to complete the company. They conversed about religion and war, and the English King Henry VI, in whom the chatelaine was interested because he was still a child, and the French King Charles VII, whom he lady-in-waiting had seen on the Loire, but whom she did not like, on the pretext that his legs were too short. And after all that fine reasoning, they came to talk about stories of amour.

Guy d'Albrot had remembered the captain of the archers of Rouen right away, and felt a harsh emotion in consequence, but he thought that the latter could not have recognized him. Even so, he was troubled by it and did not say much, except in a low voice and leaning over the armchair of the genteel widow, who responded to his tender words with tender gazes, for she did no longer made any attempt to hide her preference.

If the lady had not been as lovely, the Sire de Mauny would not have fallen in love with her suddenly, for such was his usual form of malady. But, finding her so well-provided with attractions, he could not support the idea of such a rival; anger took hold of him, and he announced that he was going to narrate the singular adventure of a young beauty smitten with amour for an old man.

The chatelaine laughed loudly at the announcement; the lady-in-waiting declared it impossible.

"Yes, Mesdames," added the young archer, "not a graying old man but an old man whose forehead was a wrinkled as the bark of an oak, and covered with silky hair as white as snow."

Scarcely had he begun his story than he encountered the gaze of Guy d'Albrot. He was troubled momentarily, but then collected himself and tried to relate the encounter of the archers and the old Saracen in the main square of Rouen. Then he stammered and became troubled again, for he had just received the affliction of that indefinable gaze. Turning his head and accelerating his narration, he hastened to talk about a young and beautiful chatelaine with white hands and a swan's neck, and the disguise of the man in the kaftan. However, as he spoke he went pale and red by turns, and felt himself trembling; for, whatever he did, in spite of himself, by an involuntary, forced movement, his eyes incessantly turned toward the superannuated gallant and incessantly encountered his fixed, motionless, penetrating stare.

Obstinate in his malevolent enterprise, be continued nevertheless, but when he returned to mock and snigger at the old man's white hair, his laughter, against his will, was augmented in its force, took on a frightening and convulsive character that cut off his speech, and only did away leaving the narrator plunged in a sort of lethargy.

"How pale he is!" said the window. "Saint Christopher preserve him from sudden death!"

"Laughter doesn't befit him," added the lady-in-waiting. "He isn't pretty when he shows his teeth."

The chatelaine gave him essences to respire, and when he had recovered his senses she had him taken to his military lodgings.

The next day she sent a page to obtain news of him; the day after that, the Sire de Mauncy came in person to thank her, but he only approached her after making made sure that she was alone. Immediately, he explained himself clearly on the matter of the old Saracen.

She laughed heartily, or pretended to, and refused to believe in the reality of the white hair. After the captain's departure, however, the window remained pensive and anxious. She had already thought about it the day before, because, in the tangled story half-told be the Sire de Mauny she had believed that she perceived his intention. Her resolution was made to clarify the matter as soon as possible, but without compromising herself. A woman's cunning is worth as much as magic.

At the accustomed hour, when Guy d'Albrot, with his pace brisk and his head high, presented himself at the château, gallantly dressed and nicely coiffed, musked and rouged, as usual, he perceived the lady on her balcony, and, as he removed his hat to salute her, a chambermaid on the opposite balcony, feigning clumsiness, emptied a large pot of warm water over his head. Who remained confused and aghast? It was the poor old man with the young heart and the foolish imagination; for the water, in its fall, had carried away all the yellow powder and his hair had been laid bare in all its whiteness.

The chatelaine uttered a cry, and withdrew from the balcony.

Guy d'Albrot proffered a long groan and left the château. But he left swearing to avenge himself, not on the beautiful widow, whom he still cherished, but on the insolent archer, the sole cause of his cruel misadventure, who doubtless hoped to profit from it. He had scorned the old man's white hair, and the old man cried: "Woe betide him!"

And woe did, indeed, arrive.

"But you're asleep, I think," I said to my young Picard, who had not interrupted me for some time.

"Not at all," he replied. "On the contrary, I'm very interested in your magician, and found the pot of hot water very moving. Go on—I'm listening, and listening so well that just now, I heard the captain of the boat announce that we're no more than four leagues from our destination."

I therefore resumed.

The Sire de Mauny did not take long to succeed Guy d'Albrot in the good graces of the chatelaine d'Oudales, even though the lady-in-waiting had made the observation that he had one eye larger than the other. From time to time, however, she felt regrets for her former suitor, for the new one was far from having a tongue as amusing and a heart as tender. When she tried to say anything about it, however, the captain responded with so many jokes and gibes about the poor man's age and white hair that the chatelaine felt ashamed and fell silent.

At first Mauny had envisaged nothing more than a liaison with the pretty widow, a fling, but when he thought about it at leisure, he calculated that a marriage of that sort could make a rich and powerful lord of him, who only possessed, and not without debts, his warhorse, his armor and his embroidered jerkin. He became increasingly covetous to possess her and her domains.

One evening, his tenderness showed itself so vividly and his amour so impatiently that the good lady, mortified in the depths of her heart to find herself constrained to change lovers to promptly, understood that it was nevertheless necessary to make a decision, amour and the laws of the realm demanding it. She asked the young suitor for three days to reflect, gave him a rendezvous in her oratory at dusk on the third day, and by means of a tender smile, allowed him to glimpse that the decision would doubtless not be contrary to him.

The following morning, as Sire André de Mauny was admiring himself complacently in a Venetian looking-glass, smiling at his good looks, his youth—for he was scarcely older than thirty—and examining his abundant black hair proudly, he suddenly took two steps back, with an expression of amazement, and then approached the mirror again, interrogating it anxiously. There was no mistake. It really was a white hair that he had just discovered there, over his brow.

("Ah!" said my auditor, sitting up straight on the bale that was serving him as a seat, for he had been listening to me for several minutes in a semi-horizontal position, almost reclining.)

The first white hair always causes us a painful emotion, for it seems to announce the imminent arrival of its companions. It is the scout who prepares the ground for the troop.

Mauny remembered all the jovial remarks he had made about white hair, and did not want to leave his own exposed to the gaze of his beauty, on parade at the front of his head. He carefully moved the others away, grasped it skillfully and pulled it sharply—but to his profound alarm, the hair stretched without breaking. A more forceful tug only gave it a greater length. The unfortunate fellow felt faint.

Pulling himself together, he thought of making it disappear by another means; he picked up a pair of scissors; but he exerted all his strength in vain; the scissors were blunted by the hair, without cutting into it, but not without elongating it further. He understood then that he was under the influence of a magic spell, and divined easily who the sorcerer was.

In order to break the spell he went to find Jean de Bourbon, abbot of Saint-Wandrille[136] who was reputed at that time to be a great exorcist and conjurer of demons. The abbot found the case serious, and initially ordered him to plunge himself into the miraculous waters of the spring of Notre-Dame de Caillouville. He obeyed, even placing his head beneath the surface of the water, which, by virtue of its repulsive force, drew a little of the hair with it, but which did not shorten it at all.

After that preparation, the abbot gave him communion, and after various ceremonies, having sprinkled his head with holy water, he took hold of the hair as close as possible to the root, and then, pronouncing the words of the exorcism, by a movement from base to tip, he pulled the hair sharply—which, obedient to the hand that was lifting it, followed it, but without breaking. The abbot was astounded; each of the monks, in order to verify the fact, tugged in his turn, and Mauny went back to his lodgings desolate and consternated, with the hair three times as long as before.

Thus the first day passed.

A fever had gripped him; he was confined to bed. In the agitations of feverish sleep, each of his spasms and disorderly twitches, which made his head creep and bound on his pillow, elongated the fatal instrument of his shame and torture further. n awakening, he found himself enlaced and garroted by it; the hair snaked around his forehead, his limbs and his body. Galvanized by rage, he leapt out of bed, and in his transport tugging at it with all his might, he tried to break it, to wear it away, to put an end to it—but the fatal hair, supple and inexhaustible, was still growing, still elongating, extending in nu-

---

[136] Jean IV de Bourbon was abbot of Saint-Wandrille from 1431-1444.

merous coils over the floor, as fine as silk and as white as snow.

When he saw it heaped up at his feet, the fear of being surprised calmed his delirium. He reflected and remembered that, according to common belief, only the person who had cast the spell could destroy it. He resolved to go and find Guy d'Albrot, to soften him with his prayers, since he was said to be sensitive and obliging, and, if he resisted, to constrain him to make the sign of the cross, after which, he would plunge his dagger into his heart, and would at least be avenged. But he ran around the surrounding area asking everywhere for news of the old man, in vain; the latter had quit the area some time ago, and no one could say what had become of him.

Thus the second day passed.

The third day commenced, at the end of which an amorous decision could render André de Mauny the possessor of one of the most beautiful fiefs in Normandy and one of the most beautiful women in the realm. But how could he dare to present himself before her with the sign of reprobation that could only attract the mockery of the widow?

He still hoped to be able to destroy it; he tried to do it by fire; he put it in an ardent brazier, which he stimulated and maintained himself; but, like pure asbestos, he drew out the accursed hair no less supple, no less silky, but even whiter than before. He plunged it into vinegar, but that substance, with which, according to the storytellers of our great histories, Hannibal has dissolved the rocks of the Alps, was impotent against the hair. He summoned to his aid a physician, who employed by turns the most destructive and corrosive agents; he attempted to sever it by means of a file and a saw, but the saw and the file were smoothed out by it; he tried to break it between an anvil and an ax, but only the ax broke. It was all in vain!

Finally, the hour marked by the chatelaine approached. *Perhaps*, he said to himself, *the charm that is bewitching me and making me unfortunate will cease later of its own accord, may it please God!*

He got ready to depart, but he was so pale, so distraught, those three days had savaged his good looks to such an extent, that in his turn it was necessary for him to doll himself up and rouge himself in order still to rejoice his beauty's eyes with an appearance of youth and health. Then he put his hair in a packet, rolling it around his hands, and carefully hid it beneath his toque, which he fastened with a chinstrap. Then he looked at himself in the Venetian glass again, and hope returned to him. Time was pressing; he mounted his horse and set forth.

Scarcely has he passed the final enclosure of Saint-Vigor than his chinstrap comes undone, a gust of wind gets up, which removes his toque, and the hair unravels behind him to attach itself to a thorn bush on the edge of the road.

With an abrupt movement, the unfortunate fellow tries to restrain his horse, but the frightened animal pursues its course with greater speed. Excited by the cries, blows and convulsive transports of its rider, deaf to his voice and insensible to the bit, it carries him with incredible speed through the paths, the woods and the mountains, leaping over fences, ditches, hedges and ravines, fuming and foaming, seeming to redouble its vigor and celerity at every obstacle, as if an invisible supernatural being breathing flame were attached itself to its rump, and spurring it on.

And in the meantime, the fearful Mauny feels his White Hair, still retained by the bush, extending and growing, elongating relentlessly. In front of him, fields, trees and stony roads that scintillated under the feet of his charger all disappear, and along his route he measures the further growth of his Hair. Seized with vertigo, he thinks he hears, roaring and spinning in his head, the inexhaustible bobbin that is alimenting the endless thread; and, when he reaches the summit of a hill and looks back at the route he had traveled, he sees with horror, in the moonlight, the White Hair shining like a silver thread rising from the depths of the valley all the way to him; and when he reaches the plain again, he can still see the fatal thread, to which his destiny is attached, shining and descending from the crest of the mountain.

Finally abandoning himself with resignation to that impetuous course, which, in his idea, lasts for several hours, he thinks that it will soon end in the sea, and that he will find in its waves the end of his life and his torment, when the horse, which has some habit of lodgment, stops dead in front of the old manor of the ancient Comtes d'Oudales, and dies there of fatigue.

Having come round, the poor lover contemplates the château sadly. Everything there seems to announce wellbeing and joy. In the first courtyard the pages and valets are going back and forth with flowers in their caps and making preparations for a nocturnal feast. And he hears murmurs: "He isn't coming!" And through the stained glass windows of the genteel oratory, he sees a soft light trembling. There, someone is doubtless waiting for him, to announce his happiness. He is so close, and he cannot go! Oh, how terrible the vengeance of Guy d'Albrot is!

Distraught and doleful, more dead than alive, cursing his evil fate, and above all the old Saracen who had subjected him to it, André de Mauny retraced his steps, through the valleys and the mountains, picking up and reassembling his White Hair, so considerably increased, extracting it from hornbeams and trees. And when he held it entirely in his hands, he uttered long sighs, and certain that it was necessary for him to renounce the chatelaine and the castellany of Oudales, he resolved to die; for could he, having previously been so mocking, show himself henceforth, even before his companions in arms, without exciting their hilarity?

He wandered all night and also the following days, drawing further and further away from his lady, only nourishing himself with wild fruits, jorroises and cernels picked from bushes; then, finally, as he was going along the River Seine, between Caudebec and Duclair, he ended his days by drowning himself.

Pushed back by an effect of the rising tide, which made itself felt at that moment, his body reached the opposite bank, and on the two sides of the river the White Hair became so entangled in the rocks at water level that exist at that point that it was an obstacle to navigation for some time, for no impact of a vessel, however impetuous it might be, could break it. Finally, it stretched sufficiently to allow the liberty of passage, except in the case when the movement of the waves brings it back to the surface. That is what happened to us today; such is the obstacle that retained us this morning above Caudebec, and now you know the true explanation of that phenomenon.

"I understand," said my interlocutor, uttering a sigh like that of a man relieved of a weight that was oppressing him. "It's a local tradition; but it's finished just in time, for I've just perceived the steeple of Rouen cathedral."

"It's more than a tradition," I replied, "it's a story, and I haven't finished yet, for I assume that you wouldn't be sorry to receive news of our old friend Guy d'Albrot? Don't worry—I'll keep my word and you'll be quit of my story before we dock in Rouen."

I therefore resumed, after my Picard had sat down on his bale again, with a slightly sulky expression.

Humiliated by the beautiful chatelaine, the old bastard of Oudales had attempted one last effort of rejuvenation, which went very badly. Far from recovering suppleness and elasticity, the skin of his body had become so slack and distended that, under the influence of the heat and the sunlight, he saw the aqueous part of his blood evaporate, the excessively relaxed and impoverished dermal network no longer being able to retain it. In order to conserve his days, it was necessary for him to live in the manner of the small amphibian animals that populate marshes, and which likewise dry out under the ardors of the sun. Thus he withdrew from society, and the Sire de Mauny looked for him in vain. The magician was, however, not far from the old manor of Oudales.

Have you sometimes, during your sojourn in Le Havre, gone through the outlying district of Ingouville and directed your stroll toward the celebrated Abbaye de Gravile and the

no-less-renowned little town of Harfleur? In that case, by prolonging your route a little and then turning right, you have
found yourself on the height of Orcher, from which the eye
embraces such a beautiful horizon, with the river at your feet
already taking on an oceanic appearance. You have gone past
the château and the park of Orcher and, in descending toward
the shore, visited the singular spring that, flowing through a
vast landslide of earth and rocks, immobilizes by petrifaction
the mosses and flowers that grow round it. You have doubtless
been shown the marvel of the region that the local villages, in
their naïve language, call "Madame de Nagu's big piss"?

Well, that spring once departed from a spacious grotto in
which tall columnar stalactites formed the support and the
decoration. The tapestries that ornamented it were great gray
lichens falling along the rocky walls, and on the ceiling, a
double layer of bats. But the spring maintained a soft freshness
there.

It was there that Guy d'Albrot retired, between the hills
of Gonfreville, so dear to his memories of youth, and the Château d'Oudales, which contained the treasure that he had
ceased hoping to possess one day. In his solitude, a double
idea still pursued him with tenacity: that of his amour and his
vengeance. Had his spell taken full effect on the Sire de
Mauny? Had the chatelaine returned the amour of his young
rival? He was to know everything.

One evening when, doubtless driven by a presentiment,
he was going along the bank, a cadaver that was drifting toward the sea caught his eyes, and especially his instinct of
jealousy. He drew it toward him, and recognized the detested
features of the Burgundian archer. The White Hair still held!
His science had not been impotent, then—but another mystery
remained for him to clarify. Before dying, had Mauny been
more fortunate than him with regard to the chatelaine? In order to inform himself, who could he interrogate? The dead
man himself!

He carried him to his grotto and there he reanimated him by means of the secrets of his art—doubtless galvanism pushed to its utmost degree of perfection.

The Sire de Mauny was still pale and his eyes were closed, but he raised his head, opened his mouth and spoke. He recounted at length his great mishap, his sterile attempts, the panic of his horse and his torture at the sight of the light shining in the oratory into which he no longer dared penetrate. He spoke, and died again forever.

Guy d'Albrot took him in his arms and rendered him to the waves, which drew him toward the ocean, the White Hair still extending and unwinding, and perhaps extending for as long as the waves collided with and impelled the cadaver, until its debris was caught and retained by the ice of the pole.

The next day the grotto of Orcher and its columns of stalactites collapsed completely; it was there that Guy d'Albrot had marked his tomb.

The water of the spring had great difficulty traversing all the rubble in order to flow once again in the sunlight. It is to the bastard of Oudales that its petrifying virtue is still attributed today.

My story is concluded.

"You can tell your tale," my eternal interlocutor said to me, "for all that must be somewhat allegorical and doubtless contains a double lesson: that in the research of vain sciences one loses the most precious thing there is in the world, youth and common sense; and your Sire de Mauny is also there to teach us that when our head begins to go gray, we struggle in vain against the first white hair; one tears it out, but another succeeds it, incessantly and forever."

"Don't look in that story for vain moralities!" I exclaimed, raising my voice and suddenly adopting the tone of force and authority that conviction gives. "All the facts are true, exact and incontestably proven, for me at least, for I was a witness to them."

At that point my traveling companion opened his eyes wide enough to make his eyelids burst. He tried to get to is feet, and sat down again. Finally, after having examined me for a moment with a sort of alarm and stupefaction, he was about to speak, doubtless to provoke a further explanation, but a general movement had just become manifest in the boat; everyone ran to his packages and bales; a host of commission-aires and porters ran into our midst. We were separated by the flux and reflux of the comings and goings.

We had docked in the harbor of Rouen.

The Story of the Academy of Berchtolsgarden in Austria
and of the Albino that was exhibited there by a Celebrated Voyager

Every evening, in a hostelry placed under the protection of Saint Paphnutius, the most notable inhabitants of the small Austrian town of Berchtolsgarden assembled. For a long time they had been content to smoke and drink there, when one day, the ideas of the century having reached them in spite of the customs officers of the Rhine and the Commission of Vienna, they took it into their head to give their society a nobler goal.

The hostelry of Paphnutius counted a few virtuosos who sometimes, on feast days, made their daughters and their neighbors dance as best they could to the violin or the flute. Nor was there any shortage among them of strong and powerful voices capable making the windows of a church or a tavern tremble alternately, with a *confiteor* or a drinking song.

In less than three months the fortunate town saw born within its walls more songs than had been fabricated there in the previous three centuries—but that fine fervor soon calmed down; ideas thickened; malevolent critiques troubled the triumph of our improvised poets. The musicians entered the lists in their turn, and, in order to sustain the lyrical essays of their colleagues, resolved to shore them up with tunes of their composition.

The landlord, landlady and waitresses of Saint Paphnutius swooned with ease on hearing the new masterpieces. Competition was felt, they strove; finally, in a surge of vanity, it was decided that, in order to inoculate all the town's inhabitants with a taste for the fine arts, a public session would be held every year, and that a concert would be executed with a full orchestra. The concert took place, but the racket was such that in the middle of the execution, the instruments suddenly stopped. Everyone looked at one another, stupefied; they hesitated, and then the singers, musicians and spectators united in chorus in a noisy and universal burst of laughter, which concluded the session.

A mortal blow had just been dealt to the lyrical society; the discouragement was great, however; for people so long cradled by flattering hopes, it seemed cruel and humiliating to do nothing. After long discussions, it was decided to form, quite simply, a scholarly society.

The idea was good, the project was sage. One can be scholarly in so many different ways and on so many different subjects; it is so comfortable and so facile to know a great deal about little things, quietly to explore the traditions and antiquities of one's town, the growth of its woods, the cultivation of its fields—and all of that is science.

The new society nurtured other views. At first its members only thought about elevating themselves in their own eyes, and then in the eyes of their relatives, friends and neighbors; now they aimed higher. It was time for the town of Berchtolsgarden to make itself known to Europe other than by its children's toys, the honor of whose fabrication was even reflected on Nuremburg and Augburg. Fine regulations were meditated, a suitable venue was sought, a sumptuous title was adopted, after which corresponding members were named in all the capitals of the world. No illustrious name was forgotten. Cuvier, Laplace, Alexander von Humboldt and Geoffroy Saint-Hilaire were elected as free associates of the Academy of Berchtolsgarden. By virtue of too much precipitation and doubtless a want of necrological annals, even honest great men dead for many years were unable to escape. They were inscribed among the non-residents, and noted for impoliteness, for not having acknowledged the receipt of the diploma.

Some having caused mention of them in Paris, London and Mexico, our scholars thought that their town was finally about to emerge from its obscurity and become, with time, the Athens or the Benares of Germany.

They would remain at the hostelry of Saint Paphnutius in order not to renounce their habits entirely; it is so pleasant to smoke one's pipe, drink beer and play faro between two grave dissertations. But they would choose the largest room and have it arranged in the most extensive fashion.

An armchair in Bohemian leather with gilded nails for the president; benches with backs before which each member had his glass and his ash-tray; a little trellised cupboard in which each of them could put his pipe under a number: nothing was lacking. I ought to add that a stuffed crocodile of medium size, which had, unfortunately, allowed a few tufts of straw and thread to escape from its truncated tail and its unstitched sides, was suspended from the ceiling, as if to announce that its occupants were occupied with natural history. A few small bottles ranged on the mantelpiece and two retorts placed the extremities also gave the location the appearance of a chemistry cupboard.

A set of bookshelves had even been constructed in the emplacement of a false door; a few brochures were already aslant on the shelves, and every member had been invited to enrich them with any works of science that he might perhaps possess; but as the smokers had no scruples about removing, first the covers and then the chapter titles in order to light their pipes, the response to the appeal was slow.

However, everything was making progress; and in order that the town of Berchtolsgarden could, as well as any other, glorify itself with possessing in its bosom a scholarly society, nothing was any longer lacking but scholars. But a further discussion was held regarding the regulation, which lasted all winter, and allowed time for the most zealous to revise their Latin a little and to prepare to sustain some unexpected thesis brilliantly before their colleagues

Since I have undertaken to make the endeavors of the Academy of Berchtolsgarden known to the world, I shall indicate here succinctly the objects toward which their first investigations were directed. An ambulant bookseller who passed through the town one morning had been perceived by some of our Academicians. By way of works of erudition he only possessed a few voyages undertaken in the second half of the last century; that was already good fortune. A few odd volumes of *Les Pères de l'Église* completed the collection, a precious source from which our scholars would extract their subjects of argumentation.

Thanks to the bookseller, as soon as the first session, the members of the Academy of Berchtolsgarden were outbidding one another as to who would reveal to his colleagues the most marvelous things concerning the usages and mores of distant countries; then they occupied themselves with the different physical forms relevant to the human race; after that it was resolved to compose a kind of monography of man, taking care to avoid all error and all exaggeration; and, thanks to that sublime resolution, in less than a year, they succeeded in proving completely:

The existence of the Giants that Commodore Byron had seen on the Magellanic coasts;

That of the Pygmies of Nubia;

That of the Hermaphrodites of Florida and Mongolistan;

That of the Men of the Woods or Orangutans endowed with speech. The thing appeared incredible at first, but it was known that the inhabitants of Apollonia had presented a similar individual to Sulla; the fact was verified and admitted.

After the Man of the Woods, the Marine Man had his turn. The *Philosophical Transactions* and the *Journal des savans* of 1676 spoke of them at length. A sworn deposition made at Martinique had established the appearance of one of those singular beings in the vicinity of the island of Diamant. The attestations affirmations and proofs by testimony were no more lacking for that than for the miracles of the blessed Deacon Paris. His existence was therefore recognized without difficulty.

The Marine Man was succeeded by the Maine Woman, presenting all the attributes of her sex as far as the half of her body that is terminated by a fish's tail. She is the Spaniards' *pece-muger*.[137] So many estimable voyagers had seen one that it was only minds hardened by doubt that were able to deny the reality. Furthermore, a living marine woman had been exhibited at the Saint-Germain fair in Paris in 1758.

After having resuscitated the Sirens and Tritons they went back to antiquity and occupied themselves with the Cyclops and Satyrs.

Saint Augustine affirms that he preached the Gospel to a population of Cyclopes in Lower Ethiopia.

Saint Jerome composed a dialogue between a hermit of the Thebaid and a Satyr.

It was, therefore, not permissible for our savant Academicians, who were all filled with respect for everything touching religion, to dare to cast doubt on what those two great saints, the light of the Church, had proven sufficiently.

Pliny's acephalic and cynocephalic humans were rejected as fabulous beings.

It was thus that the nascent Academy labored to establish and bring to light great verities. Another question no less important surged from the midst of those lively and curious discussions. A volume of Linnaeus, no one knew how, happened to be among those exposed on the bookshelves. One of the members of the society, a former student of the University of Ingolstadt, perceiving that it was written in Latin, thought that the majority of his colleagues unlikely to consult it and, without fear of being compromised, he detached a page fortuitously in order to light his pipe. The book had already been eroded as far as page 33, which our savant removed, thinking that he was only touching a half-title page.

Astonished, he scanned the text mechanically, took it home with him, and spent the night translating a fragment.

---

[137] This allegation, made by Jean-Baptiste Robinet in *Considérations philosophiques de la gradation naturelle des formes de l'être* (1768) seems to be devoid of support elsewhere.

435

The next day, accosting his colleagues with the tone of superiority and satisfaction that pierces us involuntarily when we feel that we are bearers of unexpected news, he said to them: "Messieurs, until now our work on anthropomorphism"—he emphasized that word—"has doubtless been crowned with success. I believe, however, that we have neglected the principal division, which ought to have served us as a point of departure and formed the first base of our important work."

At those words, the Academicians opened their eyes wide, turned to the orator, and poured themselves a drink in order to dispose themselves to listen patiently.

"We have already distinguished," the latter continued, "the terrestrial man from the marine man, the complete man from the incomplete man; but is not the first of all the sections, when it is a matter of individuals of the same species, indicated to us by nature herself, by the course of the stars, by night and day. It was, therefore, with the diurnal man and the nocturnal man that it was necessary to occupy ourselves before anything else."

There was in the assembly then such a confusion of exclamations, interjections, laughter and vehement invective against the orator that the bells rang in the neighboring church without the Academicians thinking of making the sign of the cross, as they usually did. All the learned individuals, believing that they had a interest in sustaining their original ideas, spoke at once, and with such lung-power that the unfortunate speaker repeated in vain, ten time over, in a loud and menacing voice: "Messieurs, I am speaking in the name of the celebrated Linnaeus, of Uppsala in Sweden"—no one heard him.

The racket only ceased when the landlord, the landlady and the waitresses came running, alarmed, in order to discover the cause of so much noise. Then they calmed down. Everyone relit his pipe, which had gone out during the argument, and the orator, who obtained permission to develop his idea, resumed in the midst of the most profound silence:

"Messieurs, it is in the name of the celebrated Linnaeus, of Uppsala in Sweden, that I am speaking. Man, he says in a work of which I do not recall the title,[138] and which is in Latin, ought to be divided into two distinct species: the man of the day, who is reasonable and prudent, *Homo diurnus, sapiens*, and the man of the night, who is troglodytic and savage, *Homo nocturnus, troglodytes, sylvestris*. The latter has a pale body, round eyes and a saffron color. By day he is blind and hides, but at night he can see, he walks, he talks, he reasons: *Die caecutit, latet; noctu videt, exit, furatur, loquitur, cogitate, ratiocinatur*, etc., etc. Thus, Messieurs, one of two things must be true: either that nocturnal man exists, or the celebrated Linnaeus is an ignoramus. Now, we cannot admit that latter case, if only by virtue of respect for our sister Academy of Uppsala, which, like ours, has already rendered great services to science.

The orator then referred to the white negroes of whom several voyagers speak. "But," he said, "it is difficult to admit as a distinct race isolated individuals brought to the state that the celebrated Linnaeus describes, by accidental causes. It is up to us, Messieurs, to decided this great question and complete hereby our immense discoveries regarding man."

This time, the assembly had adopted in part the orator's ideas, and the end of his discourse was only greeted with murmur of approval.

The research was long and laborious; time went by, and, in spite of its keen desire for celebrity, the Academy of

---

[138] Author's reference: "*Systema naturae* vol. I p.33, edition of 1766." Linnaeus does indeed suggest that *Homo nocturnus*, which he also classifies as "troglodytes" might be an alternative nomenclature for *Homo sylvestris* (the orangutan), which he had boldly and controversially attributed to the same genus as humans on the basis of second-hand reports." Saintine might not have known that Nicolas Restif de La Bretonne's *La Découverte australe par un homme volant* (1781; tr. as *The Discovery of the Austral Continent*, Black Coat Press, ISBN 978-1-61227-512-3) includes an elaborate speculative description of a species of nocturnal humans.

Berchtolsgarden was still only making a noise in the hostelry of Saint Paphnutius when it was learned that a celebrated voyager had just arrived in Salzburg with Linnaeus' nocturnal man, an Albino—a veritable Albino—of pure race, such has had not been seen, it was said, in the countries of Europe.

The opportunity was such that they could not allow it to escape without having extracted all the academic advantage possible. The great question was about to be decided by a conscientious examination of living nature. It was a subject for a dissertation, a report, a paper, even a public session! The memory of the concert restrained them on the last point, but they agreed that, without paying any heed to the expense, a deputation would be sent to the voyager and his Albino, to ask him to honor the learned Academy of Berchtolsgarden with a visit, and the deputation set forth.

The savant voyager alleged at first that he was awaited at the courts of several sovereigns; furthermore, his banker having not been exact in sending him funds, he found himself temporarily embarrassed and could not stay in the region. All those difficulties were smoothed over.

Finally, the great day arrived. (I should have said the fine night, for, in order to honor the newcomer, it was arranged thus, even though he was the only person in the town who could see without light.) Everything had been prepared to welcome him worthily. The room was decorated and, by an excess of delicacy, lampshades had been placed over the candles in order not to injure the sight of the singular guest they were getting ready to welcome. Contrary to the habits of the Academy, a sumptuous meal was to close the session.

The president had already taken his place in his Bohemian leather armchair and all the members were present when the sound of a carriage that stopped outside the hostelry of Saint Paphnutius announced the arrival of the celebrated voyager and the return of the deputation.

The Albino made his entrance amid a murmur of astonishment. He was young, of medium height, with a rather delicate complexion; his eyes were orange brown, and long white hair hung down over his shoulders. His bizarre costume was composed, according to the explanation that the savant voyager gave, of broad trousers and a kind of hooded tunic, woven with the silky fibers of an American palm tree. (One of the members of the society, a draper at least as much as an Academician, observed that the cloth closely remembered English lustrous serge.) The young foreigner also wore necklaces and bracelets of fine gold and a workmanship that attested to the industry to the worker, all of which came from his homeland. (Another member of the Academy, a goldsmith by trade, found some resemblance to the copper jewelry that emerged from the factories of Schwartz in the Tyrol.)

After our doctors had examined the Albino at leisure, verified all the strange characteristics he presented, and the secretary had drawn up the official record, the president, agitating his hand-bell, announced that he was about to make a speech on the Albino, which would summarize all the discoveries of the Academy regarding that second order of the human species.

Everyone took his place, the nocturnal man on a platform set up in the middle of the room, in order that everyone could see him, and the celebrated voyager next to the president. The latter commenced in these terms:

"Gentlemen, and most illustrious colleagues,

"The existence of the nocturnal man, called Albino by the Portuguese, Blafard by the natives of Darien, Dondo by the Africans and Kackerlake by the Oriental Indians, can never have been in doubt for minds as enlightened as yours. Linnaeus, known for his estimable works on natural history, believed that he was making an important discovery in identifying the noctambulant and troglodytic race that is so closely related to ours. In addition to the fact that his definition is shockingly inexact, it is astonishing that Linnaeus, who is a member of an Academy, has forgotten or completely ignored the fact that the race in question has been known since time immemorial.

"In fact, Gentlemen and most illustrious colleagues, you all know that it existed in Albania between the forty-fifth and fiftieth degrees of north latitude. Has not Fernand Cortez made a detailed description of those he encountered in America? I shall say more, without going so far to search, everything tends to prove that Albinos, or Blafards, or Dondos, or Kackerlakes, were once numerous in Europe, and that they were known in France under the name of Gobelins or Drusions; in Sweden under that of Trools; in Holland under that of Klabauters; in Italy under that of Gobalis; and in our Germany, finally, under the denomination of Keilkraefs.[139]

"Thus, Gentlemen, the race of Albinos was once powerful and numerous; it was thought to be extinct, but it belongs to our Academy to enable it to resume its rank in the human hierarchy, to correct the errors of false savants and to close the discussion of the subject with a incontrovertible argument. Now, Gentlemen, our illustrious guest will give us some details of the homeland, the mores and the usages of the nocturnal man. We beg him humbly to speak slowly, in order that the secretary can take notes."

The celebrated voyager rose to his feet.

"Gentlemen," he said, "you are not unaware that, in the depths of America we have two large islands, one of which was once populated by Negroes and the other by Albinos."

Member of the Academy asked the celebrated voyager whether, for the sake of greater exactitude, he could indicate the part of the New World in which those two large islands could be found, and give their degrees of latitude and longitude. The celebrated voyager declared that it was impossible for him to speak when people interrupted him, and continued.

"Now, Gentlemen, you know that good neighborhood is a rare thing, and the Negroes and the Albinos, as they are own locally, rarely live in accord. Great wars broke out between those two peoples. In order to triumph, each had recourse to

---

[139] Every name in this list is misrendered, presumably deliberately; I have refrained from correcting them.

the means in its power, and more than once, the Negroes attacked their adversaries in broad daylight, ravaging their fields and cabins. The Albinos waited for night in order to avenge themselves. There were ambushes and continual ruses on both sides. The people suffered on both islands; the damage did not profit anyone, and there were negotiations. The Negroes were good people. It was put to them that, in order to prevent any subject of discord, it was necessary to unite the two people into one; they consented to that.

"The Albinos were greedy and avid by nature, but indolent, and their island was sterile; they abandoned it and came to settle among the Negroes, whose well-tilled soil could provide sufficiently for the subsistence of all. So the black and the white were amalgamated to such an extent that the assembled population presented to the eye a perfect resemblance to the squares of a chessboard.

"The Albinos, living at the expense of their new compatriots, became accustomed to regarding them as vanquished enemies, and became indignant at not seeing everything organized by them and for them. As they were ill-adapted to work the land or make the most of industry, they were attributed all administrative employments and the senior positions in the army; but the soldiers, being Negroes, were at odds with their officers even regarding the hours of service, for the midnight of one was the noon of the other. It was the same in the city. The Albinos could only see, act and, in sum, live by night, while the cultivators and merchants, almost all of the black race, only opened their shops and held their markets during the day.

"It was necessary to settle the difficulty, however. In those critical circumstances, a great council was assembled, composed of nocturnal men; and, after having debated for form's sake, a law was passed against the sun.

"Yes, Gentlemen, what was called a curfew was rung, and everyone beat a retreat at seven o'clock in the morning. But, in order to soften the rigor that the law might have for the larger part of the population, street lighting was introduced.

441

"Everyone was discontented, night people and day people alike. The Negroes demanded the return of the sun, the Albinos swore the extermination of street lights. Every species of light wounded their sight; in everything that shone they thought they perceived the devil, even under the appearance of a glow-worm, so irritable was their retina, as you can verify with respect to the countenance of my young friend here present.

In doubt, the Supreme Council charged the priests with interrogating the gods in order to decide the question. What were the priests to do? On their orders, an enormous kite was constructed. That might seems bizarre to you, but you cannot be unaware, Gentlemen, that in those countries, religious acts are essentially emblematic. That kite, the entire left-hand part of which was painted black and the right-hand part white, represented the two factions that divided the nation. The head that dominated both of them, and was closest to the sky, was the clergy; the tail that regulated it, moderating the movements of the machine, which, if it were heavy or too light, prevented it from rising up or caused it to go astray, was the government. As for the two flaps that were supposed to maintain its equilibrium, the priests had imagined that they represented the taxes without which nothing moves. Like taxes, they had to be furnished by the people, and if, in its flight the kite inclined to the right, the victory would go to the Albinos; if, on the contrary, they inclined to the left, the Negroes triumphed and the sun would recover its ordinary prerogatives.

The Negroes hastened to send the priests a sufficient quantity of ingots of iron, copper and lead to give weight to their flap; their adversaries, better informed, furnished gold, and necklaces of pearls and topazes.

When the kite rose up before the people and the great assemblies, the crowd was not very surprised to see it, scarcely having quit the ground, suddenly lean toward the right and beat the air with its black wing, entirely denuded. That, Gentlemen, is because the flaps of the kite belonged by right to the priests, and vile and gross materials were not received in the

442

temple. In consequence, the iron, copper and lead offered by the people had been rejected.

Such, Gentlemen, is the story of the great *coup d'état*; the same evening, all the luminaries were extinguished and broken by the Albinos. The indignant Negroes ran to take up arms. Troops were sent against them in vain; the soldiers were of the black race and could not see in the dark. Daylight rendered the advantage to the rightful side; the vanquished Albinos were returned to their island and the law against the sun was repealed. Thus was accomplished the lamp-post revolution,[140] of which you have doubtless heard mention."

All the Academicians responded with an affirmative nod. The voyager continued.

"Although a stranger to any kind of faction, this young man, Gentlemen, found himself a victim of the proscription decreed against his race. I took him under my protection; he consented to come with me to Europe, and he cannot congratulate himself too much for that today, since he owes to that voyage the honor he has of hastening the decision of a great scientific question, and of appearing in person before the illustrious members of the learned and celebrated Academy of Berchtolsgarden."

Considerable applause greeted the end of that story, whose effect was so marked that the president immediately proposed to the assembly to admit to the number of members the extraordinary men who had just communicated such precious historic and scientific documents to them on the race of Albinos. The proposal was received with enthusiasm, and passed unanimously. The illustrious voyager thanked them

---

[140] The reference to the *révolution reverbère* [lamp-post revolution] is a joke, the more familiar French term for lamp-post being *lanterne*, During the 1789, when lamp-posts were frequently used for lynchings, the cry "À la lanterne!" became the equivalent of the English "String him up!" and "*Les aristocrates à la lanterne*" became a popular slogan, featured in the Revolutionary song *Ça ira*.

with a perfect modesty, and in order to testify all his gratitude to the members of the learned company, after having raised his eyes toward the stuffed crocodile suspended from the ceiling of the room, he promised, in order to augment their cabinet of natural history, to make them a gift of various very rare objects collected by him in his long expeditions.

The items in question were: the skeleton of a lamprey; one of the carbuncles that are commonly found in the head of an Indian bird; the operculum of the little fish that stopped Caligula's vessel in spite of the effort of the winds and the oarsmen; a ruby formed of sanguinary dewdops; a couple of pyrales or salamanders, which live in fire and drown in air; a duck engendered spontaneously on the coast of Scotland in the species of multivalve mollusk known as an anatife or poucepied; a branch from the sycamore with which King Xerxes fell in love; the feather of a phoenix; the wings of a dragon; and the head of a sphinx.

In order to conclude the memorable evening worthily, *coena apponitur*,[141] they sat down at table. No effort was spared by the scholars to fête their new colleague and his young Albino. The most sought-after dishes, the strong beer of Bamberg and the wine of Rhinegau were all delivered in profusion. The landlord, the landlady and the waitresses of Saint Paphnutius performed marvels of service, and academic solemnity had given way to joyful words and shining eyes, and heads had lightened, when the hour of separation arrived.

The hero of the fête, after having expressed his regrets in departing, requested for his young friend the favor of being able to contemplate at leisure the features of the distinguished men who had welcomed him with such touching hospitality.

"You know," he said, "that the faintest light harms the clarity of his vision. Allow him, in quitting you, at least to carry away a memory of your image!"

Everyone was glad to grant such a natural request immediately. All the lights were extinguished, and when the obscu-

---

[141] "Thank you for supper."

444

rity was complete, the interesting Albino, guiding the illustrious voyager by the hand, made a tour of the table, testifying his gratitude to his host by means of expressive gestures and the most frank and naïve caresses.

Everyone, in the stupefaction of pleasure, awaited his turn impatiently, and that nocturnal scene, those blind adieux, seemed to them so singular that they were added further to their disposition of joviality when the rumble of a carriage was suddenly heard in the street.

Vehicles were rare in the town in those days, and the noise of that one did not fail to astonish them. The lights were reilluminated, and it was perceived, to the general surprise, that the illustrious voyager and his young friend had already gone, along with the silverware of the hostelry of Saint Paphnutius!

The Albino had just given conclusive proof of his nocturnicity; the scholars might have been able to find a compensation in that, but the landlord nevertheless demanded his silverware, the carter his carriage and his two horses. Our learned men denied their responsibility. A lawsuit followed, whose loss caused that of the society, and it is in the records of that long procedure that I found, not without difficulty, the traces of the Academy of Berchtolsgarden and its Albino.

Jonathan in Paris

*(Excerpts from the Frame Narrative of the 1866 edition
of* Jonathan the Visionary*)*

> I shall speak, but will anyone believe me?
> *Cagliostro.*

I was born both indolent and sedentary, a true idler, incurious about everything that was not Paris. One morning, however, twenty years ago and more, after having leapt over the Alps, I woke up in the heart of the kingdom of Naples, and there was no question of railways in those days! How did that happen? I was madly in love; one of my friends, who was departing for Italy and whom isolation was annoying in advance, indicated to me, as the soul means of cure, absence and a change of country.

The remedy was good, for scarcely was I at the customs barrier of Fontainebleau than I was feeling its beneficent effects. I could have stopped in Essonne, but that would have caused my friend chagrin and paid the man to whom I owed my cure with ingratitude. We therefore continued our journey.

Having visited Genoa, Florence, Rome and Naples, discouraged by the dust, the heat and fatigue, it seemed to me that a nice armchair voyage, book in hand, without leaving home, such as I had once made, or even a peregrination along the Quai Voltaire in Paris or the Boulevards de la Madeleine and de la Bastille, inspecting the views, the sites and the monuments of all the countries in the world in the shops of the merchants of engravings, from one display to the next, had a charm no less vivid, and offered the inestimable advantage of fatiguing the body less and sparing the purse more.

Finally, while awaiting the resumption of my excursions behind closed doors and my voyages in the fireside, I was being patient, thinking that we were approaching the return to France, when my friend announced tranquilly that we were leaving for Calabria. He had acquired the habit of disposing of me without consulting me; for my part, I had contracted the habit of letting him do it. I contented myself, like anyone of a philosophical and meditative organization, with exhaling my ill humor internally.

After a few days, my ill humor had disappeared. We were traveling in the company of Frenchmen and foreigners, men of intelligence and taste, whose conversation excited my curiosity; I had always been, not only a great reader, but also, which is rarer, a great listener. We walked together, glad to lend ourselves mutual aid in that way against the ennuis of the journey.

[*At this point the narrative offers an abridged version the account of the encounter with Jonathan contained in the 1823 introduction. That continues to the point at which the introduction to* Les Soirées de Jonathan *takes over the story, and then paraphrases that text up to the point at which the narrator asks what other narrator could have summoned to his aid the knowledge of all places, all times, and centuries of experience, adding in this version: "But also, where could he have found a better listener than me?" The 1866 text then deviates from that version.*]

In the home of Madame de la Chabeaussière,[142] a few humorists had nicknamed us Mohammed and his prophet, others, even less well-intentioned, Don Quixote and... Fortu-

---

[142] Madame de la Chabeaussière is the hostess (unnamed in the previous versions) who reintroduced the narrator to Jonathan, perhaps the wife of the playwright Ange-Étienne-Xavier Poisson de La Chabeaussière (1752-1820), whom Saintine might have met in his youth.

nately, those malicious comments did not reach Jonathan's ears; for my part, I took pity on them.

One evening, we were in a small gathering at Madame de la Chabeaussière's house, and the conversation turned to fatality, the persistent hazard thanks to which certain men fail in their best calculated enterprises while others, much less provided with common sense and prudence, arrive at success in each of theirs.

"Such is good and ill fortune," said our charming hostess; "the wisdom of nations has informed us of it." Then, after having added by virtue of pious reticence: "Let us refrain, however, from thinking that the hand of God intervenes in the caprices of fate!" she turned to Jonathan, who had remained silent until then, and said: "What do you think of fatality?"

"I believe in it," he replied, briefly.

"I believe in it too," I murmured, softly.

"God! Fate! Fatality! Those are very big words for something that is self-explanatory," riposted a member of the audience. "The men who have succeeded in nothing are those who have thrown nothing into the balance in which our destinies are weighed. Victory is always on the side of the big battalions, Bonaparte said; for myself, I say that good fortune—which is to say, success—belongs to the man who can put into the balance a great name, a fine fortune and powerful connections, especially," he added, with evident self-satisfaction, "if his intelligence is at the height of his other advantages. As for the poor devil possessed by the desire to succeed nonetheless, I see scarcely any other chance for him than in obstinate intrigue and subterranean and fraudulent maneuvers. That is why parvenus are generally and justly scorned."

"Say generally and unjustly, Monsieur le Marquis, if only out of respect for the first gentleman of your family. The grain of sand that, by the agglomeration of other grains of sand, becomes the stumbling-block against which the triumphal chariot breaks, can also, by the will of fate, serve as the first stepping-stone for the poor devil of whom you speak. Providence has its calculations as well as its mysteries; more than once the frail boat without a deck, aided by a favorable wind, has been able to cross the open sea and land victoriously where, the day before, the vessel with the triple deck has sunk; the army does not only count the likes of Masséna and Augereau, as it once did the likes of Fabert and Jean Bart; there are parvenus who, without a uniform, and even, I admit, without any great personal merit, but also without intrigue and without cowardice, have astonished the world with a good fortune, perhaps unmerited, but at which they do not have to blush."

"In an epoch of upheavals like ours, yes, that can be seen," said the Marquis, with a sort of groan. "Men destined to vegetate in the social depths have emerged accidentally from their mire to rise into superior regions—but without any intrigue, that I doubt; I do more, I deny it. The tempest, to continue your imagistic language, my dear and respectable Monsieur, often enables some wretched marine weed to bloom on the surface that would otherwise never have seen the light of day; when calm resumes, thank God, the tide soon casts it up on the shore and justice is done. Let us not give a serious, incontestable principle an exception for a basis," Jonathan's worthy interlocutor added airily, "or a few miserable facts collected in the midst of a time of disorder."

That interlocutor bore a great name, possessed a large patrimonial fortune and probably thought he had the very best connections. A colonel at thirteen under Louis XVI, he had occupied high employments under the Empire and even under the Consulate, and the Restoration had recompensed him for services rendered under all regimes by opening to him both the door to the Chambre des Pairs and that of the Institut.

After having, with a rounded gesture, taken a pinch of tobacco from a rich gold snuff-box decorated with a portrait of Louis XVIII painted by Madame de Mirbel,[143] he continued:

---

[143] The miniaturist Lizinska de Mirbel (1796-1849) became the official portraitist of Louis XVIII not long before his death in 1925. The citation confuses the chronology of the narrative

"Save for exceptional cases, in a time of calm and social regularity—under the reign of the old kings, for example—I defy you or anyone else to cite a negligible man who arrived at a high position honorably, without any stain, visible or invisible. Similar to the man of the people, a bourgeois can only rise by base means, and the well-born man cannot fall unless by virtue of some shameful vice or an incurable stupidity. Invoke fatality, hazard, or secondary causes as much as you like: wind and smoke! Under a legitimate government, as well-organized as ours is, all those fine things disappear, annulled beneath the solid gears of vigorous institutions, which your grain of sand cannot prevent maneuvering regularly and for the good of all. If a few adventurous spirits and ideologues try to make theories subversive of any social order prevail, the Chambre des Pairs has not been created for nothing. We have laws to put everything back in place and in good order."[144]

"But God also has his laws!" said Jonathan, suddenly animated in sensing that he was being attacked, "and fatality, Monsieur le Marquis, is one of those mysterious, inexplicable, incomprehensible laws, which it is necessary to recognize even though it had not been passed by the Chambre des Pairs."

---

slightly, because the date of the narrator's death is recorded as June 1937, so Jonathan's demise in Honfleur must have occurred prior to May 1921, in which case this scene and those that follow must be set before then, some of them dating back several months, at least.

[144] It is not only the scathing satire of *Histoire d'une civilisation antédiluvienne* that might have attracted the attention of Napoléon III's ever-eager censors to the volume containing the present text; such remarks as those made by Jonathan to the Marquis might have seemed to them to have some relevance to the political situation of the 1860s. If, however, the text is adapted from chapters of an aborted novel written in the early 1830s, they might well reflect the consciousness of the immediate aftermath of the Revolution of 1830, in spite of their earlier setting.

That sarcasm caused a few faces to frown and others to smile; personally, I found it in perfect taste.

Madame de la Chabeaussière put her hands together in a suppliant fashion.

Jonathan went on: "As for the secondary, infimal and miserable causes that might so easily crush your gross governmental machine, believe me, Monsieur le Marquis, don't be too scornful of them, since the Restoration of the legitimate throne of the Stuarts only had for its direct, fatal cause a grain of sand that, fortunately for them, came to lodge in Cromwell's urethra."

"Absurdity!" muttered the Marquis, shrugging his shoulders.

"That absurdity was pronounced by Pascal, Monsieur le Marquis; I am only repeating it, and I will add that God has permitted and still permits today the tiny imperceptible worms of corals and madrepores to oppose dykes to the sea, to form coasts, and even continents, which, one day, will contain great realms in which a certain number of sovereigns will be counted, and perhaps upper chambers, and, in consequence, Ducs, Marquises..."

At this point, among the listeners, the left and the right, which had only been sketched at first, stood out more clearly. The right murmured, the left burst out laughing; personally, I laughed louder than all the rest.

Madame de la Chabeaussière, anxious and agitated, tugged her bell-cord forcefully and shouted; "Jean, serve the tea immediately."

For a few minutes, already, the whist table had been abandoned.

After having demanded silence with a gesture full of nobility, the Marquis reclaimed the floor, which his adversary had the good taste not to dispute with him, although he was in the middle of a sentence, whose conclusion was left in the air.

"Monsieur," said the Marquis, addressing Jonathan, "Let us not give the discussion too great an extension, as the great partisan of referenda Monsieur Decaze said to us recently;[145] between us, it's only a matter of proving whether petty individuals can achieve fortune and honors without intrigues and indignities."

"Exactly, Monsieur le Marquis; you even advance that a worthy gentleman only ever descends from his hierarchical position—in a well-constituted State, of course—by virtue of his vices or his stupidity."

"Did I say that?"

"You did say that, Monsieur le Marquis."

"Monsieur le Marquis, you said exactly that," I repeated, perhaps a little too impetuously—which earned me a severe look from Jonathan.

The latter, addressing the Marquis again, added: "You even challenged me to prove the contrary by an example. That challenge, I will take up!"

There was an immediate stir in Madame de la Chabeaussière's salon, in which everyone expected one of the stories that the master was able to tell so well. The left and the right declared a truce by tacit agreement; a few people who, pressed for time, had already taken their hats in hand, resumed their seats. Perhaps the announcement of tea had something to do with that. As for our worthy hostess, delighted to see the stormy discussion terminate with a story, she slipped a few mollifying and soothing words into the Marquis' ear and went to take Jonathan's hand, indicating an armchair next to the fireplace to him.

Jonathan passed his handkerchief over his forehead, as if to efface the cloud that had obscured it momentarily, and suddenly reappeared with a calm gaze and a smile on his lips. He had changed masks. I had, I believe, already heard the master

---

[145] The versatile statesman Élie Decazes (1780-1860) was one of the staunchest supporters of the Bourbon Restoration, having been abruptly converted to that cause after the fall of the Empire. He survived the July Revolution in 1830 and continued his career.

adopt in a salon the tone and manners of a man of the world as easily as he adopted the costume.

"Toward the end of 1749, if my memory serves me right..." He interrupted himself to salute the Marquis courteously. "You see, Monsieur that I'm observing the conditions of your program strictly; the scene will pass under the reign of Louis XV the Beloved... Oh, don't think that I recall that title in a spirit of mockery; for all those who knew him, who were close to him, that was not a vain nickname; at any rate, he deigned to honor me with his amity."

The Marquis started in his chair.

Jonathan continued "So, it was at the end of 1749..."

[*At this point, the text includes the story translated in the present volume as "Good and Ill-Luck."*]

Having finished his story, addressing a salute to his adversary with his hand that resembled a compliment of condolence, Jonathan said: "Well, Monsieur le Marquis, you see that it pleases God to subject some to the proofs of prosperity and others to that of adverse fortune. There is a destiny, a *fatum*; without that *fatum*, decreed in advance, how would astrological science, I ask you, be able to fathom the future, if nothing were stable there?"

Until then, the Marquis had only made rare appearances in Madame de la Chabeaussière's salon and he had never had occasion to encounter Jonathan there. At the word "astrology," being a member of the Institut de France, he looked at him with wide eyes and a stupefied expression, and then transported the same gaze to the mistress of the house, accentuated by a question mark.

"He's our visionary," she whispered in his ear. "Let him speak."

"You won't deny now, I'd like to believe," the storyteller continued, "the influence of secondary causes? If you, Monsieur le Marquis, whose fate appears to me to have been accomplished under the influence of good fortune rather than

453

ill-fortune, go back through your life step by step, perhaps you'd be surprised to encounter there, as a point of departure of your fortune, and our social and scientific position, one of these infinitely small active, incessant and innumerable agents of Providence. Who knows? Perhaps a few lines of verse addressed to a beautiful lady's parrot, a pinch of tobacco offered at the apposite moment…search, Monsieur le Marquis, and if you care to make us party to the discovery, I dare to assure you on behalf of everyone that you will be listened to as a man of your merit deserves to be."

The Marquis stood up majestically, rounded his elbow again, introduced the thumb and index finger of his right hand into his gold box, decorated with the portrait of the King of France then reigning, took a pinch of tobacco, shook the ruff of his sleeve, and without any other response, ordered his carriage.

After the departure of the Marquis, Madame de la Chabeaussière's regulars formed into two groups. Some of those in the former claimed that Jonathan, a skillful improviser, had just told us a tale fashioned for the needs of his cause; the others denied the possibility of improvising thus, with such chronological precision, events in Persia, France, Russia and even the coasts of Africa. They recognized in the anecdote, very curious in any case, a character both historical and philosophical. In order to have retained its details he had probably heard it repeated in his youth by his father or his grandfather.

To what epoch might Jonathan's youth go back? Even I, then, in spite of his semi-confidences, which excited rather than satisfying my curiosity, would have been very embarrassed to say.

In the second group, a young professor at the university, previously in the number of those who mocked us but to whom faith now seemed to have arrived, claimed to know a Baron de Pigafet, whose ancestor had indeed been suspended nobility for commercial affairs; he promised to ask for information. As for Bernard, the Comte de M****, he was none other, according to him, than the Comte de Saint-Germain, the famous thaumaturge, a precursor of Cagliostro—and, in consequence, Jonathan himself, for the latter had declared overtly to several people that that was the name and the title he bore at the court of Louis XV. Had not that Saint-Germain, part-jeweler and part-aristocrat, who was said to be the son of a Portuguese Jew, come back one day from a voyage to Africa with barrels full of gold and precious stones? Had he not been pampered and caressed by everyone in Paris, even in Versailles? Had not the King, madly infatuated with his adventures, made him a Comte, and even a Councilor of State? So, Jonathan had just related to us his own history, or at least one of the phases of his life, so long and so complicated—of which I had no doubt.

After having collected the remarks of the first group I approached the second. As soon as the young universitarian had stopped speaking, I took him to one side.

"Monsieur," I said to him, "I can only rejoice in seeing you less skeptical, less incredulous than before. Be careful, however; you are ready to fall into the exaggerated zeal of new converts. My illustrious friend's long existence is sufficiently full of extraordinary events and it is unnecessary, and perhaps dangerous to add others to it, in which he has not participated. I enjoy his confidence, as you know, a confidence of which I am proud; well, between us, I believe I am able to declare to you that Jonathan has never be an advocate or a physician, like that Bernard. Just Heaven! Him, a mediocre advocate and a routine physician! Above all, I can affirm that he has never, absolutely never, been married."

"How do you know? Perhaps he hasn't told you everything."

That remark caused me to reflect.

"Look," continued my young man, pointing his finger at Jonathan, who, with the appearance of a mere mortal, his feet in the fireplace, was chatting with our hostess while he finished the traditional glass of sugared water legally due to all poets and storytellers, as to all orators and all rabble-rousers, "Do you see on his face, at the base of the nose to the left, that mole garnished with hairs? I have an idea that it was the famous mole that served Monsieur Bernard so well with the independent Tartars."

The mole was, in fact, there. I had not previously paid any attention to it. Struck by the observation, I dared not affirm or deny it. It was a new mystery, with which I counted on reckoning one day—but how many others remained for me to penetrate!

In Paris Jonathan lived in a small house in the Faubourg du Roule, with an adjacent garden, and an elegant kiosk in the middle of the garden. A laboratory of chemistry, or alchemy, whatever you want to call it, occupied the basement of the house; but it ought not to be imagined as akin to the somber and hideous laboratories of the necromancers of old, such as Flemish painters have represented them to us, with a black cat, an owl, a death's-head and a stuffed crocodile suspended from the ceiling; although order and cleanliness did not reign everywhere there, the senses of sight and smell would scarcely have been more disagreeably surprised than in other establishments of the same sort. On the far side of the house, at its culminating point, the roof flattened into a terrace. There stood a large telescope, which he maintained that the neighbors mistook for a telegraph; it was an astronomical observatory.

It was in the garden, the kiosk and the ground floor of the house—where a few shelves laden with old books, a table and a large low divan backed up against the wall formed the entire furniture—that I heard and was able to collect most of the tales that follow. As for the laboratory and the observatory, Jonathan was only preoccupied there with his calculations and scientific schemes, and when I was permitted to enter there it was to play a role very different from that of listener.

The master often spoke with his eyes closed, looking inwards, as they say, in order to see more clearly the events, people and things of old filing before him, which had only existed in his memory for a long time. Rightly suspecting mine, not only did I lend him all my attention then, but sometimes I wrote down the principal points of his story without his knowledge. Like all fine talkers, he spoke slowly, not very emphatically, and while talking or narrating he sometimes smoked his large Indian pipe—which he owed, he assured me, to the munificence of Tippoo-Sahib—forcibly interrupting his narration from time to time in order to expel the tobacco smoke, which favored me all the more in my sly recording.

How were his stories produced? Was it on my solicitation? Was it sufficient for me to question him? Refrain from thinking that. Although he sometimes treated me with great benevolence, and even lavished me with the title of friend—valueless except between equals—I would not have dared to ask him for stories as people asked the Abbé Gallant for tales. That would have been to lack the respect that I owed to his science, and above all to his age. It was necessary for him to come to it himself.

Fortunately, at the sight of an object utterly insignificant in appearance, an anecdote rose to his lips spontaneously. Thus, one evening, with regard to Tippoo-Sahib's pipe, he told me the simple and touching story of a poor Indian of the Maldives.

[*At this point, the story translated as "The Island of the Coconut Palm" is inserted.*]

Every day, early in the morning, I went to Jonathan's house. More often than not I found him lying down on the divan in the drawing room. He had no other bed; his only cover was a vast cloak, a sort of furry dalmatic; in cold weather the same dalmatic served him as a dressing-gown.

An Abyssinian negress he had bought in Africa composed his entire domestic staff. She was fearfully ugly and only spoke Arabic; in consequence, he had nothing to fear from her gallantries or her indiscretions. She only opened the door to me after having inspected me through the little judas-hole. That was an instruction, for, although he did not detest society, and sometimes showed himself amiable, and even joyful, and collected successes there as a mysterious individual as well as a eccentric story-teller to which he was far from insensible, Jonathan condemned himself to the most absolute solitude at home, never admitting anyone except his tailor and me.

When I met him, I enquired first whether he had any intention of going out, ready to accompany him anywhere he wanted to go, for a walk, to a museum or library. If he projected some indispensable visit, I also accompanied him, resigning myself to waiting at the door if the house was unfamiliar to me. In the evening, if we went to a play or to the Hôtel la Chabeaussière, I only separated from him after having escorted him as far as his domicile. As I said, he lodged in the Faubourg du Roule; Madame de la Chabeaussière lived in the little Rue du Marais-Saint-Germain while I lived on the Île Saint-Louis; but I was young then and exercise was salutary for me.

We had thus become inseparable, save for meal-times and bed-time.

When he woke up, if he perceived me already at my post, he smiled at me with his eyes, for smiles rarely descended as far as his lips. I bowed before him humbly, and he touched my forehead with his hand; that was his most amicable salute. Then he indicated a place on the divan to me; sometimes he went back to sleep or meditated, and not daring to disturb either his contemplation or his slumber, I remained mute, almost motionless, occupying my forced leisure by examining the objects on a desk-table placed in front of me.

Those objects simply consisted of various implements necessary for writing, such as an ink-well, pens, paper, a powder-box, and erasing-knife, etc., but the powder-box was a large and very curious American fruit, which nature herself seemed to have designed for that function. The ink-well was a large nacreous seashell cut transversally, each compartment of its helix containing a different ink: black ink, blue ink, yellow ink and sympathetic ink;[146] those various colors of ink, spar-kling under the reflections of the nacre, a veritable writer's palette, genuinely relaxed the sight. Figuring as pens in a pret-ty Chinese ironwood rack, finely ornamented, were little piec-es of Indian rattan and bamboo from Africa, as slender as wheat straw. The pen-knives, annealed and damascened, were Arabic, as were the erasing-knifes. A number of stamps of various substances, in agate, malachite, ivory antique bronze and gold bore various strange symbolic imprints. As for the paper, it was simply Weynen paper at two sous a pad, which was in wide usage then.[147]

Certainly, there was enough on that desk-table to attract the curious attention of a lover of trinkets, such as I was by temperament, but every morning, for a long time, I had made the same detailed examination; it could not suffice to distract me for long. In order to emerge from the heavy idleness to which Jonathan's silence condemned me I riffled through a few stacks of paper thrown on to the table. The master, whose confidence in me was increasing by the day, had authorized me to do that. There were notes from his suppliers, his boot-maker, his waistcoat-maker, his manufacturer of chemical products and his optician. I checked the figures and regulated the accounts.

In the meantime, Jonathan got up; while dressing, he dic-tated a few letters to me in response to importunate individuals who obsessed him with their solicitations. Some requested an interview or an audience, because they had to consult him about a great event that was to occur imminently; others invit-ed him to dinner, doubtless to show him to their guests in the quality of a curious beast; some offered him considerable

---

[146] "Sympathetic ink" is an alternative term for invisible ink.

[147] Notepads of "Weynen paper," sold by Parisian street-hawkers, often featured in chronicles of the period, cited by Honoré de Balzac, Georges Sand and other writers as items of local color. It was named for the Dutch manufacturer Jan Wynen, although the term became generic.

sums of money in exchange for a few chemical secrets; others consented to share a lottery prize with him if he cared to indicate the winning number to them twenty-four hours in advance. To all of them I only had to reply with a refusal. That refusal I took care to sweeten as far as possible, the master's epistolary style generally being curt and almost acerbic.

After having only been his companion at first in his excursions and his walks, I became his private secretary. My functions of confidence did not stop there. When he had dined rapidly, which seemed to be more a matter of habit than necessity for him, if we were not going out in the morning, Jonathan went into his laboratory, where he sometimes remained enclosed on his own for entire hours; but sometimes, he deigned to admit me thereto—a signal favor of which I was glad and proud.

As I have said, order and neatness were not what most distinguished that sanctuary of science. For want of space, the furnaces easily became encumbered with ash and scoria; a thick dust tinted the matrasses, retorts and serpentine flasks black; the mortars were coated with residues of all sorts; the alembics and copper basins seemed corroded by verdigris as if by a leprosy.

I have never been able to bear the spectacle of disorder. For my personal satisfaction, as much as to come to the aid of the Master, who would never have consented to introduce his maidservant, much less a stranger, to such a place, I dusted, I rubbed, I scratched and I scrubbed, and like all people fond of neatness, I hardly every left that *sanctus sanctorum* without being blinded by dust, my hands, face and garments stained, strangled and suffocated by acidic vapors and almost as black as a chimney-sweep at the conclusion of his task.

At Madame de la Chabeaussière's house, where that detail of our intimate relationship had got around—I don't know how—the humorists did not fail to say that Jonathan was initiating me in the occult sciences my making me scour his saucepans. How, I ask you, can vessels in which the most precious substances are amalgamated, alembics in which gases, vapors and perfumes are condensed, cucurbits in which potable gold and diamond are digested, be compared to ignoble kitchen equipment?

Did they not dare, also, to say that I had paid him considerable sums as the price of my participation with him, and thanks to him, in the benefits of an exceptional longevity? There had never been anything of the sort, I affirm; my illustrious Master had enough to satisfy his needs, and even his whims, without trafficking his science. Had I not had the proof in my hands, via his correspondence, that people were offering him funds from all directions, which he refused, often with a certain brutality? I knew, pertinently, that it was from him that Lavoisier and the Comte de Lauraguais obtained the famous secret of composing rubies, garnets and even diamonds—at a rather considerable price, it is true—but when those resources were lacking him, being able to make gold at will, as I had the conviction, what need did he have for me to divert the meager contents of my purse into his, in the depths of which the philosopher's stone could be found?

In any case, in spite of his eccentric attire, which, moreover, he soon set aside, Jonathan lived without ostentation and with an incredible sobriety. We had only, therefore, to scorn the rumors, propagated by people, some of whom were envious of his science and genius and others jealous of the honor that the extraordinary man in question did me by admitting me—and only admitting me—to his narrow intimacy.

No matter! How had those rumors spread outside? That intrigued me for a long time. The master was uncommunicative; Baba, the Abyssinian, did not understand a word of French, and only spoke her frightful guttural jargon. On thinking about it hard, I ended up recalling that one evening, at the Hôtel la Chabeaussière, in a moment of expansion, I had mentioned to the young universitarian my interesting occupations in the little house in the Faubourg du Roule, not hiding from him that, for those petty services rendered, I would find myself more than sufficiently recompensed by a single drop of the elixir of long life.

461

The universitarian had been talkative—after me, it is true.

Certainly, to live for a long time, to live or centuries, conserving, like the master, the appearances of full maturity, healthy and strong, without too many gray hairs, without senile weaknesses, tempted me acutely, as everyone will understand. Several times, surrounding my temeritous wish with a host of more or less adroit circumlocutions, I had tried to discover from him whether the beneficent gift of longevity could be acquired and communicated. Stripping it of its character of personal interest as best I could, I disguised my question under an appearance of scientific curiosity, knowing that he did not like to be interrogated. In spite of my skillful oratory maneuvers, however, I obtained no response, and judging by his air of preoccupation I might have thought, and did think, that for him, my words had evaporated in the air before reaching his ear.

Several times, without being discouraged, taking new roundabout ways, I returned to my thesis, with the same result. He had not heard me, he had not understood me, or, rather, he had pretended not to hear me, for one day, while he was taking a siesta in the kiosk and I was preparing his Indian pipe, he pointed nonchalantly at a little picture hanging on the wall.

That picture, a rather mediocre engraving that I had encountered twenty times over in stalls on the quay, represented a stag-hunt, by Carle Vernet.

"Have I told you the story of Georges Corati?" he asked me.

"No, Master," I replied, with less urgency than I normally put into it when he asked me an analogous question—which was rarely. But just then I was thinking of renewing my attempts regarding the famous secret of longevity, and for the moment, an intimate conversation, purely confidential, would have been better than the most beautiful story in the world.

Nevertheless, once the pipe was ready and lit, I presented the flexible stem to him, terminated by a magnificent amber mouthpiece circled with gold. Then I struck my pose of listener and he adopted that of story-teller.

He commenced without any other preamble, and I, the listener, only lent a scarcely attentive ear to it to begin with, as once before in the foyer of the Opéra during the second act of *Fernand Cortez.*[148] Absorbed by an idea, still the same, my eyes fixed on an elegant carafe in Venetian glass, which stood on the little side-table placed in the middle of the kiosk, I seemed to see a very particular liquid fermenting therein, and in a few gilded arabesques that ornamented it, I thought I could read the magic words: *Elixir of long life.*

Perhaps Jonathan read my thoughts better than I did. This is the story of Georges Corati.

[*At this point in the text the story translated as "The Young Boyar" is inserted, with very little changed except for the forename of the protagonist.*]

Having finished his story, Jonathan let the amber mouthpiece of his pipe fall and looked at me with a gaze full of malignity. Evidently, his story of the young boyar was the official response made by him to my ambiguous obsession with longevity.

"You see, my friend," he said to me, like the Englishman Seyton, the Wallachian Georges Corati found himself prey to one of those unreflective avidities that cause human reason to

---

[148] This is a confusion of internal chronology, the scene at the Opéra taking place much later in the present; if the text does drive from an aborted novel, its chapters must have been rearranged. On the other hand, the story of Jean de Milan's prophecy, which the Opéra scene introduces in the present text, is placed before that of the young Boyar in *Les Soirées de Jonathan*, which suggests that the pieces of this frame might have been intended to frame the stories in that collection before the removal of the most substantial section of Jonathan's story to a prologue.

go astray. One aspired to an immense fortune, the other to long days of existence, only to direct it foolishly, with regard to time as well as to gold, without any benefit to their happiness."

"Oh, if a long life were granted to me," I exclaimed, "I would be able to find sage employment for it."

If two hundred years of existence in the fashion of Kaboul the Zingari tempts you, I can satisfy you; antimony powder, the juice of hellebore and henbane, a few wild cucumber flowers and a few wisps of hemp would suffice."

"I can dream at even less expense, Master," I said to him, with a certain vivacity and without being able to disguise my chagrin completely, "but dreaming isn't living. You've lived for centuries yourself!"

Jonathan's face suddenly resumed its character of somber austerity. He stood up abruptly and stated striding back and forth in the garden, where I heard him murmuring in a breathless voice: "Men, men! Can they only envy those for whom they ought to lament?"

Left alone, I approached the little side-table. I picked up the vessel of Venetian glass that had attracted my attention so keenly at first; I examine it at my leisure. The liquid that it contained was neither colored nor fermenting; in the gold lineaments of the arabesques I could no longer find the fantastic label whose sight had so forcefully impressed me an hour before. In reality, it contained nothing but water.

One morning, I present myself at Jonathan's house; I ring, and ring in vain; I do not see the little panel slide in its groove. Might Baba have gone out? She never goes out? Might she be dead? For she might die, like anyone else—like me, for example! As for the master, a similar supposition is not admissible.

I ring again: same result.

I wait, patiently; and while being patient, I reflect...I think about the refusal Jonathan made me to initiate me in the secret of long life, of living forever. I think about the bitter irony with which he proposed two miserable centuries of existence to me; two centuries in ten minutes; a drug to drink, a hallucination, that was all! Is that the way that he ought to recognize my devotion to his person? And his irritation! Did he not reproach me for being jealous instead of pitying him? Pity him for what? For the fact that he knows everything, even how to change base matter into pure gold and into precious stones? For the fact that he is able to do anything, even prolong my life indefinitely? Yes, I'm convinced that he could to it if he wished. But he doesn't want to! And I remain in thrall to him, as if I still conserved some hope. I have none...certainly not. Nevertheless, this morning, like every other day, here I am in front of this door, which seemingly might no longer open to me. Coward! Coward!

Since that refusal, since that irritation, two months have gone by, and I'm glad to render him this justice, in the course of those two months, Jonathan hasn't addressed any reproach to me regarding what he calls my "avidities." For my part, I've been able to contain myself and repress all my aspirations internally. Thanks to that feigned retention, he's rendered me his favors fully; as before, I'm admitted to his laboratory; only yesterday I tidied everything up here, inspecting each flask minutely, one after another; not one seemed to me to contain the precious electuary that preserves life. It's true that all the labels were in Arabic or Coptic.

As before, the master has told me tales of all lands and all ages, very interesting, I have no doubt, but as they contain nothing that seems to me to be personal, and, moreover, he seems to be choosing them in such a fashion as not to touch my preoccupying idea. Contrary to my habit, I scarcely listen, only watching out for the passage that I didn't find there and neglecting the rest—which is to say, everything. I was wrong; I reproach myself for it; perhaps I've let some marvelous story escape, a revelation for science or for history.

But why, then, is Jonathan persisting in refusing me any participation in his blessed secret? Would the prolongation of my life abridge his to the same degree? Doubtless he thinks me more covetous than I am. My God! One or two hundred years more than other men, and I'd be satisfied. Is that an unreasonable request? But time has hardened his heart; profoundly egotistical, he wants his discovery, his privilege, his arcanum, as they say only to profit him, him alone. He would cede me anything! This life, which I devote almost entirely to him, he won't voluntarily extend for an hour!

Aren't the humorists of the Hôtel la Chabeaussière right, then? I'm playing relative to him the role of dupe; that's definite. What am I doing here, then, in front of this closed door? Wouldn't it be better to go home, not to come out any more, to resume my interrupted work, and forget the route to the Faubourg du Roule forever Well said, well thought, a good resolution, of which it's a matter of taking advantage, and right away! I'll wait one more minute, just one...and when the minute's elapsed, if that door doesn't open. I'll leave and never come back.

Ten times already, at least, I've counted the sixty seconds that divide a minute into sixty equal parts; the door remains motionless, the little panel remains closed, and I, with my eyes fixed on the door and the panel, I continue to count my seconds. Finally, a surge of legitimate rise rises to my brain; my resolution made, and firmly made, I button up my coat, I jam my hat down over my head and I turn round, in the direction of the Rue Saint-Honoré. I'm about to start walking, when a reflection stops me.

Before accomplishing my great act of eternal rupture, I'd go away with a clearer conscience, it seems to me, if I rang one last time.

I rang.

The same silence, the same immobility in the house.

Evidently, I said to myself, I wasn't mistaken; either Baba has gone out or she's dead; in either case, it's a matter of indifference to me. With her rough black skin, her glaucous eyes, her overflowing lips and her yellow teeth, the woman is hideous; she must have all the evil instincts revealed by her physiognomy; she frightens me. I want, therefore, to suppose her dead, which doesn't make things any worse for me, but after all, Jonathan isn't dead! That's one of those unfortunate accidents that he doesn't have to fear, like us. At this moment he must be waiting for me; it's the time of my habitual, daily visit; he has keen hearing, and the sound of the bell has certainly reached him, whether he's in his observatory consulting the stars in broad daylight or even in his laboratory, which is more likely. Can he not disturb himself momentarily and leave his calculations or his operations of sorcery to come to open the door for me? Who does he take me for, to leave me on the doorstep like this? It's too much scorn…adieu!…I'm going home. One doesn't abuse the patience of a man one calls one's friend like this…

His friend? But, except between equals that's a title without value, and Jonathan believes his nature to be too superior to mine for equality to exist between us. In any case, can that cold dry heart know amity? I've only ever seen him moved in that fashion before memories that date back at least two thousand years. No, no! The time has passed when I allowed myself to be abused by fine words and false appearances. But if I'm not his friend, I'm at least his disciple…his fervent disciple. Have I not proven that to him sufficiently by my concentration during our intimate conversations and my enthusiasm in Madame de la Chabeaussière's house and elsewhere? And for that reason, he ought…

Let's see, am I even truly his disciple? From a master to a disciple there's a communication of ideas and doctrines. What has he taught me of what he knows so well? Those long philosophical theses, perhaps sublime, but murky and incomprehensible, and those interminable monologues, which it's not permissible for me to interrupt in order to obtain a simple clarification, are they lessons? If he's opened the sacrosanct sanctuaries of science to me, if he permits me to touch his big telescope occasionally, it's in the conservatory interest of the instrument; if—which is what I stupidly estimated as an unparalleled favor!—he has admitted me to his hermetic, cabalistic, diabolical parlor, it's not in the quality of disciple but that of valet! It's like a valet that he treats me! Me, his valet—O shame! And I'm going to expose myself again to such an insult? A thousand times rather die! A thousand times rather set fire with my own hands to his house, his kiosk, his laboratory and his observatory!

While cursing thus, overexcited by chagrin, anger and indignation, as if the flames of the terrible conflagration whose ignition I was projecting were already surrounding me, I felt an ardent heat burning my breast and cheeks, although I had frozen feet—a common effect in such cases. I had uncovered my forehead and unbuttoned my coat, but, my impetuous peroration concluded, babbling confusedly the words "adieu" and "valet," I buttoned up my coat again, jammed my hat on my head with so much energy that it came all the way down to my ears, with a furious expression, I made a second about-turn resolutely, in the direction of the Rue Saint-Honoré...

A slight sound that seemed to emerge from the interior of the habitation fixed me in place again.

I listened; the sound grew louder; then the stairway resounded as if under the impacts of an item of furniture or a heavy box hopping from step to step; a dull and regular rapping reverberated its feeble echo along the vestibule and all the way to the entrance door. Even the little panel received a slight vibration therefrom.

I began my third monologue, shorter than the other two, for reasons you will understand.

Have thieves, informed that someone in this house is fabricating gold and diamonds at will, broken into it? That's why the negress hasn't come to open the door...perhaps they've killed her! All right...but Jonathan, the unfortunate Jonathan, what if they've killed him? A man whom the years haven't been able to lay low might be able to succumb to a violent death, by iron or fire. I seem to remember him having said so himself. Let's run...! Let's run to the police! No, that's an idea of cowardly prudence! That's giving the crime time to be consummated, if it hasn't been already! Whatever wrongs he might have done me, he has called me his friend... Let's rouse the neighbors! Let's break down this door…! However, before crying "Fire!" and "Murder!" and putting the entire quarter in turmoil, let's ring ne last time...

I approached the door, I rang forcefully, violently, several consecutive blasts; that ought to do it. And I resumed counting the seconds.

I had not reached the sixtieth when I heard Baba's wooden-soled clogs clicking in the vestibule. At the sound of those clogs, my sang-froid returned. Evidently, I had become alarmed too quickly, or I had not rung loudly enough in the first place. Everything bore me to believe that Jonathan, engrossed in his calculations, like Archimedes, had not been any more stirred than he had by the Roman squadrons; as for the negress, she had doubtless been in the garden, or the cellar, or the attic.

A large trunk stood on end at the bottom of the stairway caused me to settle on that last supposition; at least it explained the impacts and jolts that I had heard. I had, therefore, no one but myself to criticize for my stupid alarms. However, when Baba had opened the door, I hesitated to cross the threshold of the house. Since everything was following its habitual and regular course, what was I going to do there? Could I forget so quickly the revelations that had just been born in my soul before that same door, the unworthy conduct of its master in my regard?

The word "master" only awakened painfully within me that of "valet." Had I not promised myself, irrevocably, twice over, not to see him again? Because his abode had not been invaded by thieves, did that mean that his wrongs toward me were diminished?

Oh, certainly, the only decision I had to make, in the interests of my future, and my offended dignity, was to keep my word and go away immediately. But what would Baba think then? I had rung the bell, she had opened the door, I had seen her, and as if that satisfaction must have made me suffer, I left. That was too ridiculous. It wasn't that Baba's esteem and the opinion she might conceive of my conduct put the slightest embarrassment into my heart or mind, but she couldn't fail to go immediately and render an account of it to her master. The latter, astonished and perhaps irritated at not seeing me return again, would not fail to recount the story maliciously to Madame de la Chabeaussière, and how my last visit to him had been solely for his frightful negress. It was inevitable that our friends the humorists would have a good time mocking me. I wouldn't dare show myself in Paris any longer.

The position was difficult. Baba not knowing a word of French and me not knowing a word of Arabic, I could not charge her with any explanation to transmit to the person who had a right to it. On the other hand, I could not remain on the doorstep indefinitely looking at Baba, who, with her large eyes fixed on mine, addressed a few guttural croaks to me that I could only suspect of being insulting.

I made my decision, and went in, my mind a trifle troubled by my attitude dignified, saying to the African with a haughty gesture: "Announce me to your master."

Baba closed the door and returned to her kitchen.

I was firmly resolved to explain myself to Jonathan in a full and rude fashion; to remind him of my devotion to his person and his interests, and how he had recompensed me for it; after which, signifying my firm intention to stay at home henceforth, I would take my leave of him conclusively. My head risen to that high pitch, equally distanced nevertheless from weakness and getting carried away, I headed for his laboratory, where, in accordance with my previous supposition. I thought I would find him. To importune him thus in his sanctuary of my own accord was bold, but I no longer had anything to lose.

Again, I found a closed door in front of me. I paused there; I knocked. Obtaining no response, I knocked more loudly, and named myself.

To my rapping, another replied. It was the one that I had heard at the same time as the somersaults of the trunk on the steps of the staircase. Interrupted since my entry into the house, it suddenly resumed, and, from the direction of the sound, I was even able to conclude that it was coming from the ground floor, from the chamber of the divan.

In the absence of the negress, whom I have left devoting herself to her subaltern occupations, who then, if not Jonathan, would have dared to penetrate into that room, his favorite refuge? But had the hand of the master, habituated to manipulating the noble tools of science, ever deigned to raise a hammer?

I opened the door quietly and recoiled, gripped by surprise.

The great telescope, dismantled, was lying in the middle of the room, with its supports, its spare tubes and its zodiacal scale. With his back turned to me, Jonathan had his arm raised, and for a moment, I thought he was in the process of making some evocation by means of cabalistic signs; but at the end of that arm I perceived a hand, and in that hand, a hammer, a genuine hammer. In view of the telescope, I then supposed that he was occupied in some labor of celestial mechanics. But around him I saw drills, pincers, a saw and wrapping materials. His arm came down, and I heard the noise and the sharp friction of a nail sinking into a plant.

There was no doubt about it. Jonathan was accomplishing not so much a work of astronomy as a work of carpentry.

On perceiving me, he said: "I was really worried about you. Why are you late? Have you been ill?"

To each question I responded with a negative shake of the head.

"So much the better!" he said. "You're always welcome, today above all, since it's necessary for us to separate..."

I uttered an exclamation. Such was the idea I had conceived of the man's supernatural power that I believed at first that everything I had just been thinking and everything that I had just resolved had been revealed to him by divination.

It was nothing of the sort, for he added: "...to separate for some time."

While speaking he had stood up in order to extend his hand to me, dropping the hammer. By virtue of an irreflective, irresistible movement, I took possession of it. It was stronger than me. It was repugnant to me to see such a great philosopher lowering himself to such occupations. In any case, I was habituated to some extent to manual tasks. When I did my degree in law I distracted myself from my serious studies with a lathe; I made tops, egg-cups and other small items.

Jonathan tried to raise an obstacle to my good will; I was so obstinate that he had to give in. It was simply a matter of packing up his big telescope; he indicated to me the precautions to take, and naturally came to tell me in the process the circumstances that rendered the packing necessary and the instrument's change of domicile.

While listening to him and driving in my nails, I started my fourth internal monologue.

What fly has stung me? I said to myself. For what do I have to reproach him, then? I doubted his affection for me; I was wrong. Has he not just enquired with interest about the state of my health, and extended his hand to me, like one friend to another, like a father to his son? One does not extend one's hand to one's valet. The same actions change their nature in accordance with the fashion in which one envisages them. He has made me clean his basins and alembics, it's true, and even this telescope, which I'm in the process of enclosing in its box; but that box, it's the master who prepared it; has he hesitated to saw the plants and ply the hammer himself?

A true philosopher, he has often said to me, is nothing but wisdom putting itself at the service of humanity. Jonathan is not humanity, but he's more than human; his name is Legion; he has lived for a long time among many peoples; he is wisdom, he is science; if, instead of being his friend, his disciple, I were his domestic, that would be enough to render me proud of myself and my social position. Insensate, a thousand times insensate, that I was! Does scarcely a year of assiduity in regard to his person merit a gift of two hundred years of existence? Has he not given me enough retribution already for my devotion by means of his instructive conversations and the honor that I have acquired in everyone's eyes from his intimacy? And I was thinking of fleeing! I have cast anathemas upon him! What fit of madness shook my brain? Cold feet must have had something to do with it—a great deal. Yes, it's cold feet that rendered me irascible, unjust and ingrate...I'll watch out for that...

Thus terminated our first quarrel—in which, moreover, Jonathan only played a completely negative part, for it always remained a secret for him.

While I was indulging in that monologue, taking care to keep an ear open in his direction, he explained to me how Mercury and Venus, one advancing toward its apogee and the other its perigee, would come into conjunction before long. It was because of that—an important event, in view of certain ephemeric concordances, which I was not yet able to understand—that he had, for particular personal reasons known to him alone, to observe it in one place rather than another.

My first thought was that he was about to return to Egypt or India, but as he had fixed the date of his return for a month hence, feeling semi-reassured, I asked: "Can't I go with you?"

"What's the point? Many concerns, various in nature, in which you cannot take part, await me out there. Only life in Paris attracts you—enjoy it!"

"But for a year, have I known any other pleasure than being with you, and aiding you in your work, which I can't share, in sum, enjoying your society while recognizing myself unworthy of it? In which direction are you going, then, where I can't follow you?"

"I'm simply going to visit Calvados," he replied, darting an anxious glance at his telescope, already completely covered in its sheath.

"Calvados!" I exclaimed, completely tranquilized as to the fatigues and dangers of the voyage. Take me with you. Master! To spend a month without you would be impossible for me. What will I do in Paris if you're no longer here? Do you want to condemn me to solitude, to languishing, to the decline of my intelligence, which will no longer be able to stir without your powerful direction? In any case, for a long time I've aspired to see that beautiful Normandy, whose picturesque locations and marvelous vegetation are praised. I've traveled the south of Italy, why should the north of France remain unknown to me? I've seen the Mediterranean, I want to see the Atlantic!"

In brief, by dint of prayers, supplications and persistence, I succeeded so well that, for once, my will triumphed over his.

At five past four on the same day, we left together for Calvados via the large coach-station in the Rue Notre-Dame des Victoires.

We were going to Honfleur, a rather sullen and dirty little town, reeking of the tide rather than the sea, with an amphibious port that plunges between two waters, with the river to its right and the sea to its left; but it appears that it there that one is best placed to witness the marriage of Mercury and Venus, as well as that of the Seine with the Atlantic Ocean.

Whence comes the importance that Jonathan has attached to being a witness to that planetary wedding? That is of no importance to me, he deigned to tell me, because I probably wouldn't understand any of it.

Once arrived in Honfleur, however, no sooner were we installed in the Auberge du Dauphin, still stiff from the jolts of the diligence, without giving himself time to unbuckle his trunk or visit his telescope, than he started running around the town. In a long, narrow, tortuous, and decrepit street, where a few worm-eaten houses still bear dates from the sixteenth and seventeenth centuries on their facades, he rented a mansard—at a high price, I have every reason to believe, for he was dealing with a Norman proprietor. He obtained authorization to repair it, consolidate it, and even to heighten it, all at his own expense.

That same evening, the carpenters and masons were there, with double pay, working in shifts all night long. After three days, the work was done, and done well—I can answer for that, the Master having charged me with supervising the workers. On the new roof, flattened at the center, was a little gallery, only covered at one of its extremities. It was to there that the telescope was hoisted.

More than once, while supervising the work, I wondered why, instead of going to such great expense to construct an observatory in a petty street near the port, and consequently low and malodorous, he had not sought to establish himself in one of the higher and better aerated parts of the town, on the Montagne de Grâce, for example. But that question I dared not address to him. The Master knows what he is doing.

When his construction was finished, he no longer budged. As soon as a star shone in the sky, he installed himself there; he spent the entire night there, his eye to the telescope, and more often than not, he did not emerge during the day, sleeping there or occupying himself with his calculations and computations. He found himself freer and more solitary there, more distant from the noise than at the Auberge du Dauphin.

I soon learned that he received people there, that black-clad men came to visit him there frequently. I thought at first that they were local astronomers taking advantage of his sojourn in Honfleur to confer with him on the great event that was occurring a few million leagues above their heads. It was nothing of the sort. The men in black proved to be notaries, notaries' clerks, advocates and attorneys; I don't know whether there were judges among them, but there were certainly no astronomers. In the Norman lands, people are more occupied in legal procedures than astronomy.

Jonathan has a lawsuit, then? He is not in Honfleur with the intention of Venus and Mercury? However, one does not bring a telescope with one on a journey with the sole aim of coming to see one's advocate or notary! One does not built an observatory merely to have a venue for judiciary consultations. That is what I said to myself, without thinking of interrogating him on that point. What would be the point? If he wants me to know, he will inform me.

I ought to render myself the justice that my confidence in the Master was then limitless; the spirit of revolt was entirely alien to me. Discreet and resigned, though doubtless not without effort, I strangled my avidity to know with my own hands.

But what had become of the pleasure trip that I promised myself in visiting beautiful Normandy? I was living alone, without a companion, without a book; I ate alone, and in consequence without an appetite. I had tried one day taking a place at the host's table at the Dauphin, but the society I found there had sickened my heart. A man like me, habituated to the words of poets and sages, can no longer live in the midst of coarse and vulgar men.

In order to distract myself, I made a few excursions outside the town; I roamed the charming valleys suspended over the edge of the sea, on the flanks of the little Norman town. I extended my travels as far as the forest of Touque; I visited Pennedepie, Criqueboeuf, and Villerville, but before Villerville, that nest of fishermen, a delightful oasis in the midst of the sands of the shore, and before Criqueboeuf and its picturesque little church, three-quarters buried under a mass of ivy, I remained cold and insensible, with no more emotion than the fat heifer that was contemplating the same spectacle as the same time and with the same indifference as me, leaning its head on the stairway, with a stupid expression.

I was alone. Today, far from Jonathan, I can no longer be stirred or passionate; I sense that I can only really live in the company of his speech, in the midst of the world that he resuscitates, in the midst of the people and the strange countries that he resuscitates before me. Otherwise, my thoughts and my imagination remain becalmed by inertia; I am nothing more any longer than an automaton, a machine that needs to be restarted, and the key to that machine, he is keeping in his pocket for the moment.

My situation was about to get even worse. The rain, ordinarily frequent in Normandy, especially at the time of high tides, became continuous and diluvian. I no longer had the resource of walks. Forcibly imprisoned in the inn, I did not know what occupation to create for myself in order to escape ennui, spleen and complete discouragement.

Fortunately, Jonathan, who came to see me from time to time in passing, understood the suffering of my frightful idleness, and took pity on me. One morning, I saw him coming into the Dauphin with an enormous wad of papers under his arm. He charged me with making an exact copy of them, thus giving me a new proof of his confidence, for that wad was mainly composed of business documents. But was it a matter of his own personal affairs?

Even when the work was done, I was not convinced of that. For the most part, they were bills of sale, purchase and transfer, financial settlements, documentary certificates of all kinds coming from the land registry or the mortgage bureau; there were maps of terrain in accordance with all geometric systems, either in obsolete measurements still in local use, in arpents, or even in hectares in accordance writhe the legal exigencies of today. But it was impossible for me to admit that Jonathan was a speculator in land or in houses; nor could I imagine him as a landed property-owner in Normandy, given that he belonged to all lands by virtue of belonging to none. In any case, his name did not figure in any of those documents. Did he even have a name, a patronymic, though? Could he have one?

That was a new mystery, which, digging up the ground, seemed to want to attract my gaze; heroically, I closed my eyes to it.

It was nevertheless the examination of those papers that enlightened me as to the role played by the black-clad men with regard to Jonathan, but for which, even today and perhaps forever, they would remain astronomers so far as I am concerned.

As I progressed in my task, in spite of the aridity of such labor, I found agreeable distractions in it, albeit rarely. Many of the title-deeds went back to the reigns of Charles IX or Henri IV. I obtained a certain pleasure from studying the naïve phraseology and the procedural forms of that epoch, entirely borrowed from ancient Norman custom. In the same stack there was a stray sheet, yellowed by time, stamped with a cross that the figure of Christ, which attracted my attention very particularly. It was the certificate of the baptism of a certain Anthoine-Germain, son of François-Anthoine Gougimel, exercising in Honfleur the estate of legal note-taker: *the said infant, presently Christian, being born in the said town, in his father's house, on the seventeenth of May of the year 1609, in the Rue des Galliasses, on the harbor facing the little spring.*

I do not know what crazy idea went through my mind at the phrase "on the harbor." I thought, by virtue of a sudden revelation, that I was on the track of a great discovery. We were approaching the middle of May, the epoch in which "the said infant" had been born; that dark and miry street situated near the harbor, along which dates prior to the eighteenth century were distributed, and where Jonathan, without any appreciable reason, had installed his observatory, could only be the "Rue des Galliasses."

Without giving myself time to reflect, taking my hat, between two downpours, I headed for the said street at a run.

It bore an entirely different name and no "little spring" existed any longer. But if it had, in fact, been named the Rue des Galliasses—or Ships—and a little spring had still flowed there, which would not have harmed its cleanliness at all, what could I have concluded therefrom? That Jonathan, a century or two before, had lived in that same house, having made then, necessarily at the same time of year, his first observations of the passage of Venus and Mercury, and being comfortable there, had judged it good to recommence them from the same point, in order to verify the exactitude, the concordance or discordance, of his ancient calculations? A fine discovery![149]

I know that it still remains to be explained how that certificate of the baptism of the infant Anthoine-Germain came to

---

[149] And completely without consequence in the present text, reinforcing the suspicion that it might be a fragment escaped from an aborted novel, in which the narrator was intended to succeed in tracing the Jonathan's birth in his present incarnation.

be in the midst of Jonathan's papers. Does Jonathan even know of the existence of that document? Has he ever put his nose into that stack of papers? He is only a man of affairs today by procuration, by virtue of complaisance. The role suits him so poorly! It has been imposed on him. By whom? I can only think of Madame de la Chabeaussière—she has property in Normandy. Come on! That's it! I've finally got it! And yet…?

But enough rambling, enough of fragile suppositions that break in accumulating one atop another; I'm in haste to return the Master's curious stories, stories from which I've been weaned for some time and which ought not to be long delayed in resuming their course.

Profoundly humiliated by having fallen back into fault so easily, having believed myself to be so well-armed against myself with resolution, I went back to my room in the inn piteously, and for three entire days I scribbled and scribbled, without seeking to understand what I was writing any more than bailiffs' clerks making duplicates of their assignations. The work was hard, extenuating and soporific; I rendered it supportable by repeating to myself in a low voice: "It's in expiation of my foolish curiosity; the Master will be grateful to me for my zeal, and my submission to his orders. Pythagoras imposed seven years of silence, of absolute mutism, on his disciples. If Jonathan doesn't like to be interrogated, at least he allowed people to soak to him, and doesn't impose any more difficult proof on them than that of scribbling; let's scribble then, and resign ourselves to it for love of him!"

That good resolution did not take long to have its recompense. The rain forbidding any visit to his telescope, Jonathan came to spend two successive evenings with me, and on each of those evenings he told me one of his finest stories. Stories is saying too much; the second was simply a tale, a tale of *The Thousand-and-One-Nights*, if you wish, but with a meaning so profound, and completing the first so well!

You already know how Jonathan proceeds with his narrations; the most indifferent object, the smallest item of furniture, that attracts his gaze, or a word, is sufficient to awaken his memories.

In the miserable room of the inn where I was, unable to stretch himself out as on the large divan in the house in Roule, while smoking—not the Indian pipe by a wretched red clay pipe bought in Honfleur—he was sitting with his legs crossed in the Turkish fashion on an old woolen carpet three-quarters threadbare, which was showing its weave everywhere. He picked up a corner of it, and said: "A Khorassan carpet!"

Like "*Fiat lux!*" that single phrase as sufficient for an emergence from a word of chaos.

He had lived in Persia for a long time, from the middle to the end of the sixteenth century; he talked to me about what it was then, its productions, its climate, and the mores of its inhabitants; and it seemed to me, brutalized by my notarial documents for a week, impregnated with contentions, almost downcast by the endless rain of Calvados, that warm Oriental breezes were blowing around me and that its great sun was illuminating me. Gradually, his account became animated, descriptions were mingled with people, among whom was the illustrious sovereign of the land, whom Jonathan had known particularly, and finally, came the story of "Bébut the Honest Man."

[*At this point the story previously translated as "Ambitious Bebut" is inserted to the text.*]

The next day, at the same hour, sitting on the same threadbare carpet, smoking the same red clay pipe, Jonathan commenced the other Persian story, in which Abbas and the former worker from Julfa, it is true, only figured as accessory characters.

[*At this point the story previously translated as "The Fisherman of Ormus" is inserted.*]

In that double story of Bébut the jeweler and Ismael the fisherman, had Jonathan had the intention of putting his finger once again on my ambitious aspirations and my avidity for knowledge? I cannot believe it; however, at certain passages in his story, blowing away the cloud of smoke that surrounded him, raising his partly-lowered eyelids, he turned a gaze full of malice toward me.

At any rate, that double story was the sole benefit I obtained from our untimely voyage to Calvados. The thrice-blessed day came when, ceasing to scribble, I had nothing further to do than pack our trunks and nail the telescope in its wooden case again.

Finally, we quit Honfleur—only to return later, alas! Embarked on a little boat with sails and oars, which then served as a connection between Le Havre and Rouen, we headed for the latter city, where Jonathan intended to stay for a few hours, doubtless in order to visit one of this men in black. Furthermore, he was in a charming humor for the time being.

[*At this point, the story previous translated as "The White Hair" is inserted, with the amendment that the narrator is present in the story alongside the inquisitive Picard, and the story within the story is separated out as "The Story of Guy d'Albrot and the Chatelaine d'Oudales."*]

As soon as we returned from Honfleur Jonathan had sent me to the Rue Marais Saint-Germain to inform Madame de la Chabeaussière that he would visit her the following day at two o'clock. That haste to see her almost immediately affirmed me further in the idea that, with regard to the men in black, he had only been the representative of his old friend.

When we arrived at her house, the weather was magnificent, the June sun shining in all its splendor. She was in her garden, under a large arbor, shaded by a old vine-stock said to have been planted by the author of *Phèdre* and *Athalie*—and Jonathan asserted that he had known Jean Racine in a similar small house in the same Rue des Marais Saint-Germain. The maidservant who was to announce us marched in front of us, pinching her lips, a corrective movement that I simply attributed to the fact that our employment of the door-knocker had interrupted her in the middle of a pleasant conversation; but that laughter, contained with difficulty, had another cause entirely

As soon as our names had been cast into the entrance to the arbor there was a great stir, and twenty people rose to their feet at the same time before us. I thought at first that they were the ordinary habitués of our soirées, but nothing of the sort, and, except for the young universitarian, I did not see any face there that I knew.

Jonathan saluted Madame de la Chabeaussière courteously, but after a rapid inspection of her entourage, his brow darkened. For vulgar people like me, scientists resemble the common run of men, and even, quite often, common men, in view of the sometimes excessive neglect of their costume. It could not be thus for him, as great a physiognomist as Lavater, or even greater. Time having not found him wanting in completing his examination in the blink of an eye, only seeing around him broad and prominent foreheads and gazes brightly illuminated by an intelligent flame, he divined what is known as a "prepared coup," and he was not mistaken.

Warned by me of our impending visit, the good lady, indiscreet with the best intentions in the world, had slyly informed those of her friends most capable of appreciating the knowledge of her dear Visionary, and not only did she have intimate friends in the Académie des Science and the Académie Française, but, recognizing the flair of all young future academicians, she liked to add them to the cortege of her friends on her days of literary solemnities.

That day, the cortege included Arago, Ampère, Biot and Humboldt, illustrious names already clad in all their authority; Richerand and Marjolin, two luminaries of the École de Médecine; Joseph Roux, the beloved disciple of Bichat, who was already following in the footsteps of his master; the botanist Desfontaines, a naïve mind and child-like heart who firmly believed that God had only created the world in order to give birth to flowers and him to study them and enrich his herbarium; and Geoffroy Saint-Hilaire, a audacious genius and pitiless generalizer, in whose eyes men and mites, science and art, were only a single fact, a single clarity and a single bloom. History was represented there by Lacretelle, known as the Younger, and Augustin Thierry, still at the beginning of his career;[150] philosophy by La Romiguière, the enfeebled athlete of idealism, by Victor Cousin, the former grand prize-winner in the general competition but who had quarreled with the government for having dared to declared man a free force from the height of the chair of the Sorbonne.

There was a third philosopher there, or rather a hardened metaphysician, a disciple of Cabanis imbued with his sad doctrines; that one I have my reasons for not naming.[151] I shall similarly pass over in silence the rest of the audience, composed of men of the world or litterateurs, among whom it is necessary, however, to distinguish Alexandre Soumet,[152] reputed to be a great poet in that epoch when Victor Hugo was stammering his first verses and Lamartine was burying his in the depths of an ambassador's briefcase.

All that information was given to me later, of course.

Although that elite assembly had the good taste to resume the conversation at the point at which our arrival had interrupted it, and only a few gazes remained fixed on him, Jonathan's frown deepened gradually. It displeased him to have been drawn into that trap, to be figuring there in the capacity of a curious beast. Like an old lion, tracked, surrounded

---

[150] This remark sustains the dating of this scene to 1820; Thierry was a significant contributor to the *Mercure du dix-neuvième siècle*.

[151] If Saintine is referring to himself, this confirms that he had been a materialist in his days as a medical student.

[152] Saintine, signing himself "X." reviewed Soumet's tragedy *Jeanne d'Arc* (1825) in the *Mercure du dix-neuvième siècle*.

and cornered by a band of young panthers, he remained silent and attentive, anticipating the struggle without dreading it—he was soon to prove that—but without desiring it. He found it compromising for his great and august science, the daughter of India and Egypt, the iniatrix of the Greek and Roman world, the errant and persecuted enchantress of the Middle Ages. He had always taken care to envelope her in veils and sacred bands, and found it repugnant to submit her to contact with modern sciences, most of them based purely on sensual observation or adventurous systems vanishing from one day to the next.

So, he thought at first that it was more sage and more prudent to beat a retreat, and we were already preparing to take our leave when Humboldt and Arago, quitting their places, came to offer him their hands and sit down next to him.

He had known Humboldt in Cumana, when the latter, getting ready to explore Mexico, had first set foot on the American continent; that was in 1799. He had been twenty years old then. That savant voyager recognized Jonathan perfectly, however, of whose physiognomy, he said, not a wrinkle had changed. He had owed to him then precious information about ancient Mexico that Jonathan claimed to have received from the mouth of a certain Jean de Milan, an Italian astronomer of the sixteenth century.

As for François Arago, his relations with the Master did not go back as far. Everyone knows that in 1808, that scholar, who was scarcely twenty-two years old, after measuring the arc of the meridian in Spain, had been captured by an Algerian corsair while returning to France. Jonathan had spent long years in the African continent, also experimenting in favor of science, but his own science. Having conserved numerous relationships with the sovereigns of those lands, he contributed to the young French astronomer's return to liberty.

It was thus that those three men, all three so great in their knowledge, already linked by services rendered, came to shake hands under the arbor in the little Rue du Marais, and, in spite of his project of retreat, the old lion found himself a prisoner.

At first, they exchanged their mutual congratulations in low voices; then came the inevitable questions, as frequent among scientists and litterateurs as among more vulgar artisans. "What are you doing, with what are you occupied now?"

Humboldt spoke about general physics, statics, and how he thought that he had discovered a new direction for mechanical forces, capable of doubling their power. Jonathan congratulated him for it, but he observed that the ancient Egyptian architects had already profited from that discovery in building the pyramids.

Arago talked about the theory of imponderable fluids, according to which magnetism, electricity and light were only modifications of the same phenomenon, resulting from various vibrations of a single fluid, the ether, in space. Jonathan seemed delighted by that theory, which, he declared, belonged to true science, while nevertheless remarking to the young scientist that it had already been produced in the middle of the thirteenth century by the monk Roger Bacon, and that it had remained a fundamental verity ever since for all the enlightened adherents of occult science.

Arago did not deny the origin, he merely claimed for himself the honor of having furnished the evidence and the demonstration of a principle that tended to do nothing less than shake the entire Newtonian system.[153] Jonathan did not believe in Newton; he congratulated him for that shaking, after which Arago introduced his friend Ampère; for his part, Humboldt introduced his friend Biot.

Although living in almost absolute retreat far from the noise of the school, the Master had been able to keep up to date with matters of science; he congratulated Ampère on this mathematical theory of games, tending to prove that hazard

---

[153] In fact, Arago's measurements, which gave the impression that the globe was not flattened at the poles, as Newton had predicted, turned out to be incorrect.

infallibly escaped all the best-calculated schemes. He had been all the more satisfied with that theory because, in work undertaken fifty years earlier, Jonathan had reached an identical conclusion. Hazard being divine in essence, purely mathematical schemes could not rise high enough to encounter it.

To Biot he talked about his aerostatic voyage, undertaken with Gay-Lussac, and departed from that to discourse on the supposedly new discovery of balloons, which the ancient peoples of the Far East had known before Messieurs Charles and Montgolfier. "Like you," he added, "the Brahmins of Benares and, in even more remote ages, even those of Auxuma in ancient Ethiopia, according to the precise information that I was able to obtain from an antediluvian manuscript that escaped the cataclysm, were able to make use of it in the interests of the physical sciences, but will you, like them, ever find the art of directing them? I doubt it.

"Knowledge of few fixed stars, summer and winter monsoons, and trade winds, that Monsieur Arago, after Halley, has explained by the influence of the tropical sun and the expansion of the air in the vicinity of the equator; easterly winds frequent in certain given circumstances and other meteorological phenomena might have been sufficient for marine navigation, but they are insufficient for aerial navigation. You are only ever occupied with terrestrial meteorology, which, as even Monsieur Biot, whom I invoke here, says, is still a science in a state of germination; in order to find the secret of the direction of aerostats—which is to say, the veritable origins of the greater number of air currents—it is necessary for you to go higher, in the upper layers of the atmosphere, and even beyond.

"Believe me, those great celestial bodies whose weight, at equal times, raises the seas, have even more reason to act upon the fluids of the atmosphere; that is what the ancients knew, Messieurs and dear colleagues; they consulted the Sun, the Moon, Mars and Saturn, not only to enquire into their volume and their distance from one another, but also their influence on the ocean of air on the bed of which we live. That is because the ancients cultivated a science that you have denied for a long time; they believed in astrology."

The heads of those five scientists had not drawn together without attracting general attention, and although the new friends were still only talking in low voices, the silence became so profound and so attentive around them that each of their words carried an echo with it. At the word "astrology" the rumor that rose up under the arbor swelled so much that the foliage of the vine planted by Jean Racine seemed to agitate as if under a storm wind. In spite of its tumultuous quality, let me hasten to say that the movement had nothing aggressive about it. People had come to the good lady's house to see a visionary, an astrologer, a lost race in our day; thus far, only the scholar had revealed himself; scientists could be procured without even emerging from the arbor, but the astrologer was about to show himself, or, at least, they expected it—hence the rumor, only testifying to a keen sentiment of curiosity hoping for satisfaction.

Nevertheless, in the midst of that inoffensive noise, a mocking snigger made itself heard.

Jonathan stared at the jeerer, whose features suddenly contacted, and who turned away with an effort from that gaze. "What is astrology? What has it demonstrated? What is its degree of certainty?" Before those interpellations, which overlapped on all sides, the Master maintained silence, a glacial and sullen silence."

With a perfect courtesy appropriate to the spirit of the country and the race that distinguishes it, François Arago turned to the audience then. "Messieurs," he said, "it's doubtless to me that those questions are addressed. I understand it; the people of Paris are obstinate in regarding me as a certified astrologer, but alas, you suspect that, compared with my honorable colleague Mathieu Laensberg, whose authority was incontestably greater than mine, I know nothing about astrology, except that on arrives by that means in prognosticating rain and good weather, in predicting the future..."

"Yes, the great adventure!" said a voice.

Arago was speaking again when Jonathan stood up abruptly. He had understood that maintaining silence any longer would be a desertion of his doctrines. Resuming his ordinary impassivity, in a firm and emphatic voice he demonstrated how the science of the stars is divided into two distinct parts, astronomy properly speaking, which measures the celestial bodies, taking account of their evolutions and their weight, and astrology, which penetrates their own substance, studying their influences, not only on inert matter but on the thought and determination of humans.

At that point, the snigger that had already resounded once, was reproduced. Jonathan did not seem to have heard it, and, pursuing his thesis, he declared that in his view, astrology limited to predicting rain and good weather he also regarded as a science, equal at least by virtue of its services rendered to its sister, astronomy. If people had not been pleased to pour scorn upon it, if charlatans and empiricists had not usurped the place of philosophers, what marvels might astronomy not have engendered in favor of agriculture, navigation and humanity? But what man, even a philosopher, would consent to use up his life and strength to the benefit of ingrates who scorned him?

Of that ingratitude there was no lack of examples. The same Mathieu Laensberg whose name was no longer pronounced without irony, almost as an insult, was a saintly man, a canon of Saint Bartholomew in Liège, who had not wanted to lie either to God or men, a savant mathematician; his almanack, the only one he had ever composed, in 1636, was a prodigy of astrological exactitude. Who suspected that today? The incalculable number of observations that it had been necessary for him to make for such a work with the aid of a telescope had cost him his life. Who, then had taken pity on him? Of his vast science, his unworthy successors, far from inheriting it, had only profited from its momentary renown.

"Although to enlighten yourselves on the phases of the weather, the variations of the atmosphere, so capricious in appearance and often as fatal, you consult without repugnance, and sometimes with reason, a flower that opens or closes, a croaking frog, a flying bird or a buzzing insect, you stand attentively before the ascension of mercury in a glass tube, you request information from simple metals, resins, stones, and even strings borrowed from the intestines of the most abject animals, but you feel ashamed if you raise your heads toward the glorious stars, the first, unique cause of all those indicative phenomena. While invoking the progress of human science, blind and superstitious, you only have faith in oracles delivered by swallows, frogs, flies and intestinal strings."

Sensing that the audience was fortunately disposed by that beginning, the Master widened the scope of his argument. He depicted the constellations of the sky as living, mobile letters traced in space by the hand of God. Fortunate were those who succeeded in assembling them, able to interpret them in their veritable meaning; that had once been the occupations of sages; those signs, as adepts still called them, were the true figures of the great mathematics, the numbers of Pythagoras. The ancient gymnosophists of India, the Platonist school and that of Alexandria; in the Middle Ages the principal luminaries of the Church, Albertus Magnus, the hermetic doctor, Saint Thomas, the Angelic doctor, had all recognized in the stars not merely a blind attractive or repulsive force, but reasoned tendencies, and even passionate impulsions.

"On that point, Messieurs," he said, "I have neither the time nor the hope of imposing my convictions upon you."

And in his firmest and most vibrant voice, dominating a slight murmur of astonishment and doubt, he represented the planets, heavenly bodies circulating in space, no longer as great insensible bodies, but attracted to one another by mutual penchants; gravitation was no longer anything but a universal law of amour that filled the immensity with shudders, palpitations and electric shocks. The planets, with their satellites, the very suns, in the midst of phosphorescent vapors, filled the ether, their common element, which rainbows and fecundating aurorae, communicating between them by means of vagabond comets. Worlds reproduced worlds. Galaxies, vast swarms of nascent stars, blazing bolides, were preparing the constellations of the future, which were to replace extinct constellations. Over the millennia, was not the sky increasingly populated, before the eyes of observers?

Finally, Jonathan, developing a luxury of grandiose images, seducing his audience by means of a poetic power that, for my part, I was far from having suspected, depicted in such a gripping fashion the ensemble of the universe as a single being, animated by a single principle, that unanimous applause greeted the end of his brilliant peroration.

Among the most enthusiastic, Alexandre Soumet called attention to himself; he could no longer contain himself, and wanted to write a poem about astrology; he even improvised the first line: an invocation of the great unity, the universal soul.[154]

At those words "the universal soul" the nasty laughter was heard once again that had already protested twice again the Master's science and opinions. Jonathan, who disdained to be offended on his own behalf, was wounded by the insult to the poet; still calm, however, affecting to turn in the direction opposite to that of the obstinate sniggerer, he said: "Those of you who believe in the immortal soul, let me tell you a touching little story about someone who did not want to believe in it."

There was a murmur of general assent in the assembly; then, when silence was established, he began.

[*At this point the story previously translated as "The Metaphysician" is intruded, in the more elaborate version included in* Les Soirées de Jonathan *under the title "Un Coup de Soleil."*]

---

[154] Although it is a stretch to say that the poem is about astrology, the reference must be to *La Divine épopée* [The Divine Epic] (1840), which Soumet might conceivably have begun to write twenty years earlier.

At the moment when Jonathan reached the conclusion of his story, someone slipped away furtively. It was remarked that in his precipitation to quit the assembly he had forgotten to take his leave of Madame de la Chabeaussière.

"It's necessary to forgive him," she said, smiling maliciously at Jonathan. "One owes indulgence to a man who had just suffered a touch of sunstroke."

A moment later, the cenacle had resumed its scientific discussions, but soon, excited by the attentive interest that was being accorded to his stories, Jonathan replying to a question from Barbié du Bocage, the celebrated geographer, and an objection by Georges Cuvier, recounted the story of an extinct people and a vanished race.

[*Here the story previously translated as "The Arinzes" is inserted, under the slightly different title of "Les Arintzes."*]

As Jonathan finished that story, which had put a hint of seriousness on all faces, a valet announced that supper was served. Madame de la Chabeaussière had conserved in her house the tradition of serving supper. She rose to her feet, and presented her arm to the narrator, which put an end to the philosophical discussions that the story of the Arintzes would undoubtedly have provoked, before they began.

Sometime after that, having gone to Jonathan's house in the morning, in accordance with my custom, it was him and not his Abyssinian maidservant who came to open the door to me. The Master's face, ordinarily so calm, testified that day to such an interior agitation that, in spite of my habitual respectful discretion, I could not conceal a start of surprise and an intention of curiosity.

Anticipating my question, Jonathan said to me: "Would you believe it? It's to and absurd dream of Baba's that I owe this disturbance."

"Master," I said, a poet who must have counted among the number of your acquaintances said, or very nearly: 'A dream! Ought one to be worried by a dream?'"

"Jean Racine," he told me, "was more or me than a mere acquaintance; I had the honor of being one of his friends and predicting to him the glorious rehabilitation of his *Athalie*." Then, returning to his maidservant, he went on: "Baba has suffered horribly; I've been able to calm the atrocious dolor, but human science does not go so far as yet as creating again those of our organs that we have destroyed. I cannot render light to her left eye."

"She's become one-eyed, then!" I cried. "All she lacked was that adornment."

"She had the means of not becoming so, but she took it into her head to bathe her eye with sulfuric acid."

"By mistake, of course."

"No, on the contrary, voluntarily. The old fool dreamed about her homeland last night; it appears that she once loved one of those Abyssinian sorcerers known as rain-makers, who are considered as public benefactors in those lands condemned to the scourge of drought. Baba, having lost one day the necklace of golden scarabs and emeralds that the women of her land wear, is still obstinate in believing that if the sorcerer was insensitive to her amour it was because a rival had stolen the ornament that 'made her beautiful.' Now, that rival, whom she had once tried in vain to identify, last night's dream enabled her to see in the sorcerer's hut; her old rancor awoke again, and as she has religiously conserved all the superstitions of her homeland, she is convinced that the harm she has done to herself, with a intention of vengeance, is only half of the measure of harm that her enemy will suffer."

"So she rendered herself one-eyed in order that the other would be blind?" I said. "But after so many years, since she lost the necklace that had the astonishing power of giving her charms, her amour for the rainmaker must have calmed considerably."

"Her amour, yes; but not her desire for vengeance; that is a fire that is never extinguished in an African heart. I know strange stories on that subject; I'll tell them to you, but first let's go see my one-eyed servant."

I followed Jonathan to Baba. She was lying on a carpet, her head supported by a cushion; one of her eyes no longer let anything show but a bloody wound; the other darted a gleam of joy from time to time; from her lips, twisted by suffering, the word "*Insh'allah!*" escaped from time to time.

"What is she saying?" I asked Jonathan.

"She's suffering, and confiding to the Almighty the care of making her enemy suffer: *Insh'allah*, God grant that it be so."

Baba was asleep, or pretending to be. Jonathan and I sat down.

"What you see astonishes you," he said. "Listen to me, and you'll know how far African vengeance can go."

[*At this point the portmanteau formerly translated as "Vengeance," is intruded into the texts, all of its subsidiary narratives being retitled, as indicated in the introduction. The texts of the stories are abridged, and many of the footnotes included in the original versions are deleted.*]

Baba, who would have been very scornful of the King of the Congo if she had been able to understand that conclusion, did not have the displeasure of seeing a new infirmity added to her ugliness; the following night, a bout of fever bore her away to the somber places where, it is said, souls unable to forgive have to go.

One evening, I accompanied Jonathan to the Opéra; he was curious to see a performance of *Fernand Cortez*;[155] by the

---

[155] *Fernand Cortez, ou Le conquête de Mexico*, by Gaspare Spontini, with a French libretto by Étienne de Jouy, was prem-

end of the first act, however, he had already show more ennui than admiration; when the second act started, he could no longer contain himself and we left our box in order to take a turn around the foyer, then deserted.

"Are you indisposed, Master?" I asked him.

"Yes," he replied, "I'm ill." Nevertheless, he conserved his habitual calm appearance, save for certain shaves of tiny wrinkles in the form of a fan, hollowed out more than usual in the corners of is eyes and lips. "Your Parisian idlers," he continued, "in returning home, will think they have made the acquaintance of the valiant conquistador; they have not even had his parody, for every parody supposes some point of resemblance. Personally, I knew that planter of Santiago!"

"What! You had the good fortune of seeing and approaching the great Cortez!"

"Yes, and it's a good fortune for which, until today, I've neglected to thank Providence. He was wrathful and brutal, your great Cortez, by nature...and they've made him a fop, a singer of songs. It seems to me that I can still see his gray eyes gleaming, and his huge hand, rough and dark, covered with hair, rising... But that Amazily, that beautiful Mexican, did she really exist? That's not a Mexican name, and I've never heard it said, even in Mexico...it seems to me, however, that Garcilasso[156] mentioned an amorous fling...yes, Garcilasso...a liar like all the rest."

As these words emerged from his mouth, his voice gradually lowered. He soon fell into one of is reveries, during which he went to "live elsewhere."

I dared not trouble him in his meditation, and was sitting silent beside him on one of the divans in the foyer, regretting, I admit, the music of Spontini and the fine verses of Monsieur

---

ière in 1809, but a revised version was staged in Paris in May 1817, which fits the chronology of the story better.

[156] The reference is to the poet Garcilaso de la Vega (1501-1536).

de Jouy, when suddenly, divining my thought, Jonathan raised his head again and looked at me in surprise.

"You're still here?" he said.

"Where can I be better than with you?" I replied, with more politeness than frankness."

"Well, I owe you a compensation for the second act, lost to you by my fault, Events have just passed through my memory that have their importance and their significance. Listen."

I did not doubt for a moment that while a conventional Cortez was strutting on the stage, there, in the foyer of the same theater, the true coarse planter with the hairy hand was about to appear to me. I adopted a comfortable position in order to listen better, and he fashion in which Jonathan began his story only affirmed me in my first thought.

[*At this point in the text the story previously translated as "The Prophecy of Jean de Milan" is inserted, supplemented with three interjected thoughts on the part of the narrator. In the second, he observes, with momentary regret, that the story is not actually about Cortez at all, while the third calls special attention to Jonathan's repetition of a remark made by Cortez to Zacatl, absent from the first version of the story, regarding Jean de Milan's prophecy, to the effect that time would tell "which of the two"—referring to the dual nature of the prophecy—would be fulfilled.*]

"A fine lesson," I said, when Jonathan had concluded his story. "That Zacatl, falling into the trap of his feigned virtue, finding in his execution the punishment for his base avidity, and, in the glory that was to survive him, the recompense for his voluntary devotion, makes me indignant and touches me at the same time; it's beautiful, of a high morality, and Providence certainly..."

"It's not a matter here of Providence or morality," he said, interrupting me with a certain abruptness, "but do you think that the prophecy of the Milanese was entirely accomplished?"

Put on the alert by his preceding "which of the two," I hastened to respond: "Entirely!"

"Well, Cortez was not of that opinion. When he returned to Cuba, in front of Velasquez and his principal followers, he reproached Jean de Milan violently for having almost compromised the success of the expedition by pushing that young Mexican, then the army's sole interpreter, by means of fables and a lying horoscope, to desert his post to run after an illusory fortune.

"Lying horoscope! That was what that ignorant soldier called one of the finest and surest calculations of astrological science! I ask, you in any case," Jonathan went on, "was the Milanese responsible for the Mexican's evil passions? If the prophecy had not been made, would not the destiny of Zacatl, written in the sky, have been accomplished regardless? That is what the impetuous adventurer did not want to understand, and getting more and more excited, in one of those crises of wrath to which he let himself yield too frequently, he put an end to the discussion by raising his hand against me."

"Against you?" I said interrupting in my turn. "What! Are you Jean de Milan, then?"

"I was, yes," he replied, after a momentary hesitation. "Why should I keep silent with you, my friend, who already know a part of my multiple and singular existence? Yes, I was then accomplishing my last but one spagyria."

I waited for an explanation of that last word, but the second act of the opera had just finished; the public invaded the foyer; various people had even been able to overhear a few snatches of our conversation, and among them I recognized one of the habitués of the Hôtel la Chabeaussière. A rumor in our direction was beginning; I escorted Jonathan back to his dwelling without addressing a single word to him on the way.

What preoccupied me most insistently then was not Zacatl, nor the lovely Axa with the black hair and the flat nose, nor old Rhaomazi with the face encrusted with gems, nor the perhaps-imprudent prophecy of Jean de Milan; I was not even seeking to divine whether the thick, hairy hand of the Conquistador had attained its intended objective or whether it had stopped in mid-air; what absorbed my thought was what I could not understand, although I had the complete and entire conviction of it, was how Jonathan, after a lapse of three hundred years, was still holding a grudge against Fernand Cortez.

One day, I went to take my compliments of condolence to Jonathan; I had been told that the loss of a lawsuit in which he was interested must have reduced his fortune by at least half.

"They're mistaken," he said, smiling. "I've lost nine-tenths. You feel sorry for me; thank you for that, but permit me in my turn to console you for my misfortune."

Without waiting for me to reply, he continued: "Indian philosophy says 'On the banks of a spring or the shores of the Ganges, one still only has one cup to fill and one thirst to satisfy.' What is true for India is true everywhere and in all times, as you shall see.

[*Here the story previously translated as "Sethos and Cleophas" is inserted, immediately followed by the beginning of "Tam-Garaï." The latter story is interrupted at the point where Tam-Garaï is summoned before the king and exiled.*]

"And I, voluntarily, shared his exile," Jonathan continued, having become suddenly pensive, and addressing himself less to me than himself.

"What!" I said to him. You lived in Gujarat, then, under the reign of the young prince so vainly tormented by the desire to do well?"

"I was one of his subjects."

"The old Brahmin, then; that worthy centenarian and good counselor? I could have guessed that."

"And you would have guessed wrong," he replied, smiling. "Buddha himself, in his numerous avatars, did not always

497

play the role of a god, or even that of a philosopher; it happened once that he reappeared on earth under the appearance of a mendicant dervish. My condition in Gujarat was much more humble; I was the poor halalkhor, scorned even by the pariahs, the wretch whose life Tam-Garaï had saved, and whose touch had just sufficed to have him condemned to exile."

"You, a pariah! A halalkhor!" I exclaimed. "But," I went on, "in order to get out of that state of abjection, did you no longer have your universal science, your profound intelligence of everything?"

"In India, my friend, as you are not unaware, science is only permitted to Brahmins; everyone there lives imprisoned in the caste into which hazard has caused him to be born. Yes, in that epoch I was only a poor olive-skinned Indian, in the last place in the last rung of that pitiless Brahminic hierarchy. In any case," he added, "it wasn't only in India that I had to complain about the unfortunate hazard of my birth; later, in Persia, the profound knowledge that you are kind enough to attribute to me, similarly obscured by an infimal birth, only earned me the title of a fool. In the court of the great Abbas, I exercised the profession of buffoon under the name Kel-Anayet."

"Kel-Anayet!" I said, exclaiming for a second time. "So, the philosophical buffoon who told the two ambitious individuals the beautiful moral tale of the fisherman of Ormus was also you? I almost suspected it!"

"You divine everything, my friend," Jonathan said to me, with the same smile, "but an interruption is a fragment of ice thrown into the middle of a story; let us return, if you please, to our young prince, who, by means of exile, thought he had finally rid himself of the only man who could dispute with him the admiration of his people."

Ceasing to interrogate, I became a listener again, and Jonathan continued.

[The remainder of "Tam-Garaï" is inserted at this point.]

"Yes he was good," Jonathan murmured then, falling back into his long retrospective thoughts. "He was not one of that world's powerful men, nor even a superior intelligence, but goodness is a power too, and the affectionate impulses of his heart took the place of genius. Never—no, never—has a human soul contained more true grandeur, or shone with a more transparent splendor than yours, good Tam-Garaï!"

And, in recalling the man who had saved him from the panther, whose exile he had shared, he seemed to be seized by one of those rare fits of sensibility, of which he had only previously given me the spectacle in Calabria, at the memory of his other friend, Epaminondas.

"Master," I exclaimed, ceding to the admiration that he inspired in me and ready to kneel before him, "you are so great, will you not permit me one day to be magnified by your lessons? You honor me with the title of your friend; will you not accord me the favor of being your pupil?"

Jonathan reflected for a moment; then he took a scroll of paper out of an ebony box and, holding it out to me, he said: "Go read and meditate on this at home; when you bring it back to me, we will see, you and I, whether you still want to be my pupil."

I took away the precious manuscript, and hastened to go and shut myself away at home, where I read the following.

[The story previously translated as "The Sorcerer's Child" is inserted here.]

The story of Maugis' disciple had moved me but had not discouraged me. The next day, when I returned Jonathan's manuscript, I said to him: "Master, I await your lessons."

"So be it," he said, "but we'll only begin after our return to Paris. I took my leave of Madame de Chabeaussière yesterday, and if you wish, I'll take you once again to Normandy."

There is no need to ask whether I accepted that proposition; now that I had the promise of being initiated into his marvelous secrets, less than ever would I have wanted to be parted from Jonathan.

[*At this point, the narrator's story reconnects with the version contained in the prologue to* Les Soirées de Jonathan, *at the point where the two of them see the long blue flame from the shore near Le Havre. The remainder of the text is simply a slightly abridged repetition of the remainder of that prologue. The most important deletion comes at the end, when the narrator is in possession of the arcanum and is deciding what to do with it. In this version his contemplation is cut short and he does not make the decision to market the secret; instead, he postpones any such decision until "plus tard"— i.e., later—and with the repetition of that phrase, his manuscript ends. It is then supplemented by a significantly different version of the final note.*]

Important Note

On the very day when Monsieur P****, Jonathan's friend an editor, wrote those last lines—which is so say, on 12 June 1837, the terrible storm occurred of which all Paris has retained the memory. As he was rummaging through the old books outside the shop of a bookseller in the Boulevard des Capucines, Monsieur P****, who hoped to live for two centuries, thanks to Paracelsus, and to recommence thereafter thanks to Pythagoras, was struck by lightning and died on the spot, without having had the time to prepare his avatar or his spagyria—a deplorable accident not foreseen by the two great philosophers.

Asked by his family to cast an eye over his literary papers, I was able to extract a certain number of stories, by turns light or grave, naïve or philosophical, some of which were obviously of Monsieur P****'s own crop. To please the family I published them all under the same title, *Jonathan le* *visionnaire*, that I am employing again today. But in this new edition, circumstances authorizing me to do so, I thought I ought to remove a few of those stories and replace them with the *Histoire d'une civilization antédiluvienne*, which had not yet appeared in the work of that contemporary of all ages.

As the second editor of this work, only one thing more remains for me to say; it is the last.

These stories, which can be called romances, tales, novelettes or stories, as the reader pleases, although varied in form and tone, all have the same objective; they are all the expansion of one great thought, and in their ensemble complete a system of moral philosophy. If some of them are found to have a certain resemblance to the productions of our modern writers, you will recall that Jonathan the Visionary dates from long ago, in literary terms. A date responds to many things today.

[Presumably, when he wrote that line for the second time, X. B. Saintine did not know that it would only be republished posthumously.]